The Charity Shop Murders

By Wat Taylor

© *Wat Taylor 2013*

This book is a work of fiction and any resemblance to actual people or events is purely coincidental.

Wat.taylor@yahoo.co.uk

Chapter 1

Martin Keynes was bored. He needed a murder.

Northampton was not the most exciting place to work, and that was even more apparent for a homicide detective. When people did die, they tended to do it in unspectacular ways that needed little police involvement before or after the event.

While he was never satisfied with his status and always felt he could do better, the numbers spoke for themselves: he had made Detective Sergeant after three years, drove a two-litre Toyota, and earned thirty two thousand pounds per year. His wife was a solid seven, possibly even eight, out of ten, looks-wise.

He was probably an eight himself, with merely basic grooming. He had a full head of light brown hair, looked as though he might at one time have played rugby, though he had not, and was always clean-shaven. He had a decent semi-detached house in an area with a low crime rate, and had locked in a low interest charge on his mortgage. All were attractive character traits, he felt.

He had laid the foundations for a very successful career. One day he would be making his name at Scotland Yard, but for now he would have to make do with Northampton: a town in decline; a morass of mediocrity, in the Midlands geographically and intellectually. It wasn't hard to outperform here, as long as events could provide the opportunities for him to prove himself.

Martin Keynes was, by and large, oblivious to the fact that most of his colleagues did not like him. Had he known, it would not have bothered him particularly. He did not go to work to make friends, and if his job made him unpopular that meant he was doing it well.

He was not fond of the nickname bestowed on him by his colleagues. They called him Milton Keynes because he was focused entirely on business and no fun to be around, and also because it was obvious.

As long as he was busy, he could ignore these petty annoyances and show his talents at their fullest, rather than wasting them casting his eye over dead drug addicts or fatal domestic disputes. The trouble was, he was not busy enough.

All he needed was a proper murder, and, fortunately for him, someone had obliged. Even on his day off, he did not need to be asked twice.

**

"I am not working with Keynes," said Mike Gunnett.

Gunnett was an angry man most of the time, and liked people to know it. He was not particularly big, but he shaved his head close to the scalp and his shoulders seemed permanently tense. He made people think of an irritable referee, undecided whether to red-card a quarrelling footballer or headbutt him.

At this moment, however, he was doing his best to maintain his calm and present a reasoned rebuttal to a terrible suggestion.

Chief Inspector Shepherd cleared his throat. It was a big throat attached to a big, hairy man, and that small gesture was all he needed to do to attract the attention of a room, especially when there was only one other person in there. He was like a mossy mountain that only needed to rumble to warn people that a volcano lurked beneath.

"I wasn't asking," said Shepherd. "Sergeant Best has gone to the West Midlands, D.I. Harper is…unavailable, so there you go."

"We know why Harper's not at work. The Keynes effect."

"Unless you're a certified medical professional, I'd prefer you not to talk about D.I. Harper. He's on extended leave, and that's all we have to say about that. Got it?"

Shepherd folded his arms. This seemed to be a subtle way of reminding people how big they were, but the thick curls of hair on his forearms were also off-putting. At the Christmas party two years ago, they had all bet on how many pencils Shepherd could hold in the curls of his arm hair. Shepherd had guessed eight, and won.

On this occasion, the sight of those arms was enough to silence Detective Inspector Gunnett. Everyone in the station knew that once Shepherd had folded his arms, he had made up his mind.

"All right," said Gunnett, after a pause. "But he's not good with people. Send him out to interview a calculator and he'd be fine."

"You'll be leading the investigation. He'll do what you tell him to. He's bright."

"Fine. As long as he doesn't try using his initiative."

Shepherd grinned, yellowing teeth shining through his beard.

Chapter 2

Detective Sergeant Keynes parked his patrol car outside Blazers nightclub, or whatever it was called these days. It had a habit of catching fire spontaneously whenever it was losing money, then re-emerging with a different name. Locals had remarked that its regular demise and return were a fairly close parallel to the fortunes of Northampton Town in the next-to-bottom division of the football league, except with a better attendance.

The car park was about sixty percent full – fairly typical for the town on a Saturday afternoon these days. Northampton was not really anyone's first choice for anything. Only the elderly and unemployed would venture out on weekdays, and although both populations were growing, proportionally, the town centre was becoming increasingly quiet.

One shop on Gold Street, not normally a hub of activity at the best of times, would be even quieter today.

Keynes had a buzzing feeling inside his chest. This would be his first real murder investigation. All of the other deaths he had investigated during his four years on the force had turned out to be crimes of passion, lethargy or stupidity, or, increasingly, tainted drugs.

Despite the status of the crime, the initial signs were not promising. The scene of the crime was a charity shop and the victim was an unmarried seventy-two-year-old. To Keynes, though, that was hopeful: it meant there was no husband to become an obvious suspect, and it was unlikely to be a lovers' quarrel or a dispute over an unpaid skag bill. It would be a true test of his considerable abilities.

Gold Street had once been an appropriate name, but now most of the jewellers had gone and it was dominated by everything-for-a-pound shops selling liquidated stock, bookmakers, charity shops and a discount off-licence. The British Cancer Foundation's shop was sandwiched between a greasy spoon café and an insipid-looking health food store of some kind.

Keynes nodded to the officer outside the charity shop, but the officer, a young man who looked like he needed a haircut, held up his hand to stop him.

Gunnett emerged from around the corner, where he had been smoking, and flicked his cigarette stub on the floor. Keynes watched with annoyance, but did not say anything.

"It's fine, Stu," said Gunnett. "It's D.S. Keynes. He's with me."

Keynes held up his warrant card anyway. He could have sworn the young officer had rolled his eyes at the mention of the name, but he let him pass all the same.

"Follow my lead," said Gunnett. "And don't talk too much." Gunnett opened the door and a tinny bell rang.

It was not a pretty sight. Vera Hope, the victim, did not give the impression that she had been very cheerful in life, but she was even less personable in death. The killer, either for convenience or through a twisted sense of humour, had broken off the metal pole from a mannequin and impaled Miss Hope upon it, using a naturally occurring point of entry. Such was her featureless expression and outdated clothing, that at least two customers had been and gone, grumbling inwardly at the lack of service, without noticing there was a dead body in the shop window.

A woman in late middle age stood leaning behind the counter, accompanied by a female constable. Gunnett ignored his colleague and addressed the staff member.

"Madam, I'm Detective Inspector Gunnett and this is Detective Sergeant Keynes," he said. "I understand you worked with Miss Hope."

"Yes, I did, but can you move her, please?" the woman said. "It's eerie, having her stare at you. And the smell…"

"That's only natural," said Gunnett. "And someone is coming to remove the…Miss Hope. They've already taken the photos, but we're waiting for the coroner."

Keynes knew for a fact that the coroner had borrowed the van to move house at the weekend and had failed to return it, probably due to the quantity of slivovitz he had imbibed at his housewarming party. Keynes had not been invited.

Gunnett produced his notepad and pen. "So, Miss…?"

"Mrs Wade," said the woman behind the counter. "Vicky Wade."

"You could have just asked me," muttered the female constable, under her breath.

"Mrs Wade," said Gunnett, ignoring her, "Did you work with the deceased?"

"We were on alternate shifts," said Vicky Wade. "I do Tuesday, Thursday, Saturday, she does Sunday, Monday, Wednesday, Friday. There's another girl who sometimes helps out, but she's no good. Large." She held out her arms to demonstrate.

Gunnett made a big show of writing this down, and Keynes did the same. "And when did you first notice Miss Hope was..?"

Vicky took a sudden intake of breath. "I like to try to keep the displays fresh. No one else bothers. You can't keep the same outfit in the window for more than a week. People notice. It looks like you're not getting any new stock. Plus it gets faded by the sun."

Keynes looked out of the window at half-hearted cloud cover and thought that last statement unlikely.

"I was moving the mannequins around," Vicky continued. "Then I tried to move that one and realised it was actually…" She broke into a sob, then stifled it with a handkerchief.

"What time was this?" asked Gunnett.

"About 11.30. I'd just opened the shop half an hour earlier."

No wonder the British high street is losing out to online shopping, thought Keynes.

"Did anyone come in or out during that time?" said Gunnett.

"There are a few regulars who like to come in early and see if we've got any new stuff. Beat the rush."

"Was the front door locked when you came in?"

"Yes."

"What about the back door?"

"It's on a latch. You can just walk out and close it behind you, you don't need to lock it with a key."

"Did Miss Hope have any enemies?" Keynes realised that was a stupid question as soon as Gunnett had asked it.

"She could be a bit rude sometimes," said Vicky. "But, honestly, who's likely to have killed a seventy-two-year-old woman? She didn't have any kids, her husband died ten years ago, which was half the reason she started working here, and she hadn't worked while she was married. Unless she rubbed someone up the wrong way at the Darby and Joan, I don't think she had any enemies."

Keynes looked around the shop. It was the usual array of dead people's clothes – some of them still being worn by a dead person – incomplete jigsaws, bad books and scratched records.

"Was anything taken?" he asked, knowing that question too was probably redundant. Gunnett glared at him.

"I'll have to check the inventory," said Vicky. "I don't know who's got it, though." Of course, it was not computerised, it was all recorded in biro and wide-margin ledger.

Keynes looked around the shop, which had a general layering of a couple of millimetres of dust, and thought he could safely say nothing had been stolen. There was nothing here worth more than ten pounds at the most, and that was if the villain had thought to drag off a full set of heavily-used golf clubs. Keynes hated golf.

He also ascertained that the shop had no security camera, so there was no record of the incident. The killer had almost certainly made his entry and exit by the back door, so unless the cameras on Gold Street showed someone entering and not leaving, the footage would be worthless.

"We'll need to take your prints, madam," said Gunnett, trying to assert control over the questioning.

Vicky Wade reddened. "Surely I'm not a suspect?"

"It's just a matter of procedure. Your fingerprints will be all over the shop, as will Miss Hope's, so we need to eliminate them. Although obviously you are the only person we can place at the scene at the moment."

Keynes thought he could hear the W.P.C. mutter something under her breath like: "Jesus, Gunnett."

Vicky became flustered. "I volunteer here. I give up my time to give something back to the community, and then I get accused of murder."

"No one's accusing you of anything at the moment," said Gunnett. "Just procedure."

Keynes did a quick mental calculation of the value of a forty-year-old woman's time in a shop full of tat that barely anyone frequented.

The arrival of Dr Lech Rutkowski at that moment defused the situation somewhat.

He was a short, balding man with an uneven goatee beard, which, like his personality, was slightly off-centre. Having arrived in Northampton from Warsaw in the mid-2000s, he had discovered a penchant for overweight

British women, which Keynes suspected was why he had remained even after many of his countrymen had realised around the end of the decade that their prospects were better back in Poland. Keynes wondered whether Rutkowski favoured fat girls because their blubber made him forget the bones and fragile structures of gore beneath the surface, which occupied his working days.

Gunnett made a show of checking his watch. "Late night?"

"D.I. Gunnett, D.S. Keynes," said Rutkowski, touching a finger to his brow. "I came earlier to do the preliminaries. It's not a crime to disco."

He looked Vicky up and down admiringly. "Do you like to disco?" he asked.

Before she could answer, Gunnett filled the silence. "I think we'd better get Miss Hope off that pole before her insides become her outsides," he said.

**

Dr Rutkowski was actually very good at his job, which went some way to explaining why his superiors tolerated his quirks. Dressed in his surgical apron, gloves and somewhat redundant hairnet, he looked like he should be delivering babies, rather than working at the other end of the mortal coil.

He gently parted Miss Hope's hair near an incision to point out a dark bruise. "Cause of death was a blow to the head. A very concentrated area. Not much blood, barely broke the skin."

"Forensics found traces of blood on the corner of the shop counter," said Keynes. "Could she have hit her head on that?"

"Don't get ahead of yourself," Gunnett started to say, but the coroner was already replying.

"Possible," nodded Rutkowski. "No other injuries of note. The usual physical condition of an old lady."

"So she's having an argument with something and there's a push, or else she just trips and falls." Keynes suddenly had the sinking feeling that perhaps there was no murderer. An old lady had hit her head in a shop and died. By sheer misfortune, she had stumbled onto an upright metal pole and turned herself into a morbid window display.

"Do you think she could have…?" Keynes began.

"Slipped and fallen?" Rutkowski interrupted. "Unlikely. Death was instantaneous. Also, the entry into the rectum is too clean. No abrasions. She couldn't have landed there by accident."

Keynes' mood brightened, so much so that Gunnett and the coroner looked at him strangely. So he was looking for a murderer. At the very least, he was looking for someone who had been involved with an argument in the shop and had, for unknown reasons, decided to impale Miss Hope in the shop window. There would be a charge for interfering with a cadaver or bodily harm, or perhaps something more serious.

That was the good news. The bad news was that it was hard to see any leads. This was the kind of case in which the only way to reconstruct the events was by ringing doorbells and tramping the streets.

Chapter 3

Keynes returned to Gold Street later that day, on Gunnett's orders. The Inspector seemed to have been slightly tired after their work together that morning and had retired to his desk, not saying much.

The sun had come out, relative to earlier, and there were more shoppers around, including many of working age and several women too young to employ but old enough to be pushing prams.

Keynes had learned from his investigations that the charity shop's tradesman's entrance – he had avoided using the term, in the circumstances – also backed onto three other businesses: Groovy Smoothies, Joan's Café and a discount shoe shop that had once sold cheap imports from China and Spain, but looked like it had been abandoned for at least six months, judging by the dust and mountainous pile of post behind the door. A heavy padlock on the shutters and a lack of footprints or other disturbances in the dust made it seem unlikely that anyone had used the shoe shop to access or escape the crime scene. There was no sign of a break-in.

His first stop was Joan's Café. As soon as he walked in, he was irritated by the punctuation on the chalk board that passed for a menu, which, he was well aware, would put him on the wrong foot for the rest of the interview.

He walked to the back of the café and showed his warrant card to the cook, a sweaty, barrel-chested teen, who went very pale.

"If you've been speaking to Jayde, she's talking rubbish," the cook said. "I wasn't even there."

Keynes paused, reached for his notepad and took his name and details. Adrian Shadwell, 19, living with his parents in Duston. He would pass that onto someone who dealt with domestic crimes, making sure that he took some of the credit. "No, but I'll be coming back to ask you about that, whatever it is. There's been a disturbance next door, so I'm asking whether anyone saw or heard anything."

"In the charity shop?" asked the cook, rubbing his face with both hands and not thinking to wash them. "What happened?"

"An argument that turned violent, we think," said Keynes. "Yesterday afternoon, early evening."

"The fat bird or the old dear?"

"The – the elder one," said Keynes. "Did you notice anything unusual?"

"I wouldn't have heard anything, the kitchen's pretty noisy." As if to bear him out, a fried egg began to spit in a frying pan, burping hot oil onto the stove. Above, an extractor fan droned continually. There were no windows, but the back door was propped open for ventilation. Keynes could feel his suit absorbing airborne grease.

"Would you have seen anyone leaving the charity shop?" asked Keynes.

"I didn't see anyone dripping with blood if that's what you're asking," said Adrian. "There's a fair few people who go through the back way. Sometimes people drop stuff off for charity after the shop closes – it'd get nicked round the front. Then you get the hippy from the smoothie shop dumping his rubbish, a few homeless looking for boxes…"

"Homeless?" said Keynes, his interest suddenly piqued.

"Yeah, junkies and that. You get a few sleeping in the doorways round here. Not our café though. I pour bacon fat on the doorstep when I lock up." Adrian grinned, revealing a missing tooth.

Keynes barely listened after that. Like it or not, once you had ruled out friends, family and work colleagues – and Keynes had all but done so – you could always rely on a drug-addled transient to commit an irrational, lazy murder, and, more importantly, to be caught easily.

He called in at Groovy Smoothies, on the other side of the charity shop, and, though his mind was racing ahead with thoughts of apprehending a slow-moving smackhead, he managed to take the owner's statement.

Ian Pruitt, a thirty-something with a beard, who had an organic smell about him, had not heard anything unusual. The shop was far quieter than the café, though the noise from the blender was incredibly loud and would have prevented him from hearing anything.

"I wouldn't have noticed if Genghis Khan and his hordes had been next door," said Pruitt. "Especially not when there's carrot or beetroot in this thing. It's hard to blend. Very noisy. Was it Vicky or Vera?"

"Vera."

"That's a shame. Nice lady. Used to go carol singing down the street at Christmas. I think she had a dog – German wolfhound or something. Or maybe it was a Siamese."

The shop was decorated with rock memorabilia from the 1970s, and Keynes got the impression that Pruitt had imbibed a few too many organic substances in his time.

"Does anyone else go around the back of these shops?" Keynes asked.

"There's a few dossers," said Ian. "You know, some homeless. They seem to prefer this street. I think it's less windy."

"Drug problem?" asked Keynes, innocently, and watched Pruitt's eyes widen.

"What do you mean?"

"Would you say any of these, er, street dwellers were on drugs? You know, glazed eyes, funny smell, slow reactions?"

Pruitt took a few seconds, then said: "Hard to say." He paused. "You know, a lot of people don't look after themselves. That's the angle for the smoothie business. Get your five-a-day in a convenient way. Can I interest you in a beetroot, celery and wheatgerm?"

Keynes consulted the menu. "For four quid? You'll be lucky."

Pruitt looked offended. "I'm sure if you looked closely at the kind of stuff you put into your body, you'd be appalled. And if you could see inside your bowel…"

"I think that'll be all," said Keynes.

**

At that moment, Keynes was convinced that the man he was after was a homeless addict, someone who had gone in to steal a worthless piece of rubbish or raid the till and had unexpectedly run into Vera, perhaps returning from a toilet break. He had noticed that the shop did not have its own facilities, meaning that she would have had to go all the way to the shopping precinct on the corner of Marefair.

It would not be quite the masterpiece of detection he had hoped for, but it was his first murder case and the main thing was for him to solve it. It could be worse: if he worked in Australia, all of his murder cases would be attributed, ultimately, to transient nutters.

Mid-afternoon was when you could expect to find a few homeless people on the high street. Whether or not they slept there, or were genuinely homeless, they would try their luck looking pathetic and hoping for spare change. Keynes had noticed with suspicion that there were an increasing number of young, supposedly homeless, people with fairly good mobile phones, and they were often quite overweight.

Anyone sleeping rough on Gold Street would know the daily routine, and, most importantly, would have noticed anything out of the ordinary. Assuming, of course, he was not under the influence of narcotics at the time Vera died.

It didn't take him long to find one. A tall, slim man in his early thirties, though it was hard to tell his age accurately, since he had been neglecting his appearance for several years. He wore his dark hair in matted dreadlocks and had irregular stubble dotted across his face. His clothing consisted of worn-out hiking boots, army surplus trousers, and three or four thin jumpers or hoodies that seemed to have been tangled into one over the years. There was a scab on his lip and a look of absolute apathy on his face – perhaps reflecting the look he most commonly encountered.

Keynes stood over him for a moment before the young man noticed. "Spare some change?" he said, then looked up. His expression hardened.

"Hope you're not begging, sunshine?" said Keynes, in what he imagined was an intimidating manner.

"Not me, mate, my hat must have fallen off." The other man scooped his floppy cap up from the ground and pushed it onto his mass of curly, matted hair before Keynes could notice whether there were any coins in there.

Keynes shoved his warrant card in front of his face. "DS Keynes. I'm investigating a suspicious death that took place on this street earlier today. Who are you?"

"The name's Zulu," said the homeless man.

"Clearly it's not," said Keynes. The homeless man's complexion was as grey as the weather.

"It's actually Zigga Zumba, but people find that hard to remember."

"Look…"

"It's an ethnic name," said the man, and Keynes decided not to force the issue.

"Well, Swampy, whatever your name is, where were you this morning?" Keynes asked.

"I'll have to check with my secretary, but I think I was sleeping off a hangover." Keynes glanced among Zulu's possessions. Bundled among a threadbare duvet and sleeping bag, and surrounded by back issues of the local newspaper, was a two-litre bottle of cheap cider, the kind that teenage girls drank before going out on the town. Clearly Zulu was already working on his next hangover – if that was all that had contributed to it. From looking at his shrunken pupils and twitching hands, Keynes suspected that other substances had contributed Zulu's fragile physical condition. If he got the chance, he would take a look at the inside of his elbows.

"Do you, er, stay here?" said Keynes. Zulu gave him an amused glance. Keynes could feel himself struggling. "I mean, is this your regular..?" He couldn't think of the right word. Pitch? Or was that for prostitutes?

"My regular abode, yes," said Zulu. "When I'm not snorkelling in the Algarve."

"So you know all the regular..?" Again, Keynes struggled for the right words: precise but inoffensive descriptions.

"Hookers? Junkies? Smackheads? Mentals? Vagrants?" Zulu seemed to be enjoying himself.

"Yes, vagrants, that's it," said Keynes. "I mean…the transient…lawbreakers. You know most of the ones in this area?"

"Yeah, we break out a bottle of White Lightning and it's like the Algonquin round table."

Keynes frowned. "Who? Look, I just want to know if there are any known undesirables with a violent streak, who might have done in the old lady in the charity shop."

21

"Which one?" Keynes pointed out the British Cancer Foundation shop and Zulu frowned. "Why would anyone rob a charity shop?" Zulu asked.

"We don't know that they did. But there was an unnatural death."

"But why would you even go in there? There's nothing worth stealing, it's not the kind of place you can sit around all day without being bothered, and that old mare wasn't even friendly."

"You mean the homeless turn up their noses at it?" said Keynes, with sarcasm that went to waste.

Zulu shook his head. "I'm saying it's not a natural fit. If it was a McDonald's or a coffee shop or something, you could stay there for an hour or so before they kicked you out. In a library, you can stay there all day as long as you don't smell too bad. You can't do that in a poky little charity shop."

Keynes could see a certain amount of logic to Zulu's comments. Unfortunately, it might mean that his solution would not fit.

He pressed on, regardless. "Look, the crime itself was not logical," he said. "Whoever was in there turned that old lady into a shop dummy. He put a metal pole up her…" He trailed off, making a vague gesture with one hand. "Body," he concluded.

Zulu considered this piece of information for a moment, then gave a grin. It was as though a light had gone on behind his eyes, though they were still a little glazed.

"Was that the cause of death?"

"No, she was already dead." Keynes had the feeling he was telling the smackhead more than he should, but for some reason this conversation seemed to be helping him think clearly for the first time on this case.

"Seems like someone was sending a message, don't you think?" said Zulu.

Keynes had to admit, he had a point. But what was the message?

He asked Zulu further questions about what he had seen this morning, but there did not seem to be anything useful to help him. Zulu had been in a stupor from the night before – Keynes had his suspicions of what had caused it – and had not woken till late. He had no idea for how long, but the shops on Gold Street had already been open for a while. He could not give a reliable account of the visitors to the shop, and, anyway, whoever had interfered with Miss Hope could have entered by the back door. Zulu slept in a side alley that was opposite the charity shop, but at an angle, so he did not have a clear line of sight, had his sight or his head been clear in the first place.

**

Keynes found it hard to think of anything else the next day, but occupied himself by putting up a set of shelves, badly. All he could think of was their capacity for causing fatal concussion should an elderly lady collide with them.

All day he thought about the killing, and in the evening, he could not help himself. He poured half a bottle of milk down the drain, then showed the empty container to his wife and told her he was going out to fetch more.

Once he was in the car, he took an unnecessary detour to Gold Street and cruised slowly down the road, just watching. He was not looking for anything in particular. He just wanted to soak in the atmosphere, streetlights reflecting off puddles and windows, knowing that somewhere in that damp, dark array of shops, people and litter was the answer.

Chapter 4

He began Monday morning full of enthusiasm, for a change. Before beginning his investigation, though, there was one stop he had to make first.

He parked his Toyota two streets away from Kottler Avenue and walked the rest of the way, sticking close to the splintery wooden fence that seemed to be a characteristic of the housing estate. This end of Harpole was quiet during the daytime, and he did not want to draw attention to himself, especially in a Neighbourhood Watch area.

From his vantage point, half-hidden between the obtruding parts of a leylandii bush, he could see a car in the driveway of number forty-three.

Keynes advanced slowly. The street was deserted. Number forty-three's curtain's were drawn, even though it was 10.30 in the morning. He strained his hearing, but could not make out any noise from a television or stereo that would indicate whether the occupant was at home.

He made it to the front door, confident that he had not been spotted. He stood slightly to the left, out of view of the peephole or the glass panels either side of the door, and rang the doorbell. A knock might have given away his identity.

As he waited, he glanced up at the bedroom window. No movement.

Out of the corner of his eye, Keynes saw the curtains twitch in the living room window. He turned to look, but was not quick enough. It did not matter. He knew who it was.

Keynes rang the doorbell again. After only a couple of seconds he realised this was futile, and lowered himself to his knees. He removed the newspaper from the letter box and peered through.

"Hello!" he called. "There's no use hiding, I know you're in there."

From what he could see of the hallway, the house was a mess. There was an empty cereal box next to the telephone, and a crumpled towel on the stairs. He could not be sure, but there seemed to be a pair of underpants in the kitchen.

Keynes waited there, staring through the flap in the door, for another five minutes. There was no movement from inside the house.

"I can wait here all day," he said.

He waited for five minutes more, then lowered the flap and stood up.

The newspaper caught his attention, and he bent down and picked it up. 'Charity Shop Murder!" screamed the headline.

Keynes muttered to himself, shoved the newspaper inside his jacket and walked back to his car, in a mood that had continually worsened since waking up that morning with such high hopes.

**

The offices of the local newspaper were on Market Square, next to a pharmacy. The reception on the ground floor was small but decorated with plenty of photographs, taken by the newspaper's cameramen, of various historical moments and sporting triumphs. At least, as close to triumph as Northampton's teams had managed. The rugby team had done fairly well for itself, but the most the football team could boast, apart from one brief season in the top flight during the 1960s, was a second division play-off win against Swansea.

The receptionist, a substantial blonde woman in her early twenties, saw him looking at the photo of that particular moment, and mistook his interest for nostalgia. "Ah, John Frain," she said. "Sixfield boys. I've still got that song in my head. Are you here for reprints?"

Keynes shook his head, trying to hide his disdain for organised sport.

"I'm looking for the editor," he said.

"He's not exactly here," said the receptionist, looking a little uncomfortable.

"He's not here, or he's not exactly here?"

"Is this about the sausage roll story?"

"No, it's not about the sausage roll story." Keynes showed his badge, then pulled out the rumpled copy of the afternoon edition. "I've got a few questions for him."

The receptionist straightened her hair. "Just go upstairs," she said. "There'll be someone there – just, it won't be the editor."

Keynes did not have the enthusiasm to ask for an explanation. He mounted the stairs, which were clearly intended for someone far smaller than him, and rounded a pile of newspapers that were curling at the edges.

The offices of the Northampton Tribune looked as orderly and hygienic as a teenager's bedroom. There were four desks crammed into enough space to comfortably accommodate two, which might still have been workable if someone had bothered to clear away the piles of yellowing back issues and print-outs, not to mention the grey and furry mugs on the desk nearest the window.

At that desk sat a thin, unhealthy looking man, whom Keynes would have placed in his late teens, but who was actually a decade older than that. He looked up grumpily from his screen as he noticed Keynes.

Keynes nearly tripped over a pile of newspapers near the door, but managed to extricate his foot. "Did you forget bin day or something?" he said.

"That's our archive," said the thin man. "It's not fully online yet, so please don't kick it. Can I help you?"

"Detective Sergeant Keynes. Who's in charge here?"

"That would be me, Chris Shingles."

"You're the editor?"

Shingles blushed. His face had the tendency to flash red in stripes on each cheek when embarrassed or annoyed, both of which applied now, highlighting how pale his normal skin tone was. "Assistant editor," he said. "Acting editor today. The editor's not in. Sick leave."

"Working from home, I thought," piped up an even younger and thinner youth from a pile of newspapers near the door.

"It's the same thing," muttered Shingles. "Why are you here anyway, officer? Come to arrest Donny for offences to English grammar?"

Keynes produced his copy of the newspaper and unrolled it to show the front page. He shoved it in front of Shingles.

"Did you write this?" he demanded.

Shingles looked very pleased with himself. "Guilty as charged."

"Who gave you this information? This could prejudice the case."

"Don't ask me who my sources are, but let's just say we keep our ears pretty close to the ground at the Tribune."

"You and the tea boy."

"He's getting some work experience for his diploma," said Shingles, stopping short of standing up for Donny. "Look, if you're not happy with our coverage, there's not much I can do about it. Maybe the police should be a bit more co-operative with us in future. You know, inside the tent and all that."

"Your story's wrong and you're going to look pretty stupid when the truth comes out," said Keynes, who had established by now that he did not like Shingles. "Maybe you should look in your legal dictionary for the meaning of the word 'murder' before you stick it on the front page." He gestured towards the shelf of hardback reference books beside Shingles' head, noticing that most of them were ten years out of date.

Shingles' ears pricked up. "You mean it wasn't a murder?"

"I'm not here to write your story for you, but it's too early to say. Plus you spelt the victim's name wrong."

"We were in a hurry. It was breaking news."

"Too much of a hurry to check your facts? It's only four letters."

"It's a competitive market, officer. There are a dozen ways people can get their news, and some of them they don't even have to pay for. This issue will sell." Shingles took a breath and calmed down. "So, what's the progress with the case?"

Now it was Keynes' turned to be annoyed. "There's no progress to talk about. It only happened two days ago."

"What would you call that expression, Donny? Bemused? Baffled? Police are baffled…" Shingles picked up his notepad and pretended to write.

"We're not baffled, we're following proper procedure, which is something you would obviously know nothing about, since you're prepared to put out a story without checking your facts."

"We stand by our story," said Shingles, though he looked a little less sure of himself.

Keynes was also not quite sure what to do. By and large, people treated him, or at least his job, with a certain respect, if only because they did not want to draw his attention and have him digging into their affairs. This muckraker, on the other hand, was from the other side and stuck his nose into everything.

"Just watch yourself," he said vaguely, pointing at Shingles.

"Is that a threat?" Shingles whooped, as Keynes turned to leave. "Maybe you think you're a tough man, but I do my talking with words."

Keynes paused on his way out and said over his shoulder: "So does everyone, you moron."

**

Outside, he slightly regretted losing his cool in the newspaper office. He had stopped using the term 'cretin' after learning that it referred to a genuine medical condition, and did not want to be accused of discrimination against the disabled, but 'moron' was a favourite word of his, and he worried that he overused it. Keynes was always careful not to upset those who could be useful to him, whether it was Julie in human resources, Ray the maintenance man, or any of his superiors, but everyone else who demonstrated incompetence or got in his way was fair game.

He headed back to the station, hoping that the coroner might have more news on the cause of death or any other leads. Keynes was not expecting to be called up by the Chief Inspector, but barely had he sat down at his desk than he was summoned to see him.

Chief Inspector Shepherd was an ungainly-looking individual. He looked as though he had been born aged fifty, and Keynes struggled to imagine how Shepherd's beer gut could have started life. It was a solid mass of hops and malt that would not give an inch when wedged against a doorway or a desk, as it was now.

Shepherd looked as though sleepiness had overcome the annoyance he had meant to express, and the faint waft of beer provided the likely explanation.

"Take a seat, M...Keynes," he said. Keynes did, but found himself looking down on the Chief Inspector, whose chair had sagged over the years and was on the verge of buckling under his mass.

"The investigation's going well, Chief," said Keynes. "Early days, but I've got a few leads and possible suspects."

Shepherd flapped his hand. "That's not what I wanted to talk to you about. It's D.I. Harper."

Keynes was wrong-footed, but tried to recover his composure. "Oh, how is he?"

"Keynes, you know very well what I'm talking about," said Shepherd, evenly. "Leave him alone. He's on sick leave, and you hanging around outside his house isn't going to make him feel any better."

"I just thought I'd check in on him, see how he's doing. It's been two months since he was at work." At taxpayers' expense, Keynes felt like adding.

"I'm aware of that," said Shepherd. "Just let everything go through the proper processes and don't make things more complicated. He's already phoned me to say you were loitering on his street. I don't want this to become a formal complaint. And he seems to think someone nicked his newspaper."

"I'll make a note, Chief," said Keynes, lowering his eyes.

"Look, Keynes, I can't go into the specific details of his…medical problem because it's confidential, but suffice to say it won't be helped by you banging on his door."

Keynes already knew what it was. Harper was off with stress, the least tangible of all the workplace injuries. He could be on leave for six months, still earning his salary while watching daytime television and feeling sorry for himself. If he could find a job without stress of any kind, or if he thought it was less stressful to be unemployed, then good luck to him. Keynes had absolutely no sympathy. If you lived in Bogota or Darfur you were entitled to feel stressed, but not if you lived in Northampton.

"Sorry, chief, it won't happen again," said Keynes, trying his hardest to sound sincere. "I was just checking on him, hoping he'll be back in action soon."

Keynes tried not to sound sarcastic, but really he was frustrated. Either Harper should come back to work or give up and leave police work to those who actually wanted to do it. Keynes had been hoping to catch Harper in the act of washing his car or doing the laundry – which, as he understood it, were the kinds of things you could not do if you were clinically depressed.

Harper had already demonstrated weakness of character. Keynes didn't know how long ago it had started, but just three months after Keynes had joined the force, Harper had already started to turn up late or make excuses why he couldn't join him on calls. Having initially accompanied Harper to lunch in the staff cafeteria, Keynes later found out that two weeks after that he had started to make a habit of eating his sandwiches in a locked cubicle in the gents' toilets on the second floor.

Keynes had known something was wrong from the way Harper rolled his eyes whenever his younger partner made a comment during case briefings, but he had not been able to put a finger on it. Now, he would probably guess it was a failure to deal with pressure, or just plain ineptitude, but Harper had certainly seemed like a reasonably confident and competent Inspector in those early days.

"Look, Keynes," Shepherd went on. "I know you're enthusiastic, and that's commendable, but go steady, OK? Build up your experience first."

"Right, sir," said Keynes, though he disagreed entirely. 'Experience' as he had encountered it in his working life tended to be a way to describe inertia. After twenty years in the same job, people stopped trying, stopped questioning their assumptions. A newcomer could spot the laziness embedded in the system. "Have there been complaints?" he asked, warily.

"No…no," said Shepherd, who seemed to be looking for another word. "Just an observation. Just remember, they're not all murderers."

"Got it. Appreciate your advice, chief."

"And don't go running off on your own without letting Gunnett know. You know he'll get upset."

As Keynes was getting up to leave, Shepherd called him back. "Keynes?" Keynes immediately sat back down, expecting the worst.

"I heard you paid a visit to Chris Shingles at the Tribune."

"How did you hear that, chief?" Keynes asked.

"None of your business." Shepherd curled his lip, then relaxed. "But well done all the same. I can't stand that jumped-up little scrote. Thinks he's leading the Iraq war enquiry when really he's writing about dog poo and council cuts."

"I think he's in over his head, chief," said Keynes. "Seems like he's in charge while the real editor is on sick leave or something."

"Alan Richards?" The chief inspector frowned. "When I saw him in the Fox and Grapes at lunch time, he seemed healthy enough. Good bloke."

On his way out, Keynes was not sure whether or not he had been reprimanded or praised.

Chapter 5

Keynes did not sleep well that night. It frustrated him to leave his case notes unfinished, but he realised he did not have enough pieces of the jigsaw to start putting them in any kind of order. He hoped fervently that this would be complicated, a true test of his intellect and policing skills, but at the same time he had a nagging worry, which so far he had not completely acknowledged to himself, that if the case was too difficult, he might not be able to solve it.

Jenny had shown her usual polite interest in his work, but he knew it was not worth going into the details, any more than it was worth him asking about her day at school.

He woke feeling mildly grumpy, and this feeling strengthened as he got ready for work. He could not get his shave right; Jenny had left empty shampoo bottles in the shower; and the milk smelled suspiciously like she had left it out on the side for too long. Nothing seemed right. The day had started off on the wrong foot, and he had the vague but unsettling feeling that he was heading into unfamiliar territory where he would not always know where to tread.

**

He was glad to have gone into the office early, even though he could still feel a patch of stubble at the corner of his jaw that would annoy him all day. There had been another murder; at least, assuming the first one had been a murder, rather than an extended, fatal stumble.

Keynes was close to losing his cool when he heard about it, though secretly he was pleased to have been handed another piece in the jigsaw.

"Why wasn't I told about this last night?" he demanded of Jimmy Biggs, a portly presence in the office.

"I only heard about it this morning when they put me on it," said Biggs. "Wouldn't be in this early unless I had a good reason. Anyway, how do you know it's related to your case?"

"It's another Charity Shop Murder," said Keynes. He had started to think of the case with initial capital letters ever since seeing the headline in the Tribune.

"Is that what we're calling it now?"

"Why don't you ask D.I. Gunnett?"

Biggs went quiet. Keynes was not sure whether the mention of Gunnett had scared him, or whether he had seen the opportunity to offload some work.

The situation was not as clear-cut as Keynes made it sound. The body of Paul Whitcroft, a student at the local university college, aged 19, had been found half-in, half-out of the Donkey Salvation League shop at the end of Abington Street. He appeared to have suffered a fatal blow to the head, then either fallen or been pushed through the plate glass of the door, which was set back from the shop front. Only his trainers could be seen from the high street, but plenty of people would have missed the body and seen only the broken window, assuming it to be routine post-pub damage.

Whitcroft's body seemed to have broken the window when he fell backwards, given that there were several bloody lacerations on his back and arms. The photography had already been done by the time Keynes arrived, but the body had not yet been collected. A hastily-erected screen shielded the scene from public view, not that there were many people on the street to bear witness.

Keynes stood back and framed the scene with his fingers. This was more for the benefit of others than himself. He knew he was supposed to look for something, but he still was not sure exactly what.

"Got any film in that?" said Gunnett, breaking his concentration. "Biggs seems to think it's one of ours. We'll see." He sounded unconvinced.

Gunnett wandered off to talk to one of the forensic team, while Keynes lowered his hands sheepishly, but continued to examine the scene.

What evidence was there? Another victim lying dead in the window of a charity shop. A similar cause of death, it seemed, although this time the blow was on the forehead, meaning he had been face-to-face with his attacker, and presumably the confrontation had taken place outside. How could anyone have been attacked and killed in the street without being noticed?

Admittedly, the shop did not have a burglar alarm; the monthly payments would have wiped out the proceeds. On top of that, Keynes learned from an officer in attendance that the entrance was in a blind spot, since obviously it made more sense to train council security cameras on shops with more valuable stock.

Still, he was stunned that there had been no witnesses, even on a Monday night. Either the deed had taken place late at night, or it had happened very quickly.

Keynes suddenly had a thought. He looked at the doorway again. It was one of the few on Abington Street to be set back from the road, meaning that it was not exposed to the wind. He sniffed, and noted, though it was far from conclusive, that there was no tang of urine. As they said, you did not do it on your own doorstep. This place could have been an ideal sleeping place for the homeless. There might be witnesses after all.

He looked at the body more closely. There seemed to be only one wound to the forehead. Presumably either that impact or the blood loss from falling through a plate glass window had done the job. There was certainly a substantial pool of blood beneath and around the body. Had the killer gone inside to remove any items, like a wallet, his footprints would have been left behind in the congealed dark red mess.

This was better: now Keynes was thinking more logically. After just one real crime scene, he was learning to spot the things that were missing, as well as the things that were present. He was getting the hang of it, with no help from anyone else.

Keynes approached one of the officers who had been first on the scene, a Constable Reeve. He was a gawky young man who looked like he should have been in class with the victim.

"D.S. Keynes," he said, holding up his card, though it was entirely unnecessary.

"Ignore him, Reeve-o," said Gunnett. "Martin here gets a bit over-excited. Did the victim have anything taken? Wallet, ID?"

"No, it looks like it's all there," said Reeve. "Hit him and ran off. Still had a fiver in his pocket, plus his bank cards."

"Anything unusual?"

"He was a chugger."

"Cider, probably," said Keynes, knowingly. He always thought the worst of students, having once lived among them.

"No, a charity mugger," said Reeve, as Gunnett rubbed his eyes. "I mean, not literally, that's just the term. They're the ones in bibs that get you to sign up for direct debit for charities. They work for an agency, for different charities. For commission."

Keynes dimly remembered hearing about the practice. Even charities had cottoned on to outsourcing. Good business principals were universal. He had once made a list of bullet-points outlining the benefits of outsourcing the police emergency hotline to Mumbai or the Philippines, but he was waiting for a good time to present it to Shepherd.

"He had the sign-up form in his back pocket," said Reeve. "All the payment details of everyone who'd signed up for charity yesterday."

Keynes thought it through. Would that piece of paper have been valuable to anyone? It contained bank details, but presumably not enough for anyone to be able to withdraw money. And anyone agreeing to monthly donations would see it on their bill, together with the name of the person or company they were paying it to, so it would be almost impossible to transfer money without them knowing the identity of the recipient.

He sucked his teeth. This could be an interesting angle to follow up, but not if he had to do so alongside Gunnett. It would be like taking a caveman to a motor show.

"What was the name of the charity?" he asked, finally.

Chapter 6

Keynes had a lucky escape. As they left the scene of the crime, Gunnett received a text message and looked at his phone with concern. He did not explain the nature of the emergency, but it definitely seemed to be something that needed to be addressed immediately.

Keynes was on his own. He could talk finance to his heart's content, while Gunnett was off following his secret lead.

Someone else would speak to Whitcroft's parents, and undoubtedly they would find out that a nineteen-year-old Sociology and Philosophy student had no enemies who wished him dead, but Keynes was becoming aware of a bigger theme. Certainly it was easy to draw a straight line when you had only two points on the graph, but there seemed to be a connection of some kind with local charities, and he wanted to be the first to find out what it was.

While he had wanted complexity in this case, rather than the open-and-shut business of dead junkies, this was starting to become complicated. He had too many leads. Keynes had never realised how many charities operated in Northampton. His head started to swim as he wondered whether he would need to contact all of them.

For now, he could cover all of the leads himself. First, he visited the offices of the Donkey Salvation League. While it was not the obvious target of the attack, he could not ignore the possibility that Whitcroft had been pushed into the shop as part of a deliberate message, one that Keynes had not yet understood.

Unfortunately, the staff at the Donkey Salvation League's main office were not especially bright. They were all middle-aged or older and seemed to have been hired for their affection towards donkeys, rather than any other skills. He spoke to three different elderly women and explained the same facts in increasingly simple terms before coming to the conclusion that no one could furnish him with any useful information, or, probably, name the current Prime Minister. It was highly unlikely that anybody there was running the kind of criminal conspiracy that could provoke a murder. Keynes had to assume that the killing had not been intended to send them a message. Perhaps it was simply the location that had been important, in keeping with the earlier murder.

Keynes then went to the offices of AfricAlms, the charity for which Whitcroft had been collecting on that day. The staff there had no record of him: he had been employed directly by the agency they used to secure new donations, a company called UGivInc. AfricAlms merely hired them once or twice a year to send people onto Northampton high street for a few days and drum up supporters.

Realising his journey had been a waste of time, Keynes asked for the address of UGivInc. Fortunately, it was a local firm. Though it covered the whole of the Midlands, its headquarters was based in an industrial park in Daventry. The building looked like a warehouse with windows, and the park itself had as much personality as a digestive biscuit.

Still, Keynes was impressed that such an obvious money-spinner kept its overheads low. Apart from a receptionist and a few staff who seemed to be accountants, the office was small and almost empty. This was purely a back office, not designed with visitors in mind. When he arrived, the receptionist showed him straight through to meet the person in charge.

Keynes was rarely intimidated. The two criteria if you were to have a chance of unsettling him were to be a male over six feet five, or an MBA holder.

Isobel Lett, the Midlands managing director of UGivInc, was just short of six feet, but she was scarily well-qualified and met his second condition. Keynes had been expected a fluffy-minded liberal who wanted to save trees and seals, but she was a businesswoman who treated the charity industry the same way she would run a chocolate factory or a prison. As he noticed the MBA certificate in a frame behind her desk, his only consolation was that it was from a British university. Actually, two consolations: she had also ended up working in Northamptonshire.

"If you're asking about the connection between UGivInc and AfricAlms, we have barely anything in common, aside from the charity angle and the compound words," said Lett. "Although, personally, I don't think theirs works. One word has a short A, the other has an elongated one. Ours is consistent. If I were them, I wouldn't trust the public to know the correct spelling. Probably had to buy an extra couple of web addresses because people don't know there's an L. It sounds like they're gun-runners for some kind of coup."

Keynes found himself agreeing with her. He wondered whether his Bachelor's degree in criminology and economics would be a suitable platform to move onto an MBA, and also whether the police force would pay for it.

"About the victim, Whitcroft," he said, trying to bring his attention back to the case. "What contact did your company have with him?"

"We hire a large pool of charity enablers –"

"Chuggers?"

"If you want to call them that. We hire them and then send them out as our client charities require. It's hardly a long term career. We rarely see anyone working for us for more than three months at a time – usually during university holidays."

"And the charities pay you commission for every donation?" said Keynes, still trying to piece together the business model.

"They pay per client acquired. So effectively just for the first donation."

"How much?"

Lett bristled. "I hardly see that it's relevant. But you can assume that the charity enabler would receive about fifteen pounds and we would receive an appropriate margin on top of that. It's more cost effective in many ways, especially for those charities that can't afford to operate a shop on the high street or run expensive advertising campaigns."

"So, potentially, people could sign up, the charity enabler and yourself would earn a fee, and then they could cancel the direct debit after the first payment of, say, twenty pounds, and the charity would be out of pocket?" Keynes said, staring at a blank patch of the wall as he tried to concentrate.

"Look, unless you're accusing me of something…" Lett looked like she was about to lose her cool, then she recovered her poise. "Everything we do here is completely legal and completely ethical. We pay our taxes in an efficient way and our fee structure is totally clear. I'm not sure what you're driving at, Inspector."

"Sergeant," Keynes corrected her, feeling himself shrink in stature.

He cleared his throat. "I'm just trying to establish motive. Is there some way to register a load of bank accounts of friends or accomplices, make the first payments and then cancel them?"

Lett explained that would be almost impossible: charity enablers were paid only for new sign-ups for each charity, and since they had to give all of their bank account details, it would require a vast number of accomplices to generate any considerable sum of money.

It was disappointing. He had formed the inklings of a crime to defraud charities, but it refused to work. At least he was thinking in the right way. If there were to be any kind of financial fraud involved in a crime in Northamptonshire, there were not many people on the police force who would have the knowhow to track it down.

"There must be something," said Keynes, half to himself. "Why would anyone kill a chugger?"

"They can be quite annoying," said Lett.

Keynes left the building frustrated that another door appeared to have closed on him. Had he been a smoker, it would have been a good time to light up a cigarette and weigh up his progress so far. Instead, he just stood there in silence, took a deep breath and tried to think. His breath came out in a cloud that dispersed as quickly as his leads had done. The sun was going in and it was already starting to turn chilly.

He noticed a man from the building opposite, tidying up a pile of flattened cardboard boxes, and a memory stirred. Perhaps there was another lead he could revisit.

Chapter 7

Zulu saw Keynes approaching from the end of the street and was quick to move. He shoved his bottle of cider under one arm and disappeared into an alleyway.

That would probably have been enough to elude most of the constabulary, but Keynes kept up a regular fitness regime including jogging with sprint bursts, and he used it to catch Zulu before he had reached the end of the alley. It helped too, that Zulu had already consumed most of the contents of the plastic bottle in his hand and was unsteady on his feet.

Zulu turned around, conceding defeat. "Didn't see you there, officer," he said.

"Hardly surprising," said Keynes. He sniffed, in mild disgust. "Is that you or the alley?"

"People do some nasty things in here. I expect you're going to pin that on me, too."

Keynes paused. That had not been his original thought.

"If you've got nothing to hide, then you'll be all right, won't you?" he said.

"Yeah, yeah," said Zulu. "Round up the usual suspects."

Keynes was frustrated. In all honesty, he would have liked to have brought Zulu into the station for questioning, but he had no strong reason to do so. He had questioned some of the shopkeepers in Gold Street about him, but none had suspected him of any criminal activity that would have linked him to the killings. They viewed him not as a violent type, but as a self-destructive waste of space who caused them little inconvenience, other than having to step over him once in a while. A couple of people had said he looked like he was on heroin, while some others had said it was more likely to be meths. Keynes was open to either suggestion, and was keeping it as ammunition just in case, but for now he did not want to waste his time on such small transgressions.

It did not help that he had been unable to find out Zulu's real name in order to run a background check. It would not have been too difficult to obtain his fingerprints or haul him down to the station, but he needed a good reason before wasting police time and resources. Keynes needed to have reasonable suspicions before bringing him in, otherwise it might make his later evidence look like it had been assembled with the suspect already in mind.

"Look, you're lucky I don't bring you in for…" Keynes made a vague gesture as Zulu grinned back at him.

"It's a social visit, then?" said Zulu, starting to enjoy himself now that he knew Keynes was helpless. "I'm afraid I don't have any glasses, but you're welcome to take a swig from the bottle. I believe it's a '42 Chateau Neuf du Pape – wait, it's paint stripper and 7-Up." He proffered the bottle to Keynes with an innocent look in his eyes.

Keynes resisted the growing urge to knock the bottle out of his hand. "I'll bear that in mind if I've got any drains that need cleaning," he said. "Right now, I want to ask you some questions."

"Shouldn't my solicitor be present?"

"I'm not charging you with anything, you moron. I just want to know what you've seen. There was another death last night."

Zulu sucked his teeth. "Last night? Then I'm afraid I can't help you. I was sharing an intimate evening with one of my counter-culture lady friends near the bins round the back of the Chinese. The manager will vouch for me – he threw a bucket of prawns at us."

Keynes tried to ignore that image and pressed on. "A student got his brains bashed in on Abington Street. Fell through the window of the donkey sanctuary shop."

Zulu stroked his unkempt beard and a light seemed to go on behind his eyes, as if being offered a new puzzle had sobered him up temporarily. "Another charity shop murder?"

"We're not saying they are connected at this point," said Keynes. "But obviously it looks a bit…"

"It's not quite the same thing, though, is it?" said Zulu.

"It's pretty similar. Blow to the head, found dead in a charity shop window. He fell through it this time. Deceased was a chugger, died some time overnight."

"Attacked in the street?" Zulu stared at some invisible object before him. "That was pretty risky. He could easily have been spotted." He glanced at Keynes. "You must have CCTV pointed at that shop."

"No, it doesn't cover the area between the bookies and the old Woolworths," said Keynes, then kicked himself.

"Thanks for the information."

"If anything happens on that street…"

"Relax. What is there to nick on Abington Street? If you see me with a new pair of factory reject trainers or a skimmed milk latte then by all means voice your suspicions." Zulu was thoughtful again. "There are a few pubs around that area – The Angus, The Crown and Thistle, round the corner you've got Jerry's…there was a good chance he'd be spotted."

"Well, he wasn't," said Keynes, annoyed. "The only people up at that time of night are drunks and criminals, which gives me two reasons to ask you about it."

"What I'm saying is, if this is the same perpetrator, he's changed his modus operandi," said Zulu. "The one on Gold Street was public, in a way, but he made sure no one would find the body until he was well away. With this one, he didn't care if he got caught in the act."

Keynes pondered this, and hated to admit that Zulu had a point. Either the killer was getting reckless or he had changed his approach deliberately. What did that mean? And did it increase the chances of him being caught? That would be good in a way, obviously, but it also meant that the chances of the killer being caught by someone else would increase. Keynes really wanted this one for himself.

"So you didn't hear about any of this last night? No one you know who might have seen it? No one who sleeps on that patch?"

"No. You seem to be under the impression that homeless people all know each other. Trust me, they smell just as bad to me."

"He's coming to the end game," said Keynes, half to himself. "Speeding up his plan."

"Either that, or he's getting frustrated because you're too thick to catch him."

Keynes shot a warning finger under Zulu's nose, but he did not flinch. "You're lucky you're not spending the night in the cells, matey," said Keynes.

Zulu looked around at the darkening skies, the drizzle that had just started to fall on stained, greying pavement, and the general aroma of the alley. Then he looked down at the filthy sleeping bag under his arm and picked out a brown prawn. "Yeah," he said. He unscrewed the top of the bottle and took a deep swig from its murky contents.

**

Keynes had absolutely no desire to visit the pubs around the top end of Abington Street in any capacity, but realised he could not avoid it in this case. He hated pubs and did not drink alcohol unless compelled to by a social situation. The hard, swollen bellies surrounding him at the police station were enough to deter him from drinking, and on top of that it was a huge waste of money. People paid out twenty or thirty pounds to sit in a grubby, smelly room with other drunk people and to feel ill the next day, or sometimes on the way home, as parts of Northampton town centre illustrated.

Sometimes Jenny might drag him out to a canal-side village pub for Sunday lunch, but even then he would avoid drinking. He could not understand why anyone would voluntarily impair themselves, even for just a few hours. He did not know anyone who operated with a surfeit of mental ability.

As a result, he was not the best choice of person to interview bar staff and try to trace Whitcroft's last steps.

At least the pubs did not smell of smoke these days, he told himself.

Keynes got off to a poor start in The Crown and Thistle by asking the barman to turn down the music before he spoke to him. Then he made a very visible show of displaying his identity badge in front of the handful of customers, two of whom finished their drinks quickly and left.

"If you've finished scaring off my customers, can you get to the point?" said the barman, who went by the improbable name of Sharky and bore a matching tattoo on his upper right arm.

"I just want to know if this young man was here last night," said Keynes. Whitcroft's parents had sent over a photograph, and he slid a print-out across the bar.

"All students look the same to me," said Sharky. "They get puke-drunk on a tenner and annoy the regulars."

"I'm not asking whether you liked him, I just want to know if he was here."

"There was a group of students in here about 7pm last night. I had to kick them out."

"Why?"

"They had two or three drinks, then a couple of them started getting mouthy. Going on about famine and debt relief in the third world. That's not the kind of subject you want to raise in here, with half the regulars on the dole or disability."

Keynes was at that moment staring at a red-faced man, aged around forty, who was dividing his time between a pint of cider and a fruit machine, while managing to balance on a state-supplied crutch. He snorted.

"Wouldn't do to hurt their feelings," he said.

"They contribute as much to society as students," said Sharky. "They may take from the state too, but at least they're keeping the economy going." As if to prove his point, the man on the fruit machine signalled for another pint. Sharky reached for a fresh glass from above the pumps, then started to pour.

"Any idea where the students went after you kicked them out?"

"I couldn't care less. But you might want to try the Royal Angus. They actually market to that crowd. Pound a pint. You're looking for a crime, try a pint of that stuff and tell me what's in it." Sharky set the glass of cider down on the counter and waved his hand behind it. "Try doing that in the Royal Angus and see if you can see your hand through it."

The man on the fruit machine was suddenly alongside Keynes, and grabbed the pint. Keynes could not help noticing that he had left his crutches behind.

Chapter 8

The Royal Angus bore all the signs of a student hang-out: it was stripped down, so that very little damage could be caused by fighting or vomiting; the prices of drinks were as low as the quality; and people kept stealing the 'G' from the sign.

A different calibre of waster occupied the seats here, but it was hard to argue that they were any more noble a breed than the benefits claimants in The Crown and Thistle. Two baggy-clothed students were playing pool in the corner, but taking an inordinately long time to play each shot, suggesting that they had recently partaken of a substance which made it difficult to perceive both distance and reality.

A group of eight others were sitting around a table in the middle of the bar. There were three drinks on the table.

The barman here had proven to be no use at all to Keynes' enquiries. He was a student himself and had not been working last night. In any case, he said, the Angus was packed every night of the week. It was almost impossible to remember faces. All he saw was hands shoving through cash and showing their student discount cards. People were coming and going all night, and groups would disintegrate and merge with each other as the night went on.

The Crown and Thistle had regulars: people who had been drinking there for years and who had formed their own society and pecking order. The Angus refreshed its clientele every year with interchangeable teenagers who started most conversations by asking what the other person was studying.

Keynes looked at the group sitting around the table and listened in on their conversation. One boy in a woolly hat was trying to convince the others that they were all robots and he was the only real person. "You can't disprove it," woolly hat said. "There's nothing in your perception that's objective."

"I can falsify it," said a slightly overweight girl with a pierced nose.

"Can you, though?" said woolly hat.

Keynes felt a rare violent urge. He was sure that when he had been a student he had been considerate, thoughtful and had certainly spent more time planning his career than he had sitting in pubs in the daytime trying to impress plain girls possessed of mediocre hygiene.

He told himself to restrain his contempt. If the barman was going to be no use, he might as well try the patrons. Whitcroft had studied Sociology and Philosophy. Perhaps someone here had shared a class with him, or even accommodation.

Keynes stepped over, brandishing his identity badge and feeling slightly old. "D.S. Keynes. Can I ask you all some questions?"

"We know our rights," said woolly hat.

"Just imagine I'm a robot," said Keynes. "Know this man? Died last night not far from here. I believe he was in your cohort." He pushed a photograph into the centre of the table.

"That's Whitcroft," said one of the students, to be met by glares from the others. He gulped, and his outsized Adam's apple bobbed. "He was my flatmate. The police already came to search his room."

This was true. They had found nothing of note, apart from an eighth of cannabis in a sock and several bank letters warning that Whitcroft had breached his overdraft limit. Neither was particularly surprising, so they had been brushed under the carpet.

"Any idea why someone would want to kill him?" asked Keynes. The one thing he liked about dealing with students was that he made them visibly nervous – probably because they all had socks at home with dubious contents.

"No idea. He was a Philosophy student. They have some pretty weird ideas," said Whitcroft's housemate.

"I think you'll find the major philosophers never endorsed murder," said woolly hat. "Seneca and some of the others endorsed suicide in certain circumstances."

"Immanuel Kant said you should actually point out someone running away from a murderer rather than tell a lie," said another, to Keynes' growing annoyance.

"Was he mixed up with any dangerous people?" asked Keynes. "Any dealers, for instance?"

"Immanuel Kant?"

"No, Whitcroft."

There was an awkward pause. "He didn't touch any of that stuff," said his housemate.

"Well, he did," said Keynes.

The housemate sighed. "Well, maybe he did, but you can get that on campus from friendly sources. You wouldn't need to get involved with any of the townies."

"Were any of you here last night?"

"Some of us," said woolly hat. "It's student quiz night. You can win a case of beer or a carbon monoxide detector. Whitcroft wasn't in our team."

"But he was here. Did you see him?"

"I did," said the girl with the pierced nose. "He was here already when I got here at 7.30. Him and the other charity collectors were at the bar. They looked pretty wasted. He'd probably been here for a while."

"Any idea what time he left?"

"I don't know. Before closing time. Most of the people who weren't doing the quiz left when it started – the locals and the students. It's too loud, you can't hear yourself."

"And he didn't get in any trouble while he was here?"

"His group was getting a bit loud and obnoxious, but the barman told them to keep quiet."

"Any idea who he was with?"

The girl with the pierced nose glanced involuntarily towards a skinny young man at the pool table. Keynes frowned and walked over to him. The youth already looked unwell, but took on a more sickly shade when he saw Keynes' I.D.

"D.S. Keynes. I'm looking into the circumstances of Paul Whitcroft's death last night. Still, you seem to be taking the news rather well."

"I hardly knew him," the skinny youth protested. "We'd just been doing Abington Street for AfricAlms, thought we'd get a few beers with the others after we'd finished. We deserved it, you know. We'd been doing something altruistic."

"At fifteen quid a pop," said Keynes. He took down the youth's name and contact details: Lawrence Wade, aged twenty. "So what do we have here: a falling-out amongst chuggers?"

"No, nothing like that! We were just having a good time, but the old blokes at the bar kept complaining. Pathetic, really. I left before the end. Whitcroft was still here. That was about 10."

Keynes made a note of the details, but felt like he had made no progress. He needed a witness to the murder, or some kind of incriminating evidence. Anything prior to that was too vague. The killer did not necessarily have to have been one of the bar patrons; there were dozens of people on the streets at night.

He left his card with the youth and put a couple more on the table with the other students.

"Call me if you hear anything or your memory improves."

"Memory?" said woolly hat. "Thanks, but I'll be treating you as a manifestation of the over-active conscience until I see further evidence." The student looked very pleased with himself.

Keynes paused on his way out. "You want some grim reality? Fine: when you graduate, you'll start paying tax. Basic rate's twenty percent, increasing to forty once you hit thirty-four K, then add National Insurance contributions on to that. You'll pay full price for beer, prescriptions and train tickets, and I expect the Bank of Mum and Dad will cut your credit line too. It'll take you seven to eight years to pay off your student loan, assuming you can get a job fairly quickly, at the end of which you'll be old enough to hate students. You've got more spending money now than you're ever going to have."

He walked out, his contempt for students rekindled.

The girl with the pierced nose turned to the youth with the woolly hat and said: "I warned you about solipsism, but you didn't listen!"

In the background, Wade left the pool table and made quickly for the gentlemen's toilets, looking like something he had consumed did not agree with him.

**

Outside, as the cold air hit him, Keynes could not help thinking how much more he would enjoy his job if the public were not involved. He envied Rutkowski, to a certain extent. He dealt in raw forensic evidence and could rebuild events from mere fragments. He did not have to pick through people's lies or attempts to be funny or clever. He just had to look through pieces of people: honest, tangible, silent testimony.

Keynes felt, after just a few years of working for the police, that you could lock up most people and not be wrong.

He felt like he would be more comfortable with a cigarette in his hand, to give him an excuse to stand outside the pub while he thought about his next move. Instead, he twirled a stumpy pencil between his fingers. A lot of people would have thrown the pencil away by now, but he made a point of avoiding waste whenever possible by resharpening. He had saved the taxpayer more than three pounds over the course of his career through this measure alone, not that he expected any thanks.

He walked away from the Angus and headed for his car, which was parked outside the Guildhall. He would head back to the office and type up some of his notes. At least he had a rough idea what time Whitcroft had left the pub. It barely helped the investigation, but it was one of those irksome details that needed to be confirmed sooner or later.

He noticed a Big Issue seller on the other side of the road tense up as he approached, giving him a momentary pang of pleasure.

A thought occurred to him.

Keynes stopped, then headed back to the Big Issue vendor, a hairy giant with one ear festooned with gold earrings.

"I'm licensed," said the giant. "I've got it somewhere."

He produced a laminated card. Keynes read the name: 'Wazz.'

"Afternoon, Wazz. I don't suppose you know anyone called Zulu?" Keynes asked.

"Zulu? Yeah, sleeps on Gold Street. I don't have much to do with him. What's he done?"

"Never mind that. What do you know about him? What's his background?"

Wazz rubbed his chin. "Bit of a know-it-all. Does a bit of H. Usually drunk or off his head on something. I heard he once swallowed ten live goldfish he nicked from the Saint Crispin's fair. Wasn't even for a bet."

"Any criminal background? Apart from the goldfish."

"Don't think so. He's too lazy. Spends most of his time begging or in the library."

"The library?"

"Look, that's all I know." Wazz looked worried now. "Anything he's done is nothing to do with me. It's not to do with these murders, is it?"

Keynes took a moment to reply. "Too early to say," he replied. "What's his real name?"

"Zigga Zumba," said Wazz.

"I suspect that's not his real name, Wazz." Keynes put the pencil away.

Chapter 9

Keynes returned to the station, feeling a little deflated. He had done the routine parts of the investigation, but he was frustrated at how long it was taking and how little progress he had made. He had nothing that even approximated a hunch so far. Keynes suspected that Gunnett had a promising lead and did not want to share the glory.

He dropped in to see Rutkowski at the morgue. Rutkowski had Whitcroft's body spread out on the slab, and had carefully sliced it open then repaired it.

"The parents have not seen it yet," said Rutkowski. "I like to make it nice for them. In the circumstances."

"There's not much icing you can put on this particular cake. Did you confirm the cause of death?"

Rutkowski grasped the body by the shoulders and turned the head slightly to show the purple swelling among the hair at the corner of Whitcroft's temple. "This was the first wound, but it wasn't fatal. Concussion. Attacked from in front. I cannot tell you the shape of the weapon, but something heavy and blunt. A rounded edge." Rutkowski placed the head back carefully into its original position, and reached down to the forearms, showing rust-coloured scars. "Cuts on both arms. He tried to stop himself falling, but only cut his wrists as he fell through the glass. Heavy bleeding from arterial wounds. He never woke up."

Rutkowski replaced the body delicately. "You know, he drank a lot of beer. High alcohol level in the blood, and no dinner. You need the dinner."

"So he wouldn't have put up much of a fight?"

"His reflexes would have been very slow. He knew nothing before it was too late."

Keynes muttered something inaudible.

"Pardon me?" said Rutkowski.

Keynes hesitated, then asked: "Did you find anything up his bum?"

"The usual."

"Right." Keynes tried to brush over his previous question. "So no tissue samples, fibres, DNA..?" said Keynes. He was clutching at straws, and Rutkowski seemed to know it, judging by the sly smile that crept around his lips.

"Nothing to help find your killer," said Rutkowski. "The possessions are over there, but nothing unusual." He gestured to a steel petri dish on a table to Keynes' left. "You know, I was a medical doctor before, for ten years. Then, they don't care what it is, they just want to cure it. Now, they only want to know the reason, and already too late. My job now is a history teacher."

"It's always nice to have the facts."

"But nicer to have the facts before this happens. You know, there is a very famous Detective Rutkowski in Poland. Poland's most famous detective."

"Oh."

"He finds kidnapped people, brings in criminals from overseas when there is no extradition treaty with the country – everything the law cannot do. He is a private contractor, so he can think and act differently. That has given me great respect for detectives. So when I hear you asking me unusual questions, I know that is because you are thinking outside the lines. Like a Polish detective."

"Thank you," said Keynes, glad that Rutkowski had stopped talking.

Keynes looked at Whitcroft's pallid features, his cloudy eyes staring at the ceiling. His skin had tightened, but he still looked gormless, unaware of the fate that had befallen him. Keynes studied him careful, trying to work out whether Whitcroft was a criminal or a victim.

Chapter 10

Keynes returned to his desk. This time he made a good stab at compiling his reports. He really excelled at this part of his job. There were no people to complicate things, only facts, and he could be selective with those in order to support whatever argument he was trying to make.

The important thing was to show that he had covered every angle and left nothing out. Other officers had made their own contributions. Whitcroft's parents would be questioned, once they had identified the body formally, and Keynes, fortunately, would not be involved in that part of events. He had been told before by his superiors that he had no talent for sympathy. He went into every encounter with the public treating it as an interrogation; as though the other person had something to hide and it was his job to find it.

Shepherd had asked him during his first month whether he had ever served in the army, suspecting that Keynes' brusque manner had come from training, rather than his inherent personality type. Keynes had considered the army prior to joining the force, but had decided in the end that the police offered more opportunities for those with initiative. Plus, the police had a fast-track scheme for university graduates which should, the advertisements had claimed at the time, mean he would need to serve only three years as a Sergeant before being promoted to Inspector. That claim was now looking rather suspect itself.

Gunnett approached without Keynes noticing, and perched himself on the corner of the desk.

"Doing the paperwork? Good lad."

"How's your other assignment?" asked Keynes, watching Gunnett's reaction closely.

Gunnett looked drained. "Not easy," he said. "It's a lot of work. A lot of work." He rubbed his hand across his face, pinching his brow. "It's going to take more time than I thought."

"Perhaps you'd better file a preliminary report, just to let people know."

Gunnett peeled his hand away from his face to see Keynes staring accusingly at him.

"Don't start," said Gunnett. "I'll be back with you tomorrow. This is something that needs my personal attention."

"It's just – this is all taking longer than it needs to."

"Is it?" said Gunnett, suddenly energised. "What, two days in and you haven't found the killer? What a surprise! You mean you've actually had to go around and talk to people, and no one's admitted it yet? What a startling turn of events. Normally murderers just turn up at the station and hand themselves in. Maybe you should check at the front desk in case Jack the Charity Shop Ripper is sitting there with a hot chocolate."

Gunnett stood up. "Or would you like me to go? Since you're obviously worried about preserving your shoe leather."

Keynes felt infuriated, but at the same time helpless to show it. "I just feel, Inspector, that we would be more efficient working as a team, and probably wrap this up earlier," he said, calmly.

Gunnett snorted. He looked almost amused. "That's what you feel. Do you know how long I've been doing this? If this merited my twenty-four-hour attention, it would have it. As it is, there's an old lady who went for a burton, and a drunk student who fell through a window. Do you need me to hold your hand?"

"No," muttered Keynes.

"I've got to take the high-level view. You've got to go around ringing doorbells, tramping the street, or whatever else I decide you've got to do. If I decide the investigation is being hampered because my car's too mucky, I'd expect you to wash it." Gunnett leaned back, breaking eye contact with Keynes, as if worried what he would say next if he continued talking.

"Where are your notes?" he asked. "The clean ones, typed up."

Keynes handed him the printed version of his latest report. Gunnett took them without a word, then headed into Shepherd's office and closed the door behind him. Keynes had the feeling that, whatever conversation was going on in that office, his own contribution to the investigation might be somewhat under-emphasised.

He wondered whether it was in his best interests to type up his notes so promptly and so neatly. It just made it easier for other people to take all the credit.

Keynes could see Shepherd in his office, nodding in agreement as Gunnett said something – blatantly reading from the notes in front of him.

He wondered exactly what Gunnett had been doing that was more important than investigating a double homicide.

It was raining again, and Gold Street was even emptier than usual. Keynes noticed that the British Cancer Foundation shop had not bothered to make much of a change to its window display. Vicky Wade had simply moved a new mannequin, clad in a pastel blue cardigan and green skirt, into the spot once occupied by her late colleague. He wondered if anyone had even disinfected the area. Dead people's clothes were one thing, but this was another, less sanitary, matter.

"Spare some change?" said a dirty, hopeless figure, holding out his hand as he felt a shadow fall over him, but keeping his head bowed. When he noticed Keynes had not moved, he looked up.

"You again?" said Zulu. "This is police harassment. Can't a man get any privacy?"

"Well, you do insist on sleeping on the public thoroughfare. It's a bit of a goldfish bowl."

Keynes waited for his words to sink in. He looked annoyed when Zulu did not react.

"A real goldfish bowl," he added.

There was still no reaction.

"Do you like eating goldfish?"

"For a minute there, I thought you were being subtle, officer," said Zulu, with a grin.

Keynes leaned closer. "Oh, I know all about you," he said, tried to sound menacing. "The goldfish...all of that stuff."

"The goldfish wasn't me, by the way. I mean, I stole them, but it was my girlfriend who ate them."

"What a classy pair you must have made," said Keynes.

For the first time, Zulu looked at him with undisguised contempt. Keynes took a step back, in case he was about to be attacked, but Zulu slowed his breathing and steadied himself.

"You really have no idea who I am, do you?" he said. The way he spat out the words made it sound like an insult.

"If I cared enough, I'd find out, believe me," said Keynes.

Zulu's eyes, suddenly clear and shining, burned into Keynes, unsettling the detective for reasons he could not explain. It was something of a relief when he turned his gaze back to the ground. Keynes wondered what kind of character he had been before the sedative, deflating effects of toxic substance abuse had taken effect.

"Anyway," said Keynes, trying to regain his composure, "I was just checking whether you'd remembered anything about the murder across the road, or heard any chatter on the one in Abington Street. From the intellectual types you must associate with."

"I'll ask," muttered Zulu, keeping his eyes on the pavement. For the first time, Keynes wondered whether perhaps he did have a violent side. If Zulu could abuse his own stomach and liver with the chemical grot he put into his gullet and veins, there was no knowing what he could do to other people if he had the right reasons. It was always worth watching people who had nothing to lose.

Keynes realised he was playing with his pencil again as he stood awkwardly on the edge of the pavement. He had the uncommon feeling of being totally lost. His investigation had come to a total dead end and he had no idea what to do next. He did not have a hunch, or even a strong prejudice against any of the people he had met in the course of his questioning. Forensic evidence was one thing, but in the end it always came down to people either giving themselves away or being spotted in the act.

He had been reduced to pestering a probable heroin addict who had not even seen anything useful, but just happened to sleep near the scene of the crime. It had been a good idea at first, but it had not worked, and he had not managed to think of a better one.

Rutkowski had not even managed to come up with a possible weapon used in the Whitcroft attack. Something fairly heavy and blunt. A round bruise on Whitcroft's head – or did that just reflect the shape of his head?

There was probably something simple tying the two attacks together. Or was it all a coincidence? Nearly a quarter of the shops on Northampton's high street were charity shops. If you hit someone over the head as they were walking along, there was a reasonable chance they would collapse outside a charity shop and a one-in-sixteen chance that two in succession would. Perhaps it was just a statistical quirk that had led him to chase a connection there, when Whitcroft could just as easily have expired in the doorway of a newsagent or a bookies.

But no, there was a connection there, the donations. Admittedly, it was all too easy to draw a straight line and find a correlation when there were only two data points on your graph, but the charity angle had to mean something.

Keynes had been twirling the stubby pencil between his fingers, but as his thinking process became more involved he dropped it. It bounced on the pavement and landed in the folds of Zulu's bedding. For a moment he considered the kinds of things that might live in that sleeping bag and the sheets of filthy newspaper, and contemplated leaving the pencil there, but the policeman within him knew that would be littering of a sort.

He bent down to pick it up, doing his best not to get too close to Zulu. The smell was terrible, like sweat layered exponentially on dirt, with an undertone of the alcohol that had soaked into his clothes and sleeping bag. Keynes wondered if Zulu ever washed his clothes or himself, and, if so, how.

As his fingers closed around the pencil, Keynes noticed the newspaper it had landed on. It was an old, and extremely weathered copy of the local paper with a photo of an overweight middle-aged woman in a hunting jacket and hat. The newsprint had been smudged almost beyond recognition, and the paper was crispy and washed out from becoming damp and drying out, but he could just make out the words "charity" and "dead" in the headline. The body copy was unreadable.

Zulu noticed the attention Keynes was paying to the newspaper article and allowed himself a smile.

"I wondered when you'd notice that," he said. He coughed inelegantly into Keynes' face, just a few inches away.

Chapter 11

Keynes rounded the stairs to the Tribune office feeling a new sense of hope, of doors opening, but this was tempered by the frustration he felt at overlooking an existing piece of information for so long. If Gunnett had not been so pre-occupied with his mysterious extra-curricular assignment they might have noticed it much earlier.

Chris Shingles was sitting at his desk, looking agitated. Three mugs of cold, stale coffee were beside his keyboard and he was cradling a telephone between his head and shoulder while attempting to type.

"It's just our policy," he said, not noticing Keynes enter. "No corrections for names, unless it's a vicar or a member of parliament." He paused to hear the response from the person at the other end. "It's not significantly different. Well, I appreciate it's significant to you, but to run a correction every time we have a slight typo..." This evidently elicited an angry response from the caller. "I don't know, probably because I'm on the phone to people like you when I'm trying to type." Shingles listened for a moment, then carefully replaced the phone back in its cradle.

"Spirit of the community, eh?" said Keynes, flicking idly through a stack of printed notes on one of the empty desks.

Shingles jumped as he noticed Keynes was there. "The usual timewasters. Can you leave that alone, please, that's confidential information."

Keynes read it. It was a press release about a new road safety campaign for schools.

"Look, officer...Keynes, I'm on deadline. Can this wait?"

"Maybe if your website wasn't so rubbish I wouldn't have to come in here to find things out. Ever heard of a searchable archive?"

"Donny's supposed to be uploading stuff for that," grumbled Shingles. "It'll be restricted to subscribers, though. I don't see the point of giving everything away for free."

"I need a back issue of the paper from November the fifteenth."

"And that's all?"

Shingles rose from his desk and walked to the ceiling-high wooden bookshelf behind the door. It was stuffed full of faded newspapers, which were piled three deep in front of it. Despite the huge mass of newsprint, he found the right issue immediately and pulled it carefully out of one of the piles to avoid bringing the rest of it down.

He handed it to Keynes, watching him with interest.

Keynes flicked through the newspaper, looking for an article above the fold on the right-hand side. He found what he was looking for: the same photo of the ruddy-cheeked woman in her hunting pinks, under the headline: 'Countryside charity campaigner found dead.'

Shingles ran a hand through his hair, dislodging flakes of dandruff.

"So now there are three?" he said, allowing himself a smile. "Looks like the school dinners story just got bumped off the front page."

Keynes shot him a warning look, but held his tongue in case he gave any more away. Right now, it seemed as though everyone else was one step ahead of him and not giving him any clues.

**

Wendy Bevan, fifty-four, had died a week ago, but the death had not seemed suspicious and, since it had taken place in the small village of Litchborough, no one would have drawn any connection to the deaths in Northampton town centre.

She had died of a combination of respiratory troubles and cardiac arrest. To put it less tactfully, she had stopped breathing because she was too fat to sustain her vital functions. Her lifeless body had been found wedged, standing upright, in an old-fashioned red telephone box between the telephone apparatus and the rear window. The robust construction of the booth's framework, not to mention the high replacement cost and the fact that the urgency of the situation had passed, had meant that rather than cutting through the metal frame to extricate her, a couple of unfortunate employees of the state had been required to lubricate Mrs Bevan's broadest points with washing-up liquid until she could be squeezed through the doorway.

The death had not been investigated at the time because it had not been viewed as suspicious. Perhaps it was as it seemed, and she had died simply of Darwinian consequences. Mrs Bevan had used an inhaler, which was found on the floor of the phone booth, out of her reach since the dimensions of her own body had prevented her from bending down.

What made Keynes look again was the charity connection, and the timing. Mrs Bevan had been a vocal and highly public supporter of the Rural Defence Association, a charity organisation devoted to upholding traditional countryside pursuits, such as riding horses through other people's vegetable gardens to assist dogs, in some capacity, in the shredding of individual foxes.

It seemed to Keynes, a town-dweller, an incredibly inefficient method, requiring dozens of people, horses and hounds, and several hours of effort per fox. He was amazed that no one had come up with a more efficient method. Even a motorbike would be more manoeuvrable than a horse, and would probably produce fewer emissions.

These days, it was illegal to hunt a fox deliberately, so the hunt chased a smelly rag on a string, but if they happened to encounter a fox on the way – perhaps one that had moved to the area, encouraged by employees of the hunt building an artificial shelter in the woods for them or blocking up badger setts in which they might have hidden – then it was perfectly fine, and in accordance with natural animal instincts, for the hounds to dismember it. This happened far more often than statistically likely.

Mrs Bevan had been a member of this happy troupe, and had been the face of its fundraising efforts. Keynes was unsure why fundraising to support a sport should be exempt from tax, but Bevan and her peers had done a good job of persuading the relevant authorities that British heritage was at risk were fox hunting and other traditional crafts to be allowed to die out. The money raised was used to lobby against proposals to ban or restrict hunting, and had been at least partially successful, given that the sport, while technically illegal, had not been impacted in the slightest.

Perhaps the charity angle alone was not reason enough for Keynes to reopen the case, but he had noticed unusual elements to it. Mrs Bevan had been a wealthy woman, the granddaughter of a successful estate agent whose chain of shops still dotted the high streets of Northamptonshire towns. She had probably never used a coin-operated pay phone in her life, and, call records showed, she had not used one that night.

What was more, the telephone booth was just a couple of hundred metres from her driveway. Even though no mobile phone was found on her body, it made no sense for her to use the booth if she had wanted merely to make a call. Keynes had checked the weather report from that night and it had been clear. She had not ducked inside to shelter from the rain.

The only reasonable explanation he could come up with was that she had been protecting herself from someone outside, knowing that she was too portly to outrun them and reach her own house. Perhaps she had run as far as the phone box, and that was why her heart had burst. Once she got inside, she had become wedged, found it hard to breathe, and so she had found herself in a couple of perfunctory paragraphs in the local newspaper.

Keynes acknowledge that there had been no reason at the time to examine her death more closely, but now that there was perhaps a potential lunatic pursuing people with a connection to charities – and now that Gunnett was too preoccupied to stop Keynes following this lead – he had good cause to look for clues.

He parked his car at the top of the gravel driveway, which stretched several hundred metres back from the road. The grounds were bordered by a high, sandstone wall, so most people would never see the house or the ancillary buildings around it. The house itself was impressive, and probably three centuries old, while the conservatory and patio area looked somewhat newer. The nearby stables, housing half a dozen horses, accounted for the slightly unpleasant smell that met Keynes as he stepped out of his car. He glanced down at his shoes in case there were any equine deposits closer to hand.

As Keynes rapped the door knocker, a bevy of barking responded. There was a wait of several minutes and he could hear several doors being opened and closed, presumably as the owner put the dogs out of harm's way.

Geoffrey Bevan opened the door, his mouldering breath reaching Keynes before he noticed the face.

"Detective Sergeant Keynes, Mr Bevan. We spoke on the phone."

"Ah, yes," said Bevan. "I only wish you people had shown this much urgency a little closer to the time of her passing." He made no attempt to shake Keynes' outstretched hand, but turned away and headed back inside, leaving the front door open. Keynes took that as his cue to follow.

Keynes followed Bevan into the living room and took a seat without waiting to be asked. The room was immersed in a muggy mist of animal odours. He realised too late that the armchair he had chosen was not actually brown but had grey upholstery that had been covered over many years in layers of dog hair.

"That's Freddy's chair," said Bevan. "I suppose you can sit there if you must."

Keynes could tell from the smell that Freddy was an elderly and rather leaky dog. At times like these, he reflected that people from the highest and lowest classes of society seemed equally happy to live in squalor, and that only the ones in the middle bothered with things like mops and detergent. He had been in crackhouses that smelled better than Mr Bevan's living room.

"Do I take it that this visit means the police have acknowledged the inadequacy of your earlier efforts?" Mr Bevan asked.

"No, sir, I've read the reports and it does seem as though there was nothing unnatural about the death itself. It's the circumstances leading to it which I'm interested in, given recent…events."

"These, er, charity shop murders?" said Mr Bevan, gesturing at a folded copy of the Tribune by the side of his chair.

"That's their catchphrase, not ours. There has been a bit of irresponsible reporting on the matter."

"The Rural Defence Association doesn't have any charity shops. They sell tea towels and things by post, and sometimes they have stalls at the agricultural shows. That's all."

"I think the charity angle is more important than the tea towel aspect," said Keynes, leaning forward with care. "Were you aware of any threats to Mrs Bevan or to the Rural Defence Association as a whole?"

Bevan snorted. The unseen dogs responded with muffled but frantic barking. "There were many, many instances," he said. "What a silly question! Surely you must have seen the records of the numerous times we contacted you with reports of intimidation."

Keynes suspected that these incidents, had they even been taken down, would have been filed in the system as a 'TW' – standing for 'Time Wasters'. Going to the police with an upper class accent and a bad attitude, he had noticed, tended to lessen the chances of receiving full co-operation. Depending on Mrs Bevan's own telephone manner, she might even have been logged as an 'LN', for 'Local Nutter'.

"Young people, usually," Mr Bevan went on. "The same sort who go around firebombing animal research labs, I expect. The kind of things they would shout at us on the road. Disgusting."

"Do you remember any specific threats of violence?"

"The tone was generally violent."

"But do you remember anyone threatening any specific act of violence against Mrs Bevan or the group?"

Mr Bevan sank back in his chair. The effort of trying to think showed on his face as he paused, his outrage lapsing temporarily.

"I'm sure there were," he said quietly, after a moment's thought. "Absolutely certain. I just can't remember specific times and places off the top of my head."

Keynes was not sure whether this admission was because Mr Bevan had been exaggerating earlier, or because he genuinely could not remember. Either way, this was not getting him very far, and he was slightly regretting driving this far from town on a low tank of fuel because he knew the petrol out here was about two pence per litre more expensive than in town, and he was trying to keep his claims down.

"Can you remember anyone who may have made persistent threats or who stood out as having particular violent intent?" asked Keynes.

"The young people," said Mr Bevan, waving his hand vaguely. "With their hoods and vegetables. The 'Save The Planet' types. They don't seem to realise how the countryside works. They buy their Spanish tomatoes in the supermarket and that's as close as they get to it. Then they get upset when they find out there's a bit of mud or viscera involved."

"Any names of individuals or groups?"

"Just the general townies and yobbos. There were one or two organisations that would hold banners and try to disrupt things – use air freshener or curry powder on the dogs to confuse the scent, and so on. There was 'Stop Blood Sports Now' and 'End Animal Torture'. 'Stop Fox Cruelty', that was another one."

Keynes gently lowered his head and pinched the bridge of his nose. Mr Bevan appeared to be simply recalling the things he had read on protesters' signs, rather than the names of any groups.

"Any people you recognised?"

"They're all the same type. Unwashed, long hair. Baggy clothing. Things through their noses, some of them, like bulls. I couldn't tell them apart."

He tried a last gambit. "Did Mrs Bevan know Vera Hope? She worked in the British Cancer Foundation shop on Gold Street."

Mr Bevan shook his head. "All of her friends were in the hunting community or the village," he said. "She went to see her sister in Towcester occasionally, but I don't think even she would have known anyone who worked in a shop."

Keynes felt like he had wasted an afternoon, and probably ruined a good pair of trousers, for nothing. The prospect of a connection to the other charities had drawn him out here to investigate the fairly straightforward case of a fat woman dying of a heart attack.

At that moment, the front door opened and the barking recommenced. He heard the sound of it closing and someone removing their shoes, then the living room door opened and an elderly, timid-looking woman peered through.

"Sorry, Mr Bevan, I didn't realise you had a visitor," she said, and quickly withdrew.

Mr Bevan sat up suddenly. "Wait!" As the old woman returned to the room, he turned to Keynes. "This is Mrs Shaw," he said. "She cleans for us." Keynes doubted that, until he saw how frail she was, which explained the quality of the cleaning. "She saw who murdered Wendy."

Keynes was dumbfounded. He looked at the woman, who nodded.

"Tell Sergeant Keynes what you saw, Mrs Shaw."

"I was walking home from chapel," she said, unbuttoning her coat. "It was late, very dark already. Bitterly cold as well. And my eyesight's not what it was."

Keynes felt sure this was going to end up in the 'TW' file.

"I was passing the village hall, heading up to Tim and Betty's," Mrs Shaw went on, as if Keynes was expected to know these people.

"Wendy was coming back from Janet's," said Mr Bevan, nodding.

Mrs Shaw went on: "Well, I didn't think anything of it at the time, but I looked back and I could see someone in the phone box, which is unusual, and the strangest thing – there was a wolf outside."

"Could it have been a dog?" asked Keynes, as politely as he could manage.

"No, it was a big old thing. Six foot, I should say."

"Standing upright?"

"That's right."

"Making a noise? Howling?"

"I don't think so."

"Could you have been mistaken?"

"I didn't hang around to find out what it was, but it looked like a wolf to me. It was about twenty-five yards back."

In the dark, with your terrible vision, thought Keynes. It could have been a garden gnome.

"Scared to death by some kind of wild creature," said Mr Bevan. "If that's not suspicious, I don't know what is."

"I see," said Keynes. "I'll check back at the station, but I don't think we've had any reports of anything similar happening since then."

"Aren't you going to write any of this down?" said Mr Bevan, with annoyance.

"They've got computers now," said Mrs Shaw, hanging up her coat.

Chapter 12

This job would be better, even positively enjoyable, thought Keynes, if it were not for all the people. If it were just a matter of tipping out the contents of a box and rearranging the pieces into something logical, he would have a good day at the office every day.

Instead, he had to speak to fantasists and geriatric wellwishers who thought the Hound of the Baskervilles was terrorising Litchborough and cocking its leg on phone boxes.

He was trying to do the right thing and it was backfiring. He was being punished for being responsible, which was not a rare consequence, he had to admit. There was still no sign or message from Inspector Gunnett, so as far as Keynes was concerned he had been left to his own devices.

Keynes genuinely could not think of an avenue he had left unexplored. He had chased up every loose end, and if he had not done it, someone else had. It seemed impossible that anyone could have seen the evidence he had seen, interviewed the people he had interviewed and done any better. There simply was no answer in sight, whichever way you looked at it.

This approach was not working. This was not how people did things on an MBA course, and he had read multiple books claiming to impart the MBA style of thinking.

He had been doing things the conventional way. That was bound to produce a predictable outcome, but this was not a predictable case. This was not a dead girl in the

Grand Union Canal with her arm covered in needle marks. This was not a husband laying in the kitchen with fatal head injuries while his wife stood holding a frying pan. With those cases, everyone knew the answers going in, and it was a simple matter of going through the motions, without missing any incriminating evidence that would be needed later.

In the case of the charity shop murders, whether or not they were murders, and regardless how many there were, he did not have an obvious suspect in any of the deaths – other than natural causes in one. The old methods did not work, so he had to try new ones.

He would think like an MBA graduate. Imagine if he solved the murders. What would be the benefit? He would look good in front of Shepherd, and perhaps he would even achieve the promotion he was suppose to have been given two years ago, before the budget freeze.

Those were both good things, but in the grand scheme of things, the bigger picture, the benefits were fairly minimal. Someone would go to prison, depending on the skill of their defending barrister, and that would be the end of it.

No, what would be really useful, a tangible benefit, would be to view things differently. Imagine there were a serial killer on the loose and targeting charity workers. View that proposition in terms of value at risk. The real benefit would be to identify the probable future targets and see to it that they were not murdered. That was pro-active thinking, he thought to himself. What was more, as long as they did not die, the potential victims would know that they had been spared from a horrible fate thanks to his efforts – again, making him look good.

That gave him a clear set of tasks. Firstly, draw up a list of all of the prominent individuals associated with charities who could be potential victims of attacks. Secondly, warn them of the risks that might be facing them. He did not want to go as far as acting as a bodyguard, but he could advise on their security arrangements, which would look good on his C.V. if he wanted to do a similar thing after leaving the police force.

In the course of all this, he might stumble across a common connection – something linking all of these charities together with the murderer.

Keynes was not so naïve as to think all charities were inherently altruistic. He had seen enough scams to deter him from charity donations altogether, until the tax benefit rule had been introduced. Being on the inside, he might be able to uncover murky behaviour, embezzlement and so on, which might prove to be the motive behind everything so far.

This all sounded like a great idea, but a nagging feeling at the back of his mind told him this approach did not quite make sense. Vera Hope had not been a particularly prominent figure on the charity scene, and nor had the student found with his head bashed in. They probably would not have figured in any list he would have drawn up at the time.

The other thing to consider was the breadth of his list. Where should he draw the line? What if he restricted it to charities in Northamptonshire and it turned out the killer had an East Midlands remit?

He had not even drawn up the parameters of his list yet, and already the input looked rather shaky.

Still, Keynes preferred to be doing something forward-thinking, rather than waiting for someone to give themselves up – or waiting for the next murder. He had to push things forward on his own terms.

He would make an effort not to use this tactic simply to meet influential figures he wanted to meet, nor to establish some left-wing credentials – which he had to admit he lacked at present. No, he would judge for himself, based on recent events, which individuals in the charity sector were most at risk. They might be little old ladies in charity shops in forsaken parts of Northampton town centre, or they might be successful tycoons who had turned to philanthropy after achieving their business goals. They might be upper-class, white women, or they might be of British-Indian origin and have worked their way up from working in a corner shop to create a local business empire, defying both class and race barriers.

It did not matter one way or the other to Keynes. It was not down to him to choose which members of the community he wanted to represent, and he certainly was not in this line of work for selfish reasons. Although, obviously, if he were to earn a reputation for being tolerant of other cultures, there would be nothing wrong with that.

Before he did anything, he called Gunnett's mobile number. As he expected, Gunnett did not pick up. In Keynes' eyes, that meant he had free rein to use his initiative. Should he do anything foolish, the blame would fall entirely on his shoulders. Likewise, should he do anything progressive, intelligent and supportive of integration with ethnic minorities, the credit would be his and his alone.

Those were small considerations, though. Keynes told himself his priority was solving the case.

Chapter 13

Harpit Singh was one of the few local success stories in the business world. He had made his fortune from his own efforts, with only a little help from his family, who had emigrated to Northampton to escape a life of hardship and persecution in Coventry. The family business had, rather stereotypically, been running a corner shop, but a teenaged Singh had leveraged on his business contacts and his experience working behind the counter selling sherbet dib-dabs to open his own venture.

His first business had been floor furnishings, under the name 'Harpit's Carpets', a brand that survived to this day. One thing had led to another, and he had expanded into a field of unrelated businesses in the early 1990s as other companies slowed down or cut jobs. He was unknown outside the Midlands – an ill-timed expansion into the caravan business with a Manchester partner had been his first and only attempt to widen the company's footprint – but within the region he was a household name, and generally well-liked.

His popularity was helped by his decision ten years ago to launch a local charity, Singh's Kids, for underprivileged children. Since then, he had raised millions of pounds for causes that were, admittedly, somewhat vaguely defined. This had helped the region's youth and had had the associated effect of raising Singh's profile and, it seemed, increasing the ease with which he could obtain planning permission for some of his business projects. This was, Keynes thought, most likely due to his increased public profile and the perception that he was a person of integrity, likely to give something back to the community through his combined entrepreneurial and charitable efforts. He was like the council and the Red Cross rolled into one. Plus, he was Indian.

Keynes had walked around the back of the carpet warehouse reminding himself to play it cool. He was there to warn Singh of a possible threat and to enquire about potential enemies, not to engage in hero worship or to try to win his favour or personal mobile number.

The rest of the warehouse was functional and a little run-down. It did not seem to have any operational machinery but was simply a place of storage for large amounts of carpeting. Men in overalls walked through the building holding either rolls of carpet or pieces of paper. The larger rolls of carpet arrived either by forklift or lorry and were transported to their appropriate places in the building. Keynes noted that the lorries had Spanish licence plates. Presumably that country was even lower in the economic pecking order than Northampton.

Singh's office was surprisingly plush. It had leather armchairs and carpeting too thick and lush to have been supplied by its proprietor's own business, which, it had to be said, was aimed more at the lower end of the market. Singh's secretary, a relative beauty in local terms, showed Keynes into the office and offered him a choice of beverages, including several types of coffee. Keynes opted for English breakfast tea, but was reminded that he had intended for one of his eight New Year resolutions to learn all the types of coffee, and even to learn to like some of them.

He sat uncomfortably in his leather chair examining the photographs behind Singh's desk. There was Singh with the head of the local chamber of commerce, the mayor, and even somebody senior at the charity commission. A space was quite clearly left blank on the wall in the middle of the other pictures. Keynes was sure Singh was saving that for when and if he met either the Prime Minister or the Queen, probably in the course of obtaining recognition for his charitable efforts. You would struggle to get that kind of recognition from selling carpets alone, Keynes reflected. How far had Singh's charitable efforts boosted his business ventures?

That was a sturdy-looking desk, Keynes noted. He wanted to turn the spare room into a study, but for some reason Jenny wanted to keep it free. A nice solid desk like that would be perfect, if he could convince her. Perhaps she could have that for her lesson planning, or something. He was not sure, though, that it would fit in the spare room. Could they repurpose part of the living room, or put flooring in the attic? He pulled himself back – they did not need a new desk, especially not one so extravagant.

At that moment, Singh arrived and interrupted Keynes' train of thought. He was slightly disappointed. Singh was shorter and fatter than he had expected. The businessman was well-dressed, in a tie that matched his turban and a well-cut three-piece suit, but even so, Keynes could tell he had enjoyed too many long lunches. Singh was doing his best to maintain his jaw at an angle that would not disclose his double-chin.

"Inspector Keynes, I presume?" he said, extending a warm hand. Keynes took it and gave a practised corporate handshake: firm, but not too aggressive, and held for exactly three seconds.

At the age of thirteen, Keynes had filled a surgical glove with custard powder, tied it off at the end, and used it to train himself in shaking hands for future job interviews. His mother had found it under his bed and thrown it away, fearing it was being used for something unpleasant, but by then he had already perfected his technique.

"Actually, it's Sergeant, currently. Mr Singh, I've followed your achievements closely," said Keynes. "Northampton needs more entrepreneurs."

"That's very kind of you. It's a different game now, though. The early 90s, that was the time. Swords and sandals. Blood and sawdust."

Keynes was not sure what Singh meant by that, so he waited for him to continue.

"This is an…informal visit, is it, Sergeant?" He noticed that Singh's top lip wore a fresh dew of perspiration. "My secretary said it was a routine visit – a courtesy call."

"That's right."

Singh glanced towards the telephone on his desk. "So there wouldn't be any need for me to have anyone else present?"

"No," said Keynes, looking a little confused. Singh relaxed visibly. He reached for the telephone and pressed a button, which turned off a small red light.

Singh rubbed his hands together. "Smashing. So, please, go on. Always happy to do something for the community."

"It's really more of a service to you, Mr Singh. You might have read certain reports in the Tribune…"

"I only skim it."

"I don't blame you," said Keynes. "Anyway, there have been a couple of disturbing events recently relating to members of the charitable fundraising community."

"Ah! The Charity Shop Murders." Singh beamed.

"That's not our phrasing. We haven't confirmed for sure that the killings are connected, or if they are all even murders. I just thought it would be prudent to contact one or two of the bigger fish in the charity world and apprise them of the possibility that they might be at risk."

Singh leaned forward conspiratorially. "That sounds to me as though it's not strictly in the police handbook. Sounds like you're using your initiative. An entrepreneurial mindset, and I ought to know."

Inside, Keynes was delighted that a successful businessman was talking to him in such a way, but he was determined not to show it. He decided to lean back in his chair slightly.

"Well, it doesn't hurt to be forewarned and forearmed," said Keynes. He thought that sounded modest enough, and also did not disagree with Singh's statement.

"Seriously, though, do you think I might be a target?"

"We don't know the killer's motives, and there haven't been any notes with the bodies, but I thought we'd better not take any chances. You are one of the more high-profile figures around."

Singh stroked his goatee. "Right, right. So what do I need to do?"

He was asking Keynes for advice. This was exactly how Keynes had envisaged this conversation. He was meeting a local business hero and being taken seriously.

Keynes relaxed a little. He could go with his instinct, and it would probably go well.

"I thought it would be best to have a little chat with you about possible times and places where you might be more vulnerable, and then perhaps to take a look around this facility and apprise you of possible areas where security could be compromised. Purely as a precautionary measure, of course." Keynes had the uncomfortable feeling that he had used the word 'apprise' with two different meanings in close proximity, but Singh did not appear to have noticed.

"An assassination audit," said Singh, chuckling. "Well, I always say: expect the unexpected. You know, no one in this company has ever suggested that I hire an outside security expert to look at this kind of thing.

"It's a huge oversight, when you think about it. Say what you like about succession planning, but I am the business. If I bite the dust, it's all over for Harpit's Carpets. They'd have to change the name, for one thing." Singh looked at Keynes approvingly. "The public sector out-thinking the private sector."

"I try to bring my own thinking to the job," said Keynes, wishing that he could have conversations like this every day, with people who appreciated him using his initiative. "But obviously…"

"Quite," said Singh. "My cousin – cousin-in-law – worked for the council in procurement. I could see he was wasted there, so I brought him over, in the end. Talent spotting, that's crucial."

Keynes felt the same warm thrill he had experienced in exams when he read the questions and realised he would score at least eighty-five percent. "Shall we go over your itinerary, and look at which people have access to you?" he said. "After that, we could take a look around the facility and I could give you a few pointers on security."

"Sounds good to me," said Singh.

Chapter 14

Singh had a busy schedule. In addition to his role as founder and chairman of Harpit's Carpets, he also had a directorship in a related haulage company, in which he also seemed to be a large shareholder, and frequently met with the town council to give them the benefit of his guidance. On top of that, he spent a lot of time working with his charity.

Several framed photographs on his desk bore witness to his fundraising efforts. There was Singh just prior to bungee jumping from a crane; there he was shaking hands with a third-tier member of the Royal family; there he was with his hands and neck in wooden medieval stocks, being splattered with custard pies in fine British tradition. For the more energetic stunts, he replaced his formal turban with a kind of lycra bandana.

They both looked out onto the workings of the warehouse. Below them, fork-lift trucks beetled backwards and forwards, while a truck reversed into an unloading bay and workers in boiler suits and fluorescent jackets helped unload huge rolls of carpet.

Keynes marvelled at the thought, impressive in a historical context but slightly patronising to point out now, that someone of Indian stock could be running a business commanding hundreds of white British workers. Britain, the great enabler. A nation of shopkeepers and a cultural melting pot, with Northampton at its molten centre, thanks to its unrivalled transport links.

He was slightly disconcerted as he looked more closely and realised that a large number of the manual labour force, perhaps even a majority, appeared to be African.

Judging by Northamptonshire's last census, and the growing number of restaurants in the side alleys off Abington Street, they were probably Somalian. That did not necessarily make Singh's achievements any less noble or impressive, he told himself. It was simply economic good sense. Call it salary arbitrage.

"Being a CEO is a twenty-four-hour job, and running a charity is a twenty-four -hour job, especially when they've both got your name on them," said Singh, noticing that Keynes seemed in awe of the bustling warehouse.

"Forty-eight hours," said Keynes, who had wanted to say something, but could not think of any more intelligent contribution than that. He was also watching his step as they descended a metal staircase from Singh's office onto the warehouse floor.

"Exactly," said Singh, treating it as an insightful remark. "Do you want to know how I do it?"

"Delegate," Keynes was about to say, but Singh spoke first.

"Most people will tell you to delegate. Big mistake. Remember my carpet warehouse near Farthinghoe? That was delegation. Lasted twelve months. So did the guy who suggested it."

Singh spread his arms wide. "This is all me. So are all my businesses. I can't afford any lapses, and I can't waste my time checking that someone beneath me has done things properly. It's quicker to do it myself, by instinct."

"How is the carpet business these days?" asked Keynes. "Profitable?"

Singh slipped on a step, but recovered his poise. "Leather soles," he said, by way of explanation, pointing at his brogues. "Let me tell you where the money is: remnants. You wouldn't think it, would you? They're basically worthless, but people need them. You write it off in your accounts, but then you get an awful lot of upside when you actually manage to sell the off-cuts that are basically factored in as waste."

"Broken biscuit strategy," said Keynes.

Singh grinned at him. "That would be a great title for a management book. I've often thought of writing one."

"You should," said Keynes, glad to have found a topic on which he could contribute. "I've just finished *Be Your Own Dubai: Building A Sustainable Boom*. It was written in 2007, but it's still relevant."

"Haven't read that one. I liked *Squeezing The Pips* by the orange juice fellow. Annoying, really. It covered a lot of the stuff my book would have done."

"I didn't like *What the Hell, Let's Sell* much," said Keynes, gaining the confidence to put forward his own opinion.

"Me neither! God, that was such hypocritical rubbish. That guy only got where he is because of his family connections. Old money dressed up as new, for the cameras."

Singh was not camera-shy himself, of course, Keynes noted, but there was something authentic about him. He had built his businesses from the ground up. They were not particularly glamorous industries; they were slow and steady earners that had not benefited from stock market bubbles or short-lived fads. People had always needed carpets, and they needed things moved from one place to another.

"Keep it to yourself," he said, "but I've also wanted to write a business strategy book using the lift tower as a metaphor." The Express Lifts Tower, recently renamed the National Lift Tower, was perhaps Northampton's only landmark. It was a massive concrete chimney-like structure almost totally devoid of features, in the centre of a residential area, and visible from most parts of the town.

"When that went up, I'm sure there was outcry," Singh went on. "There was a valid business reason for building it, and created jobs for a niche industry because no other towns had the vision to build a tower for testing lifts.

"The funny thing was, after enough time had passed, people started to look at it with affection. It's always been there. It's something a bit quirky that sets Northampton apart. When they talked about demolishing it a few years back, can you remember how upset people got? Now it's a Grade Two listed building."

"So you're using that as an example of planning for the long term?" Keynes guessed.

"I'm saying, forget sentimentality and trying to give people what they want. Do what's right for the business, even if it's unpopular, and people will appreciate it in the end."

Singh turned his palms up and gave a half-shrug, looking for Keynes' approval.

"I like it," said Keynes. "Don't ask people what they want – tell them."

"Bingo. Here we are," said Singh, stopping short of the unloading activity. "This is the biggest point of access. We typically get four or five deliveries a day like this. A limited number of suppliers, so we know most of the drivers."

"What about your staff? Are they permanent?"

Again, Singh seemed to lose his composure momentarily. "Mostly," he said. "Obviously a lot are temporary staff."

"Through agencies?"

"Basically."

"Would you be able to give me some of their background details, or a contact at the agency?"

"My secretary will have all that information. I'll make sure you get it."

Keynes looked the building up and down. Warehouses were inherently insecure places. There were usually far away from residential areas, operated into the small hours of the morning and never locked all points of entry. There were generally few security checks on people wandering in and out of the property.

"How many security staff do you have?" he asked.

"Two, at all times. Everyone has to be signed in. They take the licence plates, that kind of thing."

"Any CCTV?"

"Cameras? There's one outside my office, one in the payrolls room and outside, and a couple trained on our main traffic access points."

"I'd like to check out the blind spots, if you don't mind."

Singh grinned. "Why would I mind? You're giving me a free security audit."

After a tour of the ground level, Singh took Keynes to the security office, a small room with two chairs, a kettle and a bank of screens, which were in turn split into smaller screens, which alternated between different views every few seconds.

"State of the art," said Singh. Keynes did not respond. They both knew this was not strictly true. He watched for a couple of minutes, until he had seen every view repeated.

"Eighteen cameras for the building itself," Keynes said. "Ten inside, eight outside. Obviously with these cameras giving you about ninety degrees of coverage, you would need a few more to cover the full thousand-and-eighty degrees of viewing angles for the exterior, but you've got most of it. My concern is the lighting."

Keynes pointed to one of the exterior views of the staff car park, next to a chain-link fence. "See the tree at the edge of the fence? Very easy to get through there and not be picked up by the cameras. There's no lighting in the left of that area, and from there you could, if you were lucky, get access to the drainpipe or the South-East fire exit if someone's been foolish enough to leave it open while they go for a smoke break or something."

"They do that sometimes on the night shift," said Singh, thoughtfully. "When they get caught, they complain it's too far to walk around. We've tried chaining them shut..." He caught Keynes' eye. "I mean to say, one of my staff suggested chaining it shut, but I reminded him that would be a breach of fire safety regulations, and we didn't do it."

"Possible point of access, then."

Keynes and Singh checked the other main points of access. There were security measures, but Keynes knew they would be easy to breach by anyone with enough determination. It was impossible for anyone to memorise all of the faces here, especially with so many temporary staff and people working different, overlapping shifts. The one consolation was that anyone who did break in and murder Mr Singh would probably be caught on camera on their way to or from his office. The cameras outside the office were in excellent locations and well-lit.

As they rounded a corner to the front entrance of the building, they came across a couple of dozen metal canisters, slightly spotted with rust on the outside and stacked in a pile chest-high against the wall. Keynes looked at them suspiciously.

"What kind of substance is in here?" he asked, producing his notebook and pen. "There are no markings."

Singh looked concerned for a moment, then walked over and picked one up, beaming.

"You had me worried for a minute there, Sergeant. This is my next charity stunt. A world record attempt. Baked beans."

Keynes frowned. "I can't see any labels."

"They're slightly out of date. My brother-in-law runs a cash and carry in Kettering. He was going to throw them out. In fact, that was partly what gave me the idea." He caught Keynes' worried look. "Don't worry, I'm not going to eat them. Don't you read the local paper?"

Keynes had to admit that he did not. Singh looked slightly deflated, but perked up as he explained his scheme.

"I'm going for the world record for the longest time spent in a bath of baked beans," Singh said. "We'll be doing it outside this warehouse on Saturday."

"Good exposure for the brand."

"Now you're thinking like a businessman. Obviously branding for the charity will dominate, but the TV news footage is bound to have a bit of corporate signage in the background. The other thing is that I need to be within range of the wireless internet so I can do some work on my laptop when the cameras aren't on. I can't afford to take a whole day off."

"How long do you need to be in there?"

"The record is ten hours fifty-four minutes twenty-one seconds. In fairness, it's not a record many people know about. I can beat that, no trouble. Weather forecast is looking good, and I've got thermal underwear that should do the job. If I don't raise at least five grand from this, I'll be disappointed."

Singh looked more excited than he had done at any time during their conversation so far.

"That's very commendable," said Keynes, though he was secretly disappointed that Singh was putting on such a deliberately zany stunt to earn some publicity. CEOs weren't supposed to sit around in baked beans in their underpants. Not if they wanted to command respect. "How much do you usually raise from this kind of thing?"

"I'd have to check," said Singh, unusually bashful.

"I mean, how much have you raised in your charity career so far?"

"I don't have a number to hand. I could find out."

Keynes was a little surprised that Singh could not recite the number offhand. He seemed in such mastery of his brand that it was hard to believe he did not know the exact number, right down the penny.

"In fact, thank you for reminding me," said Singh. "I'll need to make sure someone checks that before we send out the press release. Local press coverage is vital. Absolutely vital."

"Does the charity have a press officer?"

"No, that's all done by my secretary, on top of her usual duties. Keeping the costs on the corporate side. Some charities use as much as eighty-five percent of their funds on salaries and administrative costs. Not us. A much lower figure." Singh stroked his goatee. "Again, I couldn't say exactly what that was unless I had the records in front of me."

Keynes had an anxious feeling in his stomach. If Singh really was this sloppy with his accounting, what was to stop someone skimming something from the books? For all Keynes knew, that could have been a motive for the other killings, too. Accounting firms: one possible lead he had not yet checked.

"All the same, I would like to see the financial records, if at all possible," said Keynes.

"Of course, of course," said Singh, slowly. He looked at his shoes.

"Well, I think that's plenty for now, and I've taken up a lot of your time. But as I said, you should probably consider moving one of your cameras to the back of the bins, and implementing some kind of pass-card system for certain restricted areas. It's very easy to copy keys." Keynes held out his hand. "Thank you, Mr Singh. It's been eye-opening."

Singh swallowed hard as he shook Keynes' hand.

"Hold on," he said, as Keynes turned to leave. Keynes stopped, wondering whether Singh was about to name a possible suspect who might have threatened him.

"We've actually got some larger-size remnants, recently come in," Singh went on, his throat sounding dry. "Actually not much use to us. Too small to be carpets, too large to be remnants. Seems a shame to throw them out. Perhaps you'd like to take a look."

He gave Keynes a meaningful glance. "On the house, of course, in recognition of our hardworking police."

"If I came home with a new carpet tonight, that would ruin the various milestones I've set for my wife's expectations," said Keynes, without thinking. "I try to be firm but realistic. I let her know exactly what she can expect, and that way she doesn't get spoiled and she doesn't try to overplay her hand. Everything is benchmarked against salary and career progression – hers and mine, but mostly mine. She knows the first carpet that's going to be upgraded is the one in the living room, and that's not scheduled for, probably, another three years.

"The same with the kitchen appliances. We sat down and worked out how long they need to last for us to have achieved a decent return on our investment. If we have a baby, and we're not expecting to, then we'll buy a dishwasher, but a new carpet at this stage would ruin the whole concept. But thank you for your kind offer."

Singh had turned pale around halfway through Keynes' speech. "Sensible," he said, still holding out his hand.

"I'll be seeing you, Mr Singh. And if you could ask your secretary to send me the details I mentioned, that would be great."

Keynes was sitting in his car, with the key halfway to the ignition, before he started to wonder whether Singh had attempted to bribe him. He dismissed the thought. Singh was an upstanding local businessman with an excellent reputation for charitable work. No one would put that at risk unless he had a very pressing reason to do so.

Right now, he was feeling annoyed with himself for failing to suggest the cross-sell opportunity he was sure would have shown Singh that he had business sense: stocking carpet cleaning products at the tills. He was not sure exactly what he had hoped to achieve by making the suggestion. Perhaps he had just wanted to have a normal conversation with a likeminded, intelligent individual, for once in his working life.

**

Singh, meanwhile, walked quietly back up the stairs to his office, closed the door and sat back in his chair, his hands at the back of his neck. He took off his turban, revealing a receding hairline that measured around four on the Norwood scale, and felt his scalp with his fingers. Singh reached into his desk drawer and produced a small canister of hair tonic, which he sprayed on the follicles that were not yet extinct.

As he massaged the substance, which had a vaguely grassy smell, into his scalp, he weighed up the extent of his error. He had made a heinous misjudgement in offering a free carpet, yet the detective had not seemed to pick up on it. Was it too much to hope that he would forget all about the offer entirely? The young Sergeant had seemed malleable and too eager to impress, yet, as Singh thought back, he was amazed at how much potentially sensitive information, or at least the beginnings of sensitive information, he had given away during their conversation.

Either Sergeant Keynes was a fool, or he was a very intelligent operator trying hard to look like a fool. Either could be dangerous. More than twenty years in the business world had taught him that.

Singh put the hair tonic back in his desk and pulled out a flat, mid-sized bottle of gin, which he poured into a mug on his desk. He put the bottle away and replaced his turban, then reached for his telephone and pressed a button.

"Shanice?" he said. "Can you ask Barry to send me last year's draft financials for Singh's Kids, please? And the ones for Harpit's Carpets, too? I know he's not finished, I just want to go over them tonight at home. Just to refresh myself."

He released the button, and leaned back in his chair. As he took a deep drink from his mug, he tried to think of happier thoughts: like which swimming costume to wear in the baked bean bath.

Chapter 15

When Keynes returned to the office, he was startled to see Gunnett sitting in his chair, drinking coffee. He could already see the brown rings on his desk where the coffee had dried. He was sure Gunnett had spilled that deliberately, to score psychological points against him.

Gunnett put his feet up on the desk. "Where have you been, Milton?" he asked.

"I've been making routine enquiries," said Keynes. "I did call you." He realised that Gunnett had addressed him by his nickname, which he hated, but since his superior already looked annoyed he decided not to point this out.

"Well, try harder. If Shepherd asks where you are, it looks bad on me if I can't tell him. I tried calling you back half an hour ago and your phone was turned off."

"It looks rude if you answer your phone when you're talking to a person of interest."

"A person of interest? Someone from the old folks' home?"

"Someone who works in a shop," said Keynes, careful not to lie.

Gunnett took his feet off the desk and leaned forward. "And did you get anywhere?"

Keynes blew the air out of his cheeks slowly, trying not to sigh, though that was his first instinct. "So far, there are no witnesses, no murder weapons, and no suspects," he said. "The only obvious connection, and possible motive, is the charity connection between all of the victims. That's what I've been pursuing."

"Have you, Keynes? That sounds nice." The suddenly softer tone was a warning Keynes had learned to recognise. "The funny thing is, I've just heard that you haven't even visited the home of the first victim yet."

Gunnett had a point, which was hard to bear. "I decided to focus enquiries on the murder scene, as it looked opportunistic, rather than planned," said Keynes.

"Did you, now? Is that what you decided?" Gunnett rubbed his jaw. "Did you decide that you're too good for grassroots detective work? You know, asking questions and stuff? Looking for things in the most obvious places? Are you trying to bring down the Illuminati?"

"No," said Keynes, quietly, his eyes boring holes into Gunnett.

"Really? Because if you were just trying to solve the case, you'd ask the obvious questions, look in the obvious places, and you'd probably just find what we always find – that the killer is a jilted lover, nutty neighbour or a junkie."

He was right, but Keynes hated to admit it. Keynes had convinced himself that there was something special about this case, even though he had yet to find the thread holding it all together.

"Pull it together, Sergeant."

It was the sheer disdain in Gunnett's voice, disdain he did not deserve, that made Keynes react foolishly.

"Have you finished your personal...assignment, Inspector?" Keynes asked. "Because then we might be able to conduct this investigation together, as we're supposed to. It would also remove the risk of one of my witnesses changing their account because there's no one else there to back up my version of events."

Gunnett took a step closer to Keynes, until Keynes could feel the stinking coffee fumes on his face. "Never you mind about my personal business," he said, baring his teeth. "If you needed to know, you'd know. Don't bother yourself with things that don't concern you."

Gunnett opened the top drawer of Keynes' desk and poured the remaining coffee from his cup inside. He walked off without another word.

"There are batteries in there," Keynes protested. He rushed to salvage the contents, aware that other people in the office were staring at him, and not in a sympathetic way. Gunnett was popular in the office in the same way that girls at school had always tended to prefer selfish, violent idiots: they took it as a sign of affection towards them that he treated other people worse.

As Gunnett walked away, aware that other officers were watching, he flicked a V-sign over his shoulder.

Keynes had a bigger build than Gunnett, and was younger and faster. Should they ever find themselves away from civilisation with a score to settle, Keynes would beat him easily in a fair fight. Sadly, in this part of the world, surrounded by closed circuit television and people who knew the two of them, he would never know the satisfaction of breaking Gunnett's nose.

That was the reason Keynes had stopped his boxing lessons as a teen after just two months: he knew he would never be able to use his skills without bringing trouble upon himself, even if he was in the right. Punch a mugger or a persistent annoyance, and someone was bound to see it from their perspective and decide that he was in the wrong. The thought of losing his job over someone as worthless as Gunnett made him focus on slowing his breathing down to its normal speed. He pulled a handful of tissues out of the box on his desk and started to dry his pens.

**

That night as Jenny was getting ready for bed, Keynes suggested that they invite Harpit Singh for dinner one evening.

"Harpit's Carpets?" asked Jenny, through a mouthful of toothpaste.

"He does other stuff, too," said Keynes, idly checking the lock on the landing window.

"When did you get friendly with him?"

"I met him through work, but it turns out we've got a lot in common. We're on the same wavelength."

Jenny finished in the bathroom and walked through to the bedroom, with Keynes following. She was wearing one of his old T-shirts, which she seemed to think looked endearing, but it annoyed him because she stretched them with her knees when she sat up in bed, ruining them.

She got into bed. "So what do you think? Chicken tikka masala?"

"No!" Keynes was horrified. "That's the worst thing you could cook."

Jenny looked hurt. "I thought you liked it."

"I do," said Keynes, trying to take a more gentle tone. "It's just it's a bit…stereotypical. It makes it look like we don't know anything about Indian culture."

"Is he a vegetarian?"

Keynes hated to admit he did not know what Sikhs ate, so he said nothing.

"I could make a jalfrezi."

"That's no good either. It looks like we only knew tikka masala, realised that was too obvious and then looked for a slightly more obscure kind of curry. It can't be curry."

"So you don't want me to cook Indian food for him?" Jenny was puzzled. "Won't he think it's thoughtful of us to cook something from his own culture?"

"It will just look patronising. Besides, if we try to go too Indian, we'll just get it wrong and look stupid – like putting poppadoms with something that doesn't require them. Anyway, he's from Coventry."

"I can do shepherd's pie. That's not patronising."

Keynes thought about it for a moment. "No, that won't work. That looks like he haven't given him any consideration at all." He got into bed and reached for his copy of *The Fountainhead*, still bookmarked frustratingly close to the beginning. Jenny had opened her book of crosswords, but was not holding a pen, a sure sign that she was not really reading it, but was using it as a prop to try to hide her annoyance with him.

"Chinese, then?"

Keynes considered this. It certainly showcased them as a multiculturally aware couple, and Jenny made a decent black bean chicken, but would it look like a scattergun attempt at being racially tolerant? Could they make it seem convincing that they had been planning to have Chinese food even before the Sikh turned up?

He shook his head. "That's too far the other way."

"This is getting silly now," said Jenny. She opened her bedside drawer and found a biro.

They sat next to each other in silence for another thirty minutes; Jenny making her way through her crossword puzzles and Keynes trying to remember who all the characters were.

Then, without saying a word, they agreed with a gesture of the shoulders to turn off the light. They lay side by side, both staring at the ceiling at the faint movements of car headlights, which sneaked through the gap at the top of the curtains.

"Mexican," they both said at once.

Chapter 16

Plans for dinner with the carpet tycoon were put to one side the next morning, as Keynes reached the office to learn that the investigation had taken on new momentum. An incident had been reported in town.

"Couldn't have happened to a nicer bloke," said Shepherd, as he passed on the news.

For a change, and perhaps signalling that Keynes' words had made some small impact, Gunnett came with him on the journey to the Market Square.

The front of the Northampton Tribune's office had been marked off with blue and white police tape. Men and women in white, rustling biohazard suits passed in and out of the building carrying plastic briefcases and scientific-looking devices.

Gunnett and Keynes stood outside in the cobbled street, watching the procession. This was the busiest the Market Square had been since the council had cut the area available for stalls on the premise that the vacant space could be better used for activities, the most common of which, it had transpired in the absence of further council funding, were littering and being rained on. A handful of elderly shoppers had gathered at the edge of the cordon to watch, but in truth there was not much to see. All of the action was taking place inside.

Chris Shingles, who was being kept upstairs, had opened an envelope to find an angry letter and a mysterious white powder inside. Naturally, he had been very alarmed and had called the police immediately. The powder, which had emptied mainly onto the crotch of

Shingles' trousers and down the front of his jumper, had been sampled and was now being tested.

"Al Qaeda, probably," said Gunnett, watching the scene with his arms folded. "If it's anthrax, I'm taking sick leave."

Keynes disagreed with that analysis, although he had not yet seen the letter. Anyone writing to a Northampton newspaper, rather than a national one, must be local, and with a fairly small grievance. The small scale of things meant it was unlikely the sender of the letter had access to complicated substances such as anthrax, and had probably filled it with talcum powder to scare Shingles. The grievance itself would probably be related to something the newspaper had printed recently.

They would dust the letter and envelope for fingerprints, and even if they did not find any, the sender was obviously desperate for publicity and would, it followed, send more letters with increasingly detailed information, that was, if they did not grow impatient after a couple of days and confess.

The ease with which he had come to that conclusion without seeing the evidence was a little depressing for Keynes. It was further proof that he needed more of a challenge.

The interesting part, which he could not judge until he had read the letter, was whether the threat was related to the killings. The local newspaper was at the centre of several contentious issues, but, as Singh had pointed out, it also provided crucial publicity for charities. If the killer was unhappy with the charities, for whatever reason, perhaps he also objected to the Tribune's coverage of them.

"Well, we'll see," said Keynes, not wanting to get into an argument with Gunnett so early in the day.

Gunnett tilted his head towards the chip van which had been based since time immemorial outside the Grosvenor shopping centre a few yards away. "Get us a cup of tea, would you?" he said. "Two sugars."

"I'm not sure they sell tea," said Keynes, with a hint of anger in his voice.

"They do, trust me."

Keynes hesitated a moment, then gave up and walked over to the van. There was little chance, he knew, of Gunnett paying for his tea. While it was only a few pounds here and there, it added up, and so did his resentment of his senior officer.

"Two teas, please," he asked the middle-aged man in the van. The grease stains on his shirt did not give a lot of confidence that food hygiene was a particular priority of his. "No sugar in one..." He paused. "Five sugars in the other one."

"Something going on over there?" asked the chip vendor. "Bomb scare or something? Should I move?"

"If there was a threat to the public, we would have let you know," said Keynes, handing over two pounds forty. The thought occurred to him that perhaps he should have waited for tests to rule out anthrax before he drank tea made downwind of the newspaper office.

He handed Gunnett's tea to him without saying a word, and nor did Gunnett thank him. Gunnett took a drink of the tea, barely twitching as he acknowledged the sickly sweet taste. Keynes allowed himself some satisfaction at this small victory, but it was short-lived.

"I said two sugars," said Gunnett, handing the tea back. "Go and get them to put another one in, would you?"

Keynes trudged back to the van, suitably chastened. As the chip man added another sugar, Keynes looked over his shoulder and saw Gunnett was watching, as Keynes had known he would be. Now the Inspector would have to drink an even more disgusting cup of tea, all just to prove a point. And, somehow, Keynes would lose.

On a whim, Keynes looked over at the newspaper seller who kept a booth at the entrance to the shopping centre. The headline printed on his booth today was: 'A5 delay nightmare.' It would not be a bad idea to check today's paper in case the motive for the letter revealed itself, he thought, although he was aware that the time taken to deliver a letter meant that any inciting article had probably been printed two or three days previously, depending on the grade of stamp. He bought a copy, glancing back at Gunnett as if to show that he had wanted to walk over to that side of the Market Square anyway.

"That's better," said Gunnett, as he took a swing of the tea, which by now must have bordered on the undrinkable.

He tapped a female forensic officer on the shoulder as she lifted the tape to pass. "Any idea what it is yet?" Gunnett asked.

"It's not anthrax," said the forensic officer. "But it is a toxic substance of some kind. So it probably wasn't very intelligent to touch my hazmat suit."

Gunnett wiped his hand on his trousers when he thought no one was looking.

A car pulled up at the barrier that divided The Drapery from the cobbled market street, and a middle-aged man with a jumper stretched out of proportion around his ample equator got out. He headed to the edge of the police tape looking pale and worried, one hand rubbing his thinning grey hair.

"Do you know if he's all right?" he asked Gunnett.

"And who might you be?"

"I'm Alan Richards. I'm the editor."

"Maybe you need to get a new letter-opener," said Keynes. He had no particular affection for Shingles, but his first look at Richards had confirmed the mental image he had already drawn up. Richards looked guilty. He probably assumed that the envelope had been meant for the editor and not for the young, poorly-paid deputy who had been covering him for many weeks.

"It's a terrible thing. A terrible thing," Richards repeated. He tried a new tack. "I haven't been well, you see."

Even from a few feet away, both officers could smell the brandy radiating off him. His woollen jumper seemed to be doused with it.

"Nothing serious?" said Keynes, acidly.

"It comes and goes," said Richards.

"Not stress, I hope," said Gunnett, looking at Keynes. "There's a lot of that going around."

They waited in silence while nothing happened outside.

"How's Sheepy?" Richards went on, to no response. "Sheepy Shepherd, that's what we call him down the Fox and Grapes."

"Fine," said Gunnett. "Any idea who might want you dead?"

"We get complaints. We get complaints every day, but not like this."

"Then that means it's something recent, doesn't it?" said Gunnett.

Keynes had to agree with him.

**

Chris Shingles had opened the letter thinking it was either a complaint or a photo from an elderly reader for the Tribune's Memory Lane section. If it was the latter, Donny would scan it and save it, before checking the details invariably scrawled in spidery biro on the back. If it was the former, Shingles would compress it into a ball and throw it away.

This was a complaint, of sorts. Shingles had torn open the unassuming envelope to reveal an ungrammatical message reading: 'Check your fact's.'

Shingles had been about to throw the message away, when he noticed a sprinkling of white powder over his hands and the front of his body. It looked like bicarbonate of soda or chalk dust, but he had read enough news stories to know that when someone sent a package of white powder to a newspaper, it was serious. If he was dying, he wanted a chance to live. If he was already dead, he wanted people to know about it.

"Get out," he had yelled at a startled Donny. "Get out and call 999!"

Chapter 17

Donny, though immensely upset and anxious, had called for an ambulance from the phone box in the Market Square, and Shingles had stood motionless for the fifteen minutes it had taken for one to arrive, taking care to breathe only through his nose and not to disturb the powder clinging to his sleeves and the front of his jumper and trousers. He had no idea whether that would help his prospects of survival, but he knew he could not hold his breath for more than a minute, so that was the best he could do.

It turned out that he had actually dealt with the situation fairly well. He had prevented others from being exposed, and he had limited his own exposure to minimum levels. The danger with poison came when you were not aware it was entering your system. Shingles had stood there perfectly still, albeit nervously, while a hazmat-suited police officer had vacuumed the powder from his jumper and, in a rather uncomfortable moment for all concerned, from his crotch. The officer had needed to make several sweeps with the vacuum until she had been sure the subject had been decontaminated.

His outer layer of clothing had been removed, and Shingles had wiped down his body with damp towelettes, before disposing of them in a plastic bag, while the crime scene officers set about decontaminating the office.

When the officers had assured him that there was almost zero chance that any of the toxic material remained on his skin or remaining clothing, he was escorted out of the building, clad only in his underpants, surgical slippers and a shiny foil blanket.

It was at that point that he saw Keynes, Gunnett and Alan Richards standing together at the edge of the cordon.

"Hold the presses!" he shouted at Richards. "I'll be back to file my story!"

"I think we can take a day off," said Richards, as Shingles was put into the back of an ambulance and the doors closed. Richards watched him sadly, then turned to Gunnett. "And you think I'm tragic," he said.

**

Shingles had survived without any obvious damage, although his throat felt raw and painful, and he was developing a bit of a cold. He was being kept in the general hospital in a special room until it could be ascertained that he was out of danger.

This infuriated him. "I'm fine!" yelled Shingles, through clear flaps of plastic hanging over his doorway. "Let me out! This is my scoop!"

It turned out that the mysterious substance was thallium. Until the 1970s it had been used in rat and insect poisons, but now it was used mainly for industrial purposes such as making semi-conductors. The main reason it had been discontinued from use in household products was because it had a tendency to kill people. A single gram could kill a man over a long and lingering three days, at the end of which his heart would stop.

Fortunately, the would-be poisoner had used too little in the envelope to endanger anyone's health – whether it be Shingles, the receptionist who handled the mail, the postman or the staff at the sorting office. Shingles was free to leave a few hours after he had been admitted, but not before Gunnett and Keynes had asked him a few questions.

"Why is someone trying to kill you?" asked Keynes. It was a fair question: the letter had been addressed to Chris Shingles personally, rather than to the editor.

"You can't be a journalist without ruffling a few feathers."

"Look, you can mess around trying to look like a big man and we can go home early, but the fact is that someone has made an attempt on your life and they know where to find you six days a week," said Gunnett. "Get to the point. Who have you upset recently?"

Shingles lost his brief sheen of bravado, and the red flush returned to his cheeks. "I haven't done a campaign for a while," he said. "There was the thing protesting about the new landfill site near Rothersthorpe, but the council ran out of money and that didn't happen anyway. We've been complaining about the town council for years, for several reasons, like the stupid fountain in the Market Square that's infected with Legionnaire's disease, but nothing that would really provoke anyone.

"We haven't had a juicy scoop for a while. The main thing I've been covering recently is the revised bin schedule for Paulerspury and the traffic lights near the Gas Street roundabout."

Gunnett nodded, understandingly. "Dynamite."

"And charities, of course," said Keynes.

Shingles looked away.

"That's mainly based on press releases," he said. "Then we send the staff photographer over, and maybe me or Donny to ask a few questions. It's hardly Watergate."

"And is there anything you're working on at the moment?"

"Not much," said Shingles, and Keynes was sure he was lying. "Harpit Singh is trying to break the world record for sitting in a bath of beans next week."

"And that's newsworthy, is it?" said Gunnett. "What a waste of beans."

Those beans are expired, you moron, and so it's actually a very good use for them, Keynes wanted to say.

"Have you finished? I need to find out what thallium is, and then go and write a story about it."

"Sorry for showing an interest," said Gunnett. "If anyone else tries to kill you, do let us know. Come on, Sergeant."

The two officers left the room, but not before Keynes had looked Shingles up and down one more time. He was sure there was something Shingles wasn't telling them. Unfortunately, that meant he was probably going to have to spend a great deal of time poring over back issues of the Tribune to try to find a motive.

"What do you think?" said Gunnett to Keynes, once they were in the corridor.

"He knows why he was targeted, but he's not talking."

Gunnett curled his lip. "That's not my read on it. Whoever sent this stuff just wanted some attention, but they're so backward that they didn't think to send it to a

126

national newspaper. We're probably looking for a farmer or a school caretaker. Check whether farms or school science labs keep supplies of thallium."

Keynes produced his pad and pencil, and started to write, then stopped midway and let his writing hand fall to his side in slow disbelief. This was not lost on Gunnett.

"Don't give me that look," said Gunnett. "Regardless of how I came to the conclusion, it's not easy to get hold of this stuff. It's supposed to be used to make microchips, and there's no factory like that in Northamptonshire. There's no real manufacturing industry anywhere in the county that would use chemicals like this, so we have to assume that someone either has a supply of really old insecticide or they have access to the raw material.

"If you went to the same kind of school I did, half the science equipment was older than me. If it was a real business, they wouldn't keep chemicals that old. Farms are the same. Farmers don't clean out their barns because it all gets passed down generation to generation. If we had the time, we could inspect a few farms and find dozens of dangerous chemicals still being stored there, decades after being banned for safety reasons."

He leaned closer to Keynes. "Despite appearances, I am actually highly intelligent. If you need to write that down, write it down."

Keynes kept his arm by his side.

**

Despite himself, Keynes felt something approaching respect for Gunnett. Whether he knew it or not, he had applied an analysis of free market principles to a police investigation. Keynes was actually jealous that he had not thought along the same lines himself.

That near-admiration vanished abruptly, however, when Gunnett excused himself on another errand.

"I need to go and meet someone," he said, after checking his phone. "I don't know what time I'll be finished. Just go about your business, check on possible sources of thallium, but keep me posted."

Keynes could not help himself. "Now?"

Gunnett narrowed his eyes and gave Keynes a long, slow look. "You think you know it all, but you don't," he said. "You do what you've got to do, and I'll do what I've got to do. And don't be a girl about it."

Gunnett turned and walked away, leaving Keynes open-mouthed. There was a remote possibility that Gunnett was investigating something so sensitive that only an Inspector could be involved, but it was far more likely, based on Gunnett's history, that he was disappearing for a game of darts or a bit of a sleep.

That was fine with Keynes. Gunnett was something of a hindrance, anyway. He lacked the subtle emotional intelligence that Keynes brought to his encounters with suspects and witnesses. Keynes had read every book you could name about body language, spotting liars and giving off an air of sincerity. He would get on much better by himself.

Since he had free rein and was in the town centre, he decided to head to the central library. As it happened, it was on the same street as the chugger murder, but his main reason for visiting was to check its collection of Northampton Tribunes. If there was a key to the attack on

Chris Shingles' life, then surely it was to be found in the past week's newspapers.

Chapter 18

The central library was dated, but it could hardly be called historic. The interior had been redecorated in the late 1970s and the council had obviously thought that aesthetic perfection had been achieved in that decade and decided to leave it alone since then. There was something depressing about the place. Perhaps it was the grey, beige and brown colour scheme, the scratchy carpets, and posters warning people to lock up their bicycles and get the flu jab.

Perhaps it was the silence, oppressive heat and musty smell.

No, Keynes decided, it was the people. This was where his tax money was going. An elderly couple were reading from a pile of books about how to use the internet. A bearded man in his thirties was sitting at a table reading a Spanish dictionary and making notes. Keynes was flabbergasted that the best use of the working day these people could find was to sit around reading books that were several years out of date, and, more to the point, hardly likely to improve their employment prospects. He was all in favour of people trying to improve their standing in life, but he hated to see wasted effort, especially when it was paid for by the local government. If it had been a Chinese dictionary, or even a German one, he would not have felt so aggrieved, but Spanish…the man was being deliberately impractical.

Worse yet, there were people of working age using a bank of less-than-modern computers by the window. He could see their screens. One or two had the good grace to be checking employment agency websites or drafting their

CVs, but one was reading about the weekend's motocross results and another was writing rapid-fire messages into a chat window, while scrolling through some kind of heavy metal website. Generations of British genius had spent their best efforts creating a device to enable idiots to exchange banal comments and smiley faces instantaneously.

The librarian, working at council speed, showed him to the newspaper archive. Only the older editions were kept as digital records, so he would have to go through the hard copies of the recent issues. Keynes gathered the past month's copies of the Tribune and piled them on an empty table.

As he worked his way through the newspapers, he found possible reasons to explain the lack of ambition among the unemployed. There were relatively few success stories to be found in the local newspapers. A woman from Blakesley had been given a council grant to expand her mail-order jam business. A twenty-two-year-old from Earls Barton had started his own internet company – a property rental website – and was doing well, but the kicker revealed that he had needed to move to London to achieve anything approaching success. The Tribune was good at revealing that slightly famous people were originally from Northampton, but also at hinting that they would not have achieved even that level of fame had they stayed there any longer.

There were not a lot of Harpit Singhs around. He had shown the brains to adapt to his environment, using the transport links and central location to his advantage to import and distribute consumer essentials from the continent at a low price. Others either gave up, aimed low, or took the tried and tested route of going to London, where they could look important and busy.

Keynes was making good progress through the stack of newspapers, as his blackening fingertips testified, but he was struggling to find anything controversial. There were the usual articles about villagers complaining about proposed telephone masts or roadworks, usually accompanied by a photograph of some of them holding barely literate placards or pointing at things. On a few occasions, Shingles had tried to dig into the workings of the town council, which was notorious for being both ineffective and profligate, but he had clearly pulled his punches out of concern for the libel laws, or simply because he had lacked enough incriminating material to form a thorough investigation.

He had looked at the Market Square redevelopment, and about the tender process for the new bins in the town centre. Still, he never came out and accused anyone directly of impropriety. Perhaps that was the kind of thing you could not do in the newspapers anymore. Looking around the library again, it occurred to Keynes that Shingles probably would not have found much of an audience for intelligent, incisive reportage anyway. Give the people what they want: school sports days, potholes and people finding disgusting objects in their takeaways.

He kept a tally of the charities Shingles had covered recently.

Vera Hope was there, in March this year, collecting a certificate for ten years of volunteer work in the shop. Her smile gave no hint that her life was under threat and would shortly come to an undignified end on the undignified end of a mannequin stand.

Wendy Bevan and her hunting friends were there too, holding a craft fair to raise funds for the time-honoured and unfathomably expensive pastime of wildlife dismemberment through the Rural Defence Association.

In fact, the Tribune covered at least one charity effort in every issue. Sometimes there were several, ranging from a little girl who had sold cakes at school to raise twenty-two pounds for a local hospice, to a garage owner who had sponsored one of his mechanics to run the London marathon.

The list of charities featured in the Tribune was a long one, and all received glowing, or at least unquestioningly positive, coverage. There were stories about Bronchitis Support, The Dyslexic Society – somewhat undermined by the number of typos in the copy – The Green Planet Foundation, Re-Bridge, an organisation helping put offenders back into the workforce, Singh's Kids, several times, Heart Help…the list went on.

There was no hint that Shingles was working to expose any of them as scams. In fact, most of them followed the same format of bland congratulation. Occasionally he would try to get a pun into the opening sentence, then would explain why the person in the photograph was raising money, what they were going to do, and how much they had either raised or planned to. Should there be a local business donating something, they would receive a few paragraphs about their services and a mention of the address. Keynes wondered whether a donation and accompanying free publicity was more cost-effective than taking out a print advertisement of the same size, in the same place on the page. He suspected many of the smiling donors pictured in the Tribune had pondered the same thing and checked the advertising rate card before signing their cheques.

Keynes jotted down the names of all of the charities and the people in the photographs. Disappointingly, Whitcroft, the dead chugger, had not appeared in the Tribune, which poured cold water on the theory that there might be a killer choosing his victims based on newspaper photographs.

Again, Keynes felt he was missing something, but he comforted himself with the thought that, based on the information available to him, no one else was going to work it out either.

He became aware that the musty smell had grown worse in the past ten minutes. Keynes looked up over his pile of newspapers. At the far end of the room, half-hidden by the edge of a bookshelf, he could see a familiar pair of tattered boots poking out. The dirty matted hair splaying out confirmed his suspicions.

Approaching, he saw Zulu sitting on the ground, slumped against the Sociology section. Beside him were a pile of books including, Keynes could see, the Analects Of Epictetus and something about Biomechanics. Zulu was flicking through the book in his hands at a rate of a page every couple of seconds.

"You really do come here, then," said Keynes, regarding Zulu with suspicion, though he could not put his finger on why he felt worried.

Zulu looked up with surprise, but quickly returned to his usual insouciance. "I told you, it's a lot warmer here than outside," he said.

Keynes nudged the pile of books with his foot, dislodging a recent copy of The Lancet. "What's this for? Going to tear out a few pages for roll-ups? It's a bit intellectual, isn't it?"

"I was looking for the pop-up version of 'Computational Approaches To Fluid Dynamics' but they didn't have it," said Zulu. He held up the book. "Please don't tell me how it ends. I think the butler did it, but it's up for grabs."

Keynes crouched down on his haunches until he was face to face with Zulu. "What is your game?" he said. "You don't have to answer me now. I'll work it out. But I know you're up to something, and it's not reading."

"Just warming my feet and expanding my mind, Inspector."

"Sergeant." Keynes had the unpleasant feeling he was being outsmarted, and he had no idea how. His thighs were beginning to ache, but he had no intention of revealing this to Zulu. "You wouldn't happen to know anything about thallium, would you?"

"A rather unfriendly substance? No, I've never heard of it."

"Really? Well, I've got a feeling you're going to be hearing a lot more about it, after the attack on the Tribune office."

Zulu suddenly looked interested. "Is that right? How was it administered?"

"Envelope."

"Oh. They could have done a bit better than that."

"You seem to be quite the expert."

"I've always been a heavy metal fan."

Keynes did not understand, but tried not to show it. "It seems to me you're getting mixed deeper and deeper in this whole mess," he said. "Perhaps it's time you were a bit more helpful or I might start getting the wrong idea."

"How am I involved?" asked Zulu, putting down his book. "I come in here to read about fluid dynamics and you start hassling me. I sleep outdoors and someone gets murdered indoors on the same street –statistically, that's bound to happen once in a while. What does it have to do with me?"

"Just…" Keynes found his right hand had formed itself into a fist, but his tongue could not articulate a plausible threat. "Just tell me what you know. Who would want to target the Tribune, and where would they get thallium in Northampton?"

Zulu kept quiet for a moment, enjoying Keynes' impotent rage. An impartial observer might even have thought that Zulu was willing the police officer to lose his temper and hit him.

"Well, it's not exactly Shenzhen round here, is it?" he said. Keynes had no idea what that meant, so merely grunted. "You ask me, it either came from outside, or you need to speak to someone shady at the tip."

"You must have spent time on the Market Square. Top begging location. Any suspicious types hanging around the Tribune office?"

Zulu sucked his teeth. "I have to be careful around there. There are a couple of people from the transient community who are a bit sensitive about their turf. I got beaten up in the alley by Snappy Snaps once."

"Who's Snappy Snaps?" asked Keynes, raising his notepad.

"It's the photo shop that used to be there."

"Oh." Keynes rubbed his chin. "You must have seen the acting editor of the Tribune around town. Chris Shingles. Late twenties, early thirties. Skinny, likes his woolly jumpers."

"In cold or warm weather, looks like he's been slapped in the face? He has that bacon rasher effect on his cheeks."

"That's him. Have you seen anyone hanging around the office or threatening him?"

"You must think I've got nothing better to do." Zulu yawned and stretched out his legs. "The only people I've seen going into that office are old biddies with photos of the Jubilee. But I move around, you know?"

Keynes felt that he had met Zulu far too many times, but still had not worked out how to read him. He had no idea whether the young man had any useful information on the killings, or even whether he was involved. He had not even worked out how to tell when he was being sarcastic.

He glanced down at the books again. "Why don't you read a book about getting a job?" he said.

"I had a very successful career in the local apple-picking industry over at Riscote, if you must know," said Zulu. "Nearly three months. I left due to artistic differences, like not wanting to pick apples anymore."

"Why do you even need to read this stuff? 'Advanced Thermodynamics'? Is that going to be useful?"

"I'm planning some improvements to my sleeping bag."

Keynes noticed with alarm that Zulu had in his pile 'The New Industrial State' by John Kenneth Galbraith. Surely there was no way this homeless, alcoholic junkie could comprehend Galbraith's ideas about the role of corporations in shaping society, even if the idea had been subsequently built on in more accessible books by other writers?

"I'll be seeing you," said Keynes.

Before leaving, Keynes glanced down at the pile of books to see whether there were any covering poisons or chemistry. None of them seemed to fit the bill, but the convoluted titles of the scientific ones made it hard to tell.

All in all, it had been an unsuccessful trip to the library, and now he felt pangs of doubt about his own intellectual status.

Chapter 19

There was more bad news back at the station. The forensic team had been through the envelope and its contents, and drawn nothing useful. There were no finger prints on the envelope or letter. The forensic report also informed Keynes that the sender had not licked the envelope, which he would have thought was fairly obvious or someone would have turned up in a hospital by now with symptoms of poisoning. There were no useful hair or tissue fragments attached – at least none that could be traced back to the sender, rather than a postman or employee of a stationery shop.

Keynes suspected the unsanitary conditions in the Tribune office had not helped much. There were probably more health hazards growing in the mugs on Shingles' desk or between the letters on his keyboard than there had been in that envelope.

Today had been a disaster on all fronts, and the only consolation was that Gunnett and Shepherd were not at the station that afternoon to learn as much. Keynes decided to cut his losses and go home, taking some paperwork with him in the hope it would spark a new line of enquiry.

He liked to discuss his cases with Jenny, but only after they were closed. Talking about this one would only make him grumpy.

That night at dinner, he let Jenny talk about her day at school. There was rarely any overlap between their two jobs, although occasionally he would hear bits and pieces from colleagues talking in the staff kitchen or pick up on incident reports. Jenny taught at a primary school in a middling-to-rough part of Northamptonshire, and would once in a while have an anecdote about a child who had burned down his flat, or put something unusual up his nose.

"They're always putting rubbers up their noses," Jenny said, as she cut up her chicken kiev. "At least then they can blow them out eventually, but Darren Hunt got the rubber from the end of his pencil lost in his ear. You can't really use tweezers for that."

"Could you pour in water and float it out?"

"The ear canal's too curvy. It's not worth mucking about where ears are concerned. These things work their way out, or they get so waxy that you can pull them out."

Keynes had to admit that his wife's job had given her knowledge and skills that exceeded his own in certain areas.

His hopes of having his mind diverted from work were shattered when she asked, out of the blue: "Is everything all right with Mike Gunnett?"

Keynes put down his knife and fork. He rarely if ever spoke about Gunnett at home. He had not said as much, but surely Jenny had picked up that the two of them were not the best of friends. She had never suggested inviting the Gunnetts over for dinner, which he knew would have been her instinct.

"Seems fine," Keynes muttered. "But you never know with him."

"Only, I saw Sandy Gunnett in the supermarket this evening. She seemed a bit…" Jenny made a wavy gesture with her hand.

"She's always been a bit..." said Keynes, making the same hand movement.

"I know, but this time she seemed unhappy about something. She didn't say anything, but I wonder if those two are having problems."

Keynes picked up his fork again, a thoughtful look in his eyes. That could explain why Gunnett was in no mood to work the murders. Perhaps he was too busy trying to fix problems at home.

"He has been a bit distracted at work," said Keynes. "Truth be told, he's left me to pick up the slack. It wouldn't surprise me if he's got problems at home."

Jenny paused, and Keynes knew that she was resisting the temptation to tell him something moderately salacious. She was not a gossip, but she was very intuitive. In fact, she would have made a better detective than many of his colleagues.

"The thing is, judging by her trolley, she's only shopping for one," said Jenny. "She only bought one pork chop, and the premium ones were two-for-one."

Keynes felt his jaw slackening as he gazed with renewed adoration at his wife. This was why he had married her: attractive looks, better-than-average intelligence and a keen grasp of economic realities.

"It was the same for the yoghurts, the bell peppers and the grapefruit," Jenny added. "Plus – no beer in the trolley."

"So he's not just sleeping on the sofa. She's kicked him out." That explained a lot. Gunnett was probably having to move between friends' houses or cheap hotels every few days, shifting his possessions whenever he had a spare moment.

Keynes put down his knife and fork again, pushed back his chair and walked over to Jenny. He bent down, kissed her full on the lips, then sat down again.

"You always know what to say to cheer me up," he said. He ate his chicken kiev with renewed vigour.

**

He had to give himself tasks to achieve, Keynes told himself, to disguise the fact that he had no idea what to do next. At the moment, he was, if he was honest with himself, waiting for the killer to strike again and leave some useful clues, because at the moment he had nothing helpful to point him in the right direction. He had a series of fatal incidents, which Keynes suspected were related even though few people seemed to share his view, but no solid suspects.

Even Gunnett's nutty neighbour theory had not been applicable. Constable Reeve had been out to Vera Hope's house, and her neighbours were even older than her. It was extremely unlikely one of them could have mustered the force to strike her dead, let alone escape the shop in a reasonable amount of time without being seen.

With no leads in sight, Keynes was concentrating on what he knew best – numbers. Pounds and pence. It had a tenuous connection to the case, and it was intimidating enough to deter other officers from asking too many questions.

Harpit Singh's secretary, Shanice, had forgotten to send Keynes the latest financial accounts for the carpet business and the charity, so he had needed to remind her.

That was a little sloppy, Keynes thought, for the corporate world. It was bad enough when you had to ask the town centre CCTV people three times for their videos, but that was the public sector and everything was treated with less urgency.

She had eventually sent him the documents he needed, as an email attachment, though stressing that they were preliminary and unaudited. That was fair enough: Singh's businesses were not listed yet, though he had outlined plans to float in London within the next five years.

Personally, Keynes thought Singh was wise to keep the business private until growth had stabilised and slowed. Now, he could make bold, unpopular decisions quickly, without a thousand shareholders complaining or slowing him down. This had enabled him to lead the business deftly, reacting to market changes as needed, expanding and cutting it as the economy turned. There were other voices, but his was unmistakably the loudest.

Which made it harder to understand why the accounts were such a mess. Presumably Singh had run the rule over the figures before allowing them to be released, since he did have a few outside shareholders, in the form of a couple of Channel Islands-based investors.

Keynes had no formal financial training, relying on his own reading, but even he could spot some sloppy mistakes. Goodwill was higher than earnings in the latest results, and the accountant's grasp of mark-to-market valuation was risible. Based on Keynes' observations, the stock of carpet remnants delivered in 2010 had grown in value the following year, even though some of them had been sold. Unless the benchmark price for carpets was as volatile as Brent crude, Keynes thought that was unlikely behaviour. He had to admit he had not thought the accounts for Harpit's Carpets were vital to the investigation, but at least they had given him a chance to exercise his analytical skills on something tangible, rather than the ramblings of unreliable witnesses.

The charity accounts were harder to pin down. He had used rough mental arithmetic to check the figures and they seemed to balance. It was hard to know how charities were supposed to be run, never having seen accounts for them before. They certainly did not seem to be run on commercial principles: around half of donations to Singh's Kids seemed to be spent on operating expenses, not all of which were specified.

As a small organisation, it could not benefit from economies of scale, Keynes thought. It would make a lot more sense for all of the cancer charities, for example, to join together and share the administrative functions, given that they were all working towards the same end. Did there really need to be so many of them? He could not help feeling that egos were behind some of these charity efforts.

Keynes was looking for anything that could pose a potential threat, among the lists of suppliers, creditors and employees. Harpit Singh was the highest profile name in the charity business in Northamptonshire. If the murders revolved around charity work, he had to be a target, and Keynes would have excelled if he managed to prevent an attempt on Singh's life through some pre-emptive police work.

For the carpet business, most of the suppliers were from China, Spain or Turkey. That told a story about low-cost manufacturing bases, thought Keynes. The creditors were harder to place. Most were based offshore and had names like Paneer Investments or New Sunshine Corp.

An internet search threw up nothing, but Keynes suspected these were one-man private equity firms or hedge funds willing to risk a few million on an impressive businessman.

The charity accounts were much vaguer, as Keynes would have expected. It was almost entirely a cash business in terms of income and there was no way to keep track of individual donations, especially the ones made through coins tossed into buckets.

Outgoings were equally vague. Apart from the listed members of staff, many of whom also worked for Singh's carpet business, there were several large miscellaneous expenses without any explanation, and entries such as rentals and licence fees. There was also an awful lot of amortisation and depreciation recorded on unspecified assets, burning tens of thousands every year. Keynes struggled to think what those depreciating assets could be. A children's charity was hardly a coal mining company with a shed full of diggers.

Still, these simply highlighted Keynes' ignorance on these matters. He was grateful merely to have the chance to have a glimpse inside the workings of a business empire like that built up by Harpit Singh, even if Singh's support staff appeared to have let him down. No wonder Singh insisted on overseeing everything himself.

Perhaps the mark-to-market discrepancies in the carpet business and the charity's approach to amortisation were a good excuse to invite Singh over for dinner? No – that would start things off on a sour note, and make him think he was under suspicion. Better to simply extend the invitation as a friend, rather than in a professional capacity. If he had any questions about the accounts, he could ask them directly, in a matter-of-fact way during the course of his daily work. Singh would appreciate that. A clear separation between his business and social lives.

Chapter 20

Harpit Singh did a good job of pretending to look pleased when Keynes dropped in at the warehouse the following morning.

"Good morning, Detective," he said. "This is a pleasant surprise. Can I offer you a coffee?"

Keynes was tempted to say yes, even though he hated coffee and it gave him heartburn. It was the kind of thing high-powered businessmen needed to start the day. But he decided against it, since then it would leave him with the problem of finding somewhere to put the cup down later on if he wanted to write any notes.

"No thanks. Actually, I just wanted to check a few things in those accounts you sent me."

Singh adopted a fixed grin while he waited for Keynes to get to the point.

"You see, it just seemed like the earnings for the carpet business were a bit on the high side," said Keynes. "Goodwill, some big jumps in mark-to-market valuations in a short period of time, things like repayments of loans from other companies that aren't fully explained."

"Well, as you know, goodwill is intangible," said Singh, with feeling. "We do have independent valuations of things, of course. I'd have to check how they came up with these numbers, but I'm sure you'll find that it's consistent across all our peers. And the loans to other companies – that's basically putting our excess cash to work when we don't have a use for it in the short term."

Treasury management. It's like our equivalent of bank-to-bank lending in the overnight market."

"I see." Keynes had been trying to impress Singh with his grasp of financial accounting, but now he worried that he was making himself look stupid. "It's just that some of the figures for Singh's Kids seemed a bit low, so I wondered whether…" He tailed off.

Singh tapped his finger anxiously against the metal stair rail while Keynes was speaking, then started speaking rapidly. "If you're accusing me of something, Detective, I would very much like to have my lawyer present. If you're suggesting that I've been transferring funds between Harpit's Carpets and Singh's Kids, then that's a very serious allegation. Not only that, but it would be totally impossible, if you have any idea how a company works. I can understand that idiot at the Tribune getting over-excited about this kind of thing, but seriously…"

Keynes could feel his spine melting, his posture becoming weaker, his head bowing. He had over-reached while trying to impress Singh, and now he had embarrassed himself.

"Of course," said Keynes, anxiously. "I didn't mean…I'm sure there are Chinese walls."

"Damned right there are. Okay, so there are some members of staff working at both organisations, like one or two of the financial people, but they have very clear guidelines on keeping things separate. No auditor in their right mind would sign off on this stuff if they had concerns like that."

"I wasn't suggesting that, Mr Singh, I just meant…" Keynes trailed off. His collar felt uncomfortably tight and he could feel beads of sweat starting to form just under his hairline. "The charity is obviously feeling the pinch in this kind of economic climate, so I just wondered what's the secret of your success in keeping the carpet business running so profitably?" he concluded.

Singh waited a second to see whether there was a follow-up question. He was breathing heavily now. He looked like he was full of adrenaline and unsure how to use it.

Finally, Singh spoke. "I won't lie to you," he said. "Carpets are a tough business. I wouldn't recommend anyone getting into this game now. And I'll give you one tip: never choose a business just because it rhymes with your name. If I'd gone into trucking straight away, the margins were much better."

He licked his lips, finding his flow now that he realised Keynes was hanging on his every word.

"The trick is always being on the lookout for new suppliers," Singh said. "If I asked you who are the cheapest carpet suppliers, you'd probably guess the Chinese."

Keynes nodded.

"Maybe on the cost of the goods themselves, but then you've got to transport them and factor in taxes and duties. Once you start considering things like that, you may find that one or two European suppliers, especially if they've benefited from any European Union subsidies, might work out cheaper."

"The E.U.," said Keynes, rolling his eyes.

"Exactly. But look at it another way. The French, Italians, Spanish, they're all milking the system. You just need to find out where that money's going and where it distorts prices. It's possible for businesses here to benefit from those ridiculous subsidies indirectly. You just need to know how."

Keynes was deeply impressed. A Northampton businessman was beating the Eurocrats at their own game. Subsidies designed to give an advantage to lazy countries were being turned against them to benefit British consumers.

"You clearly run a tight ship, too," he said. "I noticed overheads are very low for the carpet business – much lower than for the charity, even though a great deal of the manpower works unpaid."

Singh stroked his goatee. "Charities have a lot of promotional expenses, advertising and so on," he said. "Plus you can't expect to hire the best people if they have to work for free. With Harpit's Carpets, I'm a walking advertisement. I'm larger than life! You've just got to look at the media coverage I get."

Keynes had to agree. Singh's picture had appeared twelve times in the Tribune in the past three months – almost once a week. He suspected that some of the donations announced in photoshoots with large, unwieldy cardboard cheques were, like many government spending commitments, the same expenditure that had been announced on earlier occasions, but presented as new and different.

"Detective, I'm impressed," said Singh. "You've really run the rule over those accounts. Do you have a financial background?"

"No. Some people like football, some people like music. I've always taken an interest in finance and economics."

"It's not for everyone."

"I covered a bit of economics at university, but I'm self-taught, really."

"Oh, which university?"

"Northampton," said Keynes, rushing over the answer because Singh was bound to know that the college had not yet received university accreditation at the time he had attended. "But really my teachers were Drucker, Welch and Schumpeter."

Singh nodded approvingly.

"I always say if you can't read a set of accounts, you can't manage your own life," Keynes went on. "We all run our own corporations, in a way, whether it's managing your savings or paying the gas bill."

Singh cleared his throat. "Actually, I realised those accounts aren't the latest ones. My secretary gave you the wrong version."

"They go up to the end of September."

"Yes, but there are some big one-off items that haven't been accounted for. Have you got the document with you? I can swap it."

"Sorry, it's at home." Keynes suddenly found he had an opportunity to broach the subject he had been wanting to raise today.

His heart was pounding, and now he could feel droplets of sweat running down the back of his neck. He almost never perspired. The only reason to be nervous was if you were unprepared, and he was never unprepared.

This feeling was like the anticipation before asking a girl out, but, he reflected, he had never experienced it in exactly this way. Before asking Jenny to join him for dinner at a Thai restaurant in St James, he had sat down with a piece of A4 paper and formed an analysis of his chances of success. The points in his favour, including 'quite tall', 'good career prospects', 'above-average intelligence' and 'genetically sound', had been so overwhelming that by the time he had spoken to her the following day, he knew the chances of her rejecting him were minimal.

This was, he thought, probably the most nervous he had ever been, because he was in the presence of one of his idols and was well aware that he could embarrass himself. He took a deep breath to steady himself, aware that Singh was looking at him strangely.

"Mr Singh…" he began.

"Harpit."

"Harpit…my wife and I were wondering whether you might be able to join us for dinner this week at our humble home." There, he had said it. He waited to see whether he had humiliated himself.

Unknown to Keynes, Singh's head was spinning. He suspected Keynes was plotting something, but he had been unable to establish exactly what it was. Perhaps the detective was trying to get close to him in the hope he would trip himself up and reveal more than he intended.

That was not going to happen. Singh had seen off half a dozen attempts to destroy his business and reputation, through legislative channels, blackmail and outright threats, and it was going to take more than a steak and kidney pie to bring him down.

Besides, Singh had his own motivation.

"That sounds fantastic, Detective," Singh said, putting on the most sincere smile he could manage. "I'll have to check the old diary, of course." He pursed his lips. "Did you say you had the accounts at home? I could swap them for the new ones while I'm there."

"Oh, absolutely," said Keynes. "In my study, as we speak." Actually, his semi-detached house did not have a study. Singh's financial statements were on the kitchen table, and he had panicked this morning on finding that Jenny had managed to get garlic butter on the cover.

"Great," said Singh. "That should be fine. I'll tell my secretary to set up a time, and let you know." He checked his watch, quite obviously. "I'm sorry, Detective, but I've got to run. Meeting with a new supplier."

"Of course," said Keynes, still buzzing with his success. He shook Singh's hand feeling that the two of them were equals. The dinner would be a meeting of minds, a main course of intellectual conversation about the free market and the entrepreneur's role in society, with a side helping of complaining about the town council.

He wandered back to his car in a daze, almost knocking over a roll of frieze-cut nylon carpeting leaning against the warehouse wall. Keynes pinched himself before turning the key in the ignition. This was probably how it felt to be on drugs, he thought.

Singh, meanwhile, turned and began to ascend the steps leading to his office, slow metallic clangs echoing around the warehouse. He waited until Keynes was out of sight, then raced upstairs to his office and picked up the telephone receiver.

"You stupid girl!" yelled Singh down the intercom, a vein pulsing beneath his turban. "I asked you to send him the short version of the accounts, the one with no details. You've sent him half the unaudited accounts. There's all kinds of stuff in there. I ask you for one simple thing…"

Shanice mumbled something unintelligible in response, sounding upset.

"Do you know what?" said Singh. "Don't bother. You're fired. I don't know why I kept you on anyway. You were never any good at your job, and then you got fat. Not even nice to look at anymore."

He put the telephone receiver down and reached into his desk, retrieving the gin, which was down to the halfway mark.

This was all he needed, he thought, taking a swig from the bottle. Baked bean day was tomorrow and he was going to be surrounded by the media. If they started to ask difficult questions, he would be trapped in the bath.

A thought occurred to him. He dialled a number on the phone, but Shanice did not seem to be picking up. The phone rang and rang, then went to the answerphone.

"Shanice, it's me," he said. "Where do we keep the can-opener?" He hung up and waited for a while. The telephone failed to ring.

After a few moments, Singh wheeled his chair over to the window and parted the venetian blinds to look out. A slightly overweight young woman was walking away from the factory, carrying a cardboard box and a spider plant. Her stride was aggressive and he suspected she was not planning to come back.

**

Keynes thought he was safe to drive, but after seeing an amber traffic light too late at the Sixfields roundabout and having to slam on his brakes, he decided to pull over in a layby and gather his thoughts.

His brain was pulsing. Singh was coming to dinner. They were going to talk about business and finance, and eat Mexican food. This would fill a huge gap in Keynes' life. He had no friends with whom he could discuss matters like the trickle-down effect of easing corporate rates of tax. Actually, he had few friends at all, but, without wanting to sound arrogant, so far in his life he had met very people who shared his interests and abilities. Jenny could keep up with him, up to a point, but he could generally tell when she was losing interest.

If Singh joined his social circle – well, technically, it would be a social triangle – he could find an outlet for all of his thoughts and ideas that went beyond police work. Keynes strongly believed that he could make a good businessman, but first he needed to build a strong capital base and set of contacts, and working for the police for a few years would help put him on a firm footing.

Singh knew everyone who was worth knowing in Northamptonshire, which admittedly was not a very long list of people. Still, if Singh returned the dinner invitation, Keynes could imagine rubbing shoulders with councillors,

CEOs and perhaps even the senior members of the county police force who deemed themselves too important to mix with the rank and file.

Jenny's tortillas could make or break his career.

Keynes told himself to calm down and focus. He still had a job to do, and catching the Charity Shop Murderer would do plenty to establish his name, too.

One of Singh's comments had made him uneasy. It sounded as though Chris Shingles had been bothering Singh about some kind of financial matter. Undoubtedly this was down to Shingle's financial illiteracy and misreading of something very tedious, but it meant that he had lied to Keynes when he said he had not been running any investigations. While it was totally out of the question that Singh could have sent a thallium-laced letter of complaint to the Tribune, it would be remiss of Keynes to ignore the lead completely, especially when he had little else to go on.

It also occurred to Keynes that if Shingles had lied about this, he might well have misled him about other matters. Perhaps he knew full well who had made the attempt on his life.

Chapter 21

Margaret Shingles, a dumpy, stressed-looking woman in her mid-fifties, opened the door as far as the security chain would allow.

"Good afternoon, madam, is Chris in, please?" said Keynes.

"If it's about the bingo tickets, the paper made perfectly clear that it was a misprint," she said. "I can't believe people are still calling about that. If every ticket wins, it's obvious there was a mistake."

Keynes held his warrant card up to the gap in the door. "It's not about the bingo tickets," he said.

Margaret led him into the hallway and made him take off his shoes.

"We were very worried about him, you know," she said. "I didn't realise that editing a local newspaper was such a dangerous job. You can understand in London or Peterborough, but not here."

"We are looking into it, Mrs Shingles, believe me. That's why I'd like to speak to Chris. I think he may be able to shed some light on the reasons for the attack."

Margaret crossed her arms. "He's always up to something," she said. "He doesn't tell me anything. Piles of paper everywhere. Funny numbers on the phone bill. Funny how it's none of my business." She let out a sigh.

"I suppose I'd better offer you a cup of tea," she said. "Don't expect a coffee, I don't keep the stuff."

"I can't stand coffee," said Keynes. "It raises the blood pressure and it's been linked in some studies to an increased risk of strokes and heart disease. Tea, on the other hand, lowers the blood pressure and is rich in antioxidants."

Margaret looked impressed. She uncrossed her arms and held up a finger. "Now that's what I always tell Chris he should write about," she said. "Something useful."

Keynes was always good with the mums, he reflected. It was the younger generation with whom he struggled to find a connection, which was strange considering that he was only eight years past being a teenager.

Keynes ascended the stairs, tea in hand, squeezing past a mountain bike that was balanced at a precarious forty-five degree angle. He knocked on a door at the end of the landing, ignoring a sign which read: 'Genius at work.'

Chris Shingles opened it, wearing a stripy dressing gown and two days' stubble, and was not impressed to see Keynes.

"Right, well, that's police harassment taken to absurd new heights," he said.

"Your mum let me in," said Keynes.

Shingles seemed to realise the risible nature of his situation. He tightened the cord of his dressing gown and adapted a more upright posture. He seemed to feel the need to justify his surroundings.

"I'm living here temporarily," he said, gesturing around the bedroom, which looked like it belonged to a teenager. "I was living with my girlfriend, but that went a bit… and actually it's worked out quite well because my would-be assassin is hardly going to look for me here. But, you know, just a temporary situation." He noticed Keynes looking at the sign on the door. "That was there already."

Keynes had a rough idea what reporters earned on local newspapers, and he was fairly sure that Shingles would struggle to put together a deposit for a house, unless it was somewhere like Bellinge. He would not be surprised to find Shingles living here a year from now.

Certainly, it seemed as though he had set up an office here. A laptop and a pile of old newspapers and press releases took up half of the room, blocking up much of the light from the window. In any case, the curtains were closed, and it smelt as though they had not been opened recently.

"Catching up on some work?" said Keynes, gesturing to the computer. Shingles quickly closed the screen, but not before Keynes had noticed that he had been checking an internet database of charity records.

"I'm on sick leave, for obvious reasons, but it gives me a chance to catch up on some research. I don't really get time to concentrate when I'm at work. There are too many small things demanding my attention – NIBs, obits, horoscopes." Shingles noticed the mug of tea in Keynes' hand. "Is mum making tea? And I didn't get one? That's nice."

Keynes took a long sip, never lifting his eyes from Shingles. When he decided he had paused long enough to have an effect, he said: "Shingles, you weren't entirely honest with me earlier. You're working on something, and I think you know exactly why the killer targeted you."

Shingles took a step back, then rocked back and forth on his slippers, thoughtfully. "I couldn't say," he said, finally. "I've already told you everything I know, and, as I mentioned, I'm on sick leave, so I'd appreciate it if you could leave me to recuperate."

"That's rubbish," said Keynes. "You deal with charities every day. If there's something suspicious going on, you'd know about it.

"I've only just starting looking into this, and already I've identified people at risk. Just a couple of days ago I was running Harpit Singh through updated security precautions."

"You spoke to Harpit Singh?" said Shingles, suddenly animated. "What did you ask him about?"

"He's not a suspect. I just pointed out weaknesses in his security protocol, then I ran through his company and charity accounts to identify possible threats from staff or suppliers. I'm going to do this for all the high-profile figures who might be possible targets."

"He let you look at his accounts?" Shingles' voice almost squeaked. "Have you still got them?"

"Not with me. Back at my house."

"I need those accounts."

"Well, you can't have them. He gave them to me on a confidential basis." Keynes was a little disconcerted by Shingles' reaction, and this feeling grew as Shingles rummaged through a cardboard box, producing a dossier stuffed with dog-eared A4 sheets.

"I've been looking into Singh for six months," said Shingles. "You must have heard the rumours."

Keynes had not heard the rumours, but did not want to admit as much, so he made a vague rolling movement of the shoulders that could be construed either as a shrug or the beginnings of a nod.

"I've spoken to sources who reckon there's something crooked about that charity," Shingles went on. "He's covering it up somehow, but I'm sure some of the charity donations are going into Harpit's Carpets to prop it up. That business really looks like it's struggling, but it never makes a loss."

"That's a very serious allegation."

"That's why I haven't been able to stand up a story. Don't worry, officer, I know the libel laws. But so many people are telling me the same story that there must be some truth in it."

Typical, thought Keynes. No wonder Northampton had such a dearth of success stories when people could not wait to cut down the few businessmen who had succeeded in the face of prevailing mediocrity.

"The donations for Singh's Kids are almost all in cash. It would be easy to transfer some of that money to his other businesses, under-report the donations and make up some other, overseas source for the cash. It's even easier when you think that the charity and Harpit's Carpets have the same accountant, chief financial officer and CEO. The carpet company's not listed, so it only has to make limited disclosures."

"Got proof of that, have you?"

"No," said Shingles, "but it sounds like you have."

Keynes leaned against the doorframe and took another sip of his tea. He was far from convinced.

"Look, if I was writing about tombolas and school sports days, I'd probably try to find some kind of big conspiracy theory to entertain myself, but I think you're looking for a story where there is none."

"Don't be so naïve!" said Shingles, suddenly and explosively angry. "This is happening all over the place. Do you have any idea how many companies have associated charities?" He opened the dossier and jabbed his index finger at a printed list of names. "Fifteen in the Greater Northampton area alone. It's perfect. Donations from the company cut its tax bills in the years when it's making a profit, and it can call on the cash pile to bail it out when it's making a loss. You get companies transferring worthless assets to their charities and booking it as a tax deductible amount in their own accounts."

"Who have you heard this from?"

"Obviously I can't tell you that. Good sources. It's not every charity, but there are a couple I've got my eye on. I'm sure I can prove something if I get my hand on a smoking gun."

"Steady on."

"A piece of evidence, I mean. Like Harpit Singh's accounts, assuming he hasn't doctored them to cover it up."

Keynes had an uncomfortable feeling in the pit of his stomach, but he put it down to the chicken kiev.

"He's not the only one," said Shingles. "If I get him, it'll be easy to blow the lid on the others." He selected a couple of pages from the dossier and handed them to Keynes. One was a grainy photocopy of a bearded man in a sharp suit getting out of a car. Keynes did not recognise the man, but the car looked like a Mercedes S Class.

"Simon Oakes," said Shingles. "Founder and commune leader of the Christ Resurrection League."

The Christ Resurrection League was based in a small, self-contained village on the top of a hill near the village of Riscote. The members had little to do with anyone from any neighbouring villages, since the commune had its own shop, sports hall, and, obviously, church. It was shielded from the road by tall hedges, but Keynes had seen in passing that it had quite a decent tennis court.

The League's philosophy was vague but Christian, although it seemed to be a condition of membership for everyone to donate their entire salaries to it. There was nothing illegal about that, especially considering that all of the members were living there rent-free and without paying for food. In fact, considering that a large proportion of them were actually employed by the League in its farming operations, that seemed fair enough to Keynes. A lot of people joined the League after suffering breakdowns or other set-backs in life, so they were hardly the sort to hold down high-flying jobs, anyway, he thought.

"What have you got against them?" he asked.

Shingles paused, weighing up Keynes. He was aware he had said too much. "Nothing, yet. But doesn't it strike you as suspicious that a religious organisation is running a pet food business and a fruit and vegetable producer?

Why on earth should it be running profit-making enterprises when the main organisation doesn't pay any tax?"

Keynes felt like an idiot. Shingles made an excellent point, and it was something that had been in front of his eyes all along. Perhaps financial crimes could explain the killings. That was an area where he could really shine – and where the likes of Gunnett would struggle.

"Maybe," said Keynes. "Maybe you've got a point." He hated to admit that Shingles was ahead of him in his specialist subject area.

Shingles suddenly looked alarmed. "Give me the scoop, okay?"

"What?"

"I've helped you out. If you find anything out based on this, let me know first, before the nationals."

"Fine." Keynes did not have the first idea how to go about contacting the national newspapers, and he had not worked out where the police press officer sat in his office. He had a feeling it was the fat woman he had once accused of stealing his stapler.

"So, can you give me something useful?" Keynes made a move for the dossier, but Shingles drew it towards himself protectively.

"I already have," he said. "If you get some information or you decide you want to part with Harpit Singh's accounts, come and see me. Then maybe I'll see what I can do."

I could break your scrawny neck between my thumb and forefinger, thought Keynes. He hated the thought of this social outcast having somehow outsmarted him and using that power as a bargaining tool. It was almost as if he was being ordered to run errands for Shingles, who lived with his parents and could not get a girlfriend.

"I'm following my own line of enquiry, but it may overlap with yours," said Keynes. "I'll let you know if anything comes up."

"Appreciated, Detective," said Shingles. He looked a little too pleased with himself for Keynes' liking. "I'm glad we've finally found an area where we can co-operate."

"We're not co-operating. I'm doing my job, you're doing yours. And don't ever think of coming to the police station unless you're giving me the prize for the crossword." This was more comfortable ground for Keynes: reminding Shingles of his place in the wider world.

"Fine," said Shingles. "If you get any spare time, do you think you could find out who tried to kill me? That would be great."

Keynes did not like the idea of Shingles having any kind of power over him, but it would be that way until he could do his own digging. He would love to outsmart Shingles and show how far from baffled he was.

He finished his tea. "I'm working on it," he said. "I think that's all for now. By the way, your mum wants to know if you want sausages or fishfingers."

"Fishfingers," mumbled Shingles, but Keynes was already on his way down the stairs, jarring his elbow on the bike.

Chapter 22

Keynes had a lot of leads, but what was a lead? A starting point with no proof. He had a couple of theories, too, but needed a few bits of evidence to hang them on.

Still, he was moving forward, and that had to be better than revisiting his earlier witnesses or looking for a giant wolf.

He returned to the station. Gunnett was not at his desk and Keynes did not even bother to ask where he was. This was getting to be ridiculous, but at least it meant he had free rein to explore his own theories. He hardly thought Gunnett would have allowed him to spend hours talking to someone like Singh, based on a hunch.

Now he had a new hunch, and it made sense. If Oakes and the Christ Resurrection League really were using their charity status for personal enrichment, that would be reasonable motive for murder. Perhaps that meant that the other victims had been putting their hands in the till, too.

First, though, he needed to do his homework. He checked the police records for any charges against Simon Oakes. There had been a few complaints from neighbours and ex-members of the League, but nothing had stuck. One estranged member of his flock had claimed Oakes made them work without pay, assembling table lamps.

Keynes found it hard to get excited about the claim. Even if that were true, Oakes could reasonably deduct the costs of food and board from the national minimum wage and it would probably not leave any salary for his staff, unless they were working particularly long hours. As long as he was meeting the necessary national insurance payments and tax declarations, he was not breaking the law.

He had also noticed that an awful lot of the workers-cum-residents of the League were former homeless people and, apparently, addicts. That was the kind of background that did not give you a lot of leverage in salary negotiations.

In short, there was nothing suspicious about Simon Oakes in the police files. But that did not mean he was innocent. Still, Keynes liked to have some ammunition before he went into the field.

He was preparing to head to Riscote when Biggs parked his considerable bulk on the corner of Keynes' desk.

"Incident you might be interested in," he said. "Adrian Shadwell has been picked up on suspicion of criminal damage. Smashing up a lamppost and rubbish bin."

"Thanks, Biggs, but that's not exactly my area of focus. I've never heard of Adrian Shadwell."

"He works in Joan's Café."

The fog before Keynes' eyes suddenly cleared. A violent outburst by someone who worked next to the site of the first killing was certainly worth his attention. Adrian had not seemed worth investigating, but, it occurred to him, paying a little more attention might have meant the following two attacks would not have happened.

He had not even thought to question Adrian more thoroughly. The boy seemed barely capable of dressing himself, let alone orchestrating a series of cryptic murders. Even as Keynes thought about it, he was convinced there was some kind of mistake. This was a grand, epic scheme of murder. It had not been carried out by a short-order chef in a greasy spoon café.

Still, Biggs had provided him with the details and he needed to at least rule Adrian out, or the case would become even more messy.

Keynes dialled Gunnett's number. If he was going to waste his time interviewing this burger-flipper, he at least wanted to make sure Gunnett endured it too.

"Gunnett," said the voice at the other end.

"Finally," said Keynes. "It's Keynes. We've got a possible connection to the first murder. Personally I think it's a bit slim, but we should pay him a call. Adrian Shadwell from the café next door had been arrested for smashing up council property. It shows a violent streak, so there is a vague justification to interview him."

There was silence on the other end. Keynes checked that the call was still connected.

"Inspector?"

"I'm here," said Gunnett, after a time.

"I'll head over there shortly. Will you be joining me?"

"You don't need me to hold your hand. Just don't forget your pencil."

If Keynes had been holding a pencil in the presence of Inspector Gunnett at that moment, he might very well have used it injudiciously.

"Inspector, I'm more than capable of running this whole investigation by myself. I'm just wondering whether I should be keeping you updated."

The prolonged buzz let Keynes know his boss had hung up. This was not a comfortable working environment, but there was very little he could do to change it. The introduction of Adrian Shadwell had disrupted his theory for the murders, though he could not articulate why.

Chapter 23

The complaint was in Towcester, which told him that it was probably accurate. No one would waste their time filing a complaint in Towcester unless they were telling the truth. The town was small enough for perpetrators to take revenge if they were cleared, and large enough for them to hide afterwards. There were one or two pubs where it was almost inevitable for a visitor to be punched in the face, whether or not they had made criminal complaints in the recent past. Keynes was sure they took requests.

He parked his car on Pushkin Avenue, knowing it was a waste of time, and walked up to the front door of number twenty-nine, knowing it was a waste of time. Mr Anderson, a lean man in a thread-bare green jumper, answered. This was a waste of time, thought Keynes.

He held up his card. "D.S. Keynes. I heard about the damage," he said.

"You're wasting your time," said Mr Anderson, looking puzzled. "Another officer came here."

"I have a different interest," said Keynes."I'm from homicide." He did not say anything else. He did not need to.

Mr Anderson invited him in and made him a cup of coffee, which Keynes ignored politely.

"That boy has been the worst thing that ever happened to her," said Anderson, once Keynes had explained the background to his visit. "I have no idea whether he has a violent streak, but he just has a nasty attitude."

"Could you give examples?" Keynes asked.

Anderson thought about it. "No."

"Well," said Keynes, trying to recover the situation, "can you explain exactly why you were not happy for Jayde and Adrian to see each other?"

"You've seen the bin outside, and the window," said Anderson, gesturing to the sheet of plywood that was blocking out the light in the living room. "She was seeing him for nearly two years. How many 'please' and 'thank you's would you expect in that time? And he came here a lot."

"I'm not quite following you."

"He came to Cindy's wedding. No gift. But he drank his share, all right. Not even a card."

Keynes did not even want to ask who Cindy was. In fact, he was beginning to doubt that Adrian Shadwell had even caused the damage outside. It could be any ordinary idiot on their way home from the pub.

"Did you see Adrian Shadwell cause the damage outside?"

"I could hardly miss it," said Anderson, in disbelief. "He was outside the window, singing something, then he went to the driveway and picked up some gravel. He was throwing bits of gravel at first, but that was hardly likely to do anything. He picked up a stone tortoise from next door and threw it through the glass.

"After that, he started kicking the bin and shouting stuff about Jayde. Terrible stuff. I can understand he's heartbroken, but it's his own fault."

Keynes did not care in the slightest, but he knew he needed to ask.

"Do you have any idea why she ended the relationship?"

"She'd just had enough. She's a decent-looking girl, good career prospects at the bank. Why should she throw it all away for him? No ambition, that boy. Thinks the world's responsible for all of his problems."

"Has he been in trouble before?"

"He's never been in court, but he gets drunk and gets into trouble. He had a fight in the King Henry pub a few months ago, and a few weeks before that he nicked some charcoal from the petrol station while he was drunk. He lives in a flat on the third floor. What's he going to do with charcoal?"

"Has he ever threatened you or Jayde?"

Mr Anderson thought this over. "Not exactly," he said. "Last night he wasn't exactly violent. He was more...sad."

Keynes knew this had been a waste of time, and Mr Anderson's comments confirmed it. Adrian Shadwell might think he was a tough nut, but he was really just a heartbroken little boy who had probably looked at the remaining female population of Northampton and realised his prospects were not good. There was a world of difference between drunkenly throwing a garden ornament through a pane of glass, and throwing a student through one.

He was not their man. The forensic team were dusting the tortoise for prints and would at least be able to rule

Adrian out of the investigation, which was progress of a kind, but for Keynes it was one more wasted journey.

Keynes glanced at a framed photograph on the windowsill. "That's her," said Anderson, noticing. Jayde was a beaming, heavily-freckled ginger girl in her late teens, with a rather square jaw.

"Got it," said Keynes, who did not want to be drawn into a conversation about her aesthetic merits.

He tried a long shot. "I don't suppose she ever visited the British Cancer Foundation shop next to where Adrian works?"

"Not likely," said Mr Anderson. "They didn't like Adrian one bit. They had quite a few arguments about him smoking and throwing his fag ends at the back of the shops. The miserable old one even shouted at Jayde a few times because she knew they were together."

Keynes filed that away for reference. It might be useful later, although he suspected their spat had been the usual petty disagreement that tended to spring up between neighbours. He had brought his pencil all this way, he thought, so he might as well use it.

"How is your daughter? Everything all right with her?"

"Never better, now she's got rid of him. She's already found herself a new fellow. A bit older, more mature. She spends most of her time round his house these days. I haven't met him yet, but she's a lot happier now."

Keynes glanced at the skin forming on his coffee, then at his watch. He wondered whether enough time had passed to justify ending the interview. Even when interviews were a total waste of time, he tried to avoid revealing as much to his interviewees, at least until he had left the room.

There was no obvious next step in the investigation. He could go back to the station and see whether they had the fingerprints ready from the tortoise. The forensic team had failed to find any fingerprints on the letter to Chris Shingles, so it would not tie Adrian to the murders either way. The other two murders had been committed in locations too dirty to give much clear forensic evidence, and the phone box where Wendy Bevan breathed her last had not been examined. By the time Keynes had thought to visit it, dozens of people had contaminated the scene. The medical team would probably have destroyed any fingerprints, anyway, when they had cleaned up the copious amounts of petroleum jelly that had been needed to extricate Mrs Bevan's corpse.

He would make a call at the café, just to pre-empt Gunnett's inevitable complaints that he had failed to tie up all the loose ends. Adrian Shadwell did not feel to him like a strong suspect – and Keynes would be incredibly disappointed if his first arrest in a murder turned out to be a short-order cook with a skinhead haircut – but Keynes did not want to draw attention to his investigation through the things he had missed.

Next, he would visit Simon Oakes at Riscote. Less of an obvious lead and more of an example of thinking outside the box, the kind of thing the police force hated. If he could not find the killer yet, the next best thing would be to find the victims ahead of time.

Keynes made his excuses and left. Twelve minutes. He had spent enough time there to show respect, but not to give false hopes that the police were going to waste much time on a smashed window.

He got into his car and made a brief note on his pad: 'Shadwell – tortoise – window. Drinking recently?'

It was not so much for his own benefit as to show anyone who asked what he had been doing all day. Talking to timewasters and closing down daft alleys.

As he rolled away from the kerb with characteristically excellent clutch control, he wondered, as he often did, what Mr Anderson had done as soon as Keynes had left. Had he gone to the toilet, relieved that the officer had gone at last? Had he lit a cigarette or poured a stiff drink out of nerves? Had he moved a bloody machete from under his sofa and gone into the garden to bury it?

Like the rule in quantum physics, whatever it was, he wondered how often he changed events by observing them.

It was either Schrodinger or Heisenberg, someone like that. That would annoy him all night.

His thought process was shattered, as a speeding car pulled in front of him and slammed on its brakes. Keynes braked just in time and slid to a halt just short of its rear bumper. As the panic subsided, he started to notice the details around him. This was a police car.

An angry figure opened the passenger door of the car in front and stormed over to Keynes' window. It was Gunnett, and he was purple in the face. His fist pounded on the window, and Keynes warily wound it down.

"You're testing me, Keynes, you're really testing me," said Gunnett, gritting his teeth as though trying to hold himself back.

"What's the problem?"

"Get out of the car."

Keynes unclipped his seat belt and did as his superior officer asked. He glanced around. There were a few side windows looking onto this stretch of road, but most people who were at home now would probably be in the front room watching daytime television or doing the vacuuming, and would not witness any assault by Gunnett. That was a shame; it would be a quick, clean way to remove him from Keynes' working environment and it would open up a vacancy for a new Inspector.

But if Gunnett was going to hit him, Keynes wanted witnesses. Since there were none around, he would rather avoid being punched in the face.

He stepped out of the car and walked across to the grass verge, giving himself some distance from Gunnett. Inconveniently, Gunnett followed, standing barely a foot away from him.

"You have to stick your nose into everything, don't you?" he demanded, waving a finger in Keynes' face. "You're a little rodent."

Keynes held his palms up in a gesture of peace but not submission. It would also enable him to block a punch from either side. "I have no idea what you're talking about. I've just been following up leads."

"You've got it in for me, haven't you?"

Yes, thought Keynes. The best possible scenario would be for Gunnett to hit him just as a group of witnesses walked past or opened their net curtains, but there did not seem to be anyone out walking.

"I've just been following the case. As you may know, I've had to do it alone."

"Right, right. It's all to do with the case."

Keynes was genuinely confused. Usually he had a fair idea what he had done to annoy Gunnett, but in this case he could not think of anything.

"I can update you back at the station if you intend to come in today."

He could see Gunnett struggling against the urge to hit him. "Tell me now," demanded Gunnett. "Exactly what are you following up?"

"I'm trying to find out who would want to poison Chris Shingles," said Keynes, conveniently leaving out the details. "That's our best lead right now."

"That's all, is it?" Gunnett took a step back and looked around. Keynes wondered if he was about to be on the receiving end of a flying headbutt, but then Gunnett walked over to the front right wing of Keynes' car and crouched down. Keynes could not hear what he was doing, but it became clear as soon as he heard the sound of air escaping from his tyre. Gunnett stood up, holding a flick-knife.

"What are you doing?" said Keynes. Had it been a youth vandalising his car, he would have tried to pull him away and use a little reasonable force to suppress him, but were he to do that with Gunnett, without any witnesses, it would raise too many awkward questions, especially if he injured Gunnett in the process of pinning him down.

But if Gunnett came anywhere near him with that knife, Keynes would break his arm, at the absolute minimum.

Gunnett did not answer. He reached down and stabbed the rear right tyre then walked around and did the same to the rear left, even as Keynes tried in vain to stand in the way.

"Steady on!" Keynes said. "Look, I haven't been up to anything. I've been to see Shingles, then I went to see the Anderson family."

Gunnett stopped mid-stride and watched Keynes' face carefully. He tested the blade with his thumb.

"They think Adrian Shadwell smashed their window last night," Keynes went on. "He's the cook from the café next to the first murder scene. Turns out he was going out with their daughter and now he's turned violent."

Gunnett's breathing seemed to slow down. He opened his mouth to speak, but no words came out.

"It's not much of a lead, but I think it's worth looking at, don't you?" said Keynes.

"I suppose so," said Gunnett. He looked at Keynes' car, which had now taken on a lopsided look as three of the tyres slowly deflated. He walked over to the last remaining inflated tyre and gashed a hole in that, too. "No sense leaving things half done, is there?"

He folded the knife in on itself and walked back to his car without explanation, leaving Keynes trying to work out what had just happened.

"What am I supposed to do now?" said Keynes, absolutely livid but aware there was nothing he could do about it.

Gunnett pretended to see Keynes's useless car for the first time. "That? That's what you get for parking your car in a dangerous area. Kids, eh?"

He drove away, his own car's tyres screeching with sudden acceleration, as Keynes tried to work out exactly what had just happened, and whether he had deserved it.

**

He had called the station and made up a flimsy story about his car being vandalised while he was calling in at the post office. The location of the car had made his scenario more difficult. Since the car was not outside the Anderson house, he had needed to think of a new reason for it being found abandoned a hundred metres down the road.

Even that story did not make a lot of sense, given that the post office was a five-minute walk away and had ample parking outside. He had also needed to come up with a reason for being in there long enough for teens to let down all four tyres, and had settled for paying his gas bill. The mechanic who had come out to pick up the car had advised him to make his gas payments online in future.

Shepherd, though, had sounded as though he actually believed Keynes' story. Keynes was exactly the kind of person who would park equidistant from the post office and the Anderson house to save petrol, even though he was not paying for it.

Keynes had ignored the slow handclaps as he walked into the station. Biggs was there, mirth spread wide across his gleaming cheeks.

"What's the matter, Milton?" he said. "You look a bit deflated."

Keynes was willing to bet that Biggs had spent fifteen minutes thinking of that joke.

"Very good," he said, not in the mood for a confrontation.

"Or are you just tyred?"

"That one doesn't actually work when you say it out loud, does it? You need to see it written down." Keynes headed for his desk and did not look back to see Biggs' reaction. He was a little disconcerted that so many of his colleagues kept using that irritating nickname. On top of that, there was still a faint smell of coffee and soured milk emanating from his desk drawer.

He needed to kill twenty minutes while he waited for a new set of tyres, so he made sure his notes were updated in a neat and organised fashion on his computer, then made a phone call.

"Hello? I'd like to speak to Mr Oakes, please." The female voice at the end did not sound keen. "Perhaps if you tell him it's in connection with a police investigation," he added. There was a faint buzz of panic at the other end of the line, than calm was restored. "The name's Keynes. Detective Sergeant Martin Keynes." He checked his watch, though he knew he had no other appointments. "Yes, I can be there at four."

He hung up, pleased with himself. Finishing his day at Riscote gave him a nice drive home, avoiding the town centre at rush hour.

An officer came in to tell him that his car was ready. Excellent. That gave him enough time to pay Adrian Shadwell's employer a visit, just to check there were no loose ends that might trip him up unexpectedly later on.

Gunnett thought he had ruined Keynes' day, but he was not even close. All the same, he needed to keep an eye on the inspector. Keynes had known he had a temper, but that outburst of anger had surprised him. If Gunnett was going to attack him physically, Keynes wanted to ensure it was somewhere public where he had witnesses – ideally, in the police station.

He also wanted to make sure that when this case finally came to a close, he was given due credit for his work. Gunnett had contributed almost nothing to the investigation. True, there was a chance he might be doorstepping potential witnesses, or doing something unexpectedly useful, but on the other hand there was a snooker tournament on BBC2 this week.

Chapter 24

Keynes parked his car at the bottom of Market Street car park, then thought better of it, started the engine again and moved it to the top end, nearer to the shops and the security cameras. He could not afford more vandalism to his car.

He walked up a covered walkway to Gold Street, taking everything in as he went. Blazers was still closed for renovation; the health food shop had been replaced by another discount off-licence, and the counter-culture clothes shop, Razorpop, seemed to be in the process of closing down.

Keynes also looked over everyone he passed for signs of suspicious activity. Someone in the Greater Northampton area was a killer, and, at the moment, it could be anyone.

The street was fairly quiet, and none of the passersby aroused suspicion. Keynes had a sixth sense for spotting the unemployed, though, and identified quite a few likely suspects. Baseball caps were a dead giveaway, as were tracksuit bottoms with poppers down the side, and babies. White trainers were a red herring – they could be worn by builders, some shop assistants or the self-employed.

As he turned onto Gold Street, he noticed a familiar figure slumped in the doorway of a boarded-up shoe shop. It was Zulu, curled up in his sleeping bag and looking semi-comatose.

Keynes noticed that his sleeping bag had undergone some alterations. Zulu appeared to have stitched sheets of bubble wrap packaging to the outside of the bag and run some thin plastic tubing underneath in a zig-zag pattern.

"Quite the engineer, aren't you?" said Keynes.

Zulu did not respond, so Keynes nudged the sleeping bag with his toe. "I said, you're quite the engineer."

Zulu grinned to himself, but did not open his eyes. He stank of something sweet and yet mouldy; like potatoes or mushrooms left too long in the shed. Keynes looked at the piping more closely. There seemed to be some kind of rust-coloured liquid flowing through it. He did not care to know its provenance.

Keynes pushed harder with his shoe, though he stopped short of actually kicking Zulu. "Wake up, you slacker, it's three o'clock."

Zulu's eyes opened a crack and his jaw sagged. He looked up at Keynes limply, his head lolling slowly to one side.

"I hope you're keeping out of trouble."

Zulu nodded, in incremental movements.

Keynes seemed at a loss. "Well, this is pathetic. No wonder you can't get a job." He struggle to recall the thought that had occurred to him earlier. "You know a few things about chemistry, apparently," he said. "Where would someone get hold of thallium?"

Zulu's head rocked slowly backwards, a kind of silent belly laugh by degrees. Keynes found it very disconcerting. He waited a few moments in case it was some kind of delaying tactic.

"Look, if you have useful information and you don't tell me, that's obstructing an investigation. If there's some local thallium dealer you don't mention who later…"

Keynes tailed off as he realised Zulu's attention had been taken by the flashing lights of the amusement arcade across the street. Short of an electric cattle prod, there was little that could get his attention.

"Pathetic," Keynes repeated. "You want to lay off the cider. At this time of day."

He gave up and crossed the street. Zulu gave barely any recognition that he had ever been there.

The café was half-full, even during the daytime. Who needed a fried breakfast at three in the afternoon? A couple of the customers seemed to have just finished their shift on the bin lorries, judging by their high-visibility jackets, which was fair enough, but the tell-tale plastic crutch next to one thirty-something man eating a fried egg on toast made Keynes suspect a lot of people were among the chronically unemployed.

It made him unreasonably annoyed to see people paying for tea in cafes. You could make it yourself at home for a fraction of the cost. It was madness.

Joan was a short, heavily-built lady of indeterminate age with a rather hairy mole growing on her chin. Keynes wondered whether, technically, she should be wearing a mask over it in order to comply with hygiene and regulations, in the same way that moustache-wearers needed to.

Keynes introduced himself and showed his badge. "I'd like to ask you a few questions about Adrian Shadwell."

"He doesn't work here anymore," said Joan.

"What do you mean?"

"He hasn't come to work for the past two days. What do you think that means?"

In the police force, that would mean he was a Detective Inspector on full pay, thought Keynes.

"Did he tell you he was leaving?"

"No, just didn't turn up. No great loss. He never had his heart in it. Spent half his time on the phone to that girl, or sending her text messages. Even caught them messing around on the chest freezer once." She looked up at Keynes, suddenly guilty. "We wiped it over. Those antiseptic wipes."

"What was he like, personality-wise?"

"He was a good worker. You've got to be able to do lots of things at once. Get the sausages started before the eggs, or you'll ruin them. He was good on his timings. Even if there was eight things on the plate, none of them would be cold. Ask them." Joan gestured to her clientele.

Keynes did not write that down. "I meant more in terms of his temper. I understand he was sometimes violent."

"He lost his temper now and again," said Joan, no longer making eye contact. She shuffled her slippers. "I wouldn't say he was violent, though. Just verbals."

"And he didn't get on with the old lady in the charity shop next door?"

"Oh you're not trying to pin that on him, are you?" Joan looked outraged. "Just because he's a teenager who's had a few problems. You've got to pick an easy suspect, haven't you? If it's not him, it'll be a black, or one of them Al Qaedas. You should be ashamed of yourself."

Keynes felt out a hand in a gesture meant to pacify her. "It's nothing like that," he said. "But we owe Miss Hope the duty to investigate the circumstances of her death thoroughly, and that means eliminating suspects in the area." He thought invoking a dead neighbour might calm Joan down, but it did not seem to.

"She was a misery," said Joan. "You ask around this street, see how many people she upset. Always making such a fuss about the bins."

"Did she argue with Adrian?"

"Yes, now and again. She couldn't be bothered to open the bins and put things in. She'd just leave them on top, then Adrian would have to move them to put our rubbish in. Then she'd complain that he'd moved her rubbish."

"It's true," said one of the binmen, finishing a bacon sandwich. "We don't have to collect it if it's not actually in the bin."

"How many complaints did you have about her?" asked Vera.

The binman thought it over. "In the last three months – seven. From all of the shops on this row."

Against his better judgement, Keynes wrote down 'bins' on his notepad. He did not want to be distracted from his main purpose by a grand conspiracy involving improper disposal of rubbish. All the same, he took down the binman's name and contact details. Terry Wood, aged thirty-eight, though he looked older.

"Noted," said Keynes. "So are you saying that Adrian Shadwell was not violent towards her?"

"He had a bit of a barney with her now and again," said Joan. "Called her a daft old trout, which she was. I'd have called her a lot worse."

"And how did he act towards his girlfriend? Jayde?"

"They argued too, but she was a sort. Butter wouldn't melt in her mouth, but a proper little madam. She'd yell and he'd have to come running. He got fed up with it after a while. She was always telling him to get a proper job. What's this?" Joan gestured at the café.

"So he was never physically violent?"

"Not that I saw. He never laid hands on her."

"He used to kick hell out of those bins," said Terry. He looked down at the table as Joan glared at him.

"That's just bins," she said. "Not people."

Keynes questioned them further, but it seemed Joan was too protective of Adrian to tell him anything incriminating. All the same, it seemed unlikely that Adrian could be the man behind a string of diverse murders. According to Joan, he did not even own a car at the moment, his last one having failed its M.O.T. two months ago and been scrapped. Northamptonshire's public transport network being what it was, it was nigh on impossible for anyone to travel to Litchborough and back by bus, especially in the evening. Taxis went there if there was a booking, but that would be simple to check. It was hard to imagine a cabby waiting with the motor running while his passenger offed an old lady.

It was a waste of time, as most of his interactions with the public tended to be, but as long as he was in the area, he might as well do more digging on Adrian Shadwell. At least until it was time to visit Simon Oakes.

A thought occurred to him: a long shot, but no harm to ask. "Do you keep any thallium on the premises?" he asked.

"Are we supposed to?" said Joan.

He made his excuses and left, thinking that Joan looked relieved he was going. Whatever she had told him, she obviously had a soft spot for Adrian. Culinary skills, such as they were in an establishment like this, were clearly more important to her than his personal life. Fair enough, thought Keynes.

Keynes opened the door to Groovy Smoothies, and a bell rang. Needless to say, the smoothie shop, with its healthier offerings made from fruit and vegetables and no fried goods to be found, was almost empty. Two non-threatening youths, probably students, sat at a table by the window with one half-empty plastic cup of something purple between them.

Ian Pruitt was sitting at another table, reading a newspaper. He looked up as Keynes walked in, and excitement showed on his face.

"Hello again, Inspector," he said, but Keynes did not correct him. "Goodness me, it's like Piccadilly Circus in here."

"Afternoon, Mr Pruitt."

Pruitt held up the newspaper, the latest edition of the Tribune.

"I was just reading about the poison they sent to the newspaper office. Terrible business. Do you think that's related to..." Pruitt nodded towards the British Cancer Foundation shop.

"We're not sure, but we're looking into it."

Pruitt held up his own cup and saucer. "Can I interest you in a Bhutanese lychee infusion?"

"Not while I'm on duty." Keynes took a seat opposite Pruitt. "This is not directly related to the investigation, but I just wondered whether you had encountered Adrian Shadwell from the café next door."

Pruitt nodded. "The bins. What a hue and cry."

"Is it fair to say that he and Mrs Hope had been involved in a few arguments?"

"Definitely. She didn't see eye-to-eye with anyone really, but it was worse with Adrian because he's very hot-headed. She never really got the hang of the recycling bins." Pruitt drifted off for a minute, then his eyes widened and he was suddenly alert. "Do you think Adrian had something to do with the murder?"

"I didn't say that," said Keynes carefully. "But obviously I would be remiss if I didn't follow up every line of enquiry. And he is a suspect in a vandalism case."

"Vandalism's a very different kettle of fish. That hardly makes him a serial killer."

"I'm not saying he is." Keynes was losing patience with Pruitt, who seemed to speak almost entirely in cliches and lacked much of an attention span. "I'm just asking a few questions for now, and perhaps we'll have ruled him out entirely by the end of the day."

"Aren't there supposed to be two of you? I mean, two police officers, when you question people."

"Ideally," said Keynes, and hoped Pruitt would not ask any follow-up questions. "This is just an informal conversation on background."

"On background," Pruitt murmured to himself.

"Did you ever see Adrian with his girlfriend? A teenage girl called Jayde."

"Oh yes, she was there a lot. She'd come over at closing time to meet him. I don't think he drives."

"How were they as a couple? Did they get on well?"

"A fiery relationship, shall we say."

Keynes leaned forward. "Go on," he said.

"Sometimes they were very lovey-dovey, but other times..." Pruitt rubbed his chin, then looked Keynes in the eye. "You should have seen the way he treated her when he was angry."

"Did he ever hit her?" Keynes could feel his blood pumping more rapidly. This unpromising diversion in the investigation could pay dividends. Roll enough dice and eventually you end up with a six, he thought.

"Oh no," said Pruitt, dashing Keynes' hopes instantly. "But he could be very sarcastic."

Keynes sank back in his chair. He could do with a cup of tea, but not the ridiculous flowery stuff that Pruitt sold in this place.

At that moment, the two students came over to the table, one holding a handful of poorly-photocopied fliers.

"Hi, Ian," said one. "Is it OK if we put one of these posters up in the window? We're having a concert for Darfur."

"Uganda," said the other student. "Darfur was last year."

"Good for you," said Pruitt. "What is it? Drum and bass? Hard house?"

"Acoustic sets. Kind of indie folk, if you had to categorise it."

"Fine with me. Sounds like a good night out. Just find a space." Pruitt gestured to the large window to the left of the door, which already sported a collection of posters taped to the inside of the glass. "The oxygen of publicity."

Keynes looked at the flyer. Bands with names like Corporate Lobotomy and The Toasties were scheduled to play at the students' union to raise money, although the chief attraction, judging by the relative size of the font, was the cheap bar.

He rose from his seat and opened the door, stepping outside to read the posters in the window. Northampton seemed to have charities for every kind of cause imaginable, from niche diseases to entire countries or species.

Keynes noticed that Singh was advertising his baked bean record attempt with a professionally-produced poster, but the savvy businessman had not been able to resist putting a strip ad for his carpet company at the bottom of the poster, with the justification that it was the location for the event.

He stepped back inside, as the first student taped up his poster.

"You'll be lucky if anyone notices your flyer next to all that lot," said Keynes.

"All publicity helps," said the student, sniffily.

"It's all about raising awareness," said the other.

"Yes, but a black and white photocopy. Not very eye-catching , is it? Look at Harpit Singh's one about the baked bean bath. Full colour. The beans really jump out at you."

The first student snorted. "He doesn't deserve to be on the same window as The Toasties. That guy's a crook."

"Steady on," said Pruitt. "This man's a police officer."

"Well, you should investigate Harpit Singh. I think it's disgusting that he passes himself off as a philanthropist, when everyone knows he's stealing from the charity to patch up his other businesses."

"That's a very serious allegation," said Keynes. "Some might call it slander."

"I'm just saying what everyone else is thinking. You should at least look at his accounts."

Keynes felt slightly nauseous, and it was not helped by the smell of Pruitt's lychee tea. Even though he had heard the same thing from a couple of sources, these claims were just unfounded allegations. The British had always found pleasure in trying to cut down the most successful among them. Singh was guilty only of being too good at manufacturing publicity.

During dinner, Keynes might advise him to keep a lower profile in future, or at least to find a way to rebuff rumours a bit more effectively. He realised that he had not yet set a date for dinner, and Jenny would need to take the tortillas out of the freezer to thaw.

"I'll bear that in mind," said Keynes. "And I expect there are a few rumours flying around about Simon Oakes and the Christ Resurrection League?"

"Well, yeah. That's pretty obvious."

The student's reply made it a little difficult for Keynes to press him further without revealing himself to be hopelessly out of touch with public opinion. Instead, he remained silent for several seconds until the student took it upon himself to fill the gap.

"Slavery, that's what I call it. Everyone knows what goes on at Riscote."

Everyone except Keynes, evidently.

"Exactly what are you referring to?" he said.

The student looked back in disbelief. "Do you want a list? How about paying his staff below the minimum wage and not allowing them to leave? He just makes out they're volunteering for charity, when really they're working on his farms for next to nothing and helping him get even richer."

Keynes discreetly reached into his pocket and produced his notepad and pencil. He balanced the pad on his knee beneath the table and started to take notes, not wanting the student to know the full extent of his ignorance.

"We've been aware of those allegations for a while," said Keynes.

"But because they're coming from former victims of substance abuse and troubled backgrounds, you ignore them, right?" The student was becoming angry now. "I've volunteered at drop-in centres. The League sends minibuses around town at night, offering homeless people food and a bed for the night. They don't tell them they'll be working for eighteen hours a day on a farm without pay, unable to leave or contact anyone else."

The student jabbed his finger at Keynes. "They have absolutely no contact with the outside world, no phones, and that compound is miles from the next village," he said. "I've spoken to people who ran away from there in the middle of the night and banged on the door of some farmer asking him to help them escape. Yet the police do nothing.

"All the time Simon Oakes is preaching the gospel and driving around in a brand new Mercedes. It's easy to be humble when everyone else is doing all the work. The fact that he's allowed to operate commercial businesses and claim tax relief for his charity is unbelievable. He's a hypocrite and so are the police."

Pruitt looked uncomfortable. "Dennis, I think you'd better calm down," he said. "Those are serious allegations and there might be a perfectly innocent explanation." He turned to Keynes. "I think he's overdone the guava."

"Guava's got nothing to do with it," said Dennis the student, angrily. "The police should stop oppressing minorities and look into big business, especially when they're using the smokescreen of a charity to cover things up. That's doubly disgusting. I'm sure if it was your family sleeping in a shed and getting up at the crack of dawn to pick apples, you'd feel differently."

He finished speaking, but continued to glare at Keynes, panting a little. Keynes felt uncomfortable, but at least he had some ammunition for his visit to Oakes.

Keynes' pencil, scratching frantically on the pad, finally caught up with Dennis' words. Homeless people. Apple-picking.

He checked his watch. Twenty to four.

"Thank you for your time, both of you," he said, rising to his feet. He turned to Dennis. "For your information, the police force has been aware of those allegations for quite some time, but our concern for minority faith groups means that we need to tread carefully to avoid causing offence."

Dennis was still angry, but seemed not to know where to look.

Keynes left the shop, took a deep breath of cold, damp air, and glanced across the street. The stinking sleeping bag was in its usual place, but Zulu was no longer there. He looked up and down the street, but the wild-haired irritant had disappeared, just when he might have proved useful for once.

Chapter 25

Riscote was a hamlet on top of a hill, about five miles from the nearest village, and twenty miles from Northampton town. Buses did not pass through here, and there was not even a post box or public telephone in the area. Tall, greying hedges screened the commune and its inhabitants from the road, but multiple tyre tracks in the gravel of the driveway showed that there was regular traffic in and out from, it appeared, cars and vans.

Keynes noted as he turned into Lazarus Court that he had no reception on his mobile phone here. It was also unlikely that it would be viable for any telecom company to install broadband internet lines this far away from a large population centre, and he wondered whether the postman came this far either. There had been no letter box at the entrance.

He passed a tennis court in enviably good condition, then a series of bungalows on his right and a sports centre on the left. It had a squash court and a swimming pool, if the sign was to be believed. This little community had better facilities than most council-funded leisure centres.

Keynes followed the road up to a red-brick building at the end, where a sparkling silver Mercedes was parked. The building was nothing special: solid but unremarkable. It was overshadowed by a assortment of thick trees which encircled it, screening the commune's day-to-day happenings from view.

He parked his car next to the Mercedes, and realised that he had not passed a single person on his journey into Lazarus Court. As he left the car, he glanced into Oakes' Mercedes. Through the window he could see a broadsheet newspaper on the passenger seat, a roadmap on the parcel shelf and a protein shake on the back seat. That's the car of someone who means business, Keynes thought.

Looking around, there was nothing out of the ordinary. The place just seemed like a typical, affluent country residence: either a small village or a large private property. He could not see any sheds large enough to house people, though there was one with its door ajar which housed a lawnmower and some tools.

This place certainly did not look like the home of a cult. The only unusual aspect was the almost total absence of any other people.

Keynes' shoes crunched on the gravel as he approached the front door of the main building. He tried to peer through the window, but an old-fashioned net curtain prevented him. Everything about the building, from its sandstone walls to the stained glass in the window of the front door, made it seem like it was occupied by a retired couple rather than a multi-millionaire and his staff. Perhaps that was the idea.

Keynes gave up hope of finding any clues on the outside and rang the doorbell. An excerpt from Handel's Hallelujah Chorus chimed.

The door opened a crack and a thin, impatient looking women with dirty blonde hair peered out. It was hard to explain how, but Keynes knew instinctively that she was a vegan, or at least a very sanctimonious vegetarian.

"Can I help you?" she said, her tone implying that she would rather not.

Keynes held out his badge. "D.S. Keynes. I believe we spoke on the phone, Miss Quelch."

She sighed. "The Reverend doesn't have long," she said. "He doesn't normally see unsolicited visitors. You're very lucky he's making an exception for you."

She opened the door fully. "Take your shoes off and put these on." She handed Keynes a pair of large cotton slippers.

"Is this part of the religion?" said Keynes, leaning against the door jamb as he attempted to remove his shoes without falling over or stepping on the wet doorstep in his socks.

"No, the Reverend's just had a new carpet fitted in his office. And for that reason I can't offer you any beverages."

Miss Quelch led Keynes up a varnished wooden staircase, as he tried to avoid slipping. There were framed photographs of Biblical scenes on the wall on the way up, which changed halfway to photographs of Simon Oakes with local celebrities: shaking hands with the mayor, being interviewed on Midlands This Evening, and appearing on stage with a local Christian rock group named FaithPlant. Keynes was reminded of Harpit Singh's office.

She paused outside a heavy oak door. "He doesn't shake hands," she said. "Please address him as Reverend and limit eye-contact to less than two seconds. When you are asked to leave, please leave immediately."

Keynes had known warmer welcomes, but the sheer fact that it seemed to be so difficult to fix a meeting with this man made him feel pleased with himself for having breached the inner sanctum. He had of course needed to use scare tactics, warning Oakes that he had reason to believe that his life might be in danger. Even then, Oakes had needed some convincing. Perhaps he thought he had divine protection, or perhaps he just thought he would rather keep himself away from the prying eyes of the law. Either way, he obviously had some legitimate concerns or Keynes would not have secured the meeting.

Miss Quelch opened the door and Keynes stepped inside, walking awkwardly in his slippers. It was a nice carpet, though, he thought. About an inch deep, and in the kind of mottled off-white pattern Jenny had once pointed out when they were looking for linoleum for the kitchen.

Oakes was standing at the window with his back to the door. It was an obviously pretentious pose, as though he wanted to make it appear he had no idea Keynes was about to walk in and was actually preoccupied with something in the garden.

"You made this sound important," said Oakes, not bothering to turn around. "I hope it is."

"Actually, Reverend, I hope it isn't."

The door closed solidly. Keynes resisted the urge to speak, knowing that the longer the silence grew, the more Oakes would feel the urge to see what his guest was doing.

Oakes gave in, and turned to face Keynes.

"Well, officer, what is the reason for your visit, other than trying to scare me?"

Keynes walked to the desk and took a seat, not waiting to be asked. It was the nicest desk he had ever seen; better than Harpit Singh's. It looked like the kind of mahogany that was almost impossible to find since rainforest protection had become fashionable, and it had a flawless, shining surface. In fact, the craftsmanship evident in this office was exceptional. Keynes wondered how much Jesus-money had gone into it.

"I'm not trying to scare you, Reverend. I'm just trying to make you aware of the risks we believe you may currently face as one of the more prominent figures of the local charity community."

Oakes pulled his chin into the turtleneck of his jumper and curled his nostrils. "I'm hardly a pensioner in a charity shop," he said.

"Perhaps there's no risk and I've jumped the gun. All the same, I'd rather err on the side of caution. There is a killer at large who we believe is targeting individuals linked to charities."

"We're not exactly a charity."

"Not strictly, Reverend, no. All the same, you don't pay tax, and you do have several fundraising exercises every year which bring in tens of thousands of pounds. That in itself may be the inciting factor for whoever is carrying out these attacks."

Oakes folded his arms, revealing impressively muscular arms through the Arran wool of his jumper. "I'm surrounded by five hundred followers. Exactly how far do you think an attacker would get?"

"Obviously that depends on how violent your religion allows you to be," said Keynes. "Incidentally, where do you recruit these followers of yours?"

"They come from a variety of backgrounds. Burned-out city bankers, reformed drug addicts, and everyone in between who has seen the light. We don't judge people here. The whole principle of the Christ Resurrection League is that everyone is treated equally, and everyone has the chance to redeem themselves for their earlier sins."

"Where exactly is everyone? I didn't see a single person on the drive in."

"The working day isn't over. They're out in the fields," said Oakes. "And also at the pet food supplies shop."

Picking apples, thought Keynes. He peered out of the window, but could not find a gap in the foliage big enough to spot any people working in the fields.

"If you're looking for something sinister, you won't find it," said Oakes. "I'm sorry to disappoint you, but we are a community of law-abiding, healthy-living people who happen to have a shared interest in our Lord Christ. If we liked jazz music or spaghetti, I doubt the authorities would pay us such attention."

"It would put some people's minds at rest if we could run the rule over your financials. Sunlight is the best disinfectant."

"We disclose what we are required to disclose. I suggest you ask the charities supervisor for a copy of our latest filing."

Keynes realised he was getting nowhere. Unlike Singh, Oakes was not an extrovert. He had reached this position by keeping a low profile, by sinking into the background while the organisation he had founded grew in prominence.

"Is it correct to say that members of your community are required to pay a large portion of their salary to the League, on top of other expenses?"

Oakes sighed and placed both palms down on his desk. "We ask members to pay a tithe for the upkeep of the community. They generally do. Obviously there are costs for accommodation and other living expenses, as there would be for any other job where staff live on the premises.

"But you are missing the point. We pool our resources to grow the community for everyone's benefit. If we produce more, we can put the money back into the community, to improve the facilities and spread the word even wider.

"It's a community. We share everything. We are all equal."

Keynes leaned back in his chair and glanced out of the window again. "I see," he said. "Only, I can only see one Merc out there."

Oakes rose to his feet. At the same moment, the door to his office swung open to reveal Miss Quelch.

"The Reverend is feeling tired and would like to wish you a safe journey," she said, holding the door open.

Keynes looked at Oakes, who did not say anything. Keynes waited for a moment, then admitted defeat and stood up.

"I'm trying to help you," he said. He held out a hand, but Oakes did not shake it. Keynes let his hand drop slowly back to his side, then walked away.

He stopped in the doorway and turned back, reasoning that there was nothing to lose.

"Do you drive around in a minivan at night picking up homeless junkies?" he asked.

Oakes glared at him. Miss Quelch coughed.

"Because if you do, do you really think that's a good idea now there's a serial killer on the loose?"

Keynes gestured at Miss Quelch. "Do you think she's going to protect you from a smacked-up lunatic?"

Miss Quelch quietly took two steps backwards out of the room. In her place, a giant of a man with a centre-parting and a cardigan, walked in, stopping a couple of steps short of Keynes. He towered over the Sergeant and gave the impression that his benign grin could change to something more menacing at any moment.

"No, but I think Desmond might be able to," said Oakes.

Keynes hesitated to see whether Desmond was going to hit him, then turned and walked out.

As he sat in his car, he wondered whether there was anything he could have done differently. He suspected not. Oakes had no reason to co-operate, and all of his success was down to being elusive and fading into the background.

Perhaps, Keynes thought, he could pay a visit to the pet food supplies store and start asking questions, or even find a way into the orchard, once he could establish where it actually was.

Or perhaps he could just write this off as a wasted journey and follow up some more promising leads instead. Not every roll of the dice produced a six.

Still, it was interesting to ponder whether Zulu had been one of those new recruits picked up by moonlight on the streets of Northampton by earnest Christians promising soup and shelter. If he had – and Keynes found it hard to believe he would have qualified for an apple-picking job by any other means – then there must have been some reason for him to leave. If he really believed that spending his days in a stained sleeping bag in a filthy nook in Gold Street was better than living in a rural hamlet and earning a salary, then something must have driven him away from Lazarus Court.

Keynes had his suspicions that Oakes was skimming a sizable chunk of the proceeds from the Christ Resurrection League into his own pockets, but he did not have the first idea where to start, and it was hardly a case for a homicide detective anyway. Oakes was not the type to give anything away, in more ways than one. Harpit Singh was talkative and a relentless self-promoter. If he had any dark secrets, he would probably give them away without much effort from anyone else to find them. Perhaps he already had, thought Keynes glumly, picturing the stapled wad of financial results on top of Jenny's pile of crossword books.

It seemed to be impossible for anyone to make a success of themselves without committing a few shameful or downright sinister acts along the way. You don't become a millionaire by being a nice person, thought Keynes. That would make a good title for a management book.

He still had not confirmed dinner with Harpit Singh. It had been a major ambition of his to befriend a successful tycoon like Singh, but now that he had the opportunity he was hesitant to reach for it. Suspicion gnawed at the pit of his stomach. All the same, Singh might be entirely innocent, in which case Keynes would be passing up a great opportunity to develop a highly useful contact for his life after the police force.

Singh's record attempt was tomorrow. Perhaps Keynes could call at the carpet warehouse and speak to him before he got into the bath of beans.

Chapter 26

Keynes arrived at the carpet warehouse the next day at what he thought was a reasonably early hour. He realised as soon as he arrived, however, that it would be impossible to catch Harpit Singh for a quiet word.

The asphalt driveway outside the warehouse had been transformed and the area had, against all odds, something of a party atmosphere. Balloons of various colours had been tied to the walls, and a banner hanging from the ceiling announced: "Harpit's Carpets Presents: World Record Attempt."

Singh, never the shy, retiring type, was speaking to a television news crew. He was dressed in a fluffy cotton dressing gown and slippers, and had chosen a bright orange bandana, presumably to complement the baked beans.

A quartet of passably attractive young women were dressed in orange lycra catsuits branded with the Harpit's Carpets logo. They were handing out balloons and lollipops to the children among the crowd, which had gathered to watch a man sit in a bath of cold beans for several hours. An opportunistic vendor had parked his burger van alongside and was doing a decent trade. All the while, huge speakers blared out banal pop music. This was not Keynes' idea of an entertaining Saturday morning for the family. There were probably a hundred and fifty people here. He had no idea why.

Since he was technically off-duty, Keynes had decided not to tuck in his shirt, and was wearing dark blue jeans. He could never bring himself to wear trainers, so he had opted for a pair of leather shoes, but in brown to show he was on his leisure time.

Keynes felt a sudden urge to pop inside and see how much it would cost to buy a new carpet for the staircase, but held himself back when he recognised the impulse. He acknowledged Singh's marketing prowess. He could see around a dozen men milling around the carpet warehouse while their wives and children listened to incredibly loud music and queued up for free balloons. There was even a clown offering a face painting service. Keynes wondered how many carpets Singh would need to sell to pay for the peripheral activities around the record attempt. Even if he did not sell any, the newspaper inches this event would fill would be worth more than thousands of pounds' worth of advertising space. He noticed that Singh had positioned banners and signs so that it was nearly impossible to take a photograph of the bath without including his company logo.

The bath was a classic white porcelain model mounted on little brass feet, and was raised on a platform a couple of feet above ground level. Two lycra-clad girls had climbed the steps onto the platform and were in the process of pouring baked beans into the bath, one catering-sized can at a time.

Keynes could tell from the artificial hue of the tomato sauce that the beans were not from a household brand, and in fact they gave off a slightly stale smell. As Singh had mentioned before, a good use of bad beans. This was marketing acumen in action.

Singh was still being mobbed by the press pack, such as it existed in Northamptonshire. Now the local television station was filming him signing autographs for some of the children. He was certainly more of a role model than footballers or the singers who produced the kind of dross pouring out of those speakers at an obtrusive decibel level, thought Keynes.

He noticed with interest that Chris Shingles was trying to fight his way to the front of the pack. Singh appeared to see Shingles too, and made a barely perceptible nod to a member of his security team nearby. The security guard, who had a forehead like a hunched knee and was wearing a black bomber jacket, stepped into Shingles' path.

"He's not taking interviews," Keynes heard the security guard say.

"But he's doing an interview now," Shingles protested.

"He's not taking interviews with you."

Shingles tried arguing with the security guard, but eventually admitted defeat and acknowledged their mismatch in size. If Shingles had ever been in a fight, it would have been as the losing party. As he slunk away, he noticed Keynes and brightened up again.

"Just here for the beans?" he asked, in a tone that was too familiar for Keynes' liking.

"It's the weekend. I can do what I like."

"So you're not here on official business?"

Keynes puffed up his shoulders and leaned into Shingles, who could not help but flinch, though he tried to hide it.

"Go away," said Keynes.

"If you're ready to trade, you know where I am."

Shingles walked away, trying to put some swagger into his stride to show that he had had the better of the confrontation, though to Keynes' mind he had not. His cocky insouciance was somewhat undermined when he unlocked his bicycle from a railing, put on a chunky helmet and rode off.

Keynes wondered whether, even if facts emerged to prove Shingles right, he could ever bring himself take the reporter's side. There was something about Shingles that he disliked at a molecular level. It was as if Shingles seemed to think that idealism, and trying to undermine important people, was an acceptable substitute for getting ahead in life.

Singh had not been near enough to hear that little exchange, but he had evidently seen Keynes appear to stick up for his interests. The security guard in the bomber jacket loomed over him.

"Harpit Singh wants to see you," he said.

Keynes followed as the guard cleared a path through waiting well-wishers to Singh, who was sitting on a stool shielded by a makeshift dressing screen behind the bath.

"Detective Keynes!" he said, rising to shake the officer's hand. "Glad you could make it. It's going to be a great show."

"You are quite the showman," said Keynes. "It's very slick."

"We've used this agency for a while. They know what I like, and they know what the public likes. We were trying to get a bouncy castle, too, but the council weren't keen."

Keynes nodded sympathetically.

"Tonight this will be on two local TV news programmes, at least, one radio station is giving hourly updates, and the newspapers…" Singh trailed off. "Well, they'll have to cover it. Full media exposure for a charity, just because an overweight Sikh is sitting in a bath of beans."

Keynes smiled, feeling a larger laugh was not warranted. "Good exposure for the brand, too," he said.

"It's all about the charity – but why waste the opportunity?" said Singh, grinning. He glanced up at the banner hanging from the warehouse and his face darkened.

"I had a much bigger banner than that, but someone pinched it last night," said Singh. "It was going to wrap halfway around the building. Very good visual prop."

"I can get someone to look into it," said Keynes. "Though sadly that's not my area of oversight."

Singh appeared to think about it, then shook his head. "Nah. It's probably been cut up and used by gypsies for tarpaulins by now. It makes you sick. Stealing from a charity. Who would do that?"

Keynes tried not to catch Singh's eye as he pondered that question.

"I took your advice about the security," said Singh. "If there really was someone after me, I'd be a sitting duck out here. I've hired Gerry to keep a look out for any funny business. Mind you, that would get me even more publicity, wouldn't it? Shot by a sniper while covered in beans."

"I don't think our man is that sophisticated."

"Have you made any progress in catching him?"

"We're making headway, certainly," said Keynes, trying to sound dynamic without actually lying. "Though unfortunately there's nothing I'm able to share."

Singh looked disappointed, but nodded. "Of course. Sensitive stuff." He glanced at his watch, rolled his neck around, causing a series of small bones to click, then cracked his knuckles. "Showtime."

"While I remember," said Keynes. "About dinner – how's Wednesday?"

"I'll double-check, but that sounds fine." Singh tapped his head as though trying to remember something not particularly important, then clicked his tongue. "And that print-out of our accounts, the preliminary one. Could I get that back? Nothing major, but I don't want it floating around out there with the wrong numbers."

"Of course." Keynes was exhilarated. He was going to have dinner, at his own house, with one of the leading businessmen in Northamptonshire - perhaps even the East Midlands. This probably warranted new cutlery. Jenny would be happy.

"If you'll excuse me, officer." Singh shuffled in his slippers and threw a few mock punches, looking like a boxer in an as-yet-uninvented weight division of boxing. "I wrote this," he added, as the last song died down on the speakers and a radio presenter began his introduction.

"Ladies and gentlemen, boys and girls," blared a voice from the speakers. "Here for a world record attempt, right here in Northampton, it's the king of carpets, the champion of charity, the boss with a bandana. Would you please put your hands together for Harpit Singh!"

Singh stepped out to warm applause, as families thronged around the bath. It was now almost full to the brim with cold, out-of-date baked beans. Singh mounted the steps to the platform and waved to the crowd with both arms high above his head. Then he tugged the cord of his dressing gown and two of the women in lycra helped him take it off, revealing a pair of bright orange swimming trunks underneath. Cheers and a few ironic wolf-whistles rang out from the crowd, to Singh's delight.

One of the women handed Singh a microphone. He tapped the top, then began to speak.

"I'd like to thank you all for coming here today to see me sitting in a freezing cold bath of beans." There were more cheers. "I've bungee-jumped from a crane above the Market Square, jogged a half-marathon around Sixfields stadium, but this has to be the craziest thing I've ever attempted. I need to sit in this bath of baked beans for ten hours, fifty-four minutes and twenty-one seconds in order to break the world record, and set a new one for Northampton. I get wrinkly sitting in the bath for ten minutes, so I hate to think what's going to happen." Laughter joined the cheers.

"While I'm in here, covered in beans, my lovely assistants are going to be walking around with buckets to take your donations." The women, surrounding the stage, waved. "I urge you to dig deep and spare whatever loose change you can because, after all, it's for the kids. There are a lot of kids that need your help, and Singh's Kids will put that money to good use to underlay the work we're already doing."

The crowd loved him, Keynes thought. A born entertainer. Make them laugh, then sell them the message. It was not a bad strategy, even if it meant he had to play the clown once in a while.

That was rather a strange use of the word 'underlay', he thought. He had a feeling that Singh was trying to get people thinking subliminally about carpets.

The radio presenter led a countdown, then Singh stepped forward, shook off his slippers and stepped into the bath. The slippery contents, combined with his ungainly physique, caused him to enter it faster than expected, coating his arms, neck and chin in bean sauce. Singh pulled himself back up to a seated position, taking it in good grace.

"And the clock has started," the radio DJ announced, pointing to a digital timer beside the bath. "Under the world record rules, Harpit has to stay in the beans up to at least his nipples at all times, but his arms can be out of the beans. If he breaches this rule, he will be given a warning and have three seconds to get back into position. If he doesn't do it, he will be disqualified. He is allowed to take a three-minute bathroom break every three hours. And last of all: he's not allowed to eat the beans!"

Singh's expression as he tried to wipe the beans out of his beard suggested that the bath had proved to be a less appetising experience than he had expected.

They were going to struggle to keep people entertained for nine hours, thought Keynes, as a pack of cheerleaders emerged and started a routine which involved spelling out 'Harpit'. Anyway, he had already arranged to meet Jenny for some out-of-town shopping, killing two birds with one stone while he was here.

As he headed to his car, Keynes wondered to himself whether he would take Shingle's allegations more seriously if they came from anyone other than Chris Shingles.

Chapter 27

Keynes and Jenny toured Kitchen World, a new megastore that had opened recently near the Sixfields roundabout and would no doubt be as shortlived as the other tenants of that space: the Spanish tapas restaurant and the furniture warehouse.

"It's a bad name," said Keynes, as they examined a set of bathroom towels. "If they're going to sell stuff for other rooms of the house, they need to change the name."

"They've painted themselves into a corner," agreed Jenny. "If they change the name to reflect that, they'll lose all of their brand recognition."

Keynes put his arm around Jenny and gave her a hug, feeling inexplicably affectionate to her at that moment.

"So, if Harpit Singh's coming for dinner, are we going to need new cutlery?" she asked.

"We can't expect a man of his stature to eat using cutlery with plastic handles. A spoon with a handle for pudding, maybe, but definitely not for soup."

"I haven't seen any Mexican soup recipes."

"Okay, never mind about the soup. I think we're going to need plain metal cutlery. Something with a bit of heft."

Keynes did not enjoy shopping, but it was made tolerable with Jenny because she shared his way of thinking. He could set her a specification and budget, and she would seek out something which fit it – not try to convince him to spend more money on something prettier and less practical.

"The Gunnetts have definitely split up," said Jenny, as they browsed the tableware. "I saw Sandy Gunnett again yesterday."

"Sounds like you see more of her than I do of him. What was in her trolley this time?"

"No, she actually came over and told me. He moved out a couple of weeks ago. She thinks he's living in a shared flat in town. I don't know what he did, but she's very bitter about it."

"That's a shame," said Keynes, without an ounce of sincerity.

"It's difficult to choose the cutlery without knowing the man," said Jenny. "Can we go and get a cup of tea and think about it?"

"We've got tea at home," said Keynes.

"I know," said Jenny, squeezing his arm. "But this is nice, isn't it? The two of us, just talking."

It was nice, he had to admit. Plus, the cost of petrol to drive home and back again probably outweighed the savings from making their own tea.

**

As Keynes sat stirring his tea and trying not to show his displeasure at the cost, Jenny was flicking through a catalogue from Kitchen World. They did not have a lot of visitors, although occasionally Jenny's colleagues would pop over. Keynes himself did not have a particularly large social circle, which he thought was probably an advantage in terms of keeping his viewpoint neutral and avoiding bias towards or against particular kinds of people, in

217

much the same way that often political reporters did not vote in elections.

However, he had to admit there were some advantages to having a wife who was better-connected to the community than he was.

"A couple of the children in your class are in the Christ Resurrection League, aren't they?" he asked.

"One last year, one this year."

"Do they ever talk about it?"

"Not really. The kids bully them about it, so they try to avoid the subject. The other mums do, though." Jenny took a sip of her Darjeeling. "Ashanti's dad used to be an investment banker, till he decided to pack it in and join the League."

"They have to hand over all over their cash when they join, I heard."

"That's more or less what they say. It's quite a simple life, though. It's not as though they would have much to spend it on. They've got everything they need up there already. Hardly anyone leaves."

Keynes was struggling for a breakthrough. He had a nasty feeling that perhaps the Christ Resurrection League really was a legitimate religious commune, rather than a tax avoidance scheme. There was a killer on the loose in Northamptonshire and his little diversions seemed to be leading him nowhere.

"Have you heard any rumours about Simon Oakes?" he asked.

"Not really. He keeps quite a low profile, doesn't he? People say he drives a flashy car, but that's not a crime, is it? He does have quite a tough job managing a whole religion."

"It wouldn't be the first time there was corruption at the top," said Keynes.

"You're so negative. Look at Harpit Singh, for goodness' sake. He still takes the time to do something good for charity."

Keynes rubbed his jaw and looked away. "Well, you'll meet him," he said.

Jenny checked her watch. "Is that bean thing still going on? It's not far from here, is it?"

"No, it's not far, but it's just a man sitting in a bath of beans. There's not much to see. You'd be better off going there at the end when he breaks the record."

"I'm not that interested," sniffed Jenny. "It's not worth making a special trip, but I just thought it would be nice to see him while we're here. I've only ever seen him on the news."

Keynes sighed, and replaced his tea cup in its saucer. "I suppose we can drop in for a few minutes, but I think you're going to find it a bit dull."

**

The atmosphere outside Harpit Singh's carpet warehouse was still energetic, but it was starting to feel a little forced. The music seemed to have been turned up louder, and the cheerleaders had changed shifts. There was no longer a queue at the burger van, and they had run out of balloons. Regardless, there was still a curious crowd assembled, and Keynes could have sworn some of those faces were the same ones that had been there when he first arrived.

The clock read 3:23:45. Keynes realised with a sinking heart just how long he had spent shopping. Then Jenny had insisted on stopping for lunch. If he had planned ahead, they could have brought packed lunches and eaten them in the car park.

Singh did not look as enthusiastic as the crowd. He was still trying to run his business from the bath, and was trying to avoid getting bean sauce on his mobile phone as he dialled a number. He had a hands-free set plugged into his ear, and shielded the microphone with his hand to avoid any members of the public hearing details of his business transactions.

However, he looked pale and a little queasy. His brow was bunched up in concentration, or possibly pain, and as he put down the phone he rubbed at his arms.

"Why is it so bloody hot?" Singh could hear him ask Gerry.

"Are you OK? Do you want us to top up the beans? Do you need to get out?"

"You've just had your bathroom break," the DJ chipped in, covering his microphone with one hand. "That would invalidate your record attempt."

"No, I'm staying in till I break that blasted record," said Singh. "Can you get me a glass of iced water or something?"

He writhed in the bath and seemed to be clutching his stomach somewhere beneath the surface of the beans. "Quickly," he added.

Keynes watched with growing alarm.

"Is he all right?" Jenny whispered. "Some of these canned beans have got a lot of artificial colourings in them. They play havoc with some of the kids. There are two in my class who go up the wall if they have tomato soup."

"I don't know," said Keynes, and he genuinely was not sure what was happening, or whether he should intervene. At least he was not wearing uniform and could avoid alarming the audience. "Stay here," he said, and made his way over to the side of the stage.

"Is everything OK?" he asked Gerry, who looked worried and far less menacing than before.

"I don't know. He says his arms and legs are hot, but it's chilly out here, and he's only wearing his trunks."

"Has anyone been near the bath tub while I was away?"

"No, it's impossible. And they couldn't have got near it beforehand. There's always been someone next to it."

"Is he allergic to anything?"

"I've got no idea. He only hired me last week. He said he thought someone might be out to get him."

"Any heart problems?"

"I don't think so, but look at the gut on him."

Keynes made a decision. "I think we'd better get him out of there."

"He won't like that." Gerry looked genuinely worried, and for the first time Keynes wondered how Singh behaved behind closed doors.

Keynes climbed the steps to the stage, keeping his head bowed in an unsuccessful attempt to look inconspicuous. He crouched next to the bath and tapped Singh on the shoulder. Singh looked almost delirious as he turned around.

"Harpit, are you all right?"

"It's so hot in here."

"Let's get you out of the bath."

Singh's face suddenly contorted into a mask of fury. "Over my dead body. This is my first world record and you are not going to mess with it. Harpit Singh is not a quitter."

"Have you got any allergies, or any medical history that might…you know…where baked beans might do something bad?"

"Nobody's allergic to baked beans, you idiot." Keynes recoiled.

The DJ approached. "Is everything OK?"

"Get back over there and don't come near me for another…" Singh strained to read the digital display. "Seven hours and nine minutes. Gerry, fetch my phone. I need to call Miguel about those polyprop Berbers."

Gerry brought Singh's mobile phone up to the bath. Singh raised his right arm to take it, revealing that his skin looked tender where it had been below the bean-line.

Singh dialled a number with difficulty, then held the phone up to his ear with a shaking hand. He gestured for Gerry and Keynes to clear the stage.

"Miguel? Que pasa. It's Harpit. Yeah, that's all very well for you to say…"

Suddenly his body juddered and he dropped the phone into the bath, where it sank slowly into the beans. Singh bent double, holding his stomach, then jerked backwards and collapsed, his head hanging down out of the bath.

There was a gasp from the thirty or so people remaining in the crowd. The DJ turned off the music and approached, as Gerry and Keynes rushed back up the stairs.

"What's happening? I'm going to have to start the nipple count," said the DJ.

"Forget the nipples," said Keynes, pulling out his phone and dialling rapidly. "This is D.S. Keynes, requesting medical assistance to Harpit's Carpet Warehouse, just off the Upton Way roundabout. Get him out of there!"

Gerry pulled Singh out of the bath, having difficulty since the bean sauce made him slippery, and rolled him onto the stage. Singh did not seem to be breathing.

**

Keynes sat anxiously in Shepherd's office. Singh had been taken away in an ambulance, and had looked on the verge of death as the doors had closed. Keynes had wanted to go, but Shepherd had insisted he come back to the station to explain. He was not sure he could.

The door opened and Shepherd barged in, wearing a claret and white Northampton Town football shirt and scarf. Keynes was impressed to see that Shepherd was not wearing a coat. He slammed the door, then sat down heavily.

"Kick-off's at three, so get to the point. What happened down there?" Shepherd demanded.

Keynes could feel his forehead beading with sweat. "I don't really know. We were watching the record attempt, then he seemed to have respiratory problems."

"The early word is they think he was poisoned. Now that's a bit awkward, right in front of a police officer."

"Is he..?"

"Dead? Not last time I heard, but I'm only getting updates every half hour. He doesn't look too healthy, that's all I know." Shepherd leaned forward. "Now, what I'd like to know is why a detective just happens to be down there twice in one day."

The beads of perspiration were beginning to clump together and threatening to run down Keynes' brow. "I was just there to wish him good luck," he said. "It's a good cause, and not that easy to sit still for so long."

"Is that all there is to it?"

"What exactly do you mean, sir?"

Shepherd paused, and cupped his chin in one hand. "It's a bit of a coincidence, wouldn't you say? You're investigating a series of murders that may or may not be related to charities, and then Harpit Singh gets poisoned while you happen to be there. Did you have advance information of a threat to his life?"

Keynes exhaled. "Not exactly," he said.

"You'd better explain what that means. And I'm not going to ask again, so get your story straight first time, because I'm sure I'm not the only one who'll want to hear it."

Perhaps because of the Chief Inspector's name, Keynes often thought he bore a resemblance to a worn-out, shaggy and overweight sheepdog – albeit one which could give you a nasty nip on the ankles if you strayed off course.

"I put two and two together and I thought he was the most likely target. I tried to warn him."

"I see," said Shepherd. "And did you notify Gunnett or any other superior officer?"

"No."

"Right."

"I didn't have any solid evidence. It was all just conjecture, a bit of a hunch."

"Are there any records of your conversations with Mr Singh?"

"I've written it down on my pad. I don't know if he kept any notes."

"I'll need to see that. I'll also be checking with Gunnett, but that can wait till Monday." Shepherd sighed.

"You know, if you'd come to me and told me about this, we could be celebrating a success story – catching the killer in mid-poisoning and saving a local celebrity's life. Instead, we're waiting to hear whether he's going to survive, and whether anyone's going to sue us for not warning him properly."

He pushed his chair back. "Well, I'm going to try to get to the Cobblers, but I doubt I'll get a parking space now," Shepherd said.

"You could try parking round Malcolm Drive and walking up."

"I think I've heard about enough from you for one weekend," said Shepherd. "I want your written explanation on Monday. As they say in the exam papers these days, show your working." He rose from his seat and walked out, leaving Keynes wondering, not for the first time, why he was in trouble for getting it right.

Chapter 28

Keynes' weekend was a dead loss after that. Normally he tried to do something to take his mind off work, like reading books on management or investment. At the moment, he and Jenny had only about eighty pounds free at the end of the month to invest in his portfolio, but he wanted to make sure he was prepared for such time as that amount increased.

Instead, he had to spend his Saturday night at Northampton General Hospital checking on Harpit Singh. In ordinary circumstances, given that Singh was not in imminent danger of dying, he would have waited until Sunday, but his conversation with Shepherd had lent an importance to the timing of his visit.

Shepherd was suspicious that Keynes knew something about the attempt on Singh's life. If Keynes went immediately to the hospital to see Singh, that would confirm Shepherd's suspicions and show a guilty conscience. If he waited until Sunday, that would be too casual. Even if someone like Gunnett had been poisoned, it would be only natural for Keynes to visit him the same day he found out about it. Waiting any longer than that would make it seem that he was deliberately delaying his visit.

As such, the only time that he could visit Singh and maintain an appearance of having been caught unawares by his near brush with death was Saturday night. That actually suited Keynes rather well, as it meant he could miss most of Jenny's dire selection of TV talent shows, which would invade his hearing even if he tried to read his Ayn Rand at the kitchen table.

And so, he found himself at the hospital at just after eight o'clock on Saturday night. Keynes had worn a tie, thinking it somehow appropriate, but now realised it signalled mourning, and hastily pulled it off, stuffing it into his pocket.

He was preoccupied as he walked up the stairs and showed his identification to the nurse on duty. He was not quite sure what to say to Singh. It would be an admission of guilt if he apologised. The strange thing was how disturbed he felt at the fact he had been utterly correct in predicting the Charity Shop Murderer's next victim. It seemed like pure luck, but perhaps there was something in Keynes' thinking that explained the logic behind the murders.

Keynes hesitated outside Singh's room and leaned his hand on the wall. He needed to give a plausible reason why he had expected an attempt on Singh's life and yet had failed to prevent it. There was no good explanation. The only thing in his favour was that Gerry had been present all morning and had failed to protect Singh, too. However the attack had occurred, it could not have been prevented by the time Keynes arrived on the scene.

All the same, it did not make him look good. He needed an excuse in which he seemed to take responsibility but ultimately blamed other people once the logic was followed through.

He tapped his index finger on the wall and tried to think. If he was going to blame anyone, it should probably be Gunnett.

"Why are you here? It's Saturday night. So sad."

Keynes was shaken out of his deep concentration to see Rutkowski standing beside him. He was further shaken to see that the dimunitive Pole was wearing a tight short-sleeved shirt with half of the buttons undone. Rutkowski punched him on the arm in a friendly manner, which still hurt.

"Rutkowski. Evening. What are you doing here?"

"Professional interest," said Rutkowski. "I don't only care about the dead, you know."

He smiled to himself. "Actually, I have a friend here."

That made sense, thought Keynes. Anyone who loved women with enormous bottoms was bound to cross paths with an N.H.S. nurse eventually.

"Did they tell you anything?" Keynes asked.

"I saw some interesting test results. Harpit Singh was poisoned by thallium. It looks like it was administered through the skin."

"How?"

"They tested the beans and found a very high concentration of thallium there. It's amazing he could stand it for so long."

"He kept saying his arms were too hot."

"That correlates."

"Is he going to…"

"Die? Not yet. His liver is in bad condition, but I think that started a long time ago. Thallium attacks the heart and his was already bad, but he was not exposed for very long. There might be some nerve damage in his limbs. We will see." Rutkowski beamed. "It's interesting, though, isn't it?"

Keynes had to agree.

"Is there any way this could be accidental?" he asked.

"You mean, could somebody at a baked bean factory knock a bucket of thallium into the beans, and Mr Singh bought all of the poisoned cans? Maybe I'm wrong, but I don't think so. It was added later, in a very concentrated dose."

"Looks like he was definitely the target, then."

"Yes." Rutkowski bounced from one foot to the other. "In a way, I am a bit sad he didn't die, or this would be my exciting discovery. But I have to leave it to the toxicologists. I'm sure he is a nice guy."

Keynes envied Rutkowski his sunny world view. He was no longer convinced that Singh was a wholly pleasant person. Now he had to find a theory to connect the failed thallium poisoning at the newspaper offices with the successful one at the carpet warehouse. The first one had been so amateurish, yet the second one had nearly succeeded. Could it be that the killer had simply learned through trial and error?

"Is there any way to track where the poison came from?"

"Unfortunately not. But it is used to make semiconductors and spectacle lenses."

"I know you're new here, but surely you've noticed that Northampton doesn't have a manufacturing industry.

If they used it in call centres or pound shops, we might have some leads."

"Wherever they got it from, they got a lot." Rutkowski checked his watch, then pulled up his jeans to conceal his belly a little better. "Do you want to come to Scarlett's? It's happy hour until ten, but it's a happy place all the time."

Keynes politely declined.

"Okay," said Rutkowski. "But one day, when you finish this case, you come drinking with me, okay? We talk, get to know each other."

Keynes frowned, but could not think of a suitable excuse. "I'll see if he's awake," he said.

Rutkowski patted him warmly on the shoulder, which was a bit of a stretch for him. "If you change your mind, come to Scarlett's. Ask for me," he said as he walked away, then started whistling to himself.

The coroner was probably the only perfectly content person in Northamptonshire, Keynes thought. His job was a lot simpler: he dealt only with the dead, and bore no responsibility for their sudden expiration. Keynes, though, could find himself under pressure if he struggled to make headway with the case and the bodies continued to mount up. He prepared for the possible range of reactions from Singh, who was bound to be rather unhappy that Keynes had warned him in rather vague terms of a possible threat to his life then failed to prevent it.

A nurse in reception outside Singh's room told Keynes that the patient was awake, but feeling weak and was not ready for a prolonged questioning.

"I've got a feeling he'll have a few things to say to me," said Keynes.

A tall, brown man was standing outside the room, checking his phone. Perhaps it was his posture that made him seem somehow sophisticated, or perhaps there was something about the curve of his nose. He glanced up as Keynes approached and showed his identification.

"Police," he said. "Well, we've all been waiting for this moment." The man had a tinge of an upper class accent.

"Not sure I understand," said Keynes. "I'm D.S. Martin Keynes. I'm a friend of Harpit's."

"I'm Sunny. I'm his brother."

This piece of information surprised Keynes. Singh had always done his utmost to portray himself as a self-made man of the people, who had dragged himself up by his bootstraps, but his brother was nothing of the sort. Keynes had learned to recognise people who had been privately educated, and Sunny definitely fell into that camp. He also lacked Harpit's easy charm, making his first name seem somewhat ironic.

"How is he?" asked Keynes.

"They don't seem sure. Apparently the toxin takes a few days to do its damage. I don't think they can just flush it out."

"Is he awake?"

"He is, but don't expect gratitude." A tear formed in Sunny's eye. "The number of times I've bailed him out, in school, in business, in life, and he keeps ending up in situations like this. Beans. At his age. I've driven down from Coventry."

"I'll just go in," said Keynes, feeling awkwardness overwhelm him.

"Coventry," repeated Sunny, his voice breaking.

Keynes opened the door to Singh's room warily. The businessman had been nothing but pleasant to him, but he was aware that no one ever became a millionaire without having a nasty streak. He was more worried about whether he could face any legal liability for failing to prevent the poisoning, and was trying to remember exactly what he had told Singh during their conversations.

The room was bare, modern and white, with the only spot of colour coming from several vases of flowers on the window sill. As a private patient, Singh had the benefit of a flat screen television mounted on the wall in front of his bed, but he was not watching it. He was curled up in his blankets, an intravenous drip spiralling out of his arm, and looked pale and worried.

He turned his head as Keynes knocked on the door frame.

"D.S. Keynes," he said, in a voice that sounded thin and raspy.

"You gave us all a shock, Harpit," said Keynes.

"I was a bit shocked myself." He ran his eyes over Keynes, who, despite his best efforts, looked uncomfortable and had his arms crossed. "Any idea what happened?"

"We're looking into this very seriously," said Keynes. "The poison used in the attack was a restricted substance, so that narrows down substantially the number of people who could have had access to it. Now we just need to work out who had access to the scene. It's actually quite a promising starting point."

"They say my hair's going to fall out. I might even need a liver transplant. They're waiting to see whether this stuff gets flushed out of my system. Look at the state of me. A policeman and a bodyguard, and still someone gets through."

Keynes tried not to turn his eyes away. He did not know what to say. Apologising could make him sound culpable, but he wanted to express some sympathy.

"You're made of tough stuff," he said. "This is a chance to bounce back."

He was trying to flatter Singh, but as soon as the words were out of Keynes' mouth he realised how ridiculous they sounded.

"I should be grateful that someone tried to murder me?" Singh looked like he would be furious if not for his weakened condition, but it seemed to hurt him to even glare.

No," Keynes said, struggling. "It's just a unique test of character. No one ever tried to murder Peter Drucker, did they?"

Singh paused to consider this. He rolled onto his back and studied the ceiling. "Not everyone gets their own assassination attempt, do they?" he said in a soft voice. "It means something. A measure of importance. Abraham Lincoln, Gandhi, Tutankhamen, Harpit Singh. For better or worse, that's going to raise my profile, isn't it? People are going to want to hear how I came back from this."

Keynes seemed to have deflected Singh's ire by appealing to his arrogance. This was probably an opportune time to ask questions.

"When we spoke earlier, you couldn't think of anyone who might want to harm you," he said. "Have you had a chance to think any more on that?"

"Obviously someone does. I really can't think who it could be, though. There are plenty of ex-staff who left on bad terms, but no one capable of anything like this. Some suppliers might think I've squeezed them too hard on pricing, but they know they're going to have to deal with me again." Singh turned to look at Keynes. "You don't think it's related to those charity shop murders, do you?"

"It's hard to say."

Singh looked mortified, and this seemed to reinvigorate him. "You can't lump this in with a granny in a charity shop and a student who got hit over the head. They don't have the same profile. I absolutely don't think this is connected. This is an assassination attempt of a prominent public figure."

"I agree the circumstances are different, but we don't have a suspect."

"Who could it be?" Singh held his face with both hands as he tried to think. "The only person who's really got it in for me is that newspaper reporter, but he's too much of a wimp to even think of something like this."

"Chris Shingles?"

"That's his name. He's always sniffing around, being nice most of the time, but asking questions behind my back, as though he's going to find some skeletons in my closet. Honestly, I don't know what his motivation is."

Keynes made a note on his pad, though it hardly seemed like a convincing lead. Shingles himself had been a target of a poisoning attack using thallium.

"I think he was a little concerned about the possible overlap between a commercial enterprise and a charity administered by the same person."

"Overlap?" Singh snorted. "What does he know about overlap? He should talk to Simon Oakes." He wiped his brow with a corner of the bedsheets.

"By the way, I don't suppose you'll have a chance to bring that financial print-out? It would give me something to read while I'm in here. No Wifi. I just want to run through it and see where my accountant went wrong. It's not good to have that floating around out there. Gives the wrong impression." Singh noticed Keynes' face starting to fall. "Nothing urgent. Maybe the next time you're here you could bring it."

"I'll see what I can do," Keynes mumbled. Singh was, for all he knew, on his deathbed, and yet retrieving those accounts was the only thing on his mind.

"And if you could see your way to bringing in a little nip of something…"

Keynes frowned, not understanding.

"Just a nip of gin, something like that. The nurse can be a bit of a stick-in-the-mud. I keep telling her it's medicinal, but she won't have it."

"Is that okay, with the…" Keynes gestured towards the tubing.

"It goes out as soon as it comes in."

"I see. Presumably dinner at chez Keynes is not possible now?"

"Oh…obviously dinner's off, for now," said Singh. "I don't know when I'll be on solids again. But when I get out…"

"Yes. When you get out."

Singh clutched his abdomen again. Perspiration bloomed on his face. "Perhaps you could fetch the nurse on your way out," he said.

Keynes was more than happy to leave. He had always been opposed to the use of hunches and intuition in the place of evidence and hard facts, but the more time he spent with Harpit Singh, the more he was convinced that he was involved in wrongdoing of some kind.

Singh obviously had enemies out there; people he had trampled on his way to the top, maybe even his family. The fact that he had not mentioned any of them, even after an attempt on his life, made Keynes highly suspicious that he had plenty to hide.

**

Keynes tried to have a normal evening, and did not take up Rutkowski on his offer. He watched awful television with Jenny, tried to read a book on Fermat's last theorem, but got stuck on page fourteen, and then had a small glass of ginger beer to help him sleep.

He rarely drank sugared beverages, which showed how stressed and anxious he felt. Keynes was experiencing a strange combination of two types of guilt: first, that he had not prevented Harpit Singh from injury, and second, that he had attempted to befriend someone who was, in all probability, a bit crooked. He had always felt that he was meant to belong to the business world, and thought that once he had served his time in the public sector and earned a decent pension he would tap his contacts and knowledge to develop his own company, or at least work as a consultant.

Now, he wondered if there was any way to succeed in business without being inherently dishonest. Certainly, his favourite local success story did not seem as clear-cut as it had originally.

He slept fitfully, then spent Sunday trying to clear his mind of all things work-related. He did some work in the garden, weeding the borders and trying to work out why one side of the shed was going mouldy. He did not check his phone or email, and, thankfully, Shepherd did not call the house line.

At the back of his mind was the niggling concern that Gunnett might pay a visit to his house. He knew where Keynes lived, after a housewarming party a couple of years ago, and had been unusually silent since the Singh poisoning had come to light. Surely Gunnett must have spoken to Shepherd by now, or at least watched the local news?

Continued silence was probably a bad thing, but Keynes decided he was going to embrace and enjoy it until he absolutely had to deal with whatever bad news was planned for him. He could not avoid the bombshells, but he could ignore them until they were overhead.

He sat with his legs crossed on the lawn and started to wonder whether there was room for a row of runner beans.

Chapter 29

Keynes arrived at the police station on Monday morning with all the vim and vigour of a condemned man whose last meal was not quite what he had ordered.

He started the week in the worst possible way: giving a detailed account of his interactions with Harpit Singh prior to the attempt on his life. Keynes was nervous as he began, and kept referring to his pencilled notes, but as he went on he realised that none of the events reflected badly on him. He had simply been taking precautions, but unfortunately they had not gone far enough. No other detective would even have thought of trying to identify the next person at risk. If things had played out differently, he would probably have received a commendation.

The main thing was, anyway, that Shepherd did not reprimand him. The chief constable leaned back in his chair as Keynes recounted the events of the previous week, only interrupting to check dates and times, but generally he seemed fairly satisfied.

"You can't win them all," he said. "At least you're thinking on the right lines. And maybe you prevented Harpit Singh from coming off even worse."

Keynes had not thought of that. He had reacted quickly, ordering Gerry to drag Singh out of the bath when he had been determined to stay in there for another seven, probably fatal, hours.

"Did you question anyone in the crowd?"

"No," Keynes admitted. "It seemed to be mostly families with kids."

"That might have been a good idea."

"Agreed."

"Would you recognise anyone if you saw them again? Were there any familiar faces?"

"Probably not," Keynes admitted. "The only person I recognised was Chris Shingles from the Tribune, but he didn't get anywhere close to Singh. He's got a bodyguard now, a man called Gerry Williams. I've got his contact details."

"If there had been two of you there, one could have spoken to witnesses while all this was going on. Where was D.I. Gunnett?" Shepherd asked, steepling his fingers on the desk.

"He was following up other enquiries, I believe," said Keynes, being careful in his phrasing in case Gunnett had already been caught in a snooker club or brothel.

"That's what he said, too."

Keynes waiting for elaboration, but that seemed to be the end of the interrogation. Shepherd rose from his chair.

"If you work out who this killer's going to go for next, perhaps you could give us a bit of warning this time?" said Shepherd.

Keynes nodded, and made a swift exit, pleased to have dodged the brickbats he had been sure were coming his way.

He was greeted at his desk by another surprise. A red light blinked on his answering machine.

Easing himself into his seat, he pressed the button, and readied his pencil.

The voice in the message started with an uncomfortable cough. "Sergeant Keynes, this is Simon Oakes of the C.R.L.," it began. "Unfortunately we didn't have time to finish our conversation the other day, but I would appreciate it greatly if you could pay another visit and I may be able to help you in some of the areas we discussed." There was a beep as the message ended.

Oakes had seen the evening news, even if Gunnett had not. Fear was a powerful instrument. Funny how Oakes had come crawling back once he realised that Keynes' warning was credible – even though Keynes had not realised at the time quite how credible it was.

His thoughts were disturbed by an angry Gunnett slamming both hands down on his desk.

"You keep me updated, understand?" Gunnett snarled. "I don't like hearing about this stuff out of the blue."

Keynes feigned innocence. "I left a message with Sandy. Didn't she pass it on?"

Gunnett looked confused for a moment, and then was even angrier. He reached for Keynes' mug, but was disappointed to find it was empty. He replaced it on the desk, sheepishly.

"What does it take?" he said.

With that, Gunnett walked slowly away – an act that was more disturbing than his usual crashing and smashing.

Still, Keynes had managed to keep his meeting with Oakes a secret. He did not want to share this with anyone.

**

First, though, he needed some evidence of the skeletons in Oakes' closet, and he was convinced that Zulu could provide it. Surely the Christ Resurrection League was the only employer that would hire junkies to pick fruit.

Keynes visited Gold Street, and looked in the doorway that Zulu considered his permanent address. There was no sign that anyone had slept there, and even the smell had improved. There was no sleeping bag in sight.

Keynes looked around the backstreets in the area, but could not see Zulu anywhere, nor anyone who might associate with him. This was strange.

He tried the library on Abington Street, but Zulu was not there, either. Nor had any of the staff seen him in the past couple of days.

As a last gambit, he exited the library and turned left, heading towards the Royal Angus. As expected, Wazz was there, selling magazines.

"Buy a copy, mate? It's my last one," said Wazz, then recognised Keynes. Wazz held up his identity badge. "All legit, don't worry."

Keynes dug his hands into his pockets. "I just wanted to ask you whether you'd seen a mutual friend recently. Zulu. Sleeps on Gold Street."

Wazz lowered his magazine, then crossed himself in an approximation of the Catholic ritual. "Poor Zulu," he said.

"Is he dead?" said Keynes, his voice reaching an unintentionally high pitch.

"I haven't heard the latest. But he's not in a good way."

"What happened?"

"They found him out cold on the doorstep of the old arcade. Dunno what he'd injected. He wasn't fussy."

"When was this?"

"Friday afternoon sometime. Maybe evening."

Keynes thought back to Friday and his unsatisfactory conversation with Zulu. He had seemed distant, unresponsive, yet Keynes had not thought it worth calling for medical assistance. In fairness, Zulu had played so many games with him over the course of the past week-and-a-half that Keynes found it hard to judge when he was serious and when he was either mocking him or under the influence of a variety of mood-altering substances. Ironically, Zulu would have been better served if Keynes had arrested him for drug consumption, rather than being lenient and allowing him his liberty.

"Do you know where they took him?"

"Jace said they put him in an ambulance."

"I don't know who Jace is, but thanks, that's really helpful. Do you know which hospital?"

Wazz shook his head.

Keynes gritted his teeth. He was about to walk away, then decided a change of tack was in order.

"Did Zulu ever live at Lazarus Court? With the Christ Resurrection League?"

"Yeah, did he tell you about that?"

"A bit," lied Keynes.

"I've had other friends who stayed there. It sounds OK, but then you hear some horror stories…

"And you've got no freedom. You've got to get up at 6am every day to go and work, then you can't really go anywhere. You're just kind of stuck with the same people all the time. It gets oppressive, you know? All work, no play."

"Yeah," said Keynes, fighting his urge to point out that it was still better than sleeping in an alleyway laced with other people's urine. "Picking apples," he added, hoping to prompt Wazz's flaky memory and point him in a more useful direction.

"Yeah, Zulu was picking apples. It was okay for a bit. Those two liked the rural life, you know? Mellow. After all that, another O.D.…."

"Those two?"

"Zulu and Adamantia," said Wazz, looking confused. "I thought you knew him?"

"I do," said Keynes. "Just, I don't think he ever mentioned…" He made a guess. "Her."

Wazz's face darkened and he viewed Keynes with mistrust. "Anyway, like I said, I don't know where he is." He reached into a satchel and pulled out a handful of magazines. "I've got twenty of these to sell before I can finish, so if you don't mind…"

Wazz rather pointedly turned his back on Keynes, who wondered where in the conversation he had gone wrong.

**

Keynes had been hoping Zulu would be able to give him some ammunition to use in his rematch with Oakes, but Wazz's intelligence had been weaker than, well, Wazz's intelligence. All he had learned that some people were not willing to put in a hard day's work even when the alternative was sleeping rough.

In a last effort before heading off to visit Oakes, Keynes pulled up a list of local hospitals from the bottom drawer of his desk and called them one by one to ask if any unnamed overdose victims had been admitted. Each time, when asked for the name of the patient, the best he could do was to explain that he was a white male with dirty chin-length matted dark brown hair, brown eyes, and possibly wearing a sleeping bag. When the first nurse asked for Zulu's height, Keynes struggled to remember whether he had ever actually seen him standing up.

The answer was the same in every hospital. No unnamed males matching that description had been admitted in the past forty-eight hours.

He hung up. He had very little information to arm him for his encounter with Oakes. If it was like last time, he would come away with nothing, even though Oakes was scared now. He knew that all Oakes wanted was protection, but Keynes could not very well refuse, even though it would have been a good bargaining tactic.

Keynes realised this could put him in a very humiliating position.

Chapter 30

The doorbell rang and Mrs Shingles answered the door shortly afterwards to reveal Keynes, looking distinctly uncomfortable, on the doorstep with his arms behind his back.

"Sergeant Keynes," she said. "Very nice to see you again. Won't you come in?"

He shook his head. "No thank you, Mrs Shingles. Is Chris in, please?"

"I'll just get him." Mrs Shingles went inside, leaving the door a crack ajar. Keynes stood on the doorstep, his breath forming clouds of condensation.

Chris Shingles appeared, fully dressed this time. He seemed surprised to see the detective.

Keynes said nothing, but held out the print-out of Harpit Singh's accounts. Shingles' eyes widened and he made to grab it, but Keynes pulled it back. "Bring me the dirt on Oakes," he said.

Shingles nodded, then disappeared. Keynes could hear him thundering up the staircase, then throwing things around his bedroom in a frantic search for the document, before pounding down the stairs again.

Shingles reappeared holding a manila folder with 'C.R.L.' scrawled on the front in black marker pen. He held it tentatively before him.

"On the count of three…" Shingles began.

Keynes snatched the folder out of his hand. "Don't be so childish," he said. He flicked through the contents of the file to check that it was worth the trade, then tossed Singh's document to Shingles, who caught it gratefully.

"No attribution," he said, and started to walk back to his car. Now he had ammunition.

Unfortunately, as a consequence his idol and would-be mentor, Harpit Singh, recuperating in intensive care after cheating death, might find himself in a spot of bother when he got out of hospital.

Keynes sat in his car and flicked through the dossier. Shingles had been very thorough. There were surveillance photographs of Oakes unloading boxes from the boot of his Mercedes, coupled with public records of his companies' accounts and photocopies of invoices. There was plenty of evidence that pointed to something suspicious, but Keynes could understand why Shingles had not felt confident enough to run it in a story. One small numerical error and his career would end in a very expensive lawyer's letter.

Keynes could also face the same thing if he did not make sure he was totally familiar with the facts. He did not want to take the original documents to Lazarus Court in case the hulking Desmond decided to take them away from him.

He pored over the documents, dozens of pages of them, reminding himself of the time he had learned the rudimentary history of the Tudors in half an hour. He had returned to school after a bout of food poisoning to find that the class had been learning about a totally different branch of the British monarchy and was due to face a test that afternoon. Not wanting to sit the test again the following week, he had gone to the library, found an encyclopaedia and scribbled down the brief history of the Tudors, before condensing it further and then creating a mnemonic to help remember the order of the kings and queens.

The current situation was not entirely similar, he had to admit. He flicked through the pages again and again, memorising names, numbers and dates.

**

He drove up to Riscote, his head swimming with details which he hoped he could retain in his memory at least until he had a chance to question Oakes.

There were still thing that bothered him about the case. He was treating the deaths of Wendy Bevan, Vera Hope, Paul Whitcroft and the attempted murder of Harpit Singh as though they were connected, simply because of the charity angle. Apart from that, though, the attack on Singh had little in common with the others. The deaths seemed to have resulted from opportunistic attacks that perhaps had not even been meant to kill, while the baked beans laced with thallium were a deliberate, calculated attempt to murder Singh.

The profile of the victims was totally different, too. Perhaps the first three had some connection, as their charity work defined them and were low-profile figures to which it was easy to gain access, but Singh was a local celebrity. Either the killer had changed tactics, or this attempt was not related to the others.

Keynes still had no idea what the killer's motive could be. At first he had thought it was someone who had a grudge against those particular charities, but they were all so different: helping cancer patients, fox hunting supporters, Africans and children. Surely it was not possible to have an axe to grind with all of those particular groups.

The other stumbling block was the motive. This was obvious in Singh's case: someone was unhappy that he was, probably, embezzling money while claiming to be a shining light of goodness and charity. If Oakes was the next target, as he himself seemed to believe was possible, then the motive there – exposing hypocrisy – could quite easily be the same.

However, it did not fit with the other attacks. Say, for the sake of speculation, that Vera Hope had been stealing from the charity shop or Whitcroft had used some phony bank account details to boost the commission he earned as a chugger. These amounts would have been negligible compared with the scale of Singh's larceny, and it would have been almost impossible for any outsider to know about these acts. The crimes were trifling and hardly worthy of execution by a high-minded vigilante.

Unless, of course, the killer had started off small and now had greater ambitions. Poisoning someone in front of a crowd with a restricted poison was quite a step up from bashing a drunken student over the head.

Oakes seemed to be worried, anyway. Perhaps he would be more helpful on a second visit and could shed some light on who might want to target him, and why.

Lazarus Court seemed busier today. Some of Oakes' recruits were loading boxes of apples from one of the farm buildings into a white mini-van. They looked up in mild surprise as Keynes drove in, then returned to moving boxes.

Keynes parked alongside Oakes' Mercedes, noting that there was now a packet of indigestion tablets on the back seat next to his protein shake.

He rang the doorbell and started to take off his shoes even before Miss Quelch answered the door.

"He called me," he said, before she could speak. "So I'd appreciate better manners this time."

Suitably cowed, she handed him the slippers. "The Reverend is upstairs," she said.

"Milk, no sugar," said Keynes, and headed upstairs.

Desmond was standing outside the door to Oakes' office, but was no longer smiling. He nodded at Keynes, then opened the door.

Keynes walked through and the door closed behind him. He could hear Desmond turn a key in the lock.

Oakes was standing at the window with his back to Keynes as the detective sat down. He did not turn around.

"There are some powerful sinners in the world," he said. "It seems I may need your protection after all."

As Oakes turned to face Keynes, he noticed the detective was glancing at the wooden crucifix hanging behind the desk. "That protection only goes so far, Detective. Man can destroy anything if he puts his mind to it."

"You wouldn't call me unless you were worried about someone in particular, so why don't you get to the point and tell me who it is?"

"Satan takes many forms."

"Right," said Keynes, preparing to leave. "Just make sure you keep your windows locked and you should be fine. Cheerio."

Oakes noted Keynes rising, and motioned him to stay. "Perhaps I have a rough idea of the general area of the threat," he said. Oakes looked less clean-cut than last time Keynes had seen him: there were dark circles under his eyes and he seemed not to have trimmed his beard this morning. He could not remember whether that was the same jumper Oakes had been wearing at their last meeting.

"Let's assume that you do."

"Various people wish this organisation would fail. Dark forces have long perpetuated a campaign of slander and innuendo against the C.R.L."

"That's not the same thing as trying to kill you, is it?"

Oakes perched himself on the edge of the windowsill. "Perhaps the threat is developing. Perhaps they've realised that they can't destroy us through words alone."

There was a pause as both waited for the other to speak. Eventually, Keynes broke the silence. "If you won't give me a name, this is pointless," he said.

"I can't give you a name," said Oakes, angrily. "But I can tell you that the media, the local authorities, other religious groups and apparently the police would all like nothing better than for the C.R.L. to vanish. Our success sends the wrong message."

"And that's as specific as you're going to get, is it? You want me to give up my time to protect you against some deadly threat you won't even tell me about?"

"You did it for Harpit Singh, I hear. Perhaps even saved his life. But then, he's a Sikh, isn't he? That looks better for your career."

"Don't start with that. Singh co-operated. He gave us access to his business operations and personnel records from the beginning. And I came to him because I thought he might be a target, he didn't ask us."

Keynes leaned back in his chair and glanced up at the ceiling, giving himself a blank white field of vision so he could clear his mind of extraneous thoughts and focus as he pulled the relevant strands of memory into a coherent argument. He produced his pencil from his pocket and tapped it on his notepad as he spoke.

"You were no help at all last time I was here," he said. "Now, after the attack on Harpit Singh, you suddenly want to talk. But you don't want to give away any details.

"That means you think Singh's attacker could be after you. And you've got nothing in common apart from some possible overlap between your businesses and your tax-exempt efforts. There are one or two rumours that Singh's accounting might not be squeaky clean. Some think that could be a motive for the attack. Perhaps you believe that there are inconsistencies beneath the surface of your own organisation that could also lend themselves to the same motive. Do I need to go on?"

"I have no idea what you're talking about."

"And yet your two pitbulls haven't appeared to throw me out."

"Why don't you tell me what you think you know?"

Keynes took in the ceiling again, its flawless white complexion giving him a blank canvas for his thoughts, without distractions. It had obviously been repainted recently, as it had no cobwebs or discolouration. He wondered whether the painter had used a roller or a very fine brush. There were no brush strokes visible, which he knew from experience was very hard to achieve. The ceiling in the spare room could do with a lick of paint.

He had to focus.

Keynes rose to his feet, tapping his pencil against the pad and pacing around the room, making no sound as his slippers sank into the thick carpeting.

"You think someone has information about your business operations," he said. "Either they've tried to blackmail you or they've contacted you in some other way.

"Perhaps someone has seen the ledgers from other companies you deal with and realised that your invoices don't add up. They've realised that you are understating your sales – receiving some payments in cash and not declaring them. They've spoken to your residents here and perhaps conducted their own valuation of the rental value of the rooms, and come to the conclusion that you are massively overcharging your staff for accommodation in the deductions you levy on their salaries. They've realised that some of your church outgoings are hard to explain, and that your official salary may be somewhat understated."

"Nothing but lies. Where is your evidence?" Oakes folded his arms and stared at him.

Keynes bared his teeth in a grin. It was time to show his powers of recall. Oakes had left him an open goal.

"It's hard to pick just one detail that stands out," he said, rocking on his right heel, as if getting ready to take a penalty. "But I would point out that your ledger for the balance received by Higginbotham's grocery for the month of August 2012 was short of the amount recorded in their accounts by around eight hundred pounds."

"Is that it?" Oakes snorted. "You've come all this way to quibble about eight hundred pounds. It's probably just differences in accounting methods. It may fall under a different financial year."

"In August?" It was Keynes' turn to snort. "And it's not just the once. In July, June and May you understated income received from this one supplier by eight hundred pounds each month. We could assume this has been going on for a while, but, like you say, I don't have the proof."

He started to pace around the carpet. "What we do have is surveillance photographs of you meeting your suppliers at motorway laybys late at night to transfer fruit and veg in return for cash. It looks like White's and Hayward's. Perhaps there's an innocent explanation, but I can't think of one.

"The observation on the price you charge employees for accommodation is based on conversations with former residents and an estimate from McCarthy Woods property consultancy, which valued this very property before you bought it in 1994 and which has also done extensive work in the surrounding villages." Keynes turned on his heel. "Based on that information, you appear to be charging your staff on average three hundred and eight pounds a month more than the market rate. Furthermore, your national insurance contributions do not appear to be reflecting that. It seems from other, recorded conversations with former employees that many of them were paid in cash, with no record of their N.I. contributions or payroll taxes. The very fact that so much of your business is run in cash raises suspicions that..."

Oakes had been listening patiently, but his jaw had begun to clench as Keynes went on. The blood had visibly flowed to his face and a vein in his forehead was beginning to pump. As Keynes prepared to begin his next assault with the aid of recently memorised information, Oakes rose to his feet and interrupted forcibly.

"There is no law against paying staff in cash, Sergeant Keynes, and as you may realise with a moment's quiet reflection, a great number of society's dispossessed, some of whom end up joining our community, have difficulty establishing bank accounts, especially when they do not have a postal address. Are we supposed to set up an electronic payroll transfer to someone who has been sleeping in a doorway for the past six months?"

"Well, no," said Keynes. "But there don't seem to be any employment or payroll records for the..."

"As for meeting suppliers or customers in motorway service stations, we often meet at equidistant points for reasons of fuel efficiency and convenience, especially if we have several deliveries to make. European Union regulations actually require us to provide whichever means of payment our clients prefer, which sometimes includes cash. We would actually prefer bank transfers in many instances, as the banks charge us on the basis of how many coins we deposit with them, but as I mentioned, we need to pay many of our workers in cash for obvious reasons and so we need to keep hard currency on hand."

Oakes was on a roll now, and he was starting to walk around the room. Keynes noticed, disconcertingly, that he was barefoot, and that threw his concentration off further.

"Right," said Keynes. "The accommodation…"

"McCarthy Woods, as you say, has not been here since 1994 when the CRL acquired the site, since when it has undergone countless improvements. Heat efficiency has been improved, the plumbing has been overhauled and we could add a couple of hundred pounds to the monthly rental bill were we to charge for the use of furniture. Everyone is here of their own free will and could leave at any time. You may have noticed that the main gateway is always open and there are no fences or other impediments to people leaving at any time."

"But it's a long way," Keynes heard himself saying.

"This whole community is an exercise in trust. People need to accept that and open themselves to the concept, otherwise they might as well leave, which is what some people do. Not many, but some. Those that do leave tend to be those who could not live without material comforts, such as television, or heroin. I'm not sure those are the kinds of reliable witnesses you would wish to put on the stand and question about detailed financial matters."

Keynes realised that Oakes had walked a full circle around him, with Keynes turning in small degrees each time to face him. He was now facing the window again, and blinked as the sunlight hit his eyes. Oakes had pushed out his chest and glowed with confidence, no longer the besieged victim that had greeted Keynes moments earlier. He stood a couple of feet away from Keynes, staring him in the eye, daring him to come up with another challenge.

"But the financials for the pet food business…"

"You can come up with any question about my accounts, anything at all," said Oakes. "I'm not Harpit Singh. I've got an MBA from a London college, and you've got a GCSE in Maths."

"The doggy baskets..." said Keynes, desperately. He wanted to tell Oakes that he had managed an A in Maths and it had been his best subject, but it would not have helped.

"If there is any discrepancy in the financials, and there isn't, I could explain it through mark-to-market accounting, depreciation, goodwill, a mis-statement from the previous period, or a thousand other ways you couldn't begin to understand." Oakes leaned back on the windowsill, a victorious orator. Keynes could see how he had built up such a following. He was charismatic in a smug, overbearing way, but he was also very convincing.

"We can do this all day," he continued, "or you can just inform me of the possible threats to my life and how I can best deter them."

Keynes took a couple of steps over to the chair and sat down heavily. His mouth was dry, and it seemed that Miss Quelch genuinely was not going to bring him any tea.

"Who is out to get you?" he said.

"As I told you before, many people would like this project to fail. I can't name them all. Now, assuming one of them has escalated their threats, how should I defend myself?"

Keynes looked half-heartedly around the room. "Well, you've got Mary Poppins and Quasimodo out there, so that's a good start," he said. "Keep away from the windows, for starters." Oakes twitched, but seemed to realise it would show cowardice were he to move from the windowsill at that precise moment. "You really are going to need to implement some kind of access control. Anyone could wander in and out of this place."

"But that's really the point," said Oakes, nonchalantly rising to his feet and taking a couple of steps to the side of the window, where he leaned on his desk. "We can hardly put barbed wire around the place. That would really give people something to talk about."

"You need to at least keep a record of who comes in and out, especially if there are any vehicles."

"Any vehicles would be noticed. Perhaps we could ask people to sign in and out when they left the main complex. It would have to be voluntary, though."

"Do you lock anything around here?"

"As a rule, no. This community is built on trust. There has never been a violent incident here. Anyone who does not want to conform to our shared values or trust in His love generally leaves fairly quickly." Oakes rapped his fingers on his desk, and Keynes was lost in admiration again. It looked like polished mahogany, of the sort that was totally unavailable since people had started caring about the rainforests.

"Could you provide a police patrol service?" Oakes asked.

"You're in the middle of nowhere. It might be a bit difficult to justify. Especially since you said yourself there are no specific threats."

Oakes pursed his lips. "But if I reported something suspicious, you would send somebody to investigate?"

"Yes," Keynes admitted.

"And can I ask whether you have any suspects in mind for the recent attacks on philanthropic individuals?"

"There are a few lines of enquiry we're pursuing," said Keynes, thinking: You're one of them.

Shingles' dossier had seemed so strong. Keynes had read it with excitement and convinced himself that it would create a bulletproof case against Oakes. Probably not the kind of case he was supposed to put together as a homicide detective, but still impressive, and another string to his bow.

Oakes leaned back in his chair, now totally relaxed. He waited a few moments before speaking, as if to see whether Keynes was going to add anything more.

"Then I think that's all you can do for me," he said. "Thank you for putting my mind at rest."

"That's put your mind at rest?" said Keynes, confused.

"I think I know what I'm up against," said Oakes, meaningfully.

Keynes was about to respond, but he heard the key turning in the lock and Desmond entered, equally meaningfully. He looked somehow more menacing in Keynes' eyes now that the detective was depressed.

Keynes realised he would be leaving very shortly either way, so he took a chance.

"Who's Adamantia?" he said.

Oakes could not help himself. His left eye twitched and he pulled his arms into his body. A consummate professional, he recovered quickly, folding his arms as though it had been his intent all along.

"I can't say I recognise the name."

"Really? You don't remember her being here? It was a shame the way that ended."

Keynes detected the trace of a smirk at the corner of Oakes' lips and realised he had gone too far. He felt Desmond's shadow fall over him and knew he did not have much time.

"What did you do to Zulu?"

"I don't know anyone by that name."

Keynes thought quickly. "Zigga Zumba."

The twitch returned.

Now it was Keynes' turn to smile. "That's the first time I've seen you look worried," he said.

Desmond was in front of him now, not doing anything threatening, but looking enormous, which amounted to the same thing.

"If you want me to leave, you'll have to throw me out," said Keynes. Desmond made an infinitely small movement and Keynes stood up. "It's just an expression," he said, and walked out of the room, his slippers adding little to his dignity.

He walked away backwards, keeping an eye on Oakes to watch his reaction, and Desmond to see whether he was going to attack him. As he backed through the doorway,

Miss Quelch appeared, as if to block him off should he attempt to explore any of the other rooms. He ignored her, and headed downstairs, noticing how steep the staircase felt when wearing slippers.

Keynes halted at the front door, put on his shoes, and stepped outside. Miss Quelch watched him all the way.

He walked back to his car and drove slightly down the driveway until the bend of the road meant Oakes' view was blocked by hedges. Keynes pulled over and applied the handbrake. He punched the steering wheel.

"Stupid!" he yelled to himself. He stopped and took a few deep breaths. Then, as if nothing had happened, he reached into his jacket pocket and removed his phone. He had several missed calls from the station.

He called back, to find that Shepherd had been trying to reach him.

"Why is it that as soon as something breaks in this murder case, I can't get hold of you or Gunnett?" said Shepherd. "Have you got more important things to do?"

"No, sir, sorry. I was questioning someone and my phone was on silent."

"Well, we've got a suspect now. Adrian Shadwell. His boss at the café called to say he's been acting strangely and making threats. Give it your full attention."

Chapter 31

Keynes finally got his cup of tea. He waited for it to cool down while Joan finished her story. She looked agitated, not to mention guilty for informing on her favourite member of staff.

"I'm worried about him, more than anything," she said. "He acts like a hard man, but he's very sensitive really."

"Tell me exactly what he said."

"He said he wasn't coming back because someone had ruined his life. I can't remember the rest." Joan seemed to be being deliberately evasive.

"Perhaps you could try." Joan met Keynes' stare and looked down at the tablecloth. She rubbed her finger absently at a ketchup stain on the PVC surface.

"He was angry," she said, after taking a few seconds to gather her thoughts. "I've seen him upset before, about her, but not heard him angry like this."

"What did he say exactly?"

"He said he was going to tear his head off."

"Whose head?"

"He didn't say. And then do something down the neck. I don't want to swear."

"I think I can fill in the details myself."

"Have you called his home since then?"

"Yes. He's either not there or not answering. I'm very worried about him. He's never had his heart broken before. He's not taking it very well. He tried sending her messages and buying her flowers and things, but she wasn't having it. I just didn't think he'd get so angry."

Keynes took Adrian's home address from Joan. He was sure Adrian was not the killer, but he had to admit it did not look good. He worked next door to the first victim, had a short temper and had recently suffered a traumatic event in his personal life. He was a young, single male, which was bound to put him in the frame for crimes of some kind.

All the same, he was not the type. While the early killings could have been random attacks, the poisoned letter and baked beans showed patience and skill, although admittedly they had been unsuccessful. Adrian would have had plentiful access to baked beans, which the boys back at headquarters would no doubt seize on in their urgency to close the case, but it was unlikely he would have been able to get hold of thallium, or know of its existence. Keynes had only encountered Adrian Shadwell briefly, but had formed the impression that he was not particularly academic in his capabilities.

Keynes called Gunnett. There was no reply, which was as he had expected, but at least if questioned later he could show from the call records on his phone that he had tried to follow the chain of command.

Instead, he chose to use his initiative. Adrian Shadwell was clearly not the Charity Shop Killer, but he had to assume for the purposes of his job there was a tiny chance that he was. There was always a slim possibility that Keynes could be horribly wrong and Shadwell could be garrotting a poppy seller at that very moment.

Keynes called at Shadwell's home, but it was a waste of time as far as he could tell. His parents lived in a third-floor flat in Duston, and while they both looked as though they were made of tough stuff, he formed the impression that they were not lying to him.

The father, Ken, showed him into Adrian's room, which was just big enough for a single bed and a chest of drawers. The wardrobe was in the hallway because there was no space for the doors to open when it was kept inside the room. The floral-patterned wallpaper had been torn behind the door, but other than that there was no evidence of violent tendencies.

"He didn't say where he was going," said Ken. "It's hardly a national emergency when a young lad goes out for the day, is it?"

"Between you and me, it's probably a waste of time me even being here," said Keynes. "But if I didn't follow up a violent threat from someone who works next door to the scene of a murder, I wouldn't be doing my job."

"It's not exactly a violent threat, is it?"

"Mentioning that he's going to tear someone's head off isn't a violent threat?"

"Not these days. It's just a figure of speech."

Keynes had to agree with him.

"Any idea who he would want to hurt?" he asked.

Ken shrugged.

"Jayde's father? Mr Anderson?" Keynes suggested.

"Doubt it. It's not his fault his daughter's a slapper."

Keynes looked more closely at the chest of drawers. On top was an upturned picture in a frame. As he turned it over, he saw that it showed Adrian and Jayde together in happier times.

"He really loved her, you know," said Ken. "If you think he's some kind of thug just because he's got a shaved head and he looks a bit tasty, then you've got it all wrong. He was totally different around her. He was trying to learn French food."

"What about the other night when he chucked something through Mr Anderson's window? Was that him showing his emotional side?"

Ken sucked his teeth. "Well, when he's had a few drinks, that's different…"

"Any chance he might have had a few drinks this morning?"

Ken leaned against the wall in an effort to look casual, and examined the plasterboard. His face eventually settled on a slightly guilty expression.

"Phone's in the hall if you want to use it," he said.

Keynes extracted Mr Anderson's number from his notepad and dialled it with precise but rapid key presses.

Mr Anderson answered on the third ring. "Hello, Anderson residence."

"Mr Anderson, this is Detective Sergeant Keynes. It's probably nothing to worry about, but I just wondered whether you'd seen Adrian Shadwell today."

"Adrian? Yes, he was here five minutes ago."

"Really? How did he seem?"

"Very apologetic. I tell you, he's a different lad when he's sober. Very responsible. He brought me a geranium. I've got too many already, but it was a nice gesture. Offered to pay for the window too, but I told him we can write it off to high spirits. We've all been teenagers, haven't we, officer?"

Keynes tried to think of any similar indiscretions he might have committed as a teen, and could only think of the time he had failed to report an untaxed car parked outside his parents' house.

"So that was it? He just came to apologise?"

"That's it. I tell you, officer, you've misjudged him. I'm guilty of the same thing. You see a skinhead coming towards you and you think he's going to smash something up or threaten you…" There was a pause at the other end of the line. "Well, he did once, obviously, but I'm just saying generally he's a very nice young man. Very thoughtful. I told the officer I've dropped the charges."

Either Adrian's anger had subsided substantially since calling Joan, or Mr Anderson had not been the target of his rage after all.

"Was Jayde in when he called?"

"No, she doesn't stay here anymore. Actually, he's going round there now to apologise to her too."

"Sorry? Where is she?"

"She lives with her fella now, at his place. He's taking them a housewarming gift."

I bet he is, thought Keynes.

"Perhaps you'd better tell me where that is," he said.

Chapter 32

Jayde had moved in with her new, much older boyfriend a couple of days before. Keynes reasoned that it was probably what had triggered Adrian's violent outburst. He hoped he could beat Adrian to the house, and this was possible, since Adrian was relying on the bus to get there.

Ken had admitted that Adrian had taken the news badly when he had found out that Jayde was now even further from his reach. He had gone straight to his room after work, not even bothering to drown his sorrows.

Jayde's boyfriend lived at a terraced house off Billing Road, in the suburbs of Cliftonville. Keynes travelled there as fast as he could, though he was careful to obey the speed limits and did not feel the occasion warranted using his lights or siren. If he was barking up the wrong tree, he preferred as few people as possible to know about it until everything was over and he could file his own version of events in a neat, immutable email.

As he turned into Harding Street, he could see he was just in time: Shadwell was ringing the doorbell. Keynes found a parking spot, but it was for residents only, plus it would mean a difficult parallel parking manoeuvre. He hesitated as he wondered whether he was justified in parking there. Perhaps he should see how the encounter turned out in its early stages, and take it from there. There was no point committing a parking offence unnecessarily. Adrian did not appear to be bearing housewarming gifts, but that did not necessarily mean he had violent intentions.

The front door opened and Gunnett appeared, dressed in a tracksuit. Keynes' foot nearly slipped off the brake.

Gunnett said something to Adrian, who replied. Gunnett responded aggressively, jabbing his finger in Adrian's chest and using uncompromising language, but was surprised when Adrian interrupted his tirade by punching him in the face.

Gunnett doubled over, holding his nose, and Adrian dragged him out of the house by his neck. The teen tried to punch Gunnett in the nose again, but the Inspector had slipped onto one knee, and Adrian's fist ended up hitting him in the ear, which seemed to be equally painful, judging by the reaction.

Adrian now had his bearings. He rained punches down on Gunnett's face, until the officer's lip burst open, leaving a thin, bloody stream to run down his chin. The attack was frantic, and though Gunnett was doing his best to defend himself, he simply was not fast enough to fend off the blows. His left eye looked badly swollen where Adrian's right hook had connected with it half a dozen times in as many seconds.

Keynes watched with mixed feelings. On one hand, a police officer was being attacked. On the other hand, Shadwell had gone off at a ferocious pace and there was a good chance he would wear himself out without Keynes needing to use any restraining measures, which were always hard to justify in police reports if the subject was unarmed. There was talk that they were going to get a few tasers for the office, but he had delayed applying for one until he had read more research on their effects.

He was torn, and so was Gunnett's tracksuit, as Shadwell dragged him to the ground, the gravel from the driveway scraping Gunnett's cheek. Adrian kicked him in the stomach and Keynes could hear the resulting grunt from his vantage point within the car.

That was enough, he decided. As Adrian stepped back for another shot at Gunnett's abdomen, Keynes carefully began his parking manoeuvre. It took about twenty seconds by the time he had straightened up, during which time Adrian had booted the Inspector in the gut half a dozen more times.

Keynes shut off the engine and stepped out of the car.

"That's enough, Adrian," he said.

Adrian turned around in shock, his foot still hanging in mid-air. Gunnett grunted, his eyes squinted in pain through a mushy mask of red.

Keynes walked over to the pair of them, keeping a safe distance of around four feet from Adrian.

"I think you'd better leave it there, don't you, Adrian?"

Adrian looked at him in puzzlement. He was starting to pant, and as the adrenaline began to wear off he lowered his foot to the ground and took a stumbling step backwards.

"I'm D.S. Keynes. We spoke earlier at Joan's Café."

"Come to stick up for your mate?"

"Actually, I've come to stop you doing something stupid while the shop next to yours is the centre of a murder investigation, but apparently I was too late."

Adrian looked down at Gunnett's crumpled form, as if seeing him for the first time. Gunnett's tracksuit was ripped around the neck, and blood ran from his nose and lip down to the opening of his T-shirt. The skin around his left eye was starting to swell shut.

Adrian took a deep breath and tried to slow down his breathing. He looked at Keynes carefully.

"Where's your stick?"

"I haven't got one."

"Do you not get one, or you just forgot to bring it?"

"I could request one, but it takes a couple of weeks. I've had the training."

Adrian looked Keynes up and down. Keynes was not vain about his physical appearance, but he did enough exercise – press-ups and sit-ups in the morning, and jogging with short bursts of sprinting a couple of times a week – to keep himself in robust physical condition, plus he was a little over six feet tall and knew that was usually good enough. Adrian was about five ten, but much heavier set. Keynes widened his stance a little and maintained eye contact, even as Gunnett clutched his stomach and moaned in the gravel.

"Am I under arrest?"

"I would have thought this is at least worth a chat down the station," said Keynes. "Myself and Inspector Gunnett appear to be the only witnesses, which makes it a bit tricky, though."

Adrian's shoulders relaxed and he took a step back.

"Go and stand by the car, and don't try any funny business," said Keynes. "I know where you work, I know where you live, and I know you've got pretty flowers on your bedroom wallpaper."

Adrian hesitated for a moment, then, without a word, walked over to Keynes' car and stood there silently, watching the two officers.

Gunnett spat out a mouthful of blood and rolled over to look up at Keynes.

"Have you been there the whole time?"

"I was making a three hundred and sixty degree evaluation of the situation," said Keynes. "Evaluating the optimal tactics for intervention."

"Is this the optimal outcome?"

"I restrained the attacker without laying a finger on him. I think that's pretty good."

"Because he wore himself out kicking me."

Keynes crouched down to take a better look at Gunnett, who looked at him distrustfully.

"Here's the thing, Gunnett. You're a married police officer who's been knocking around with a nineteen-year-old girl. How do you think that's going to look when it all comes out?"

Gunnett rolled onto his back, flinching at the pain, and covered his face with his hands.

"You've been bunking off work, and I've covered for you," said Keynes. "You ignored all my phone calls, which could have been highly important. I thought you had some kind of personal problems, or perhaps you were actually doing some very sensitive work related to that murder case we've been working on. Instead, I've been taking up the slack so you can mess around with a girl young enough to be your daughter.

"Your hanky-panky has basically been paid for by the taxpayer."

Gunnett muttered something, but it was muffled by his hands, and by the blood still running from his nose.

"What was that?"

"I said, do you know what it's like, being with a nineteen-year-old girl?" yelled Gunnett, pulling his hands away to show his sweaty, blood-streaked face.

Keynes was expecting some kind of crude information about the advantages of a lithe, supple young woman compared with the, admittedly, over-the-hill one Gunnett had married, but Gunnett surprised him.

"It's a very emotional age," said Gunnett, his voice breaking a little. It was hard to distinguish from the blood and sweat that spattered his swollen cheeks, but the Inspector appeared to be welling up with tears. "She's got so much to deal with. Changes with her body, with her emotions. It's a very confusing time.

"She's got so many choices open to her, it's overwhelming for a girl that age. I've got to help her. She's got no one else who understands."

"I suppose this also explains why you didn't want to spend much time on Gold Street," said Keynes. "You didn't want Adrian to see you."

Gunnett covered his eyes again, and this time he was definitely crying.

"It's all done now, isn't it?" he said.

Keynes nodded.

"You must be loving this." Gunnett looked at him with accusing eyes, which were wet but still angry.

"Not really," said Keynes.

Adrian shuffled awkwardly from one foot to the other as he watched them.

Chapter 33

Keynes took them both back to the station, nobody daring to speak. It was as though neither Adrian nor Gunnett were quite sure which of them were in more trouble. Adrian sat quietly in the back, while Gunnett stared idly out of the passenger window as if in a daze, or slightly concussed. Jayde definitely had a type, thought Keynes, as he compared the two shaven scalps and sulking expressions.

The way Keynes saw it, Gunnett was in trouble whatever happened, but if he was too embarrassed – or if Shepherd told him to – he might drop the charges against Adrian. That would not set a good precedent, but it might avoid damaging publicity, and embarrassment, for the police force.

The trouble was, though, Keynes was mixed up in this mess. Through no fault of his own, he was going to be in trouble for failing to report Gunnett's disappearing act to Shepherd. He could prove through his phone records that he had tried to keep Gunnett updated and had gone it alone in the absence of any other guidance, but now things like the failure to protect Harpit Singh were going to be attributed to Gunnett leaving a Sergeant in charge of the investigation.

Keynes was going to be forced to list what he had known and when, not to mention that he would need to explain why he had not told anyone of his suspicions. He could treat this as a job interview and give perfect, bland answers, but he knew they would not wash with Shepherd.

He sat at his desk going through the notes on his pad and making sure he could make it sound as though he had a good reason for everything he had done over the past nine days. At the time, he had thought every step he took was entirely logical, but it was a different thing to see it in writing a few days later. He would be entirely honest in his account, but might also omit a few of the trickier details if possible.

The sheer length of time Gunnett had spent in Shepherd's office told him that his own interrogation was going to be long, slow and painful. Keynes was sure that Gunnett was doing his best to lay all the blame on him. He would have loved to do the same, but Shepherd seemed to have a code of loyalty, meaning that he would view negatively any attempt to discredit another officer.

He could see Gunnett through Shepherd's window at the end of the room, but the icepack Gunnett was holding against his eye made it difficult to see his facial expression. It was quite clear, even from this distance, though, that Shepherd was red in the face. Shepherd's expressive finger-pointing underlined the impression that Gunnett was in deep trouble. Keynes had expected no less.

At length, the rather one-sided discussion was over, and Gunnett trudged out of the room, his head lowered. He glanced over to Keynes on his way out, but could not muster the enthusiasm to make one of his usual derogatory comments. Gunnett looked like a broken man.

Keynes tried to act as though he was not dreading the moment when he would be called to the headmaster's room to be read the riot act. The main thing was that he should not behave as though he had something to hide. It felt like he was about to be audited.

His hopes at playing it cool disintegrated when Shepherd leaned out of the doorway and bellowed: "Keynes! My office, now."

The whole office turned to watch, and he did his best not to give them the satisfaction of looking terrified. Biggs seemed to find it particularly amusing, and Keynes could see it was killing him not to make some kind of smart remark while Shepherd was there. His moon face creased with the effort of trying not to yell out.

Keynes strode over to Shepherd's office, calm yet purposeful, and closed the door gently behind him.

"Take a seat," said Shepherd.

As Keynes was sitting, Shepherd fired off his first volley, catching him unawares. "And I thought you were the intelligent one."

"Sir?"

"Do you realise what kind of problems we could have if there turns out to be any link – any link at all – between Adrian Shadwell and the charity shop murders? He's going to claim he won't get fair treatment because he beat up a copper. And his credibility as a witness is shot to pieces.

"D.I. Gunnett has agreed not to take his grievance with Mr Shadwell any further, and we'd better hope that's the end of it. Of course the dolly bird will know about it, and she'll tell her friends and her parents, and they'll tell their friends, and a little bit of the respect they used to have for us will be gone forever, but at least it won't get as far as court."

"It's regrettable."

"It is regrettable. I regret no one told me this situation was developing, until it had already exploded in Gunnett's face."

Keynes tried to remember the order of events. "I didn't know he was Jayde Anderson's boyfriend until he opened the door."

"But you knew he'd been bunking off work to go and see her? In the middle of a murder investigation! By his own admission, he's spent most of the past week with her. They've been more or less living together, and he's been waiting on her hand and foot. She sends him a text message saying she wants more banana ice cream and he goes running to bring it to her."

"I knew he'd been unreachable for parts of the week," said Keynes, carefully, making sure not to break eye contact with Shepherd. "As far as I knew, he was following up his own part of the investigation. I assumed it was something sensitive and he thought I couldn't be trusted."

Shepherd's colour, which had been subsiding to his usual pasty complexion littered with burst veins, grew redder again. "And did he seem to be making much progress from his enquiries in the frozen food aisle?"

Keynes looked down at his knuckles, which he had realised he was kneading. "He hadn't been giving me a lot of feedback," he said. "I wasn't sure whether that was his normal way of working on this kind of case."

"You should have let me know something was wrong," said Shepherd.

"I didn't know anything was wrong."

"You're a detective. You should have been able to work it out." Shepherd leaned forward, and even at a distance of four feet Keynes could feel the heat rising off his face. "Loyalty's all well and good," said Shepherd, "but your first loyalty is to me. I need to know I can trust you."

He had a point, Keynes had to admit. Keynes tried the line that he had rehearsed from reading similar sentiments in American management books, which seemed to boast about failure. "I'll make sure it doesn't happen again, and I'll ensure I learn from the experience," he said.

"Don't give me that nonsense. This isn't a paper round. You're a detective investigating murders. You can't make mistakes. You make a mistake and the chain of evidence gets ruined, or someone else gets killed. You've got to be like the Pope – infallible."

Shepherd looked down at the papers scattered across his desk, and pulled a handful together. "I mean, where are we at with the Gold Street murder? No progress at all, as far as I can see. I gave you a nice soft case, a little old lady bashed over the head, and you haven't got anywhere with it. Likewise with the others." Shepherd lifted a page from the bottom of the pile. "You seemed to be getting somewhere with the Harpit Singh angle, but you don't seem to be able to explain how you got there, so it doesn't help us get any closer to the killer.

"I don't know if you've done much reading on the subject, but murder cases that aren't solved in the first two weeks don't get solved."

"We're making progress."

"Forget 'we'. Gunnett's off the case."

"Is he..?" Keynes did not finish the sentence, but his meaning was obvious.

"We'll see," said Shepherd. "We're short on officers as it is, and I won't get the headcount back under this government, but it might be better if he finds work elsewhere."

Keynes was momentarily overjoyed, though tried not to show it. A split-second later, his spirits had sunk anyway, as he reflected that he probably faced a punishment of his own.

"And what about me?" he asked.

"I had high hopes for you," said Shepherd. "If we hadn't had a freeze on promotions, perhaps your fast-track would have come through by now. Now I'm wondering if you're cut out for this job."

He shuffled his papers and put them into a slightly neater pile. "For now, you finish the job, then we see where we stand. But tomorrow I'm going to put you with someone else. Someone who's going to keep a closer eye on you. No running off to pursue your little side projects. You clock in, you tell him where you're going, who you're seeing, and if you get any breakthroughs you tell him immediately. He's going to keep you on a string so that you don't wander off and step in something."

This was going to be worse than Gunnett's laissez-faire style of management, thought Keynes. He would not have been able to follow up leads related to Harpit Singh and Simon Oakes if he had needed to bring along the blustering, lead footed D.I. Gunnett to meet them. He would be suppressed, silenced, reduced to following every step in the plod's handbook rather than using new thinking to solve the case.

It all depended, though, who his new partner was going to be. With a bit of luck, it would be someone open to new ideas; someone dynamic and with a willingness to let youth try breaking with convention.

Chapter 34

Biggs leaned on the corner of a formica-topped table in one of the meeting rooms. It was nearly eleven o'clock and he was eating a Cornish pasty. Keynes could not understand why some people had to eat their breakfast at work. It showed poor time management and was incredibly unhygienic. Time spent eating was, ergo, time that was not spent working. In his view, people who ate at their desks should make up the time later, in line with his thoughts on smokers.

"I haven't been following the case, so bring me up to speed," said Biggs, adjusting the waxy wrapper so that he could access more pasty. "You've got how many victims? Four?"

"Three dead, and two attempted poisonings. The first killing we knew of was Vera Hope, who was working in the British Cancer Foundation shop on Gold Street. Her body was found in the shop window…with a pole inside her."

"It wasn't Rutkowski, was it?" Biggs coughed out a lump of potato in his amusement. "All right, it's just a joke, no need for that look. Anyway, he only likes the larger ladies. Go on."

"She had suffered a fatal blow to the head. Then two days later, Paul Whitcroft, a student, was hit over the head after collecting for charity. He was found in the doorway of the Donkey Salvation League shop in Abington Street, having broken through the glass of the door as he fell. Seems to have been a combination of concussion and blood loss that killed him."

"OK. Seeing the charity angle."

"There's also another one I think might be, which happened a few days before Vera Hope died. Wendy Bevan was found dead in a telephone box in Litchborough, having had a heart attack. A witness seemed to think she was being chased by something, or someone." Keynes did not mention the wolf, as he could imagine that Biggs would only use it as an excuse for more bad jokes. "She was a prominent member of the Rural Defence Association."

"Okay. That one's a bit flimsy."

"The two poisoning attempts were made on Chris Shingles, the deputy editor at the Northampton Tribune. He received a letter with a small amount of the toxic substance thallium, but not enough to do any harm. We've analysed the letter, but no clues.

"The second was Harpit Singh. You probably saw that one on the news. There's no chance of getting any forensic evidence from the scene. It was outdoors and there were families wandering all over the place."

"Right. Any suspects?"

"There's one, but I think he's a long shot. Adrian Shadwell, who worked in the café next to Vera Hope, has a few violent incidents in his history and had been involved with arguments with Miss Hope in the weeks leading to her death."

"That's the bloke who decked Gunnett?"

"Yes, if you want to put it like that. He had recently split up with his girlfriend, which might be an inciting factor to all this, but as I said, I don't think he's our man."

Biggs looked off to the distance suddenly, and lowered his pasty, as a thought came to him. "Hang on, is that Joan's Café?"

"Yes," said Keynes, looking at him expectantly. Perhaps Biggs was about to surprise him.

"Do they..." Biggs hesitated, then tapped the desk with his right index finger. "Do they still do that bumper breakfast for four quid?"

"I don't know, Inspector."

"Anyway, he sounds possible. No one else?"

"No." Keynes could not bring himself to name Oakes. He felt he was justified in keeping his suspicions to himself. The only evidence he had was in relation to possible fraud and employment offences. If Oakes had anything to do with the killings, Keynes had yet to prove it. He still thought Oakes was more likely to be a target than a perpetrator, but he would be happy to be proved wrong.

"What about the fourth one? Shingles?"

Keynes was suddenly shaken out of his complacency. "Chris Shingles?"

"Yes. The newspaper reporter."

"He was on the end of a poisoning attempt. I think that rules him out."

"It was a pretty harmless attempt, wasn't it?" Biggs finished the pasty and scrunched up the wrapper, then using it to wipe the remnants from the corners of his mouth. "Maybe the killer got more sophisticated by the time he came to Harpit Singh, or maybe Shingles sent the letter to himself so that he would be above suspicion, using just enough poison so that it looked dangerous. He's got no links with charities at all. I can't see why he would be a target."

Keynes felt his mind and all the information in it slanting to one side. If Biggs was right – and it did sound plausible – that meant all of his lines of investigation had been a total waste of time. Perhaps Shingles had put together the Oakes portfolio to distract him. And perhaps his obsession with bringing down Harpit Singh was more than just journalistic.

"He was at Singh's carpet warehouse on the day of the poisoning attempt," said Keynes. "He didn't get anywhere near him."

"He didn't need to. He just needed to get near the bath. In fact, he didn't even need to do that. He could have tampered with the beans when they were still in the can. If he had access to thallium to post that letter, he could have used it to poison Singh, too."

"He lives with his parents," Keynes protested.

"He's not bringing the bodies home, is he? Maybe he's got another location where he keeps his poison and his murdering clothes."

"It's possible, I suppose." Keynes thought it over from this new angle. "All of the victims had appeared in the Tribune. In fact, they'd all been in the newspaper very frequently – at least, the charities had." He looked up at Biggs, and realised that he had quite probably been outsmarted by someone who had not even bothered to read any of the case notes.

Perhaps he had misjudged Biggs. He looked like he was paying no attention, but he seemed to have good recall of information once it had been explained to him, and he had drawn connections that had been staring Keynes in the face for days without becoming apparent. It was utterly discouraging to think that Biggs might be inherently better at being a homicide detective through pure talent, when Keynes worked so hard and Biggs was so lazy. And fat.

"Do you think we should bring him in?"

Biggs held up one hand to silence him. "Calm down. There's no point panicking about this." He looked at Keynes, showing no signs whatsoever of any tension or apparent effort. "Do you know how many murder cases I've worked?"

"Ten?" Keynes guessed.

"Less than that," said Biggs, frowning momentarily. "That's not the point. The point is, the killers always make a mistake.

"Half the time they want to get caught, and they'll give you more and more rope till it's enough to hang them with. They'll be so frustrated watching us and wondering what's going on with the investigation, even if we're getting nowhere. The other half of the time, they'll make a mistake because the pressure starts to get to them.

"Either way, we could sit around in this room all day doing nothing and it would still cause something to happen that's going to lead us to the murderer."

Biggs hopped off the edge of the table with great difficulty and dusted off the crumbs that had gathered on his lap.

"Now, for today, just concentrate on proving that all of these cases are related," he said. "I'm still not sure about that phone box woman. And try to work out where Chris Shingles fits into it. Maybe he's got a motive. We've already got Adrian Shadwell. I'll see what he's got to say. He knows he's got to co-operate."

"Should I come?" said Keynes, starting to stand, but Biggs motioned him to sit.

"I think you've had enough excitement for one day," he said. "Plus Shepherd's told me you're not to go near him. He's just covering himself in case later someone decides it might prejudice the case."

Keynes' face was a mix of dismay and consternation. "So I'm just supposed to sit quietly at my desk and read a magazine?"

"If you want. Or you can firm up the motives, like I just asked you to. Or you can go home and do your ironing. Forget about today. It's a write-off. We'll get started properly tomorrow." Biggs paused for a moment.

"Call me if you need to, but not before half ten, and not after six in the evening. That's one of my rules. Work-life balance, you know.

"Get on with something useful, just don't contact any witnesses or suspects today. We don't need to make this more complicated than it already is. We'll work out how to approach this tomorrow. For all we know, we've got the killer in custody already."

Biggs patted him on the shoulder as he left. Keynes did not feel particularly encouraged. He was surprised that Biggs had actually shown some aptitude, but he was disappointed that he was not showing more urgency.

What was worse, Keynes was being sidelined. Right now, Biggs and Shepherd were working on the theory that Keynes had brought them the killer, and he was not even allowed to join the interrogation. He sensed that, had Shepherd had more free staff available, he might have been dropped from the investigation entirely. Keynes was their key asset in this case – it seemed as though Biggs had not done any preparation before taking charge – and yet he was being treated as a liability.

As it was, he knew that no one was likely to trust him with anything important in the near future. He would need to pass all of his leads through Biggs and seek approval for every tiny piece of independent thinking. In addition, he was sure Biggs would give him all of the tedious, time-consuming work to carry out, while the senior officer lounged at his desk eating baked goods. Keynes felt like he had been demoted without anyone having the decency to tell him.

The worst thing was, he was sure he had done everything properly. It was hardly his fault that Gunnett had been fooling around with a ridiculously young girl, and who had, in one theory of events, triggered a psychotic episode in Adrian Shadwell that had left several charity workers dead.

Keynes returned to his desk, ignoring the knowing glances of his colleagues, and began to plot his way out of detention. He needed to come up with something good, without interfering with the investigation. That ruled out speaking to Chris Shingles, who would have been a useful source of information about Oakes right now, given that Keynes' approach had not borne much fruit.

He wondered whether he could go back to Gold Street and just wander around. Perhaps something would inspire him. Or he could track down the magazine seller, Wazz, and try to get to the bottom of the events that had happened to Zulu while he was at Lazarus Court. He seemed sufficiently removed from the murders for Keynes to be able to contact him without disrupting the investigation.

He remembered, though, that Zulu was possibly dead.

Keynes froze for a moment, then reached for his telephone, trying not to look too energetic in case anyone noticed. He dialled one of the numbers already on one of the sheets of paper in front of him.

"Hello, this is Detective Sergeant Keynes from Northamptonshire Police. Yes, I called yesterday to see whether any unnamed twenty-something white males had been admitted for a drug overdose. I've got a name now: Zigga Zumba. As it's pronounced."

He waited for an answer. Then he dialled another number from his list. Within five minutes, he knew Zulu was alive, and he knew where he was.

Chapter 35

Zulu's ward was a world away from the one in which Harpit Singh was recuperating. While Singh had enjoyed a private ward with satellite television channels and a bed which reclined at the touch of a switch, Zulu was in a room with five others, his privacy maintained only by a curtain around the bed, which was currently drawn open. The room had a pungent odour of disinfectant, or possibly pickled onions.

Zulu looked like he had been hit by a very dirty bus. His face managed to look drawn yet puffy, and there were purple swellings around his eyes. An intravenous drip was attached to a vein in his bruised left arm, and his hair looked dirtier than usual. He still smelled of preservatives, perhaps because he seemed to be sweating out the contents of his bloodstream. As he stared at the ceiling with wide, staring eyes, his legs twitched under the covers, and Keynes noticed another clear plastic tube leading out from under the sheets.

He was startled to see Keynes standing at the foot of the bed, dressed in casual clothes – or at least, what Keynes considered casual clothes.

"Sergeant!" said Zulu. "Thank God. My bedpan's nearly full."

"Who do you think is the figure of fun here? Me or you?"

Zulu sank back into his pillow, which was wet where his face had been laying. "Did you at least bring me some grapes? Or a Baudelaire?"

"I'm not your dealer," said Keynes, uncertainly. "You got yourself into enough trouble with alcohol and skag."

"I think that Merlot was corked. I've got half a mind to send it back."

"You were in a coma for twelve hours, and you think it's funny? You could have suffered brain or nerve damage. You were found curled up next to a skip, not breathing and soaking in your own…substances. They've still got the sleeping bag, if you don't believe me."

Zulu was staring at his own hand now, though Keynes did not believe he was as dazed as he pretended to be.

"You should really give this naloxone a try," said Zulu. "The wonderful side effect is that I can't concentrate on anything you're saying."

Keynes located a chair at the side of the room and dragged it over to Zulu's bed. He sat down, crossing his arms, and then wished he had reversed the chair to look more intimidating.

The National Health Service was a wonderful thing, Keynes thought. It was a mark of civilisation, setting modern Britain apart from the pre-war era, and the Americans. But its fatal flaw was that it was open to everyone, even those who were squandering its resources through their own self-destructive tendencies. Someone who actively harmed themselves should not be bailed out by the state. Junkies, smokers, drinkers, the obese – they were all trying their hardest to waste public money.

"Are you pleased with yourself?" said Keynes. "Wasting taxpayers' money like this so that you can be scraped up and revived?"

Zulu met his glare. "This wasn't an accident," he said. "I was willing to bear the consequences."

"Rubbish. It was a cry for help. Teenage girls just write in their diaries. It's much more mature."

Zulu tilted his head back and stared at the ceiling. He did not speak.

Keynes hated this kind of silent treatment, but had to admit that he had started off on the wrong foot. Zulu was a difficult person to read at the best of times, but it seemed today he was not going to be of any use. It seemed pointless to try to match the silence, and the longer he stayed here, the more chance that he would miss a phone call from Biggs. He did not want to lie about his location. He also did not want any of the other officers to speak to Zulu. Keynes had a hard-to-fathom feeling that he had given too much away about himself to Zulu, without finding out much in return.

"I spoke to Simon Oakes," said Keynes. Zulu's face did not react, but his leg twitched.

Keynes waited a moment, then added: "He told me about you and Adamantia."

"You're lying," said Zulu, still staring at the ceiling.

"All right, I'm lying. Now I'll be honest with you, and I haven't even told my superior officer this: I'm investigating Oakes. I've got a big bundle of documents that seems to point to systemic fraud in the accounts of the Christ Resurrection League and its associated companies. I'd love to put Oakes in jail, but I'm sure he's got lawyers and accountants who would be able to explain away all the discrepancies in his accounts, or at least drag out the legal process for so long that he gets away with an out-of-court settlement."

Keynes leaned forward, and he could see that Zulu was, despite his best efforts, paying attention. "Now here's the thing: I came to Oakes because I thought he was a potential target for the Charity Shop Killer. Perhaps he still is. But I'm also wondering whether he poses a threat himself. There seems to be a code of silence around that place, and an awful lot of people seem desperate to leave.

"You seem to have been involved in something up there. You're not talking, and nor are your friends, but if there's something that incriminates Oakes, I want to know about it.

"From what I can tell, Adamantia was your girlfriend. She had a drug overdose, perhaps even died. I think it happened while you were both staying at Lazarus Court."

Zulu leaned forward and rested on his elbows. "You're making it up as you go along," he said. "You think I'm going to jump in and help you."

"Oakes was either responsible in some way, or you didn't like the way he reacted afterwards. Either way, you hold it against him."

It looked as though Zulu might speak at any moment. Keynes just needed to come up with the right combination of words, but he was running dry. He had no idea whether he had got anything right so far. He just knew that it sounded convincing to him. He took a wild guess.

"Would Oakes be able to get hold of thallium?"

Zulu, who had seemed interested for a brief moment, rolled onto his side, away from Keynes.

He had blown it. He had been close, but somehow he had reached a little too far and spoken before he had finished thinking. Keynes waited, but this witness was not going to shed any more light on whatever crimes Oakes had committed.

All was lost. He might as well roll the dice. "You know about science and that kind of thing," he said. "Though I have no idea how. Where would someone get hold of thallium in Northampton?"

He saw Zulu's back move, in what appeared to be a shrug. "Your best bet's probably the university," he said, to Keynes' surprise. "They've got a well-equipped lab, and students can hook you up with most stuff." He held up his left arm, tube and all. "Exhibit A."

It made sense, Keynes thought, and he could pass the tip to Biggs without saying where the idea had originated. Whitcroft had been a student there. Perhaps there was a connection somehow.

He still did not understand Zulu. He seemed intelligent, but seemed set on self-destruction, or at least comfortable apathy. Keynes felt that there was more he could extract from Zulu, but he did not know how. He had not exactly been friendly towards the vagrant during their first few meetings, but he had the sense that it would not have helped. Zulu did not want anyone to break the ice.

"Are you…" Keynes fumbled for the right words. "How long do you have to stay in?"

"I can probably leave today."

"That's good news."

Zulu did not respond, and it occurred to Keynes that, depending on his alternatives, sleeping in an N.H.S. ward for a few days more might actually be a better option. He rubbed his hands together.

"Right then," he said, not being able to think of anything better. "I will find out, you know."

As he stood up, Zulu spoke, still facing away from him. "What's a homicide detective doing reading company accounts?"

It was Keynes' turn to shrug. "You've got your hobbies, I've got mine."

He walked out, thinking: Zulu likes puzzles.

Chapter 36

Next morning, he waited patiently at his desk for Biggs to arrive. Keynes had made the mistake of arriving at nine, when Biggs had more or less given notice that he would not turn up to the office until after ten.

Keynes busied himself by cleaning up the file on Whitcroft. It struck him that the death had not been investigated particularly thoroughly. At the time he had assumed it was just another drunken student wandering into trouble, and perhaps it was, but neither he nor the intermittently attendant Gunnett had bothered to tie up the loose ends. They had not even asked Whitcroft's housemates for their full details.

Biggs strolled in at ten twenty-five, carrying a brown paper bag stained with grease. Keynes hoped he was not going to start eating in front of him.

Biggs sat down on the corner of Keynes' desk, to the Sergeant's discomfort, and opened the bag.

"Muffin?" he said, then looked inside and pulled out an unhealthy looking brown cake. "Sorry, I thought there were more left." Biggs tucked in to the muffin, oblivious to the crumbs falling onto Keynes' desk.

"Get up to anything yesterday?" he said, through a mouthful of muffin.

"I just went to visit a friend. He hasn't been well."

Biggs stopped mid-chew.

"Don't worry, it wasn't Singh or Shingles."

"I know it wasn't Singh. He died last night."

Keynes felt himself turning pale. "What happened?"

"That poison apparently does its damage over a few days. What was worse, the pillock somehow got hold of a bottle of gin. Not the best idea when you've got massive organ damage already."

Keynes put a hand over his mouth and looked down at the ground. His grief was mitigated by his mixed feelings towards Harpit Singh. He had wanted to get close to the great man, but the nearer he had approached, the more dubious details he had noticed.

The Inspector began chewing again. "So we're up to two victims, but a bit short on suspects," he said. "We interviewed Adrian Shadwell yesterday."

"And?"

"I'm not convinced. But he's been daft enough to commit several violent acts and he had easy access to the scene of the murder, so we can't really let him go. There's no solid link between him and the crime, but on the other hand there's nothing that rules him out. He doesn't have good alibis for the other murders either. I can't see him being able to handle poisons without bumping himself off in the process. He's a bit of a div."

Biggs finished off the muffin and coughed roughly. "There is one thing," he said.

"What?"

"They've put up the bumper breakfast by thirty pence. Nearly ten percent. They've just lost a customer."

Keynes tried not to show that his spirit was slowly sinking, crushed and buckled by the mediocrity that emanated from Biggs. It was one thing to be ignorant and lazy; it was quite another to be proud of it.

With difficulty, he pulled a sheaf of papers out from under Biggs' thigh.

"I've been thinking," he said, pulling out details of Whitcroft's post mortem. "Perhaps we should visit the university campus. They have restricted chemicals on site at their laboratory, and we have a connection through the victim, Paul Whitcroft. We should at least question his housemates."

Biggs looked unimpressed.

"We don't really have a lot of leads," said Keynes. "And there aren't many places someone could get hold of thallium in Northamptonshire."

"All right. But let's keep a low profile. Students don't like police, and I don't like being called a pig."

Keynes bit his lip.

Chapter 37

Midlands University had, until recently, been called Northampton Technical College. As the number of teens wanting to go to university had exploded, and many of them found that they were not bright enough to qualify for further study, a gap in the market opened up for new red-brick institutions with more negotiable standards. While it was not technically a university in its own right, it provided a syllabus and examinations franchised from a much older seat of learning in Dunstable.

Local youths could save money by living with their parents while they studied, instead of moving to a city and paying rent, while Midlands University could also cash in on the lucrative market in foreign students. Bemused African and Chinese teenagers who had read and believed the university's marketing materials were a frequent sight at the train station, examining the map outside the ticket office to work out exactly how far they would have to walk to get to Leicester Square.

The regular income from student nights, during which pubs and nightclubs offloaded expired beer and unpopular alcopops to an undiscerning crowd, was a welcome boost for the town's licensed establishments, though it still seemed it was not enough to save Blazers from its regular bouts of combustion.

No one really achieved entry to Midlands University: it was more that they were rejected from everywhere else. The campus teemed with people who were just happy to be there, and to have the better-than-average chance of leaving with a degree.

Keynes had ended up there through a slight miscalculation. He had been an excellent student, close to the top of his class in most subjects and a clear leader in maths and economics.

He had the misfortune to come of age after the abolition of student grants, and at a time when state-provided student loans were not much more attractive than a commercial bank loan. Keynes had evaluated his family's circumstances – he knew within a couple of hundred pounds what his father earned each year – and realised that he could not afford to go to his first choice universities in foreign cities where he would have to pay rent. That would entail going into debt, and while he might be lucky enough to find a high-paid job in London, he knew that it was more likely he would have to work his way up over the course of a few years until he would be saving any money from his salary.

He consulted business magazines and ran his own calculations and decided that interest rates were heading up, making it an extremely foolhardy proposition to take out a floating rate loan. Keynes was averse to the concept of being in debt anyway, but his economic projections convinced him that his stance was correct.

That was how he had ended up studying Economics and Criminology at Midlands University in its early years, while living at home and working part-time in jobs with titles like Data Entry Executive at a re-insurance firm.

Being back on campus made him feel uncomfortable. The quadrangle – really a grey concrete square between the Humanities block and the library – had seemed huge just a few years ago, but he was struck by how small and underwhelming it was. Wide-eyed students clutched rucksacks bulging with textbooks while trying to give the impression of being effortlessly familiar with the surroundings. Keynes could smell fear.

He had little time to reminisce, had he wanted to. He was accompanied by Biggs, who was already out of breath and sweating after ascending about twenty steps to reach the quadrangle. Keynes probably looked young enough to pass for a mature student, although his upright posture gave away his occupation, but Biggs looked like someone who either worked in law enforcement or was wanted for questioning by its representatives.

Their first stop had been the student registrar's office, where they had checked up on Whitcroft's three housemates. Two of them had been present when Whitcroft's room was searched, but the interviews had been so brief and the reports so lacking in detail that there was no useful information there. It seemed Gunnett had left it all to a couple of young constables to do the dirty work and they had done the absolute minimum.

The late Whitcroft's housemates had been Sophie Burt, Geology; Lucas Bennett, English Literature; and Matthew Weekes, Chemical Engineering.

Only Sophie Burt and Lucas Bennett were present at the house when Keynes and Biggs arrived.

"Well, we've found penicillin," said Biggs to Keynes, eyeing the pile of submerged dishes festering in the sink.

"The police have already been here," said Sophie, blocking the doorway.

"Have you got a warrant?" said Lucas, not bothering to get up from the sofa where the two housemates had been watching daytime television, in front of a table laden with half-eaten takeaways. He had upper-class features which made him look like he was continually on the brink of tears.

"We just want to ask a few questions," said Biggs. "You don't have to let us in, but we've got new information related to the killing of Paul Whitcroft and we really would like to solve the case."

Lucas and Sophie looked at each other uncertainly, so Biggs added: "Don't worry, we're not looking for wacky baccy. We'll assume that lovely aroma is a new kind of air freshener."

Sophie let them in, but reluctantly. "We're really busy. We've got deadlines for our modules next week."

Keynes looked at the television, which was showing a confrontational talk show with the strapline: 'Lindsay doesn't know her daughter is pregnant with Craig's baby.'

"We're on a study break," said Sophie.

"Is that a tea break?" said Biggs. "If you've got any clean mugs we'd be much obliged."

Keynes ignored the offer of a cup of tea. He simply could not see how any of the items soaking in oily water in the sink could ever be restored to a hygienic state again. The students seemed to use cold water for washing their dishes, which may have made them look clean but certainly did nothing to remove bacteria.

Biggs moved a pile of dirty clothes off one of the sofas and sat down. Keynes preferred to stand.

"So have you actually got any new information?" asked Lucas. "It's been like a really long time since this happened."

"We're looking into a new angle," said Biggs. "Consider this a friendly chat. We're not taking notes."

Keynes had already produced his notepad and pencil. "I'll have to take *some* notes," he said.

"All right, just the details. We don't have to say where we heard it." Biggs eased his bulk into the armchair, which squeaked under the weight. "We believe that Whitcroft's death may somehow be linked to the distribution of illegal substances."

Lucas tried not to look scared, but his eyes widened noticeably and his breathing seemed to become more rapid.

"That's outrageous," he said. "To come in here and start accusing people of being drug dealers."

"No one said that," said Keynes.

"Well, he wasn't," said Lucas. "He didn't touch the stuff. None of us did."

"Let's say that's right, and you've got eyes like a startled gerbil just because you had to wake up so early today," said Biggs. "We're not talking about a bit of weed. We're talking about a controlled substance – the kind of thing that you wouldn't take for pleasure. Not more than once, anyway."

"Some kind of chemical?" said Sophie. "He studied Sociology and Philosophy. He wouldn't have had access to anything practical."

"Oh, because Geology's a much more important subject," said Lucas.

"I'm just saying, all you need for Philosophy is books. It's hardly even empirical."

"You're going to get started on this again?"

Keynes interrupted, though he was interested to find out what information the two housemates would divulge if they continued to argue. "Just out of interest, what kind of chemicals would you use in your Geology course, Miss Burt?"

"Just the usual. Various acids. But that's a small part of the course. We don't need to actually have the rocks in front of us."

Keynes thought she was probably telling the truth, but it would not be a bad idea to check with her lecturers. Students were notoriously terrified unless they were in groups, and Whitcroft was bound to have spent much of his time socialising with his housemates, which would make them the most likely connection to the source of thallium. All the same, he doubted whether either of these two would have had the confidence to approach an underworld figure off-campus to arrange such a transaction.

"Where's your other housemate?" said Biggs, checking a piece of paper. "Matthew Weekes."

"He's at lectures," said Sophie.

"And what exactly does he study?"

"Chemical Engineering. He'll be in the lab right now."

Biggs looked up at Keynes, and said to the two housemates: "We'll come back later. Don't go anywhere."

Chapter 38

As they strode towards the Science block, Keynes wondered exactly how all of the students around him seemed to know he was a police officer. He did not think his age made him stand out, although his expression was probably more serious than the youths around him. No, it was most likely to be the shoes, he decided. Students seemed to wear trainers to lectures these days. It seemed to be fashionable to dress as though you were homeless. None of the males seemed to shave, regardless of their proficiency in growing facial hair.

Keynes was fairly sure he had worn sensible shoes to lectures when he was a student. He tried to remember whether the other students in his class had done the same.

He failed to notice in his pre-occupied state that Biggs was struggling to keep up with him. It was only five hundred metres from the halls of residence to the Science block, but Biggs' forehead was glowing with perspiration and his breathing was becoming heavier.

"Steady on," said Biggs. "What's the rush?"

"He's our best lead on the thallium."

"We don't even know if the university has any on campus."

"We can check later, but let's get hold of Weekes before someone warns him we're looking for him."

"Midlands University only has a couple of dozen courses. It could just be a coincidence that a chemistry student lived with Whitcroft."

"We'll have a better idea of that after we speak to Weekes, won't we?"

Keynes pushed on ahead, with Biggs trailing behind. He was struck by how tatty the grounds looked, even though it was one of the most modern of British universities. The brickwork of the buildings looked worn down somehow, and the paving slabs had accumulated decades of dirt already – although Keynes acknowledged that many of the youths walking on them were dirtier than average.

Walls and pillars were scarred with little bits of tape and paper, where fliers and room advertisements had been fixed. Newer A4 posters for bands with names like Razor Vomit, Mildew, and Better World Collective overlapped leaflets promoting sponsored pub crawls and trying to make people feel guilty about eating fish.

A student dressed as a camel was giving away vouchers for a shot of something called 'Humper's'. Keynes had no doubt half of those vouchers would end up on the floor and felt that the distributor should be held liable for the clean-up costs.

They entered the Science block, a wing of the university that looked like it had been built forty years ago but had been given a lick of paint and some double-glazing at around the time it was upgraded to quasi-university status.

According to the timetable, Matthew Weekes was scheduled to be in Lab 2.14, although schedules seemed flexible here. Students seemed to drift in and out of rooms, and it was hard to tell which were classes and which were simply random gatherings of students sitting and shrugging.

They found the lab. The door was ajar and a handful of students seemed to have been thrown in, in varying states of wakefulness.

Biggs knocked on the door. "Excuse me, we're looking for Matthew Weekes."

A teacher who looked barely older than the others glanced over from the edge of the desk where he was seated, then jumped up suddenly. "Are you the inspectors? I've got the lesson plan somewhere."

"I'm an Inspector, he's a Sergeant," said Biggs, very pleased with himself.

Biggs produced his identification as he and Keynes moved into the room and surveyed the class, who were not animated even by their appearance.

"Is one of you Matthew Weekes?" asked the lecturer. He turned to Biggs and Keynes. "It's a new class, we don't really do roll-call. I try to build an environment built on trust, not rules."

"Is that a good idea in a chemistry lab?" Keynes could not help himself.

"He's not here," said one of the students, a mop of unruly black hair above a retro Brazil football shirt.

"Do you have a record of the restricted substances you keep on site?" Keynes asked. "And a register of who signed them in and out? Mr…"

"Dr Kendrick." The lecturer opened his desk, which was not locked, and produced a photocopied sheaf of papers with a stubby pencil tied to it by a string knotted through the end. He handed it to Keynes. "Here you go. That's the list."

Keynes noticed immediately that some of the pages had been torn out, leaving irregular shreds of paper under the binding and a gap of several days between entries. He flicked through it. "Some pages missing. They keep thallium on the premises."

"What's this all about?" said Dr Kendrick, looking very worried all of a sudden. "Do I need to call the vice-chancellor?"

As Keynes handed the register of restricted substances to Biggs, a lanky youth ambled in, listening to music. He stopped halfway into the room, realising something was amiss, and unplugged his earphones, turning around at that moment to see Biggs and Keynes.

Keynes realised an instant later than Matthew Weekes that the two of them had met a few days ago in the Royal Angus, when Matthew had identified himself as Whitcroft's housemate.

He had not written that detail down at the time, and had barely paid attention to the skinny youth, with an Adam's apple you could hang your coat on. No one had considered the Whitcroft angle worth investigating, but that view had suddenly changed.

Weekes turned and bolted with a surprising burst of speed as he recognised Keynes. Keynes hesitated, then ran after him.

As he chased Weekes down the corridor, he realised firstly that Biggs had not joined the pursuit, and, secondly, that running shoes were a distinct advantage over conventional work shoes on a polished surface.

Keynes was undoubtedly a better athlete, but Weekes was staying twenty-five metres ahead.

The corridor was not crowded, but Weekes was forced to push a heavily-built female student to one side as she blocked his path. As her rucksack tilted, a cascade of chunky textbooks fell out, sliding across Keynes' path.

Keynes jumped over them athletically, then skidded a little as he landed. He was still not gaining on Weekes, but he was keeping a good pace, thanks to his regular jogging sessions.

Weekes came to the end of the corridor and burst through the double doors – at least he would have done, had one not been locked. He caught his shoulder on the immobile right door of the pair and spun through.

Keynes ran through the doorway, choosing the correct side, and saw Weekes turning left towards the university playing fields. If he were to reach the football pitch, Keynes' shoes would be next-to-useless in that mud.

Keynes put on a burst of speed as his soles were finally able to grip on the weathered concrete paving slabs, and could see Weekes was flagging. His unhealthy student lifestyle of beer and takeaway food, as evidenced by his housemates' living room table, had taken its toll on his stamina. Keynes visualised himself in the final stages of a ten kilometre run.

He sprinted forwards, his hands chopping the air in short vertical slices as he powered forward, then dived for Weekes' legs. Keynes's right shoulder caught Weekes behind the knees and he wrapped his arms around tightly to ensure the student collapsed.

Weekes' face slapped into the mud at the edge of the playing field as the rest of his body followed his knees to the ground. Before he could react, Keynes had readjusted and put him into a half-nelson, with one knee in the small of Weekes' back.

Weekes struggled gamely, then twisted his head to one side and spat out a mouthful of dirt. His face was streaked with it.

"I swear, I didn't know what Paul was going to do with it!" he said. "He just said he wanted thallium for one of his friends. I needed the money, so I didn't ask why."

Keynes noted with satisfaction that his rate of breathing was entirely comfortable, while the student was struggling for air, despite being seven to nine years younger.

"I didn't know anything was wrong until he got killed. Then later the thallium started turning up in places, but it's nothing to do with me."

Weekes' face slumped back into the earth as his adrenaline started to wear off, and Keynes realised he was not going to volunteer any more information.

"Matthew Weekes, you are under arrest under suspicion of supplying a controlled substance under the Misuse of Drugs Act. You do not have to say anything, but you may harm your defence if you do not mention something you later rely on in questioning."

As he finished, Biggs came out of the building, then bent over, clutching his sides. He straightened up as he noticed Keynes straddling the suspect.

"Everything under control?" said Biggs, trying to hide his rapid breathing.

"I think I can handle it," said Keynes, thinking: If he had had a pork pie in his pocket, you would have chased him.

"Looks like you've got Weeke at the knees."

"His name's Weekes, with an S." Keynes picked himself up irritably, and dragged Weekes upright.

"I think we're probably going to need to give Dr Kendrick a caution for failing to control a restricted substance, too," said Biggs. "I've told him to expect a return visit."

"Can't we just charge him with general stupidity?"

"If that was a crime, we'd never get a day off."

Chapter 39

Back at the station, Matthew Weekes stuck to his story, and looked so terrified that they believed it. He insisted that he had stolen some thallium, perhaps twenty grammes, and sold it to Paul Whitcroft with no idea what he planned to do with it.

"He seemed like a nice bloke," said Weekes. "I didn't think he'd do anything dodgy with it."

"What on earth else can you do with it?" said Biggs.

Weekes did not have an answer.

"How long ago did you deliver it to him?" asked Keynes.

"About a week and a half. I signed it out a few times in small amounts, then went back and adjusted the records."

"Then it looks like there's a good chance he'd still be alive if you hadn't supplied him with that stuff," said Biggs.

Weekes turned paler, though there was still some mud on his face. He looked like he might be ill, right there in the interview room, just as hundreds had been before him.

It seemed Weekes had never heard of Adrian Shadwell, which did not surprise Keynes. Adrian was hardly likely to have the chemistry background necessary to run a campaign of poisoning, and Keynes doubted that many of his friends were students.

In fact, he did not even seem to know his late housemate particularly well, either. Weekes confessed that he had not even known Paul's surname until he had read it in the newspapers.

It soon became clear that Weekes had told them all he knew. He had not denied anything, he had not claimed to have had an accomplice, and he could explain exactly when and how he had stolen the thallium from the university laboratory.

He had packed it in a stainless steel Thermos flask and handed it over to Whitcroft. Dr Kendrick and the rest of the university staff seemed rather clueless about the whereabouts of their toxic substances, and seemed to have little security around them. Weekes told them how the laboratory had been locked down once after Dr Kendrick had mislaid a container of mercury. It was never found, but the next week all the gerbils had died.

Students were supposed to sign in and out, but in practice it was easy to avoid doing it. If Weekes had not told them everything, it was doubtful anyone would have been able to find out who had stolen the thallium from the laboratory – or even known that it was missing in the first place.

Weekes simply looked so terrified that it was impossible to believe he was involved any deeper with the Charity Shop Murders, thought Keynes, as he and Biggs left the interview room.

"See what I mean?" said Biggs, after the door closed behind them. "Any crime, anything at all, and nine times out of ten the criminal will crack. We didn't have anything on him till he started running. Let them do all the work."

You let me do all the work, thought Keynes. Weekes would have been back at his parents' house by now if it had been up to Biggs to chase him.

"I've got to report into Shepherd," said Biggs. "He's keeping us on a tight leash, since Gunnett had his little interlude. I'll see you later."

Keynes resented being treated like a child, but there was not much he could say at the moment. He had chalked up one major point in his favour by catching Weekes – regardless of how they had worked out he was involved – and he could sit back and let that fact sink in.

Something was bothering him about Zulu. Actually, most things bothered him about Zulu, but there was something at the back of his mind. Something that, perhaps, he already knew.

For now, though, he could not put a finger on it. It was another frustrating thing that would have to wait until later, like the tangential loose ends in the murder case. Like Mrs Bevan and the wolf.

Keynes suddenly stopped in his tracks as inspiration struck him. He barely remembered how that felt. He headed to his desk to collate clippings from the Northampton Tribune.

Chapter 40

"I don't understand what we're doing here," said Biggs, as they arrived at the house of the late Mrs Wendy Bevan.

"The cleaner thinks Mrs Bevan was terrorised to death by a giant wolf." Keynes knocked on the door.

"That's that, then. Case closed. Maybe it did the others, too, and we can go home early."

"The cause of death was cardiac arrest, as a result of her size," Keynes said, trying not to look at Biggs, "coupled with what I believe was some kind of panic attack from being chased."

"You do know we investigate murders, right? Not attacks of the screaming ab dabs or the heebie-jeebies."

Geoffrey Bevan answered the door, dressed in a golfing jumper than was thinning at the elbows. "My, my," he said. "You're multiplying. Is this a sign you're taking my wife's death seriously now?"

Keynes thought this was a terrible question to ask in the presence of Biggs, who could not take anything seriously, and especially in light of the theory he was about to put to Mr Bevan.

**

The three of them sat in silence in the living room, which seemed warmer than before and with an additional pungent smell that seemed to be coming from behind the radiator. Mr Bevan seemed content to sit there without speaking, staring at the television set, which was turned off.

Keynes rapped his fingers on the manila cardboard folder on his lap. It was a silly theory, but he was sure it was right.

They heard the sound of the front door opening and closing, then someone taking off and hanging up their coat very slowly and clumsily.

After a time, the living room door creaked open and Mrs Shaw entered.

"Two of them now," she said.

"Mrs S, these two officers would like to ask you a few questions," said Mr Bevan, not bothering to get up. "They seem to think they have new information about Wendy's death."

"Not exactly new information," said Keynes, hastily. "More like a new theory. I'm Detective Sergeant Keynes, as you know, and this is Detective Inspector Biggs."

Biggs nodded, as Mrs Shaw sat down in an armchair with juddery movements.

"We'd like to know if you could identify the wolf, if you saw it again," said Keynes, trying to sound earnest.

"I wouldn't want to see it again."

"But if you did."

"I wouldn't want to."

"If you were to see a picture of it."

"That's different."

Keynes pushed a pot of dead flowers to one side and cleared a pile of letters, then put the manila folder in the centre of the coffee table.

"I have a few photographs here. I'd like you to let me know when you recognise the thing you saw that night."

"I haven't got my glasses with me."

"Did you have them with you that night?"

"No."

Keynes opened the folder and produced a pile of newspaper cuttings. "Stop me if you see anything you recognise," he said.

Biggs looked like he was about to speak, but Keynes silenced him with a gesture of his hand. In front of Mrs Shaw was a pile of clippings from the Northampton Tribune with photographs showing charity events. In each of them, there was someone dressed as a mascot in an animal costume.

Mrs Shaw picked through them with shaking fingers. There was someone dressed as a dog for a pet rescue centre; an oversized frog that was, for some unknown reason, the mascot for a local orphanage; and a man-sized sea lion to promote the lifeboat service.

She paused over one photograph and leaned closer. "I'm not sure," she said. "This could be the wolf. It's different in the dark, you know. I was a long way away. But it looked like this."

She pushed the clipping towards Keynes. It showed a person in a fox costume, shaking a collection bucket for the Anti-Bloodsports Confederation. To an elderly woman at a distance, in the dark, it could have looked like a wolf walking on its hind legs.

Keynes allowed himself a smile. Mrs Bevan had been chased down and killed, albeit unintentionally, by anti-hunt protesters. There was something ironic about killing people to stop them from hunting.

What was more, his hunch, triggered by the sight of the camel mascot at the university campus, had been correct. Mrs Bevan's death was suspicious and had a charity angle. It belonged with the others, and perhaps helped narrow down the list of suspects, at such time as there would be enough for a list.

Mrs Shaw went through the rest of the newspaper clippings, but she did not see anything else familiar. That was good enough for Keynes.

Biggs was more sceptical. As they walked back to his car, he outlined his doubts to Keynes.

"Perhaps she was scared to death by a loon in a fox costume," he said. "I'm not sure that's even a crime. Even if it is, you'd have to identify the exact costume and the person who was wearing it at the time."

"That's impossible, I know. I'm just trying to draw connections, and now I know this death is connected to the others."

"Is that really what it tells you?"

"It tells me there's a charity angle."

"It's a nice theory, but it doesn't prove that, you know."

"It gives me a hypothesis."

"It gives me a headache." Biggs fumbled in his pocket for his car keys. The width of his thighs made his trousers too tight for him to access the contents of his pockets easily. "You're generating theories left, right and centre, you're adding to the list of possible suspects, and after all that we don't have a single decent suspect or a motive for killing all these people."

"They're all connected to charities. It can't be a coincidence."

"It can, and sometimes it is. Look at the methods. They're totally different from one victim to the next. I'm not even convinced it's one person doing all this. It's all so haphazard."

"Maybe he's just not very good."

Biggs opened the car door and eased himself in to the driver's seat. "I hate to break it to you," he said. "But does it ever occur to you that perhaps we're not very good?"

Keynes was taken aback. As it happened, he had never included himself in that assessment before.

Chapter 41

Biggs' words rang through Keynes' head, making it hard for him to concentrate. Keynes had always thought of himself as a top achiever, capable of anything. He had never failed at anything that could have been accomplished by anyone else.

Until today, he had treated this case as unsolvable, given the amount of information available. He had made small breakthroughs, which was more than most of his colleagues would have managed, but still needed more before he could come up with a motive and a likely killer. Keynes certainly did not think there had been any failings on his part so far. It was not his fault that the few breakthroughs he had made had led to dead ends.

Matthew Weekes had not been able to give them much more information. He did not know where Whitcroft had been sending the thallium, but he was aware that Whitcroft had known a few older characters – in other words, people who were not students – who had seemed a little strange, a bit off-centre. Weekes could not remember what any of them looked like and was not sure whether his friend had ever mentioned being a member of a charity group, other than his work bothering passersby.

Back at the station, Keynes made himself feel a little better by doing something proactive. He drew up a list of all of the charities active in the county that were opposed to fox hunting, then contacted them to ask for their membership lists. He was not sure whether he could compel them to provide the information, but hopefully they would decide that it was better to comply than to risk the police taking a closer look at their activities, given that property damage and trespassing were usually among them.

He also wondered about the case of Adamantia. Keynes was not convinced that she was relevant to this case, but he did not like leaving puzzles unsolved, especially when they might point to wrongdoing on Simon Oakes' part. He called up all of the information on drug overdoses in the Northamptonshire region in the past three years, but there were a lot. Even so, he could not be sure that he was looking at the right time period.

There were dozens. He would have to narrow down his search using some educated guesswork. First he reduced the area of focus to women, then to those below forty. It was a little hard to know what type of women Zulu would choose, given that he did not seem to have particularly high standards these days.

There had never been any overdose victims reported at Lazarus Court. Ordinarily, that would have caused Keynes to stop looking, and reminded him never to trust the word of a junkie, but both Zulu and Wazz had seemed genuinely scarred by something. In any case, the mention of Adamantia had certainly caused a reaction from Oakes.

He looked for drug overdose cases in towns and villages near Riscote in the past three years. There were a few, but none that leapt out as suspicious. He ran through the names. They were all clear-cut cases of accidental or deliberate overdoses, with no suspicious signs. Keynes found their case files and scanned through the notes and accompanying photographs. Nothing leapt out, and none of the victims seemed particularly striking in death.

Keynes seemed to remember working on some of these deaths with Harper, before Harper had suffered his own, self-induced collapse, but could recall very little about them. A dead body in a ditch was much less interesting once you worked out that no one else had contributed to its current condition and there was no mystery to be solved.

He was interrupted by the arrival of Biggs, who slammed a meaty hand down on his desk. "Long time no see," said Biggs. "Get your coat, you've pulled."

"Where are we going?"

"It's time we paid Chris Shingles a call and gave him a proper grilling."

"We've already spoken to him a couple of times. I didn't think he had much to tell us."

"Look, son, I've read the file," said Biggs. "You and Gunnett have been all over the place, but you've hardly got anything out of Chris Shingles. To my mind, he's our most likely suspect. Oakes might be a bit dodgy, but there's nothing to make me think he's a killer, and he doesn't seem like someone who takes risks."

"Unless he's desperate."

"You and Gunnett have tried things your way, now we're going to try it my way. My way's a lot calmer and with less running around. If I'm wrong, we cross Shingles off the list and move onto the next one. But as far as I can see, the only person connecting all of these charities is the bloke who wrote about them for the paper."

Chapter 42

Keynes wondered initially whether Biggs would manage to manoeuvre his way up the narrow stairway to the Tribune office, and was on the verge of suggesting that they ask Chris Shingles to come down instead, but Biggs managed to use a sideways motion to climb the stairs without becoming wedged.

"Two of you," said Shingles, noticing them without delight. "Where's the angry one?"

Keynes' eyes registered alarm and he ran through a variety of plausible answers, before Biggs said: "I ate him."

"This is Detective Inspector Biggs," said Keynes. "We'd like to ask you a few more questions."

"I haven't got time to answer your questions. Donny's gone for a job interview. Alan turned up for work for a few days after the poison attack, but now he's on sick leave again." Shingles snorted. "Can you imagine? I get nearly poisoned – to death – but I still come into work, and he goes off sick because he's got a bit of a cold. And might I add that you still haven't caught the person responsible."

"If you think it's important, then talk to us," said Biggs.

Shingles tapped his fingers on the desk. "So you're sure that the person who sent me the letter is also the Charity Shop Murderer?" His fingers were inching towards a ballpoint pen.

"Don't write that," said Keynes. "It's still just speculation."

"There is one thing that connects all of these incidents," said Biggs.

"And what's that?"

"You."

Shingles' fingers stopped in their tracks. He scratched the two-day-old stubble on his chin instead.

**

Shingles turned his computer screen around so that Keynes and Biggs could both see it, then pulled a mound of newspaper clippings onto his lap and began sorting through them.

"This is obviously a desperate move," he said. "Shows you're out of ideas if you need to come over here and start threatening me. I'm a victim here."

Biggs leaned back in his swivel chair, which gave a distressed creak. "There isn't much that links all of the victims together," he said. "You might say they're all connected by charity work, but that still doesn't give us anyone who's connected to all of them, or any obvious motive. The only link is you and this newspaper. Every one of these victims has had their picture in the paper in the past couple of months."

"I can't help it if the killer is picking his victims from newspaper photos."

"Maybe you're right," said Biggs. "But I think you know more than you're letting on."

Shingles turned to Keynes. "Do I need a solicitor present? I would like to point out that as a journalist I'm duty-bound not to reveal my sources."

"You're not being charged with anything," said Keynes. "We just want to make sure you're not keeping any potential evidence to yourself when it could be helping our case."

"That letter, for example," said Biggs. "I read the forensic report. It said there were trace amounts of thallium on the glass of your digital scanner, but you opened the envelope on the other side of the office."

Shingles pursed his lips.

"Almost as if you scanned a copy before the police turned up. I don't know why you'd do that in a life or death situation."

Biggs had picked up on something Keynes should have spotted. It was yet another hammer-blow to his confidence.

"At the end of the day, I'm a journalist," said Shingles. "Sometimes my personal safety has to take a back seat to the pursuit of truth."

"You're not in the Tora Bora caves. You write about Bonnie Baby competitions," said Biggs.

"I sometimes freelance that out," said Shingles, quietly.

"I'm just saying it's a bit suspicious."

"Look, not only am I the victim, I'm also a journalist. I've got double the reason to find out whodunit."

"Have you made any progress?"

"No." Shingles produced a printed copy of the letter from his desk. "Poor grammar, but that doesn't narrow down my usual list of letter-writers."

'Check you're facts,' the letter demanded. Keynes felt personally affronted by the errant apostrophe.

"Could someone be sending you a message?" said Keynes. "Could they be unhappy with the way you covered a particular story?"

"Complaints go in the bin. After I've written down the name of the sender."

"And emails?"

"Not a lot of our readers are familiar with emails. But, yes, same procedure."

"Then I think we'd like to see the list."

Shingles duly produced a notebook with a black cover, though it had been scuffed away by frequent use over many years. Keynes started to flick through it, then stopped.

"I didn't know you had this many readers," he said.

"Did you receive any threats before the poisoning attempt?" asked Biggs.

"Nothing specific, really. Even the letter that came with the thallium wasn't exactly threatening. I get a few anonymous letters warning me that I got things wrong or that I shouldn't trust what someone-or-other tells me. If I took it too seriously, I wouldn't be able to do this job."

Keynes could see that Biggs was not convinced. It was a little too convenient that Shingles had destroyed the evidence and seemed not to remember any previous threats against him.

"Do any of the letters you receive have grammatical errors?" said Keynes.

Shingles took a deep breath. "It's Broken Britain, officer. No one can spell or use punctuation anymore."

"Well, what about the redundant apostrophe?"

"There's nothing unusual about that. Step outside, go to the fruit and veg stalls on the market and see how they handle plurals. God, you could arrest Donny."

"This is all a bit vague, isn't it?" said Biggs. "Have you ever met a student called Matthew Weekes?"

"I don't think so," said Shingles. "I meet a lot of people, though."

"What about Paul Whitcroft?"

"No idea. Hang on, the student who was murdered?" Shingles was suddenly beginning to look worried. "Why are you asking me?"

"We're just trying to look for connections."

"Have you ever had any strange letters from people connected with charities?" said Keynes, interrupting before Biggs could take their line of questioning further off track and antagonise Shingles more than necessary.

Shingles appeared to relax, and sank back into his seat.

"The Tribune is a lightning rod for lunatics," he said. "Every clown and his mother wants us to write about them."

"It looks like you do write about most of them," said Biggs, flicking through a copy of the newspaper.

"I'll be honest. For the less investigative kind of stuff, the press releases from the council, the village fetes, the charity stuff, the bar is quite low. It's in the public interest, and if we print something, it shows that we care about that part of the community. As long as they're a registered charity and they can provide a photo with a resolution of at least four hundred dots per inch, or they can give us enough notice to send a photographer, we'll give them half a page."

"What about anti-hunt charities?" said Keynes. He could not understand why Shingles kept describing the newspaper as 'we', when it seemed to be basically a one-man operation.

"We've covered a few events, but we have to tread a bit carefully. If we print an anti-hunt story, we alienate half of our readership. We've got to strike a balance."

"Have there been any photos recently of anyone in a large animal costume, possibly a fox?"

Shingles paused. He looked down at his biro, unsure whether it was worth picking it up. "Sorry – you think the Charity Shop Murderer was someone in a big fox costume? Wouldn't that be a bit conspicuous?"

"Answer the question, please," said Keynes. "If we've got anything to tell you, we'll send you a press release with pictures at the appropriate resolution."

"I think there might have been a costume in one of the photos recently, but the pictures are always very poorly labelled from that lot. Never any names to go with the pictures. Probably because a few of the members spend the rest of the time in balaclavas digging holes and unlocking gates. There's no way to know who's wearing it."

"I'd appreciate if you could check. It might be important."

"It's probably not," said Biggs. Keynes looked at him in disbelief. He found it hard to believe that there was any good tactical reason for Biggs to undermine him.

"Then I won't try very hard," said Shingles.

"What about other charities?" said Keynes, trying not to sound desperate. "Are there any lunatics that might be dangerous? Perhaps ones you didn't cover in the newspaper because their press releases weren't good enough, or they didn't seem legitimate?"

"Hundreds," said Shingles. "I get tons of emails from Agoraphobia Support, but their photos are always too dark to use. There's one group – I think it might be one married couple – who wants me to alert the population to the news that we are being ruled by lizards. There's the Better World Collective, which is some kind of vague be-nice-to-people thing."

Keynes had seen a poster for the Better World Collective on the university grounds, along with flyers for terrible bands. It was a tenuous link between the student body, the newspaper and the charity world, but so far none of his connections had turned into anything more substantial than a loose assortment of facts. There was no theory at the centre of his thinking. He was simply stumbling in the dark, trying to find a light switch and hoping not to step on an upturned plug.

"Can you give us the contact details for the last two, please?" said Keynes.

Shingles rummaged through his wastepaper bin.

"We can come back another time," said Biggs, stretching his arms and making it obvious he was preparing to leave.

Shingles threw a balled-up piece of paper at Keynes. "Here you go. 'Lizards are among us.' They're good at headlines, at least."

"If you find any more, can you pass them on, please?" said Keynes.

Biggs gave up any pretence of subtlety and stood up. "Knocking-off time," he said to Keynes' dismay. "But before we go – have you ever met Harpit Singh?"

Keynes' eyes unwittingly met those of Shingles, sharing their guilty secret.

"Of course I have," said Shingles. "He's a very prominent local figure. I've covered his business achievements and his charity work. He's not exactly publicity-shy."

"And how would you say you got along with him?" said Biggs, suddenly giving Shingles his full attention.

"It's a largely cordial relationship," said Shingles. "Obviously there will be times when I have to write something negative about him." He stared down at his desk, doing his best not to look towards Keynes.

"You were at the record attempt earlier, I understand."

"I was. I'm a journalist. Of course I was there."

"From what I hear, it seems like Mr Singh didn't appreciate your presence very much. Why might that be?"

"You'd have to ask him."

"I can't really do that, unfortunately," said Biggs.

Shingles turned pale. "Has something happened? Is he dead?"

"I can't tell you any more about that. Use the official channels."

The energy seemed to drain from Shingles. Keynes knew it was grief for the death of his big scoop, which he would not be able to run, at least until a suitable mourning period had passed.

Shingles was a beaten man after that.

Biggs made a few more pointed remarks and questions, Shingles gave defensive answers, and before Keynes knew it, he was walking out of the Tribune office with the Inspector. Keynes felt too shell-shocked by Biggs' flippant dismissal of his line of questioning to be angry about it yet.

"Give us a lift back to the station, and then I think we're done for the day," said Biggs.

Keynes knew enough from reading a multitude of management books to frame his complaint as a question. "Can I just ask why you didn't think the Wendy Bevan angle was worth pursuing?" he said.

"It's a wobbly theory based on a wobbly witness. However much time you spend on it, you'll never get it to stand up."

"And the other charity angle I suggested?"

"You're just throwing darts in the dark. Maybe you'll hit something, but it's a hard way to do it. I'd rather start with something solid."

"And you still think Chris Shingles is a suspect?"

"I still think he's our best lead, and our best chance of making an impact." Biggs tapped his nose. "Meet him, put the fear into him, and wait for him to make a mistake. Let him do all the work."

Keynes wanted to make his objections plainer, but he was aware he had dispatched, unintentionally, two Inspectors in the past few months, and did not want to earn a reputation for being difficult to work with.

As they rounded the corner to the back of the building where Keynes had parked, he realised something was wrong. There was a sprinkling of glass beside the passenger side door, and as he approached he could see the window had been smashed.

His chest tightened. There had only been one thing of value in the car.

"You're joking," said Biggs, who stopped in his tracks as he noticed the damage. "We were only in there ten minutes."

Keynes ducked his head through the hole and saw that the glove compartment was open. His dossier on Simon Oakes had been taken.

"Nice of them to leave the radio," said Biggs. "Is anything gone?"

Keynes felt under the seat, but he kept a very tidy car interior, and there was nothing there except a small fire extinguisher. He straightened up, and leaned back on the bonnet, one hand gripping his forehead.

Biggs was evidently becoming a little unsettled by Keynes' continued silence.

"You can swear if you like. I won't be shocked."

"I don't swear. It's the sign of a feeble mind."

Keynes had made a stupid error. He had kept the dossier in his car partly because he wanted to read it during quiet moments, but also because he had not wanted anyone at the station to see it and realise he was keeping an eye on Oakes. He had not wanted to unleash the law on Oakes until he had at least finished reading the whole thing. Now his best weapon was gone.

On top of that, it made him look like he had not learned his lesson from the quadruple puncture incident and had continued to make poor decisions on where to park.

He had nothing else to incriminate Oakes. The only thing he could do was appeal to Biggs' instincts as a detective, and he was not entirely sure from their limited time together that Biggs had any. Shepherd had already warned Keynes for overstepping the mark in his interactions with Harpit Singh, and it would not look good if the Chief Inspector thought he had done the same thing almost immediately after being warned against it.

With few options left, Keynes took a chance.

"This wasn't kids," he said. "Simon Oakes did this."

"What, the God Squad fellow? Doesn't that break one of them commandments?"

"I had some documents in my car that might have been useful evidence against Oakes, and now they're gone. Oakes knows I've got some information on him, and he's obviously worried I'm getting too close."

"You had a lead on the killings and you didn't tell anyone?"

"There's nothing connecting him to the killings," Keynes admitted. "It's just financial stuff. But I wouldn't be surprised if there's more to it than that. For him to take this risk…"

Biggs folded his arms and gave Keynes a quizzical look. "Why are you even investigating a financial crime? We've got people for that."

"It's just a hunch. I think there's a connection to the killings if we look hard enough. I just haven't found it yet."

Biggs seemed satisfied with that answer. "Just don't get into the habit of doing work for other departments. They'll come to expect it."

Keynes rounded the car and unlocked the driver-side door. "We need to get there before he has a chance to destroy it," he said. "Watch out, there's glass on the seat."

"You want to go up to Riscote now?" Biggs edged his sleeve up over his watch and tried to glance at the time without Keynes noticing, but it was a fairly obvious movement.

"We need to catch him in the act, before he destroys the evidence."

"Hang on – we've got no evidence against him, because it's disappeared, and we've got no proof he broke into the car, but you want to drive up there and accuse him of…I'm not even sure what you want to accuse him of."

Biggs' face was a mixture of confusion and laziness.

"I just want to go to Lazarus Court," said Keynes. "We can work out the details later, but if we find him with my documents then it's pretty straightforward."

"And if we don't?"

"Then we go home."

Keynes watched impatiently from the driver's seat, his key in the ignition, as Biggs stroked his chin thoughtfully.

"All right," said Biggs. "But I need to make a phone call."

He opened the door and Keynes helped him dust glass shards off the seat. Biggs spread Keynes' road atlas over the seat and sat down carefully, then found his phone and started to dial.

"Hello, Jude?" he said, as Keynes pulled away. "It's me. Can you set the video to record the darts at six?"

Keynes pulled away, restraining his urge to speed, but knowing that if he was too late the evidence would be gone. He had come off second-best in his previous visits to Lazarus Court, and now he had no dossier to help him. The presence of Biggs could be either a bonus or a liability.

He was not sure how to proceed once he reached the Christ Resurrection League's community, but he knew there was no room for error. If Oakes really had stolen the document, or ordered one of his troupe to steal it, then he was becoming desperate. That was good news if it meant the normally unshakeable Oakes would make a mistake under pressure, but it could also make him more volatile. If Oakes turned out to have some connection to the killings, they could be heading into a dangerous situation.

As he drove, Keynes considered the possibility that Biggs' earlier suggestion might have proven effective: he had gone to Oakes on a very sketchy pretext, rattled his cage and then left him to worry. His broken window was the end result. Perhaps Oakes was starting to make mistakes.

Chapter 43

As they approached Lazarus Court, it became clear that something was wrong. A thin trail of black smoke spiralled into the air from behind the trees, and Keynes thought initially that the house was on fire. They turned off the road into the driveway and as they rounded the corner to the house, they could see that the smoke was coming from the orchard behind.

"Is that suspicious?" said Biggs.

"Let's assume so."

Keynes parked and dashed out of the car, with Biggs jogging heavily behind. Keynes vaulted a wooden gate, and as the smell of burning filled his lungs, he saw Miss Quelch standing over a blazing metal dustbin, a bundle of documents in her hands.

"Miss Quelch, don't even think about burning that," he demanded. Keynes was too late: Miss Quelch, with a look of defiance on her pinched features, threw the papers into the fire.

Keynes, realising that the fire extinguisher was still in the car, kicked over the dustbin and began stamping on its burning contents. Biggs opened the gate and sauntered through, as Miss Quelch grabbed a handful of papers from a pile beside her and tried to strike her lighter.

"Now then, let's all calm down," said Biggs. He walked over to Miss Quelch and took the lighter out of her hand without a struggle. "What's going on? Have you found those documents?"

As the flames died out, Keynes dropped to his hands and knees and started to pick through the smouldering remains. There were fragments of paper with names and numbers, but nothing that resembled the dossier Chris Shingles had put together. These seemed to be payrolls and employment records, dating back at least ten years.

His fingers became blackened as he flicked through the pages. The dossier was nowhere to be seen, but he was sure there was something incriminating there, if only he knew what to look for. The names and figures meant nothing to him.

Suddenly, a scrap of singed paper caught his eye. Anthea Adams, employed from May 2006 to March 2007. He could not find the rest of the page or make sense of the partial words on that fragment, but it sparked something in the recesses of his memory. Anthea Adams. Could she have been Adamantia? The name was similar enough. He pocketed the burned fragment and stood up.

"Where's Oakes?" he asked Miss Quelch.

"He's not here."

"Destroying evidence is a serious crime. Nice that he let you do his dirty work."

Miss Quelch said no more, but her eyes betrayed her. Keynes noticed her glance towards the cottage, and as he turned he saw a figure in the window of Oakes' office.

"Stay here," he told Biggs. "Make sure she doesn't mess with anything else."

"What's going on?" said Biggs, but Keynes was already running towards the house.

Keynes pushed open the front door and stepped inside, not exactly sure what to expect. A pair of slippers were beside the door, but he would do without them, despite his muddy shoes.

He stepped quietly onto the stairs, trying to move quickly but without causing them to creak. Keynes moved his feet to the edges of the steps so that the wooden planks would not flex.

As he looked up, he realised that his caution had been in vain. Desmond stood at the top of the stairs, glaring down at him. There were fragments of glass glittering in the sleeve of his jumper, presumably from where he had smashed Keynes' car window.

"I expect you won't like it, but I'm planning to come up there and get my property back," said Keynes.

Desmond seemed almost to grow in size, giving him a more overtly threatening appearance, apart from the white slippers.

Keynes lowered his shoulders and moved up the stairs, but Desmond stepped down to bar his way. Keynes feinted to the left, but Dennis pushed him back. He tried again, and received a harder shove for his efforts, sending him into the wall.

Keynes braced one foot against the wall and another against the banister, and tried to push through Desmond's bulk with his shoulder. Desmond was a particularly obstinate roadblock and seemed to fill the entire stairway with hard, angry muscle. As Keynes pushed harder, Desmond grabbed the officer's neck under his armpit and started to squeeze it against his chest.

Keynes could feel the air being squeezed out of his body and his face turning purple. His windpipe was being squashed. He punched Desmond below the ribs with his right fist, with what he thought was a respectable jab, but it elicited no reaction. He took a wider swing, which he was sure had connected with Desmond's kidney, but the giant did not flinch.

Desmond forced Keynes' head downward, until, his face mashed into Desmond's woolly jumper, he could see only stairs and feet. As his face turned purple, Keynes felt that he had only a few seconds before he passed out. There was no way to signal Biggs for help, and he doubted the Inspector would have been much use in the circumstances anyway.

He focused on the slippers. Inappropriate footwear for a tussle on a varnished wooden surface.

Keynes took a step down, then another, catching Desmond by surprise. As Desmond struggled to maintain his grip, his slippers struggled for purchase on the wooden stairs.

Keynes parked his rubber soles against the wall and the banister, then as Desmond slipped down a step, used his momentum to throw him down the stairs. Desmond crashed into the wall headfirst with a crack that split the plaster, then fell to the ground in a heap. Keynes wondered, with slight anxiety, whether he had killed him, but that could wait. He definitely did not want to be there when Desmond came round.

He entered Oakes' office. It looked as though the head of the Christ Resurrection League had left in a hurry. The drawers of his desk had been left open and the pictures of him with local figures had been taken down. He now saw that the photograph of Oakes and the Mayor had been concealing a small safe set into the wall. The safe was open, and empty.

Keynes stepped through the thick carpet pile and checked through the drawers. There was nothing there. Presumably if the dossier had been here, it had been the first thing to be consigned to the fire.

He checked for secret compartments in the desk or the walls, and gave a quick tug on the carpet in case anything was hidden underneath, but it was hopeless.

Keynes walked slowly down the stairs, as a chunk of plaster fell onto Desmond's comatose body, revealing the brickwork. Property damage and assault, depending on how you saw it, coupled with trespassing, and there was no dossier to justify his visit.

He checked Desmond's pulse. At least he hadn't killed him. That would have made the situation even more awkward.

Keynes stepped outside in something of a daze, and walked back to Biggs.

"Not much of a talker, is she?" said Biggs. "I tried her with a few knock-knock jokes but she wouldn't bite. I made quite a good pun about cooking the books, but it's not worth repeating now."

Miss Quelch glowered at them both, but Keynes could see a hint of desperation beginning to creep in. A couple of minutes of Biggs' jokes could do that.

"Oakes isn't here," said Keynes. He turned to Miss Quelch. "Where is he?"

She folded her arms and turned away.

"Did you find that document, then?" said Biggs.

"No."

"Ah. That makes this all a bit tricky."

Wait till you see the unconscious giant on the stairs, thought Keynes, but decided that could wait.

Keynes began scooping up armfuls of burnt documents.

"Help me carry this," he said to Biggs. "It's all evidence."

"Evidence of what?"

Keynes paused for a moment. "Tax fraud, probably. Under-declaring staff salaries to dodge payroll taxes. Or over-declaring them to reduce the tax on company profits."

"Sounds pretty watertight to me."

"Look, we won't know what he's trying to hide until we go through all this stuff, and I don't fancy sitting here to read it, so help me put it in the car."

Biggs muttered something to himself, then reluctantly bent down and picked up some of the pages, trying to choose the least muddy ones.

"I don't see why we're wasting our time on something that's not a murder," he said.

"Oakes has run away. He's rattled about something, and I don't think it's just his staff payslips."

Keynes tried to read Miss Quelch's thoughts, but she stared resolutely back at him, unblinking. All the same, he could see she was worried about something. She just did not want Keynes or Biggs to know what it was.

"You can expect another visit," said Keynes to Miss Quelch, although based on his current information that was an empty threat.

Keynes and Biggs staggered back to the car under the weight of reams of singed, soggy papers, which they put in the boot. They got into the car, and closed the doors without speaking. Biggs attempted to lean his arm on the window, but realised he might knock out the remnants of the glass.

"So, did anything happen inside the house?" he said, casually, as though making conversation. "Only, you were a bit red in the face when you came out."

Keynes gripped the steering wheel. "There was a bit of an altercation and I threw a man down the stairs in self-defence."

"That's a new one."

"It was a new one for me as well."

"I imagine he'll be a bit annoyed about that."

"I would have thought so."

"Especially since you didn't find any evidence to justify being there. Let alone chucking him down the stairs."

"Oakes has cleared out the safe. He's scared. Maybe he's scared of us."

"Rightly so, as it turns out."

"We're close."

"But no cigar." Biggs checked his watch. "This is a mess. I'm too tired at the minute to even work out how much of a mess. We've got a broken window, a boot full of burnt paper that's probably got nothing to do with the murders, a missing millionaire, and a nice little charge of police brutality on the way. I don't know how your mind works, but that doesn't look like a good use of a day."

"It all fits together. I just think we need a couple more pieces."

"You've got too many pieces. Throw some away."

Keynes could not explain it to Biggs, nor, if it came to it, to Shepherd, but he was sure he was on the right track. He might not have the evidence in his possession now, but Oakes' decision to run told him that the church leader was guilty of something more than doctoring his accounts.

"It's late," said Biggs. "I'm not going to write this up tonight, and I'd appreciate it if you didn't tell anyone about that window until we've worked out how we're going to tell this story. Just drop me back at the station, I'll sleep on it, and then we'll see how we justify our actions in the morning. And when I say 'our actions', it is mainly yours."

Keynes could not think of a response, chiefly because he could not think of a better course of action. If Gunnett had gone raging into Lazarus Court, things would not have turned out any worse. He had to admit that sometimes his greater abilities did not translate into better results. For all his good intentions and talent for investigative work, he had not made any more progress than his lazier colleagues.

"On the plus side, there haven't been any more victims for a couple of days," said Biggs. "Maybe the killer's finished. We can go through the motions for a few more days, and then wash our hands of it."

Keynes started the car and pulled away, feeling lower than he ever had before.

He knew his abilities, and his limits. He might not be the best in dealing with people, but he had always trusted his skill in analysing data. Give him some solid, incontestable names, dates and numbers, and he could excel.

He dropped Biggs back at the station car park and was about to drive home before anyone spotted the broken window, when something compelled him to go inside.

He came back a few moments later with armfuls of documents: everything he had been able to find on the membership details of local anti-hunt organisations, recent drug overdose victims, and clippings on charity events from the Tribune. It was a huge amount of data, but he knew that an evening spent poring through it would be the highlight of his day.

If there were connections to Oakes, he would find them.

**

Keynes spread the documents in neat, organised piles in his spare bedroom. Now he was in his element. Data could not lie – well, it could, but he would notice any inconsistencies, any outliers.

He opened an A4 pad on a clean page and wrote Simon Oakes' name in the centre. Everything revolved around him; he was sure of it.

He wrote the words 'charity', 'tax' and 'junkies' below it. One of those had to be the source of the motive.

Students did not pay tax either. Paul Whitcroft had not been a drug addict, as far as the evidence went, but he had handled illicit substances. What was the connection with Oakes? Keynes could not envisage Oakes mingling with sozzled students in the Royal Angus. In fact, it was hard to imagine Oakes having much contact with underworld figures at all, other than meeting his suppliers and clients in motorway service stations to make cash handovers.

Whitcroft had simply been the means to obtaining the thallium. Once he had provided that, he needed to be dispatched to avoid any chance that the killer could be traced through him. There might be students or patrons of the Royal Angus in the Christ Resurrection League. Whitcroft could be explained.

Oakes was not a member of any anti-hunt charities. It was a fair bet, though, that he would not have wanted any intrusion on his property if he had something to hide. Mrs Bevan's hunt could have ridden too close to his land for comfort, making her a target.

Chris Shingles was a simple one – he was sticking his nose in, trying to find evidence of criminal activity at Lazarus Court, and had come very close to finding it. Oakes had either wanted to scare him off, or he had simply underestimated the quantity of thallium needed to kill him.

He had perfected the formula by the time of his next poisoning attempt. The bottle of gin had helped dispatch

Singh, though Keynes tried not to think about it. Why, though, would Oakes want to kill Singh? He was a fellow businessman. Perhaps they had some dealings which Oakes was worried might come to light if Singh was exposed as the crook he most likely was. Keynes had now resigned himself to the view that Singh would not have been an appropriate business contact or dinner party guest.

Oakes had a very plush, new carpet in his office. Was that proof of a link to Harpit's Carpets?

He could explain all of the victims except for Vera Hope, the first and the least obvious one. Why would an elderly lady in a charity shop be a threat to anyone? Keynes could not believe she would have stumbled on any wrongdoing by Oakes by herself. She would have had no reason to encounter him in her normal routine. She lived in Kingsthorpe, the other side of Northamptonshire to Riscote, and she did not have any children who might have ended up in the Christ Resurrection League.

Keynes realised they had not checked the rest of her family tree. Was there a nephew or niece who might have hit hard times and ended up checking into Lazarus Court? Or even a neighbour? How on earth could he check this? It did not help that the Christ Resurrection League had burned its employee roster. Keynes had recovered a lot of names from the fire, but he had no idea how many were missing.

Jenny knocked on the open door. "Tea for the troops," she said, producing a mug.

"Watch where you're putting that. There's vital evidence all over the place. I can't take this to a judge with a tea ring on it."

"I have heard of coasters, you know," said Jenny, producing one and placing it beneath the mug.

"Fine, but call it a beer mat, please, we're not American."

"Someone's in a bad mood."

"You're correct. Full marks." Keynes rubbed his eyes. There was too much to read. There was no way he could process all of this information by himself, but he had no confidence in Biggs, who lacked any concept of urgency.

On top of that, he had no idea how he was going to explain his justification for throwing a man down the stairs. It had seemed entirely justified at the time, but his violent action had produced no evidence or breakthrough in the case. He knew it would look, to an outsider, like he had assaulted a member of the public for no good reason. He certainly could not prove that Desmond had attacked him first.

That was the kind of incident that could end careers, or at least steer them down less interesting paths. That was what was in store for Gunnett, and he had not even thrown a punch.

If he did end up in the graveyard of police work, dealing with drunkards or junkies, again, it would be his own fault. He had been given an intricate puzzle to solve, and he had tried to do it through brute force. No wonder it had yielded no results so far.

It was certainly not Jenny's fault that he was an idiot.

"Want to help me with some marking?" he said. This was as close to an apology as he had ever managed with Jenny, but she never seemed to mind.

"You've certainly got a lot there."

"This is everything with any possible connection to the Charity Shop Murders. The truth is in here somewhere."

"That's a lot for one person."

"Well, you know what the others are like. They're still living in the dark ages. They think the only way to solve crimes is to keep asking questions until someone tells you who did it. They've never heard of data mining."

Jenny picked up one of the folders and looked at the photograph beneath the paperclip. "Another victim?"

Keynes glanced at it. "No, that's just a heroin death. It was something else I was checking on. That's nothing to do with the others."

He reached for his tea, a thoughtful expression on his face. He could not be sure whether it was the mild infusion of caffeine and tannin that had kick-started his thinking process, or whether his brain had begun working earlier and had only just finished running the calculations.

Something stirred in the foundations of his memory. He had a terrible memory for, not exactly names, but people in general. He only remembered the important ones, but perhaps his subconscious kept the others on file.

None of his early cases in the police force had captured his imagination. He had gone into them with high hopes, only to lose interest when Rutkowski's reports had shown the victims to have overdosed on drugs. If a death was self-inflicted, it was nothing to do with him, and the investigation ended there. There was no puzzle for him to solve, and he would lose interest immediately. Someone else would take over trying to trace the source of the narcotics, and he would forget about the body growing colder and bluer in the morgue.

Had he been able to go into the police station and search his old cases electronically, he could have found the answer he wanted almost immediately, but as he was laying low he would have to resort to a rather less sophisticated form of digging for information.

Keynes bent down and pulled open the bottom drawer, where he kept all of his old notepads, just in case he was ever called upon to defend his behaviour in an earlier investigation.

"Do you want me to leave you to it?" said Jenny, recognising a nervous energy growing in her husband.

Keynes held up a hand, his face buried in the contents of the drawer. "Stand there, don't move, don't speak, don't distract me," he said.

He found three notepads from what he thought to be the correct time period, and flicked through them. March 2007. Early in his career, yet he had already seen enough deaths by overdose to be thoroughly bored by them.

A name leapt out from his carefully pencilled notes. Anthea Adams. Adamantia, if he was right. This had been his investigation.

He read his notes: two scant paragraphs. That was all she had been worth.

She had been discovered by a dog walker under a bridge by the canal. A thin red-head, her arms freckled by needle-marks, she had been wearing a man's hooded jumper and jeans, with nothing on her feet. She would probably have been a good-looking girl, before addiction had withered her.

There had been nothing unusual about the death – perhaps it had been suicide, perhaps it had been an accidental overdose – and the only suspicious detail, as Rutkowski had determined, was that she had not died beneath that bridge. Someone had dumped the body there after death. That was not uncommon. When someone found their partner in smack had stopped breathing, they could expect the police to ask them a few questions and for their own chemical condition to be analysed thoroughly. Sometimes it was just easier to leave the body somewhere the police could find it with less inconvenience to all parties involved. People found that their ties of friendship were not as strong as they had thought, once they were tested by something as awkward as a dead body in the bathroom.

Rutkowski's examination had found synthetic fibres in Anthea Adams' hair that could have come from being transported in the boot of a car. Perhaps they could have investigated further and identified the brand of car, then tried to check the nearest security camera footage for vehicles matching that description during what would have been a fairly lengthy period of time. However, the parents had not pushed for a deeper investigation, wanting to draw a line under the whole sorry incident, and no one at the police had felt the need to take it further.

It was an open and shut case. There was nothing suspicious about it.

Apart from the fact that she had been living and working at Lazarus Court at the time of her death. According to Keynes' notes, when told the news of her death, someone from the Christ Resurrection League had informed the police that she had run away a few days previously. Perhaps she had; it could not be proved either way.

Now, though, Keynes had a theory – one that was not borne out by any data, but simply by the behaviour of the people involved. He was sure that Adamantia had overdosed while at Lazarus Court and Oakes had ordered her body to be dumped elsewhere to avoid embarrassment to the community. Zulu, or whatever his name had been at the time, had never forgiven Oakes for that. Perhaps it explained his current pattern of behaviour.

But that was lapsing into psychology. There was no point Keynes theorising in any more detail. He could not prove any of this. He just knew it was right.

Now Oakes was missing. That gave two possibilities, as far as Keynes could see. If Oakes really had been shaken by Keynes' investigation into Adamantia's death, then he might be looking to silence Zulu before he talked.

On the other hand, if Oakes really had been as scared as he had looked, then perhaps he thought Zulu could be a threat in other ways.

Keynes found it hard to believe that Zulu, armed with nothing more dangerous than a dirty syringe and a bottle of methylated spirits, could be a danger to anyone but himself, but he knew by now the benefits of questioning the received wisdom. So many things which he had taken to be inviolable facts had been torn up and discredited during the course of his investigation.

"I'm going out," he told Jenny, but he finished his tea first.

Chapter 44

Keynes looked up and down Gold Street, but could not see Zulu anywhere. The sun had gone down hours ago and the streetlights cast cold pools of light in the damp pavement.

Keynes considered it vital to track down Zulu tonight, but he was not in the mood to spend the whole evening traipsing around Northampton when it was this temperature. Shops on the street were starting to close up, and soon the town centre would be taken over by the pub crowd.

The juddering of metal shutters rolling down to the ground behind him startled Keynes and he turned around, to see Adrian Shadwell. Shadwell, who was in the process of locking the shutters, did not seem pleased to see him when he turned around.

"You again?" he said. "Are you just going to follow me until I make a mistake?"

"I'm actually not here for you."

"One little slip-up and your card's marked for life."

"It's actually more than one, isn't it, Adrian? But I'm not here to see you."

Shadwell's face was growing worryingly red. "Wasting your time on this. You should be going after real criminals. Just five minutes ago, Jayde nearly got run over by a speeding car. She could have been killed."

Hearing her name, Jayde Anderson turned around. She was all but absorbed by a dark blue puffer jacket, and

Keynes had hardly noticed her standing against the wall. She was not the most prepossessing woman he had ever seen, and found it hard to understand why two grown men would fight over her with such passion.

She had gone back to Adrian, thought Keynes, leaving Gunnett to his tattered marriage. It had probably been a bit hard for her to take him seriously after Adrian had administered a very one-sided and public beating. Even though Jayde had not seen it, she would certainly have heard about it. Youth 1, Experience 0.

Keynes had suspected that the status quo had been restored, after Jenny reported that Sandy Gunnett had started buying food in multiples of two again. There had been no frozen food in her trolley this week, though, which suggested that she was not rushing into anything.

"Great big silver Merc, it was," said Jayde, and Keynes found himself wincing at her voice. He really could not understand why she was so sought after. She was hardly Helen of Troy. "Probably driven by a councillor or someone, so I doubt you'll do anything about it," she went on.

"I'm not a traffic policeman," said Keynes, then stopped himself. "A silver Mercedes? Did it stop here?"

"Yeah, it was parked outside the smoothie shop for a bit. Then he drove off like a madman and nearly hit Jayde."

"Did you see who was driving?"

"No, I was more concerned with getting out of the way. He had one wheel on the pavement."

"Heading where?"

"Looked like St James."

Keynes reached for his notepad, and, out of force of habit, jotted down a note about it. This seemed to appease Shadwell.

The lights were turned off in Groovy Smoothies and a 'closed' sign hung in the door, but the shutters had not been pulled down.

"Does Ian Pruitt drive?" asked Keynes.

"He certainly doesn't drive a Merc. He's got a bike. Save the planet, and all that."

Keynes slowly became aware that someone was watching him. He turned around to see Zulu grinning at him from across the road.

"All right, Zigga," said Adrian, waving at him.

"I thought you hated homeless people?"

"He's all right, he stays out of my way, doesn't cause me any trouble. He helped Jayde fix her motor once when the radiator pipe kept spitting water. Knows a lot about engines."

Keynes crossed the road. Zulu was standing up, making him seem thinner than usual. The clothes seemed to hang off him.

"Checking up on my wellbeing, officer?" said Zulu.

"Something like that. Simon Oakes has gone missing, and I thought you might know something about it."

"I've been busy trying to get a place in the homeless shelter. I was a bit slow, unfortunately. Sell-out crowd tonight."

"I think Oakes was here a few minutes ago, and I want to know why."

Zulu seemed to be caught unawares by the news. "Here? What did he want?"

"If he wasn't here to see you, then I don't know."

"What would he want with me?"

"He might be trying to tie up loose ends. He might think you talk too much. It's a popular opinion."

"Charity shop's not open, so he must have been to see Ian," said Adrian.

"Why isn't the charity shop open?" said Keynes, instantly suspicious.

"They're short-staffed."

"Maybe you'd better go and check on the smoothie shop," said Zulu. "See if the owner's been impaled on a papaya or something."

Much as Keynes hated to admit it, Zulu had a point. Oakes had probably been the driver of that car, and there might well be something here that explained why he would have been at the British Cancer Foundation shop to kill Vera Hope – the one piece of the puzzle he could not yet explain.

"I'm going to take a look," said Keynes. "But not because you suggested it."

He crossed the road again and found a gap between all the flyers and posters where he could peer through the glass. There were no signs of a struggle. The door to the storage room was ajar, but he could not see in. A few cardboard boxes were scattered across the floor in a haphazard fashion, but it was hard to know whether they had been knocked over or whether Pruitt was simply untidy. Keynes suspected the latter.

"Hard to know from outside," said Zulu, who was suddenly standing behind Keynes. "Probably need to break a window and take a look around. You've got reasonable grounds."

"The day I take legal advice from a drug addict is the day I resign from the force," said Keynes, starting to become annoyed.

Unfortunately, Zulu was right. Keynes could not afford to wait until tomorrow to check inside the building. A broken window was a small price to pay if there was a man inside about to breathe his last – or if there was forensic evidence that could be saved.

Keynes took a few steps away from the others, then dialled Biggs' number. The call went straight to Biggs' answer machine. Keynes made sure to leave a message explaining what he was about to do. At least he would be able to account for his actions if he was later called upon to justify them.

He walked around the back of the smoothie shop, next to the rubbish bins. The rear entrance was locked and there was no obvious way in.

Keynes picked up a brick laying near the bins and tapped the window closed to the door handle. It failed to break, so he brought his arm back and hit it harder. The entire window shattered with unwelcome loudness. He stood there frozen, with one arm through the void, as glass shards dripped from the window frame.

Unavoidable, he told himself, and shook off the glass. Keynes reached for the latch and a bolt below, and opened the door carefully, although there was probably not much else left to break.

He took a step forward, holding his breath in case he missed a significant noise. All he could hear, though, was the glass crunching beneath his shoes and the hum of refrigerators. He stepped over a pile of cardboard boxes and a crate of mangoes which had been left on the floor.

There was no body in the shop window, which would have been his first guess. The shop had only three small tables, and the chairs had been stacked on top upside down, except for two which were set out as though ready for an after-hours meeting. The tabletop was empty.

Keynes moved behind the counter, and almost slipped over on a mashed mango that appeared to have fallen out of the crate. He recovered his poise and crouched down to take a closer look. There appeared to be another footprint in the mango, but Keynes' shoe had smeared it too much to be identified.

In the evening gloom, a dark stain on the counter caught his eye. There was a charity collection tin chained to the counter, with a reddish-brown substance on the bottom. He stood up and tried to take a closer look without touching it. It was hard to tell by the naked eye whether it was remnants of blood or blackcurrant, but it was worth noting.

It occurred to Keynes that the shape of the collection tin – a plastic cylinder that tapered in at the middle and out again at the bottom – could have produced the wound seen on Paul Whitcroft's head. Any charity tin, filled with small change, could be heavy enough to concuss someone, at least.

He turned his attention to the refrigerator, behind the counter. It was emitting an irritating hum, and Keynes realised as the chill reached him that the door had not been closed properly. There were two handles, one of which hung down loosely. Keynes grasped the other, hoping he was not destroying fingerprints. He needed to be sure.

Keynes eased the handle down, lifting the latch, and pulled the heavy steel door towards him. A cold blue light illuminated the contents. Apples, oranges, carrots and celery filled wet, stainless steel shelves on the left of the walk-in refrigerator, while opposite were plastic cartons of milk and boxes of obscure berries.

Keynes lowered his gaze to the large space in the middle. In the centre of the floor, as his eyes adjusted, he saw a shape. It was a box of pineapples.

He straightened up, relieved. He had half-expected to find Pruitt's lifeless body, perhaps mutilated by one of his own blenders.

"No body?" said a voice behind him, and Keynes banged his head on a shelf.

He turned around, his body awash with chemicals urging him to be either furious or terrified, and saw Zulu observing the scene.

"What are you doing in here? This is a crime scene," said Keynes. He thought for a moment longer, then added: "Well, it might be."

"Is it a case of Grievous Blueberry Harm? Has there been a grape?"

"Get out."

Zulu noticed a stack of cardboard boxes and picked one up to test its qualities. He seemed impressed with the thickness.

"Stop touching things," said Keynes. "I mean it, get out. I'm securing this area."

He escorted Zulu out of the shop, rubbing his head as he went, then pulled the door closed behind him. The latch clicked shut, but Keynes was suddenly aware that would not be terribly effective in protecting the premises as long as there was a gaping hole in the door.

He saw Zulu waiting patiently for him to leave and realised with aching slowness that he had played into the homeless man's hands. Keynes rubbed his eyes.

"You did this on purpose," he said. "You want to sleep in there, so you talked me into breaking the window."

"I've got no idea what you're talking about, officer. I'm just an innocent bystander. Though I am a bit chilly, now you come to mention it."

"Nice try, but it's not going to work." Keynes opened the door again and fetched one of the cardboard boxes. He flattened it out and deemed it was the right size to fill the hole where the glass had once been. All he needed now was some masking tape.

Keynes held the flattened cardboard sheet up against the window. It was too big. He would need to fold it. Even then, would a sheet of cardboard really keep anyone out? It was raining lightly and the cardboard would be soggy before too long.

As he considered his position, he noticed the text on the box. Glory Farms, Lazarus Court. It was one of the holding companies of the Christ Resurrection League, and Pruitt was evidently one of their customers.

A scenario came to him: Simon Oakes had decided to leave town in a hurry, realising that Keynes was far too close. He had emptied his safe, but decided he would need more cash, and had called on Pruitt to collect what he was owed for his last shipment of apples. Perhaps a fight had broken out, and Oakes had sped away after hitting Pruitt with the charity tin and stowing his body in the boot.

That last part was conjecture, at least until the forensic team had checked the provenance of the reddish-brown stain, but the rest made sense. Perhaps Vera Hope had seen Oakes spending time at the smoothie shop and noticed him making large cash payments – something like that. Oakes had silenced her when the opportunity arose, using the back door to enter the British Cancer Foundation shop without being seen from the road.

It was a good theory, but Keynes had no idea at the moment how to prove it.

He put the cardboard box down and closed the door. Like it or not, he would need to report the damage to Pruitt's door and have it secured. If he left it open all night, Zulu and his friends were bound to leave it in no condition for hygienic smoothie-making.

"If you like, I can look after it while you go and find a padlock or something," said Zulu. "Make sure no undesirables get in."

"I've had enough of you for one day, Zulu, or whatever your name is. This door is going to be locked and boarded up. You're not sleeping here, so if you want to find a place to squat you'll have to come up with something better."

Zulu looked off into the distance, and cracked his knuckles. Then he looked back at Keynes and punched him in the face.

Zulu's punch was not hard – his wiry frame and poor diet saw to that – and Keynes was more shocked than hurt. The officer resisted the immediate urge to hit him back, and waited to see if that was the extent of Zulu's attack. It was.

"Right, I am arresting you for assaulting a police officer. You do not have to say anything, but anything you do say may be taken down and used in evidence against you." Keynes produced his notepad and waved it in front of Zulu as a warning. He began to write, hesitated, then pencilled in 'Zigga Zumba'.

"It's a fair cop," said Zulu.

"I've been very patient with you, considering, but you've pushed your luck too far. Now you're spending a night in the cells."

As a smile crept across Zulu's lips, Keynes realised he had walked into another trap. It was too late now. Zulu had earned a night at the Hotel Cop Shop.

"Oh, you must think you're very clever," said Keynes. "But as a violent criminal you obviously represent a danger to the public and need to be restrained."

He produced a pair of handcuffs from his coat pocket. Zulu's smile dimmed a little.

Zulu held out his hands and Keynes snapped the handcuffs around his wrists.

Keynes walked him to the car and wished he had parked slightly closer. He also wished he had brought a plastic sheet or some newspaper for the back seat. The upholstery would retain Zulu's cocktail of odours for weeks.

Keynes was annoyed with this added distraction, but he had been more disappointed that he was no closer to finding Oakes. At least he had a more substantial theory in his arsenal the next time he did encounter Oakes. It might even help save his reputation when he had to explain to Shepherd tomorrow why he had thrown Desmond down the stairs and seized a pile of burnt paper.

He felt he was on the brink of solving the case, if he could only find Oakes.

He pushed Zulu roughly into the back of his car, then sat down in the driving seat. He needed to deposit his passenger in a holding cell somewhere and see about patching up Pruitt's door, but he also knew that the bigger the head start he gave Oakes, the less chance there would be of ever catching him.

Keynes put the engine into gear and pulled off in the direction in which Oakes had been headed in such a hurry.

"I'll drop you off at the station, but we're going the long way," he said.

Chapter 45

Keynes cut across Marefair to St James' Road, with no clear idea of where he was heading, or exactly what he would do if he caught up with Oakes. It seemed like a good idea to pursue Oakes, but Keynes was aware that everything he had done in the course of this investigation had seemed logical initially, only to seem slightly less justifiable when he was questioned by his superiors later on.

"I hope you're pleased with yourself," he said. "I've got murders to solve, and I have to waste my time on you."

"Sorry about that," said Zulu, who was lounging across the back seat of the car to avoid the draught from Keynes' broken window. "It gets a bit chilly out there now I don't have a sleeping bag."

"All because you want to sleep in a cell. That's very short-term thinking. We actually have similar goals. I want to put Simon Oakes away too, and your little stunt might put paid to that."

Zulu tried to pretend he was not paying attention, but Keynes could see in the rear-view mirror that his eyes were somehow clearer now that Oakes' name had been mentioned. Zulu did not speak, so Keynes went on.

"I think he's behind the Charity Shop Murders. Either he did it himself or got his trained chimp to do it." Keynes would not normally have disclosed sensitive information about an ongoing case, but he felt that Zulu was hardly likely to be taken seriously were he to repeat it. One look, or one smell, would rule him out as a credible source in most people's minds.

"I would have thought you of all people would want to see justice served after what happened with Adamantia. All you needed to do was give evidence against him."

Zulu looked out of the window. He did not say anything.

"I realise you were upset at the time, but you let him get away with it."

Zulu turned to meet Keynes' eyes in the mirror. Nothing much had changed in his expression, but his eyes were burning with anger. "So did you," he said.

Keynes looked back to the road and decided that was a good place to end the conversation. The National Lift Tower loomed above as he passed the rugby stadium, and Keynes wondered how far he was willing to travel down this road before giving up the search. He could head down a bit further to Weedon Road, and if he still had not found anything he could double back and check the car park at the train station. He needed to be able to show Shepherd some signs of progress tomorrow morning to outweigh the less positive things that had happened today.

His heart jumped as he spotted a silver Mercedes up ahead on the left. It was Oakes' car, which seemed to have crashed at very low speed into a street sign. Both the driver and passenger doors were open, and the car was empty.

Keynes parked alongside it, then walked over to the vehicle. The engine was still warm.

He looked down the pavement ahead but could not see anyone among the handful of pedestrians who matched Oakes' description. Inside the housing estate, the road curved as it led towards the lift tower and it was hard to tell whether anyone was there.

He was so close, but could not think of the right move to make next.

A prompt came from an unexpected source. There was a sudden clanging of metal and breaking of glass from near the lift tower. It was jarringly loud and sounded as though something had fallen off the structure.

Keynes made up his mind. He returned to the car and put his head through the broken window.

"I'm going to investigate a possible disturbance," he said. "Don't go anywhere."

Zulu held up his handcuffed wrists. "I went to quite a lot of trouble to get arrested," he said. "Just put something nice on the radio."

Keynes ignored him and headed towards the source of the noise. It was too dark too see much from this distance, but there did not appear to be any work underway at the lift tower. There did not even seem to be any security staff present.

As he reached the base of the tower, he saw that a door had been forced open. Keynes felt nervous for the first time and reached in his pockets for anything that might be of use as a weapon. He could use his car keys if push came to shove, or perhaps snap his bank card and use the jagged edge as a makeshift knife, but then he would have to wait five working days for a new one.

The noise had been caused by a tangled steel structure hitting the ground. On closer examination, it appeared to be the Christmas tree silhouette that was illuminated every year to lend some festive cheer to the vast concrete structure. He looked up, but it was impossible to see whether anyone was at the top.

He entered the tower. All his life, this building had been in the background, but he had never been inside and had very little idea what went on here. The owners had recently opened the tower up for abseiling, usually in charity fundraising efforts, but he did not know anyone who had descended it.

Another piece clicked into place. Another charity connection.

Keynes climbed a flight of steps and entered what appeared to be the control room. The lights were illuminated on several control panels, and there was a lift door in front of him. Presumably this would take him to the summit, but it would be hard to make a stealthy entrance. The tower was one hundred and twenty-seven metres high, he remembered. Taking the stairs was out of the question.

He pressed the button for the lift and entered it. As he pressed the only button on the wall inside, he felt for his car keys. Aim for the eyes, he told himself.

The doors slid closed and the lift began its rapid yet smooth ascent. He would not have the element of surprise he had hoped for, but he was confident he would be more than a match for Simon Oakes as long as Desmond was not involved. Keynes just needed to make sure he was alert at the moment the doors opened.

The lift shuddered to a halt. Keynes took a deep breath, adopted a crouching pose and prepared to spring.

The doors opened to reveal a blank concrete wall and another flight of stairs. Keynes relaxed slightly and stepped out. The stairs seemed to lead up rather a long way. In fact, he estimated he was barely more than halfway up the tower. It hardly seemed like a thorough way to test a lift.

He exhaled, stretched his quadriceps one after the other, one arm leaning against the wall for balance, then began to jog up the stairs. He did not know what Oakes had prepared up there, but it was not a bad idea to stretch before confronting him.

One flight of stairs ended and another began. They began to blend into each other, and the bland, bare concrete made him lose count of the floors. Every floor was identical to the last, and there was no indication of how much farther he needed to climb. His calves were burning now, and his breathing laboured and heavy. Sweat was starting to seep through the back of his shirt. He prided himself on his physical upkeep, but this was tiring him.

After what seemed like a dozen more flights, he reached a doorway. Pausing for a moment to catch his breath, his hands on his knees, he prepared himself for what he might face. He had never faced an armed assailant, but he had completed the training with full marks. Lesson one was to wear a stab vest. It was in the boot of his car.

Keynes grasped the handle, his sweaty hand slipping at first, then eased it open. He stepped through and closed it quietly.

He was outside now, and the cold wind whipped wildly at his face. It would not take much to lose one's balance here. A set of metal steps led up to the summit.

Keynes ascended the final set of steps as quietly as he could, and saw the face of Simon Oakes staring back at him from the other side of the roof.

He took a step back, then realised, as his eyes adjusted to the darkness, that Oakes had a noose of rope around his neck.

Keynes was taken aback, and was still trying to think of something appropriate to say when a voice from the darkness said: "Detective Sergeant Keynes. Glad you could make it. Eventually."

He looked to the right of Oakes and saw Ian Pruitt grinning back at him. On closer examination, Pruitt was armed with what appeared to be a small fruit knife. Keynes would need to make a few adjustments to his theory.

"Ian Pruitt," he said, while his brain, and his lungs, caught up with recent events.

"Martin Keynes."

"Yes," said Keynes, struggling for something to say.

"So you've tracked me down at last. I was beginning to think you were never going to work it out."

"Oh, I've had my eye on you, Pruitt."

Vera Hope, Wendy Bevan, Paul Whitcroft, Chris Shingles, Harpit Singh, Simon Oakes. Keynes could not think of a single possible motive for Pruitt to want them dead. His heart sank as he realised Gunnett's theory had been right: it was a nutty neighbour.

"He thought I did it," said Oakes. "He's been hounding me for the past couple of days."

"That's what I wanted you to think," said Keynes, uncertainly.

Pruitt looked a little unsettled. Keynes was glad he was not holding a larger knife, but the presence of Oakes, who was apparently a hostage, made the situation more complicated.

"How does that work?" said Pruitt. He looked to be deep in thought. "You didn't even ask me any questions about the murders. You just kept asking me about Adrian Shadwell and the homeless fellow."

"He didn't have a clue," said Oakes.

"I've been taking an approach based on empirical evidence."

"Rubbish, you've been looking for excuses to arrest me. We sell apples. That's it, end of story. There's no big conspiracy there. Sure, there are a few things that don't go through the books, but you find me a single privately-held company that doesn't do the same thing. You've clearly had a vendetta against me, so I thought it prudent to give myself some distance." Oakes jerked violently and Keynes realised that his hands were bound behind his back. "Now this lunatic's going to hang me. Excellent police work."

Pruitt ran his fingers through his scrubby beard and looked thoughtful.

"Did you really not work it out?" he said, pointing at Keynes with his knife.

"Of course I did."

"Because I thought I made my clues quite obvious, really. The first time you walked into the shop I thought I'd overdone it."

"No, I thought you got the balance just right."

"It was good, wasn't it? Cat and mouse, with me always one step ahead."

Oakes looked ready to explode. "Don't listen to Sergeant Keynes, he's making it up. He's got no idea."

"I do."

"Go on, then, what's his motive?"

Keynes sucked in his cheeks and pondered the question. He resisted the urge to take out his notepad and check the evidence again. He stalled for as long as he could, then said: "Fruit prices?"

Pruitt was taken aback, while Oakes let out a short, bitter laugh.

"Fruit?" said Pruitt. "Why would I kill so many people over fruit?"

"Is there a shortage of some particular kind of fruit? A fruit cartel?"

Pruitt looked shell-shocked and leaned on the waist-high wall for support.

"All this, and he didn't work it out after all," he said to Oakes.

He turned to Keynes. "You, sir, are a fraud."

"I'm here now, aren't I? What difference does it make?" Keynes remembered that his principal aim in climbing the lift tower had been to apprehend the murderer, and that objective had not changed just because the antagonist had. "Ian Pruitt, you are under arrest for the murders of Vera Hope, Paul Whitcroft…" he began.

"Of course it makes a difference," said Pruitt, angrily. "I've put a lot of effort into this. The medium is the message."

"I think I've got the gist of it, but perhaps you could clarify."

"I've been very clear. This has all supported the aims of the Better World Collective to support kindness and less wasteful living."

Keynes dimly remembered seeing posters for the Better World Collective around the university campus, but had to admit he had not read them closely.

"For some reason, my organisation can't get charity status and the Tribune won't print my letters. I had to try something a bit different to grab the public's attention."

"You've been killing people to promote a charity about kindness?"

"And to highlight the inherent hypocrisies in other charities. Everyone knows Harpit Singh uses that children's charity to make himself look good and to prop up his carpet business. Everyone knows foreign aid doesn't work. Everyone knows we don't need five different charities researching cancer, when one would do. Everyone knows those charity muggers don't have the best interests of charities at heart. Everyone knows charity shops are just a way to throw things away without feeling guilty."

"So you thought you'd kill them?"

"It didn't start off like that. I wanted to scare Wendy Bevan, not kill her. I got there after dark because my friend was late bringing the fox costume. Stopping animal cruelty is only a small part of the Better World Collective's manifesto, but I had the opportunity to borrow the costume, so why not? I could have done a bit more with that, but when she keeled over I was terrified. I just legged it."

"You cycled back from Litchborough wearing a fox costume?"

"No, I stayed there for the night. I was visiting my parents. You know, Tim and Betty Pruitt?"

Keynes had a familiar sinking feeling. Another lead that had not been followed up.

"And then Vera was sort of an accident. She kept putting boxes on top of the bins, and then I had to move them to open the lid. Very irritating. We starting arguing, she poked me, I pushed her back and she hit her head on the counter. Goodnight Vienna.

"I could have just left things there, but when I saw her laying there, I realised I shouldn't waste the opportunity. It was like a second chance. I took the mannequin off its pole and put Vera on there. It was a bit tricky lining her up, but I think it worked quite well, and it sent a message. I got newspaper coverage after that.

"That spurred me on. I got a bit more inventive with the murders, just to jazz it up a bit. I experimented with poisoning. Not sure where I went wrong there. I was hoping to bump off that newspaper editor to send a message about the charities he chose to cover. There's an agenda there."

"I think you just need to make sure your photos are the right resolution," said Keynes.

"Anyway, I've got their attention now. Then I had a bit of luck when Simon here walked into my shop this evening. I started buying from the Christ Resurrection League to get close to Simon, and he made it even easier than I hoped. He came in offering me a discount for cash – something dodgy going on there, I reckon – and I just bashed him over the head when he wasn't looking. Same thing I did with Paul Whitcroft once he'd served his purpose, although that was a bit impromptu because he was getting very talkative after a couple of beers."

Pruitt gestured towards Oakes, and Keynes realised that the rope around his neck was attached to a long banner. In fact, it could have been the same one that was stolen from Harpit Singh's warehouse.

"This is going to be fantastic," said Pruitt. "My final murder will be Simon Oakes, hanging from the lift tower by a banner explaining the Better World Collective's manifesto. No one will be able to ignore that."

"Why didn't you just put up the manifesto in your shop window?" said Keynes.

"It is in the shop window!" Pruitt recovered his composure and scraped his hair away from his face. "The terrific thing is all the interviews I'll be able to do while I'm awaiting trial, or even after I'm in prison. It's going to be fantastic. The Better World Collective is going to get its message to a huge audience."

"How many people are there in this collective?"

"Just me at the moment. There are a lot of closed minds out there."

"Can you just shoot him or something?" said Oakes. "This is getting ridiculous."

"I don't have a gun," said Keynes. "I could call for an armed response unit, but they're not going to have much of an angle unless they get on the roof too."

Pruitt was distracted by something behind Keynes. "All right, Zulu," he said.

Keynes turned around to see Zulu standing behind him, leaning on the wall. His eyes were fixed on Oakes, who seemed more scared of him than Pruitt.

"How did you get up the stairs so quickly?" said Keynes.

"There's a lift that goes all the way up."

Keynes cursed to himself, then noticed that Zulu had managed to shed the handcuffs. "How did you unlock those?"

"There's a fire extinguisher under your seat. I used the pin. Pretty simple stuff."

"If that fire extinguisher goes off in my car, I swear…" Keynes put his concern for his upholstery to one side for a moment and focused on the most urgent priority.

He turned back to Pruitt. "Look, you don't need to kill Oakes. You've already got everyone's attention."

"But I've spent a long time planning this."

"Then just roll out the banner and let Oakes go. It will still get your message across."

"I suppose so," said Pruitt, thinking it over. "I just wanted the fame of being Northamptonshire's first serial killer."

"You already are. You only need to murder three people. Hope, Whitcroft and Singh."

"Actually, you're not," said Zulu. "A court would probably view the death of Vera Hope as manslaughter, not murder. Wendy Bevan died of natural causes, so that just leaves you with Paul Whitcroft and Harpit Singh. You still need one more."

Oakes started to shake. Zulu seemed to enjoy his discomfort.

"You're going to let him kill me because of that girl," said Oakes, his eyes watering either due to the wind or his growing fear. "Because of that stupid drug addict. She used to eat goldfish!"

"Is he right about the serial killer thing?" Pruitt asked Keynes.

"Yes, but it depends on the judge's interpretation."

"Don't help him!" yelled Oakes.

The wind had risen since Keynes had reached the summit. It swirled around the four of them, and stirred the folds of Pruitt's banner. If Keynes waited too long, the wind might blow Oakes to his death anyway.

"Have you thought of hiring a public relations agency?" he said.

Pruitt rubbed his chin and looked into the distance thoughtfully. "What sort of price do they…?"

He snapped back to attention in time to see Keynes lunge for him. Pruitt pushed Oakes towards the edge. As he did so, the banner caught the wind, billowing out and knocking Pruitt off balance. He tipped over the edge, making a desperate dive for Oakes. His hand grabbed Oakes' jumper at the same time as another gust of wind lifted the banner into the air.

Oakes yelled something as the two of them disappeared over the edge, the banner unravelling loudly behind them.

It snaked wildly for a few seconds, then went taut. By then, Keynes was at the edge, both hands gripping the wall and a look of horror on his face.

"Quite a view, isn't it?" said Zulu.

Chapter 46

Keynes sat in Shepherd's office, feeling like he was enduring something between a hangover and a school detention. Biggs sat beside him, looking confused.

"The lesson we take from this is that we keep our phones turned on after office hours," said Shepherd. "Isn't that right, Inspector Biggs?"

"I think the battery had died or something," Biggs muttered.

"I just about understand your story about Lazarus Court. You went there to try to locate Simon Oakes, believing that his life might be in danger. That just about makes up for the rather aggressive approach D.S. Keynes took there. Then Keynes, on his own initiative, spotted Oakes' car and pursued it, where he bore witness to the unfortunate events at the lift tower."

Keynes kept quiet.

"I suppose your being there didn't make a lot of difference, but at least there aren't going to be any more Charity Shop Murders. Always nice to solve cases like these."

The chair creaked as Shepherd rose to his feet and opened the door. "D.I. Biggs, I'd like a moment alone with D.S. Keynes, please. Run along."

Biggs waddled out of the room, relieved to have escaped lightly.

Shepherd closed the door. He sat back in his seat and folded his arms. Keynes waited for the inevitable ear-bashing.

"They're still looking for Simon Oakes' head," said Shepherd. "It popped off when the rope…" He pulled his fists apart in an approximate mime.

"Right." Keynes realised he was clutching the sides of his chair with both hands.

"Your account of what went on up there is a bit hazy."

"It all happened very quickly. Pruitt pushed him over and then jumped off, as soon as I arrived."

"It's a shame there aren't any witnesses who saw it."

Keynes did not say anything.

"It means we'll have to take your word for it," said Shepherd. "Rutkowski thought initially that Pruitt's body had hit the ground first, but he couldn't be sure."

"As I said in my report…"

"Yes, we'll stick with the report. History is written by the victors, and all that." Shepherd closed the folder on his desk. "I asked you to solve these murders, and you did. It got a bit messy, but who's to say we influenced that?

"Look, Keynes, you've done well. You haven't been working with Britain's greatest minds, and it looks like you've been doing all the work. In case you're wondering, Inspector Gunnett is going to be taking a voluntary transfer for his little indiscretion to Newport in South Wales, which I'm sure he will be delighted to hear about."

"Isn't he going to be punished?"

"He's being sent to Newport," Shepherd repeated forcefully, and Keynes saw his logic.

"What about Harper?" asked Keynes.

"I don't think he's coming back. Last time I spoke to him, he was thinking of giving it all up to join the Christ Resurrection League. I don't know if his plans have changed now that they don't have a head. So to speak."

Shepherd cleared his throat. "Anyway, long story short, I'm recommending you for Inspector."

Keynes rose from his seat to shake Shepherd's hand, but Shepherd waved him away.

"You won't get the promotion, unfortunately," said Shepherd. "We just don't have the budget at the moment. I know you were supposed to be on the fast-track programme, but it got a bit slower when the economy fell over. We won't get extra headcount for Gunnett being transferred, and while Harper's in limbo he's still on the payroll. I'll see to it that you're recognised when we get our funding back, but for the time being you'll have the reward of a job well done."

Keynes felt mixed emotions. He was not facing any further investigation into Oakes' fall from the tower, but he would also miss out on promotion. On balance, he was happy with that, he decided.

"I can get someone to mention you in the press release for the newspapers, if you'd like?" said Shepherd.

"Perhaps not."

Shepherd stood up and shook Keynes' hand. "You get a handshake and a pat on the back," he said. "That's more than most of this lot ever get."

He patted Keynes rather rigidly on the back, then showed him out.

Keynes walked out, feeling at a bit of a loss. This case had consumed him. It had tested his analytical abilities to the limit, and even his physical strengths at times. After this, he could not face the tedium of the day-to-day investigation of ordinary people and mediocre deaths.

"We'll have to give you a new nickname," said Biggs, who was perched on the corner of his desk eating a bag of crisps. "Killer Keynes."

Nor could he stomach working with mediocre colleagues. The office was an intellectual desert.

Chapter 47

Keynes parked his car alongside Groovy Smoothies, which had been boarded up. In the window, he could still see yellowing flyers and leaflets, including one from the Better World Collective.

It was a rambling, baffling series of proposals which generally centred around being nicer to people and consuming less of the earth's resources. Keynes agreed with them in principle, even if they were somewhat naïve in the modern world, but failed to see how Pruitt had decided that promoting this manifesto justified becoming a serial killer.

Keynes also noticed that Pruitt had no idea how to use possessive apostrophes correctly.

Zulu was across the road, as Keynes had known he would be.

"Afternoon, Zigga Zumba, or whatever your name is," he said. Keynes still had a mountain of partially burned files from Lazarus Court, but so far he had not managed to work out whether Zulu was mentioned in there by his real name. He would find out eventually, but it could wait.

"New car?"

"Replacement. They're still fixing the window and getting the fire extinguisher foam out of the seats."

Keynes crossed the road and crouched down next to Zulu, who looked rather pathetic, sitting cross-legged on a flattened cardboard box with a checked rug over his knees.

"How's things?" said Keynes. "All good?"

Zulu's eyes flicked down to the cardboard sheet.

"You can spare me the tea and sympathy, officer. You're checking up on me, wondering if I'm going to tell anyone my version of events."

"You're not in the official report because it's too complicated. I can't explain why you were there. It's better for you, believe me. No awkward questions." Keynes tried to smile in a friendly way, but was not successful.

"Better for you too, if no one tells your boss about your hostage negotiation skills."

"Look, you little…" Keynes' voice became a hiss. He stopped, and tried a different tack. "Look, I was thinking. You're out here on the streets. It's nearly winter. I've got a spare room in my house."

Zulu's eyes gleamed brighter.

"And when I was tidying it last weekend, I found this." Keynes produced an old sleeping bag. "The zip's broken, but it's a good brand. That's yours."

He handed it to Zulu, who paused before giving a dry laugh that degenerated into a cough. Keynes looked him earnestly in the eyes.

"So we're okay?" he said.

"Oh, you're fine," said Zulu.

Keynes walked away, his shoulders back and his head held high. Northampton was not London. He was not surrounded by intellectual giants and he would have to work much harder to be noticed, but he knew he could make a difference. If he had to bide his time until the police force recognised his talents, there would always be opportunities here to test himself.

Most of all, he understood the people.

Printed in Great Britain
by Amazon